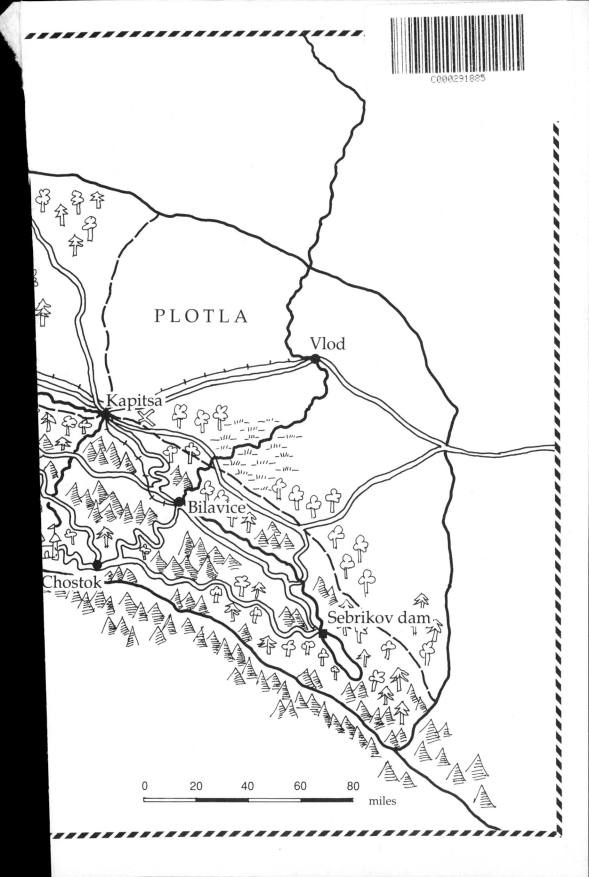

PLOTLA

Vlod

Kapitsa

Bilavice

Chostok

Sebrikov dam

0   20   40   60   80
miles

After Zenda

By the same author

After Zenda

A NOVEL

John Spurling

ANDRE DEUTSCH

First published in Great Britain in 1995 by
André Deutsch Limited
106 Great Russell Street, London WC1B 3LJ

The author has asserted his moral rights

ISBN 0233 989 196

Printed in Great Britain by
Redwood Books, Trowbridge, Wiltshire

TO NATHANIEL
red-haired, sometimes reckless and fond of opera,
but to whom the narrator bears no other resemblance

with special thanks for advice on medical,
media, middle European and military matters to:
David Gibson, Jonathan Gili, John Higgins,
Maria Melnik, John Powell and Jane's
Information Group

". . . for I love to see myself once again in the crowded streets of Strelsau, or beneath the frowning keep of the Castle of Zenda."
Anthony Hope: *The Prisoner of Zenda*

"Princes and lords may flourish, or may fade;
A breath can make them, as a breath has made;"
Oliver Goldsmith: *The Deserted Village*

"And since we are concerned with what happened in respect of its reflection in what we are, we should perhaps include our genetic past: the organisation of genes which distinguished that unknown great-grandfather which now appears in the colour of my eyes and the shape (and, in part, the skill) of my hands. What comes after may modify what went before, but it cannot expunge it. Layer upon layer; all a great and contingent mixture from which we cannot escape but to which what we are and what we do now is somehow a response."
Michael Oakeshott: *On History*

Contents

Preface

The small Central European kingdom of Ruritania was created on November 28th, 1893, when a young barrister/novelist called Anthony Hope Hawkins, walking back from winning a case in the Westminster County Court to his Temple chambers, suddenly thought of the story of *The Prisoner of Zenda*. A month later the book was written and, published in April 1894, was so successful that by July its author had decided to abandon the law and become a full-time writer. The sequel, *Rupert of Hentzau*, Hope's only other excursion to Ruritania (apart from a volume of stories, set in an earlier period), though he wrote many other novels, was published in 1898.

My own rediscovery of post-Nazi, post-communist Ruritania was equally sudden. It was set off in 1992 by reading obituaries of the Grand Duke Vladimir Romanov, putative heir to the throne of Russia, whose last Tsar, Nicholas II, began his unlucky reign in the year *The Prisoner of Zenda* was published. Was it possible that the hero of Hope's story had an heir? Not, of course, if the sequel, *Rupert of Hentzau*, told the whole truth; not unless Sherlock Holmes, whose *Memoirs* were also published in that busy year 1894, came back from the Reichenbach Falls.

And where was Ruritania itself? Many people seemed to think in the Balkans, but in that case why should the nineteenth-century visitor get there by changing trains at Dresden? And why should its capital sound so like the German name for the Polish city of Wroclaw – Breslau?

I decided to try the Carpathians and, having found the lost kingdom, to travel further into its interior than Hope needed to when there was a king in Strelsau and a rivalrous half-brother in Zenda and the main problem was dynastic rather than ethnic. I have provided a map of the whole country (drawn by Sandra Oakins) on the endpapers, but can't guarantee its absolute accuracy, since I only carried it in my head while I was there.

This story is not a sequel to *Zenda* and *Hentzau* in the ordinary sense; more a reflection in a frosted mirror from the other end of a hundred-year corridor.

John Spurling,
London, 1994

1

An Ambassador in Regent's Park

'I wonder when in the world you're going to do anything, Karl?' said my brother's wife.

I was bent over her fridge searching for a stray can of beer and the question came at me from behind without any warning except a weary sigh and a disapproving thump as she dumped a big bag of shopping next to my bare heels.

'You didn't get any beer, I suppose?' I said.

'I certainly did not. It weighs a ton, it costs a bomb and the only person who drinks it is you.'

'And I'm just the guest who's outstayed his welcome.'

'You said it, not me.'

'I can read your thoughts.'

'That's something you *are* good at.'

Written down, the conversation sounds heavy, but you have to imagine a light, bantering tone, like a fresh breeze on a thundery day. Actually Jennifer and I got on well together – my role as the useless layabout nicely balancing my brother's as the plodding breadwinner who came home every evening from his job in the Council's housing department with another day's mortgage, insurance and gas bill paid for, but not much progress on the road of life to report. Jennifer, having put in a morning at the charity shop and done the shopping on the way home and now about to tidy the house, iron shirts and prepare supper, to a steady background of chat and soap-opera on radio and TV, could enjoy feeling superior to both of us in different ways. Women, in my experience, are mostly anxious, unconfident creatures and they want their men to be either subservient or masterful. Since they can never make up their minds between the two, their ideal would be both at once, which is obviously impossible on a regular basis, short of bigamy. So with my brother playing obedient and reliable and me playing feckless and bumptious, Jennifer was as nearly happy as any woman can be.

1

Unfortunately for her it wasn't going to last. She was about to be left exclusively with my brother Freddy and I was going to have all the fun: which is what I'd always kept myself for and why – though I was a year older than my brother and pushing thirty – I hadn't so far made the mistake of signing up for either a mortgage or a wife.

I did once have a job. The fee-paying school I went to turned me out on the world with only one 'A' level – and *that* was due to having a German mother and being bilingual – but while I was drinking around on my State handout I happened to meet up with an old school friend called Bob Featherly. He was doing very nicely in the City and took me into his firm. I really enjoyed that. It was the mid-Eighties, when Thatcher had just put Socialism in the bin and there were instant fortunes to be made. I drove a Lotus, rented an expensive room in Notting Hill Gate and had a new girl-friend every three months. It couldn't last and would have got boring if it had.

Dad, of course, who had called his sons after Marx and Engels, thought it was sheer evil and wouldn't even look at my Lotus. He died of what they said was lung cancer from all his long hours smoking and arguing with other dyed-in-the-wool Socialists in sealed rooms, but I thought was really grey grief over the triumph of Capitalism. He didn't live to see the bubble burst in 1987. I wished he could have known that I had to sell my Lotus – it was a pain to me, but it would have given a momentary lift to his tight, down-turned mouth and brought a little joy to his rancorous heart. Mum, who had originally met him at some international Socialist congress in East Germany, but was far from being a convinced Socialist herself – she was the one who insisted on her children being privately educated – didn't believe in my luck either and kept warning me about investing for the future, but she could see I was insanely active for the first time in my life and thought that must be a good thing in itself. Heredity works in strange ways and just as it gave me dark red hair and a long straight nose from several generations back, whereas Mum and my brother were fair with snub noses and Dad dark-haired with a sort of beak, it must have carried secret instructions about my life-style.

My summons came that very afternoon – a scorching day in May – while I was relaxing in a deck-chair on the little patch of balding grass at the back of my brother's house. My sister-in-law, wearing her apron, came and stood in the kitchen doorway and shouted indignantly:

'Phone-call for you!'

Friends occasionally rang me in the evening to fix a session at the pub, but who would want to speak to *me* in working hours at standard rate?

'Yes?'

'Is that Mr Karl Rassendyll?'

'It is.'

'Can I speak with you, please?'

The voice was foreign, probably German. His English was silky-fluent, but he wasn't quite bilingual like me.

'Who is this?'

'You don't know me, but I shall introduce myself when we meet. May I suggest Regent's Park tomorrow at 11 a.m.? Alongside the wolf's enclosure.'

'What's this about?'

'I will explain everything, but not on the phone.'

'How will I recognise you?'

'I shall recognise you.'

'How come?'

'I believe the family resemblance is uncanny.'

And rang off.

The wolves were flaked out in the heat. Their enclosure was well shaded with trees and at first I couldn't see any of the beasts at all, only the remains of their breakfast, a discarded knuckle-bone and a bare rib-cage being picked over by starlings. The wolves had flung themselves down here and there among the patches of long grass, dandelions and cow-parsley and were dreaming of chasing Russian troikas through a snow-bound forest.

'Mr Rassendyll.'

He was a small, compact old party with a round, mainly bald head. He looked as if he might have made a living as a human cannonball. In fact, I discovered later, he taught fencing and violin at a private girls' school nearby – or had done until recently. He was wearing a thin blue suit, very creased and shiny, with a striped tie – probably some genuine club which he actually belonged to, though people got quite indiscriminate about that in the Eighties.

'Are you the person who rang?'

'Colonel Danzing, Ambassador for the Republic of Ruritania.'

He bowed and clicked his heels – or they would have clicked if he hadn't been wearing canvas shoes.

'Ah, I remember now.'

'You remember me? We have never met, Mr Rassendyll.'

'I vaguely remember there was a country called Ruritania.'

This was the wrong thing to say and he looked irritated.

'Shall we find a seat?'

We walked as far as an orientalish-looking drinking-fountain and read the inscription. It had been donated by a Parsee Knight of the Star of India in gratitude for the British Raj and inaugurated by Queen Victoria's daughter, the Duchess of Teck, in 1869.

'How curious and enticing are the B-roads of history!' said Colonel Danzing. 'Your great-grandfather, whom you so closely resemble, would have been a very young man at the time and his father, the Earl of Burlesdon, would certainly have known the Duchess of Teck.'

'The Earl of Burlesdon? So I *am* a relation of his?'

'A distant relation of the present Lord Burlesdon, but descended from the family.'

'I remember Mum once asking Dad what connection there was, but he didn't want to know.'

'That doesn't surprise me. He would have considered such a connection politically compromising.'

'What about Sir Cowarjee Jehangir?'

'I know nothing about him.'

He sounded irritated again.

'The philanthropic Parsee who paid for the fountain? Dad might have preferred a connection with him.'

He pursed his lips and walked on in silence. Like most Eastern Europeans he probably thought the English were too soft on coloured people.

'You know a lot about my family history.'

'It is part of the history of my country.'

'Dad didn't tell me anything about either,' I said. 'He was a history-teacher, but I got the impression he hated history.'

'He was ideologically opposed to that kind of history,' said the Colonel. 'I myself once invited him – in my capacity as Prime Minister of the Kingdom of Ruritania in exile – to a modest reception, but he replied that he could only regard me as a fiction and that, supporting the People's Republic of Ruritania as he did, he had no wish to be associated in any way with its feudal past. In spite of that rebuff, I may say that when I heard of his untimely death in 1985 I caused our flag to be lowered to half mast and would certainly have attended his cremation if I had been invited. I felt that my own father, who had

4

been Queen Flavia's last Prime Minister at the time of the German invasion in 1939, would have wished it. One should never confuse the man with the office or *vice versa*.'

I was feeling confused myself. The Colonel indicated an empty seat in the shade and we sat down.

'I see I must start at the beginning,' he said.

The original connection between my family, the Rassendylls, and Ruritania was off the record. A Crown Prince of Ruritania with a mass of dark red hair and a long straight nose visited England in the 18th century and slept with the fifth Earl of Burlesdon's pretty young wife. The Prince and the Earl fought an inconclusive duel at dawn, after which the Prince, who had been slightly wounded, returned hastily to Ruritania, while the Earl caught pneumonia and died. His titles and estates went to the only son, born seven or eight months later to the pretty Countess. This boy had thick dark-red hair and a long straight nose and every so often one of his descendants in the Rassendyll family would turn out to resemble him. Meanwhile back in Ruritania the Crown Prince eventually became King Rudolf III and many of his successors were red-haired and long-nosed. In 1876, as coincidence would have it, the new King of Ruritania, Rudolf V, and the then Earl of Burlesdon's younger brother, Rudolf Rassendyll, were almost the same age and looked virtually identical.

'That Rassendyll was your great-grandfather,' said Colonel Danzing. 'I never met him myself, of course, but to judge by the photographs and one miniature portrait in my possession, you are his living likeness. What is your height?'

'Six feet one.'

'He was an inch taller and usually wore a small pointed beard and a thick moustache.'

'Usually?'

'Except when he was impersonating King Rudolf V, who had shaved off his beard and moustache to please the Princess Flavia.'

'My ancestor was some sort of con-man, then?'

Colonel Danzing stamped his canvas shoes and went red in the face.

'Have you really not read the books?'

'I'm afraid not. I never cared much for reading.'

'There are also five or six films.'

'I missed them all.'

'I thought every English boy had at least read *The Prisoner of Zenda*.'

'Not this one.'

'I am astonished.'

He sounded outraged.

'I suppose we must put this down to your father's prejudice. He deliberately kept you ignorant of your heritage. Did your mother never discuss it with you either?'

'Discuss what?'

'Your connection with Ruritania.'

'She never mentioned it.'

'Incredible! What an evil era this has been! What a century of lies and distortions and worst of all self-deception on the part of those who should have known better – the educated classes of the western democracies! Whole generations of young people like yourself betrayed by the false doctrines of their parents and teachers! Fortunately they failed in their attempt to suppress all those who still carried memories of the former times. A few of us survived – enough to keep the flame alight and rekindle the ardour of a new generation for a world whose values are not those of greed, envy and materialism.'

It was a Thatcherite sort of outburst. I didn't like to say that it was in Thatcher's heyday that I'd first discovered the joys of materialism, so I just watched the passers-by – most of them walking models of greed and envy – until he calmed down.

When he did he told me the rest of the story. My great-grandfather, who was a bumptious layabout like me, but with the big difference that he had a private income, was the first Rassendyll to visit Ruritania. He went there for a holiday and to see the Coronation of King Rudolf V, but immediately got mixed up in a plot by the King's half-brother, Duke Michael, to grab the throne for himself. This black-haired, black-hearted villain intended to kill the King and marry the next legitimate heir to the throne, the King's delicious red-headed cousin, Princess Flavia. The plot was foiled by a group of loyal courtiers and the lucky chance that Rudolf Rassendyll spoke perfect German – the main language of Ruritania – and was able to stand in for the real king at the Coronation and even propose to Princess Flavia without her knowing the difference. At least she did detect a difference but thought it much for the better.

Imagine her distress when she finally discovered, after Rassendyll had rescued the King from his dungeon in the Castle of Zenda and restored him to his throne, that she had to marry the boring and traumatised genuine King instead of the romantic substitute she'd fallen in love with. She gritted her teeth, said goodbye to Rudolf Rassendyll and became Queen, but that only led to more trouble. The end result was that although black Duke Michael was eliminated, his most vicious henchman, Count Rupert of Hentzau, did succeed in murdering the King before himself being killed in a duel with Rudolf Rassendyll.

You might have thought this was a happy ending. The real King's corpse had already been consumed in a fire in his hunting-lodge near Zenda and the unrecognisable remains buried in a local cemetery as those of the visiting Englishman, Rudolf Rassendyll, whose family were regretfully informed of his accidental death. So Rassendyll could now go on posing indefinitely as Rudolf V and Queen Flavia would have the husband she really loved. What nobody allowed for was Rassendyll's peculiar sense of honour.

'Your great-grandfather was a true English gentleman,' said the Colonel.

'In what sense?'

'In every sense. He could not betray the truth.'

'But he'd been telling lies all along by pretending to be the King.'

'Only for the benefit of the true royal line of Ruritania. His conduct was always in accordance with the family motto.'

'What motto is that?'

'You don't know?'

His eyes bulged with incredulity. I shook my head.

'How are the mighty fallen!' he said, shaking his own.

'That's appropriate enough.'

'No, no, you misunderstand. I was expressing my own sentiment. The motto is in Latin: *Nil Quae Feci*.'

'Ah.'

'You never studied Latin?'

'Afraid not.'

'An approximate translation would be: "What I did was nothing".'

'Doesn't sound too difficult to live up to.'

'If you took it at face value I suppose it might describe someone who was merely untalented, inadequate and idle. Its real meaning is more subtle and contains the essence of the gentleman's code. For someone who had truly done something – something as outstandingly courageous as Rudolf Rassendyll had – it would represent the very pitch of courtesy, altruism and *sangfroid*. "It was nothing", when in reality he had given not less than everything for the sake of others. But for the same reason, by the same code, he could do nothing for his own sake. To make himself permanently King and live the rest of his life with the woman he loved but in another man's shoes, that would be sheerly selfish and quite illegitimate.'

'But if she loved him and wanted him to do it . . .'

'It would be cheating. No good could come of it.'

7

'So what happened?'

'The book tells us that he was walking in the Palace garden, still wrestling with his conscience, when he was shot in the back by a hidden assassin, a servant of the villain Hentzau.'

'And?'

'And soon afterwards, having taken leave of the Queen and his faithful courtiers, died, lay in state in the Cathedral and was buried with his supposed ancestors.'

'A sad ending,' I said, 'but a smart solution.'

'Quite so.'

I thought about this for a while, staring at the ground and the Colonel's nearest canvas-shod foot, which began to tap irregularly. I looked up to see that he was watching me closely.

'One thing occurs to me . . .' I said and then stopped, not wanting to upset him again.

'Speak your mind!'

'Did he have children *before* he went to Ruritania and met Princess Flavia?'

'He did not.'

'Then if he was such a gentleman, how come he's my great-grandfather? How come, I mean, he's anyone's great-grandfather?'

'Your father said nothing about this?'

I shook my head.

'He may not have known and probably did not care to inquire. But Lord Burlesdon certainly knows.'

'I've never met him.'

'I suppose your parents never told you that the Burlesdons paid for your education – and your brother's.'

'I did wonder how Mum and Dad could afford it, especially when he was totally against it. Haven't the Burlesdons got any children?'

This was beginning to sound interesting. An earldom, a country mansion and a fortune would suit me very nicely. There might even be a good car tucked away in one of the stables – a Bugatti or at least a Bentley.

'Lord Burlesdon has five children, three of them sons.'

I stared disconsolately at the fat plebs shuffling, wobbling and rolling past and thought how unfair life was, picking out the few for the real perks and leaving the rest of us with nothing much to look forward to beyond chips and chocolate bars.

'Apart from Lord Burlesdon,' said the Colonel, 'I am probably the last person alive that knows this – my father told me before he died and he had it from the Queen herself when she was very old and knew her country was in deadly danger from Nazi Germany . . .'

He went silent in mid-sentence. Even now his secret was too sacred or too scandalous to utter. Now that I'd lost my chance of an earldom, I couldn't be bothered with all this fitting and starting.

'What's the problem, Colonel? It's ancient history. Surely it doesn't matter any more to anyone still alive?'

'You think like your father, do you? The old days are wiped out? Marx and Engels, Lenin and Stalin have abolished the past? The truth is the very opposite: the past rises up to abolish Marx and Engels, Lenin and Stalin and all their lies, the dead rise from their dishonoured graves, nations revive and royalty will be restored.'

2

The Waxwork in the Vault

'Karl had a mysterious assignation this morning,' said my brother's wife.

'Oh, really?' said Freddy, helping himself to new potatoes. 'Did it lead to anything, Karl?'

'Hard to say,' I said, my mouth full of delicious braised liver.

Jennifer was an excellent, straight-down-the-middle cook. I used to give my stomach appalling hangovers with the pretentious and expensive restaurant food I ate when I was flush and it was an extra incentive to stay unemployed that I felt so healthy on my hostess's cooking. I'd refused to tell her anything about my meeting with Colonel Danzing, not even his name or where we'd met. This was partly on his instructions, partly because what he'd told me didn't anyway bear discussing at a kitchen table in a terrace house in Hackney. It was OTT and OTR, over the top and open to ridicule, especially from Jennifer.

'I presume it was some sort of job?' said Freddy.

'Oh yes.'

I decided it would be easier and more amusing to mislead him than stonewall.

'In the City again?'

'I don't have much expertise at anything else, but it could mean going abroad.'

'Well done!'

'I haven't got it yet. It's only at the planning stage.'

'You mean it's a new appointment?'

'More of a re-appointment. But there's been a long gap.'

'Who were you talking to?'

'One of these retired military types.'

'Personnel manager or higher up?'

'Bit of both. It's quite a small firm.'

'But international?'

'Mainly national, with international connections.'

'He must think he is going to get it,' said Jennifer. 'He's so extremely pleased with himself.'

That wasn't totally accurate. I was high, granted, but not on self-esteem. After all, if someone tells you, on a sunny day in Regent's Park, that you're the heir to a vacant throne, it's more like winning the jackpot than a game of darts. Your own talents aren't involved.

Colonel Danzing insisted we start walking again before he'd reveal what he knew. I thought it unlikely there was anyone in the shrubbery behind us collecting state secrets, but the Colonel had spent most of his life defying the Soviet Empire from a two-room service flat in Marylebone and he was quite certain, even now, that the monster was only shamming dead. We went all the way down the broad walk, past the sexy sculpture of a naked boy with a shark – through the rose garden – where the Colonel showed me a red rose which he said was exactly the colour of the royal rose of Ruritania – and he still hadn't come to the point, though he'd filled me in on a lot of history.

Rudolf Rassendyll, my great-grandfather, walking in the garden of the Royal Palace in Strelsau, capital of Ruritania, while he tried to make up his mind between being a bogus king and a genuine English gentleman, was shot by an assassin. The wound was nasty, but not fatal, and while he was recovering he decided there was no way he could go on playing King Rudolf V, even though everyone in the secret, including Queen Flavia, urged him to. So they gave out he was dead and buried a waxwork in the royal vault under the Cathedral, while Rassendyll himself left the country in a heavy disguise. It doesn't seem to have occurred to him that he was going to have to pretend to be somebody else for the rest of his life anyway. His brother, Lord Burlesdon, was in the secret, but everyone else in the civilised world thought that both King Rudolf V *and* Rudolf Rassendyll were dead. Perhaps he hoped that when people had more or less forgotten about the sensational death of the King of Ruritania, he, Rassendyll, could reappear and say that reports of his death were much exaggerated and that actually he'd been up the Amazon or down the Zambesi at the time.

But he overlooked two things. First, he and Queen Flavia couldn't really bear being apart for ever. Secondly, the secret of the original impersonation wasn't all that secure. In particular, there was a former friend of Rupert of Hentzau, a person with a name like a bottle of white plonk – the Count of Luzau-Rischenheim – who had changed sides and given his word as a gentleman not to reveal what he knew, which was virtually everything except the fact that Rudolf Rassendyll hadn't actually died of the assassin's bullet. But as time went on, Luzau-Rischenheim got restive and couldn't see the same reason as Rudolf Rassendyll for going on being a gentleman at the cost of not being King of Ruritania – or at least, in his case, Prince Consort. In other words, he fancied Queen Flavia and started suggesting – at first, no doubt, quite whimsically, but later very seriously and meaningfully – that she would surely prefer to marry him than . . . hum, ha . . . keep brooding over a dead man whose name of course he would never dream of mentioning to anybody even when he was drunk with despair at her unfriendly attitude. He also played on the fact that her subjects were fed up with having no heir to the throne. Queen Flavia was the last of the Elphbergs and she showed every sign of remaining a widow for ever. Luzau-Rischenheim cultivated the editors of *The Echo* and *The Gazette*, the two main newspapers in Ruritania, and got a noisy lobby going for the Queen to remarry, preferably with some Ruritanian aristocrat of impeccable breeding, distant royal lineage and known admiration for her, such as the handsome and popular Count of Luzau-Rischenheim.

Rudolf Rassendyll, meanwhile, had changed his name to Edwin Fenton, dyed his hair, grown a huge bushy beard and retired to a fisherman's cottage in South Cornwall, where he took up photography. He couldn't see any of his old friends any more, of course, but he made new acquaintances among the artists' colony around Newlyn/Penzance and he lived quite comfortably on his own money, which had passed, at his supposed death, to his nearest relative, Lord Burlesdon. The Earl arranged with a discreet solicitor for the income to be forwarded monthly to 'Mr Fenton' in Penzance and my great-grandfather might have been reasonably content, apart from a lot of pain from the old wound in his back, but for the thought of Queen Flavia and for her thoughts of him.

After a couple of years' abstinence, she became really ill and her loyal courtiers decided there was nothing for it but a summer visit *incognito* to the Swiss mountains. 'Mr Fenton' also visited the Swiss mountains that summer with his camera and brought back a lot of pictures of a particular lady which he showed to nobody. Nor did he spread it about that he'd made a secret marriage, but he did return the following summer to the Swiss mountains, while Queen Flavia's continuing ill-health meant she had to return there too.

This became a habit with both of them, until one year Queen Flavia became so indisposed that she had to enter a clinic in Switzerland and stay there over Christmas and into the spring before returning to her anxious subjects in Ruritania and the increasingly pressing attentions of Count Luzau-Rischenheim. 'Mr Fenton' had also been absent for a longer period than usual and he returned to England in the company of a nurse and a baby, who took up residence at Burlesdon House in Hampshire, while Mr Fenton resumed his photography in Cornwall. That baby, christened Charles Gordon after the famous martyr of Khartoum, was my grandfather. He was never called Fenton but was adopted by Lord and Lady Burlesdon and known by their family name of Rassendyll and, since he had red hair and a longish nose, it was always assumed that he was actually the Earl's son and that the Countess had behaved very maturely in letting him into the family and treating him just like her own older children, to the point of being genuinely fond of him and even in due course sending him to Eton. In fact the Burlesdons and their descendants continued to subsidise the education of Charles Gordon Rassendyll's children (including my father) and grandchildren (me and my brother), though not at Eton, because death-duties and inflation had by then made a shocking hole in the family finances.

But this is going too far ahead. Back in Ruritania in the 1890s, Queen Flavia received an ultimatum from the bottle of plonk. Luzau-Rischenheim's tame newspapers were making out now that the Queen was spending so much time abroad because she no longer cared about her people and was even thinking of abdication. He told her that it was all very unfortunate, but the only alternatives he could come up with were for her to marry him or for the truth to come out about Rudolf Rassendyll posing as the King all those years ago. As a gentleman who had given his word to keep a secret he much preferred the first alternative, but even a gentleman must put the welfare of his country before his own scruples. Queen Flavia asked for time to think and there was a panic meeting in Zurich that year, attended by Fritz von Tarlenheim (the Queen's most loyal courtier), 'Mr Fenton' and Lord Burlesdon. The plan they came up with was to take the sting out of Luzau-Rischenheim's blackmail by publishing the story of the substitute King themselves. They reckoned that when the world read about Rudolf Rassendyll's daring deeds and incredibly correct behaviour, everyone would feel sympathy for the Queen and understand why she couldn't marry anyone else. They didn't, of course, intend to give away the part Luzau-Rischenheim didn't know about – the fact that Rassendyll had survived the assassin's bullet or that he'd finally married the Queen or that they'd had a child. They felt that the Ruritanian public might possibly warm to the noble death, but no way to the waxwork in the royal vault.

The story was ghosted by a London lawyer and published under the pseudonym Anthony Hope in two instalments – Rudolf Rassendyll's own memoir of how he saved the King from Duke Michael's machinations and Fritz von Tarlenheim's account of the duel with Rupert of Hentzau, the death of King Rudolf V and the saintly renunciation of the throne by Rudolf Rassendyll with his subsequent assassination. It worked. Luzau-Rischenheim – who played a weasel role in the second instalment – was left with egg on his face and had to retire to his country estate, while Queen Flavia got so much sympathy that she must have wished she'd told the whole truth and brought her secret husband and child to Strelsau to live with her openly. There was one nasty moment when the question was raised by the editor of *The Echo* whether the charred remains of the real King Rudolf V lying in the graveyard in Zenda ought now to be exchanged with the body of Rudolf Rassendyll in the Cathedral vault. Luckily the editor of *The Gazette* – both newspapers had totally thrown over their allegiance to the luckless Luzau-Rischenheim – picked up an idea craftily floated by Tarlenheim at the end of his account. Such a gallant hero as Rassendyll, this editor argued, might not be strictly royal but surely did honour to the royal vault of the Elphbergs. He added that keeping the bodies in the wrong tombs with the wrong inscriptions would particularly appeal to tourists and that clinched his case.

It was at about this point in his narrative that Colonel Danzing pointed out the red rose of Ruritania.

'Like Mr Kinnock's,' I said.

There had been an election recently in which Mr Kinnock and the Labour Party went about sporting red roses in their buttonholes and also featured them on posters. It didn't do them any good. They went down to their usual decisive defeat.

'Not in the least like,' said the Colonel contemptuously. 'The British Labour Party symbol is a tight, forced flower of the kind you buy in cellophane which dies before it opens. The royal rose of Ruritania is a crimson climber, full, round and virile. Mark it well and learn to distinguish it from inferior versions.'

'Are you trying to tell me,' I said, 'that I have a claim to the throne of Ruritania?' It sounded fantastic, even to me.

The Colonel put the side of his shoe against a ball of horseshit which was lying on the stone path and propelled it with an elegant flick into the rose-bed. He glanced at me as if he wished he could do the same with me and then went on with his history.

Queen Flavia had continued to reign with more or less popularity until 1914. She ignored the question of a successor, which was occasionally aired in the Press, and most people assumed that, since she was now well past child-bearing age, it would have to be one of the Hapsburgs – the ruling dynasty of Austria-Hungary – who were distantly related to the Elphbergs. Kaiser Wilhelm of Germany and his family, the Hohenzollerns, also had a claim, but it was even more distant. Anyway, the heir to the Hapsburgs was shot dead and the First World War began – basically German-speakers against the rest. But although the majority of Ruritanians spoke German, Queen Flavia was such an Anglophile, for obvious reasons, that she tried to stay neutral. Kaiser Wilhelm couldn't put up with a hole in his front line against Russia, so he occupied Ruritania and shunted the Queen off to an inaccessible castle in the Harz Mountains.

When the war ended, the victorious anti-German powers were so pleased with Queen Flavia's attitude that they restored her to her throne and treated Ruritania as if it had really been on their side – even though many Ruritanians had fought in the German armies. This made the country relatively prosperous and the Queen highly popular to begin with. The problem was that during the war she'd lost the great love of her life.

As soon as Rudolf Rassendyll heard about her being imprisoned in the Harz Mountains, he set off to the rescue. He'd kept pretty fit in his Cornish retreat, but he was nearly seventy, so he obviously wasn't up to the sort of exploits he'd written about in *The Prisoner of Zenda*. The Queen wasn't particularly well guarded in her German castle and he could probably have walked through the main gate without much trouble, but he preferred to scale the walls by night. They found him in the dry moat in the morning, well dead, and since he wasn't supposed to exist, the Queen had to pretend this white-haired, white-bearded corpse was a total stranger. The grief blew her mind, so that after the war when the Ruritanians had finished waving flags and throwing virile red roses to welcome her triumphant return to Strelsau, they soon realised they'd got an old, wild woman on their backs and began to wish they'd gone republican like the Germans and Austrians, or even communist like the Russians.

Still, they took comfort in the thought that she couldn't last all that long and it certainly wasn't the moment, as her elderly Prime

Minister, Fritz von Tarlenheim, had hoped, to reveal the existence of an heir to the throne. Charles Gordon Rassendyll, therefore, who was now about forty and had survived the War by serving in some staff job behind the lines, was left to get himself a job as a school bursar and marry a middle-class Scottish lady called Mollie.

'Did Charles Gordon know who his mother was?' I asked.

'I think not,' said Colonel Danzing.

'He never went to Ruritania?'

'He would have been too recognisable as his mother's son.'

'Didn't they ever see each other after the war?'

'In Switzerland, no doubt, but he was probably not told their true relationship or that she was Queen of Ruritania. Your grandfather was not very wide awake, I'm afraid, nor a very reliable or trustworthy person to entrust a secret to.'

'He doesn't sound the right sort of person to be a school bursar.'

'That was soon evident. I believe the school had to close and your grandfather became unemployed at the time of the Depression – at about the same time as your father was born. I have always tried to see your father's political ideas as forgivable in view of what his childhood must have been like.'

'I don't remember my grandfather. I suppose he was dead before I was born?'

'Long before. My own father, General Danzing, who had become Prime Minister of Ruritania in 1926, after the death of Fritz von Tarlenheim, told me that the Queen, in the late 1930s, became determined to recognise her son and bring him openly to Strelsau. Nothing would dissuade her, not even the obvious personal disadvantages of her son, which included by then chronic alcoholism. As a last resort my father could think of no better plan than to employ an intermediary to offer Charles Gordon Rassendyll a lucrative job in Australia. He was told that the job had to be secured without delay and he went by flying-boat, ahead of his wife and children. The aircraft disappeared somewhere in the region of Sumatra. Your grandfather was always accident-prone.'

'Was it an accident?'

'Do you suggest that my father, the Prime Minister of Ruritania and a royalist to his fingertips, would have deliberately arranged the death of the Queen's only child?'

'It seems to have been convenient.'

Colonel Danzing wore his sour expression again and looked about for another ball of horseshit to kick.

'For men of honour convenience is never a primary consideration.'

We had left the rose-garden and stopped beside a curving bed of flowers somewhere in the area of the Open-Air Theatre. I shall always remember that bed – the flowers were mostly blue, of different sorts and shades. It was here that Colonel Danzing told me that although there had been no Ruritanian monarch since the death of Queen Flavia in 1939, he believed a restoration was desirable and feasible and I was the only suitable candidate. I looked him in the eyes and noticed for the first time that they were pale blue as if they had strayed from the flower bed and faded on the way.

'You think I *am* suitable?'

'In the context of monarchy,' he said, 'suitable is not a question of character or attainments, which it must be said you lack, but of birth. That is the essence of hereditary monarchy – it leaves the choice to God rather than men.'

'A bit dated, though, isn't it?'

'If our century has demonstrated anything, it is that "progressive" political ideas are no more likely to work than the old ones. In the history of mankind I should say that monarchies have generally proved more successful that democracies, especially in small, backward countries.'

'Is Ruritania so backward?'

'It has been shut up inside the Soviet Empire for forty years. You cannot get much more primitive than that.'

'So what do you want me to do?'

'Agree in principle that you are willing to claim your inheritance. Say nothing for the moment of what I have told you, not even to your brother. Wait patiently until I approach you again and in the meantime read everything you can find about your country, including those two books I mentioned. And study to be . . .'

He stopped, looked at me gloomily, looked away again.

'Yes?'

'Are you willing?'

'Why not? I haven't got any other particular projects in view at present.'

'No other particular projects in view,' he said, spreading out the words like a hand of cards which he hated the sight of.

'What do you want me to study? Court etiquette – that sort of thing?'

'That would be premature.'

He paused again, waited for two lovers with their arms wound round each other to pass and then said, quite angrily:

'Do you want to be King of Ruritania or don't you?'

'Is there any loot in it?'

'I shall find sufficient funds, but there will be few luxuries, if that's what you mean.'

'A King without luxuries seems a bit pointless,' I said.

'What is your answer?'

'Yes,' I said, 'O.K.'

'I will call you, then, in a week or two,' he said and immediately turned to go, as if he suddenly couldn't bear any more of my company. Then, over his shoulder:

'Study to be more dignified, for God's sake!'

And he walked briskly away without looking back.

3

Zenda Airport

It was a month or two before I heard from Colonel Danzing again. My brother and sister-in-law became increasingly sceptical about the job they thought I'd been interviewed for.

'Don't be so passive!' said Jennifer, as she stuffed dirty clothes into the washing-machine. 'Give them a ring! They must have made a decision by now. They just haven't got around to writing to the unsuccessful applicants.'

'Then if I'm one of them, why waste a 'phone call to save them the trouble?'

'Don't you care either way? Perhaps if you'd shown more enthusiasm, you'd have got the job.'

'Enthusiasm isn't one of the qualifications they asked for,' I said.

'Well, I wonder if you've got the other ones either. Unless they just wanted someone with red hair, like the people in the Sherlock Holmes story.'

'More or less,' I said.

'Do you have to leave all your shirts and socks inside out?'

'It saves trouble.'

I'd begun to have doubts myself about the reality of that encounter in Regent's Park. Was I really on hold for a kingdom? On the other hand, I had now read *The Prisoner of Zenda* and *Rupert of Hentzau* and my name was undoubtedly Rassendyll. Also I'd started to read the foreign pages of my brother's newspaper and occasionally found a paragraph about Ruritania and its problems. They looked terminal: a catastrophic economy, an ethnic split between Germans and Slavs and a political vacuum rapidly being filled by the same old communist party hacks now posing as democrats. Perhaps a King was the only hope. The Serbs and Romanians, with similar problems, were at least giving their ex-royals entry-visas. It was impossible to conceal my new area of knowledge and interest altogether from my relations.

'Eastern Europe is reverting to pre-First War,' said my brother, as we sat watching the news after supper.

'Further than that,' I said. 'Pre-Hapsburg Empire.'

'What would *you* know about it?' said my sister-in-law.

'So this new job is in Eastern Europe, is it?' asked Freddy.

'Not necessarily,' I said. I was afraid they'd start trying to pin me down to a particular country.

'It's not like you to take such an interest in current affairs,' said Freddy.

'For a City man,' I said, 'it's always worth keeping an eye on where the international aid is flowing. Whenever governments are involved, there's always a lot of overflow.'

'By which you mean the taxpayers' money gets diverted to a lot of con-men and corrupt officials.'

'Paying tax is voluntary,' I said with a mean smile, immediately closing my eyes and bowing my head as I waited for the blast from Jennifer.

But nothing came and when I opened them again I found she hadn't even noticed my provocation. She was gripped by the latest news on the screen.

'What a macabre affair!' she said.

It was only a short item and I'd already missed everything but the pay-off. The BBC's girl reporter – young and pretty but media-aggressive – was standing in a cobbled square in front of a large church.

'For the present, then,' she was saying, 'people seem to be more bewildered than shocked by the revelation that their principal tourist attraction is not all it seems. It remains to be seen what, if any, effect this will have on the uneasy balance of power here. Clare Studebaker, reporting for the BBC, from Strelsau.'

'What was all that about?' I asked, as casually as I could.

'You and Freddy were chattering,' said Jennifer, 'so I didn't catch it all. They're digging up some grave in East Germany and transferring the corpse to the royal vault in Strelsau Cathedral. For some reason I couldn't fathom, the corpse they've got in there already isn't a corpse at all, but a waxwork. And it isn't even one of their kings, but an Englishman.'

'Why are they bothering?' I asked.

'It seems to be a political move, but the reporter wasn't very clear about who was organising it.'

'Attractive girl all the same,' I said.

'What do you mean by that?'

'She looks nice, but of course looks aren't everything in a journalist.'
'You're suggesting a man could do the job better?'
'It was you who criticised her performance.'
'Sexist pig!' she said.

The state funeral in Strelsau was widely reported, especially in England because of the English connection. The Earl of Burlesdon was interviewed and said he was delighted that his great-great-great uncle was being brought back from the dead, as it were, and admitted that the secret of his survival and marriage to Queen Flavia had been known to the head of the Burlesdon family all along, but never divulged to anyone else.

And now, of course, Jennifer and Freddy woke up to the fact that the corpse at the centre of the ceremony was that of Rudolf Rassendyll. It's not a very common name and Freddy got teased about this at work. He was full of it at supper.

'I do believe we must be related,' he said, as he helped out the sausages and mash. 'Rudolf Rassendyll was the younger brother of the Earl of Burlesdon and I remember Mum trying to get Dad to admit that he was related to the Burlesdons.'

My sister-in-law was excited too.

'Why don't we take a holiday in Ruritania?' she said. 'East Europe's said to be incredibly cheap because of the exchange rate.'

'We're already booked for the Loire in August,' said Freddy.

'Couldn't we go at Christmas?'

'There's no way we can afford two holidays in one year,' said Freddy. 'The exchange rate may be good, but what about the fares?'

'I could go,' I said. 'I'm not booked for the Loire.'

'What would you use for money?' asked Jennifer. 'Or do people on the dole get an annual foreign holiday thrown in?'

'I'll ask the nice people at Social Security,' I said.

In fact I knew by now that I was going to Ruritania. Colonel Danzing had 'phoned and invited me to meet him on Primrose Hill. We kept moving round the paths, as before, though there was no cover at all for communist spies, and the Colonel told me that the state funeral and the revelations about the survival of Rudolf Rassendyll and his secret marriage to Queen Flavia were indirectly his doing. The state funeral went off reasonably well. People were amused and intrigued rather than shocked to learn of the waxwork in the royal vault and the local newspapers thought the story would be good for tourism rather than the reverse. But the Colonel and his friends inside Ruritania had hoped for bigger crowds and more excitement. The affair had curiosity value rather than glamour and that was disappointing. Without the glamour factor there was little hope of arousing people's enthusiasm for the restoration of the monarchy.

The next stage was to reveal that the secret marriage of Queen Flavia and Rudolf Rassendyll had been blessed with Charles Gordon Rassendyll and that his descendant was alive and available, but Colonel Danzing wanted this to emerge more gradually.

'The sense of history is even weaker in the East than it is among your generation in the West,' he said. 'We have organised an exhibition of the life and times of Queen Flavia in the Palace of Youth in Strelsau, but the attendance is poor. Most of the visitors are tourists – still rather few in Ruritania – or old people who remember the pre-war period before Nazism and Communism. The main exhibit is the waxwork of Rudolf Rassendyll exhumed from the cathedral vault, but there is still not enough interest for our purpose. It's as if people are content for the past to lie buried.'

'Perhaps you chose the wrong approach,' I said. 'You should have started with me and then revealed the back history.'

The Colonel looked at me with surprise.

'You are taking more of an interest,' he said. 'You may be right. At any rate, what we need now is an event, a news story with implications for the present rather than the past. I am proposing to send you to Ruritania.'

'Fair enough,' I said. 'And when I come down the steps from the aircraft I'll kiss the runway like the Pope and claim my inheritance.'

'No,' said Colonel Danzing, 'You will go *incognito* and will first acquaint yourself a little with the country and some of the personalities and interests involved. After that we will decide whether it's opportune for you to throw off your disguise.'

'What disguise? A black cloak? A big hat?'

'A hat would be advisable, since otherwise people might mistake you for a waxwork or think a dead hero had come to life.'

'People of my age don't wear hats.'

'I am aware of that.'

The Colonel paused. I had the impression he was stringing me along.

'A baseball hat and dark glasses?'

'The simplest solution,' he said, 'would be to shave your head completely.'

'Ah. Let's think a bit harder, then!'

'You are vain of your hair? It will grow back.'

'I'd look like a neo-Nazi.'

'It would be the simplest solution,' he repeated. 'And historically apt. Your great-grandfather shaved off his beard and moustache in order to resemble the King more closely. More than a hundred years later, you who *are* the King, need to *avoid* resembling your great-grandfather.'

'You, who *are* the King . . .': that clinched it, as the crafty old sod knew it would. As I was beginning to discover, if you know you are a king, your outlook changes drastically and you can put up with almost anything in the short term. Colonel Danzing would get me a ticket, fix me a passport in another name and arrange for me to be accredited as a journalist for an obscure business magazine. That job, he said, wouldn't be a hoax and they'd want some copy out of me.

'I hope you're capable of writing joined-up prose,' he said.

'No problem,' I said, 'but when are you going to start treating me with proper respect? Calling me "Sire" and walking backwards – that sort of thing?'

'Your saving grace, Mr Rassendyll,' he said, 'is your sense of humour. You will appreciate the name I have selected for you to assume in Ruritania. It is "Edwin Fenton".'

So I flew into Zenda airport as a skinhead journalist called Ed Fenton. Zenda is the nearest city to Ruritania's most accessible border and about fifty miles north-west of the capital, Strelsau. Both cities are built on hills and separated by a flattish area which, in my great-grandfather's time, used to be mostly forest. It was somewhere in that forest that King Rudolf V – after being murdered by the villainous Rupert of Hentzau – was incinerated in his hunting-lodge. The original airfield made by the Ruritanians in the Thirties was much smaller and closer to Zenda – hence its name – but when the Nazis occupied the country in 1939 they cleared a lot of the forest, moved the airfield nearer to the capital and added an autobahn in order to keep a tight grip on both cities.

My plane from Warsaw docked directly on to the airport building, so I didn't encounter any Ruritanian soil I could have kissed until we got to a scrubby bit of waste-ground – mainly dogshit and dandelions – round a tower-block on the outskirts of Strelsau. But going through passport control I seriously wondered if I'd make it even that far into my inheritance. Nobody seemed to have told the officials that the Iron Curtain had gone and the Soviet Empire with it. The plane hadn't been all that full, but most of its passengers were foreign – Germans and Americans looking for business opportunities, I guessed – and the passport people in their bullet-proof glass booths spent about ten minutes per person, examining them front, side, and – with the help of a large mirror hung on the wall – back. By the time they got to me I was really pissed off – mixed with a bit of worry, of course, about my alibi – and I suppose they were trained to pick up any signs of stress. After the usual close examination from all angles of my shaven head, the bloke in the booth sent for his superior.

'This photograph is you?' the superior asked in English, with a tone of complete disbelief.

'Unfortunately, yes,' I said. The photograph showed a smirking axe-murderer, but I'd certainly sat for it.

'You have come for the football?' he asked.

'No,' I said. 'On business.'

'What business?'

'Actually to write about business opportunities in your lovely, friendly, prosperous country.'

'What are your racial views?'

'I prefer the Welsh to the Irish and the Scots to both. I'm a bit indifferent to Canadians and I can never tell Belgians from French. I loathe Japanese cars but I've nothing against individual Nips as such. Have you got a race-problem here?'

'We do not need any Nazis.'

'I'm sure you don't,' I said meaningfully. Ruritanian border control was obviously a nest of them.

'Why did you cut off your hair?'

'It was too much trouble to wash.'

'This is not a joke.'

'No, it's a bloody disgrace. The first thing I shall do for my paper is warn off people looking for business opportunities in Ruritania. Especially people with hair disabilities.'

'We do not like aggressive people in our country.'

'Listen!' I said, speaking in German for the first time, 'I don't like aggressive people either and I've got a perfectly good visa there from your Embassy in London. Why don't you send for the British Ambassador and tell him what you've got against me?'

'You speak good German, but I wonder why you want to look like a hooligan.' He smiled, handed me my passport and waved me through the barrier. 'Please! Welcome to Ruritania, Herr Fenton!'

Colonel Danzing had arranged for two of his associates to meet me. They were waiting impatiently the other side of the baggage-hall. As we hurried outside and got into a down-at-heel Skoda in the car-park, I asked them why the passport people were so obstreperous.

'They thought you might be a dangerous criminal,' said the shorter and older of the two, without a smile, as he got behind the wheel of the Skoda. Anton Grabenau wore a blue, East European, Dracula-style raincoat and looked as if he'd been through every kind of hassle and compromise. There were trenches running down from his nostrils to the corners of his weary mouth, another straight down the middle of his forehead and his small eyes darted about inside dark grey rabbit-holes. He was a deputy in the newly-elected Parliament and wore a little green and blue badge in his buttonhole to prove it.

'Do I look so terrible?'

'Fairly terrible,' said the younger and friendlier of the two, tall with thick, fairish hair cut short round the sides. Vladek Tarlenheim wore glasses, jeans and a check shirt and smoked incessantly.

'Why did they get more polite as soon as I spoke German?'

'They were probably afraid at first that you were an English mercenary coming to help the Slavs murder Germans.'

'Is there a lot of that?'

'Not yet . . .' said Grabenau, leaving the sentence open as if he was really saying the opposite.

The motorway from the airport to Strelsau probably hadn't been repaired since the Nazis constructed it, but Grabenau and the other drivers seemed to know every crack and hole intimately: the traffic braked and bounced and swerved in a collective series of zig-zags, as if we were all dodging an invisible air-attack. Any newcomer – an unwary tourist, for example – travelling in a straight line would have broken an axle or collided with a deftly sidestepping ten-ton lorry. The vehicles were mostly of Fifties' design and maybe actually dated from then, but there were a few newish Mercs. Market-forces had already started to creep into Ruritania like the first tentacles of ivy taking hold of an old tree.

The tower-block, all set about with dogshit and dandelions, contained Vladek's flat-cum-studio. I was booked into a hotel near the centre of Strelsau, as befitted a supposed Western journalist with hard currency, but meanwhile we needed somewhere private to talk.

'Do they still have mikes in the hotel rooms?' I asked.

'Certainly,' said Grabenau.

'They're probably not connected up,' said Vladek, 'or if they are, then nobody's listening, but you can't be sure.'

'We can be sure of nothing,' said Grabenau. 'The old order is partly abrogated, the new one has not yet come into being. We are a disturbed ant-hill.'

Vladek's flat consisted of two small rooms and an even smaller kitchen, with cubby-holes for a loo and a bath. The whole place was tacky to a degree and more or less impassable with stacked-up canvases, thinly and messily painted with elongated figures. It didn't surprise me that Vladek had taken to politics – he obviously had no talent as an artist. We sat crushed into the only clear space, drinking tea and some sort of local alcohol, with a smell like manure and a taste to match. They didn't treat me as their potential monarch. Grabenau occupied the only arm-chair, while Vladek and I sat on kitchen-chairs. I was beginning to think that a bit of deference wouldn't go amiss, if only to prepare me for my new role.

'How much nostalgia is there for the old days?' I asked. 'The days of Queen Flavia.'

'None,' said Grabenau. 'She was mad for the last years of her reign and most people looked forward to a republic. A few people considered her death heroic – you know that when German tanks entered Strelsau she came out alone from the palace wearing her crown and stood in the middle of the square to stop them, only to be run down by the leading tank? But most people thought she was too mad to know what she was doing and in any case there was widespread support for Hitler.'

'What happened to the crown?'

'Also crushed, I should imagine,' said Grabenau.

'Or stolen by the Nazis,' said Vladek.

'Could be expensive to replace,' I said. 'But I'll have to have one.' Grabenau looked at my shaven head and scratched his wrist expressively.

'So what makes you think,' I said, 'that there's any mileage in restoring the monarchy?'

'Lack of alternatives,' said Grabenau.

'I take a more positive view,' said Vladek, offering me a bowl of Russian sweets that looked as if their sell-by date had expired some time during the siege of Stalingrad. 'We have experienced so many dismal forms of so-called "popular" government – Fascism, the First Republic briefly after the war, Soviet Communism, now the Second Republic – that we are craving for something more colourful, more inspiring. In this context monarchy would not seem so much like a return to tradition as a fresh idea.'

'Failure of alternatives, as I said,' said Grabenau.

'How much clout do you have?' I asked. 'I mean, are you just freelances or is there some kind of royalist organisation?'

They looked at each other and then at me warily. Grabenau answered.

'We are not official,' he said.

I always used to think that skinheads shaved themselves mainly to annoy the other people that had to look at them. Now I began to suspect it was to annoy themselves. At any rate, the combination of feeling like a criminal plus the alcohol, the horrible canvasses hemming us in and the general squalor of this dead-end place suddenly got to me. I stood up and started to complain.

'Bloody hell! I didn't come here to be pushed around. I may not be King of Ruritania but I'm bloody heir apparent. What have you got to offer in return for me taking an interest in your grotty problems?'

They looked alarmed, but also curiously gratified.

'The walls are quite thin,' said Vladek.

'I'm not worried about that,' I said. 'I can get on a plane and go home tomorrow. As far as I'm concerned this is a business transaction. I happen to have something you want – even if it's only a pint of royal blood – so what have you got that I want?'

'You misunderstand our position,' said Grabenau, 'or at least mine. I am not convinced that we want you or your half litre of royal blood, but Colonel Danzing's family was good to my family after the war and therefore I agreed to introduce you to our country and investigate the prospects of a royal restoration. As for you, I don't imagine that you'd be here if you didn't wish to be King of Ruritania, so I think, yes, you'd better go straight back to England if you can't take an interest in our grotty problems.'

'We are seeking something more spiritual than material,' said Vladek. 'A King in the modern world has no material power, but he supplies what we have all lost, the power of our own collective identity, the power of ceremony. You are necessary to us, Karl, because you are not a business transaction and for no other reason. Therefore I hope you will not go home and therefore I shall be happy to make you a crown.'

It wasn't clear whether he was speaking metaphorically or whether he actually intended to fashion the thing with his own hands, but I noticed that several of the figures in his paintings were wearing hideous crown-type head-dresses of various kitschy kinds and I was very much afraid it was the latter. It was at this point that I understood forcibly that one of the worst things about

27

being a King would be having to stand in for other people's dreams and live down to their stunted imaginations.

4

The Palace of Youth

Strelsau reminded me of Edinburgh: a large chunk of rock with the old city crowded up it on twisting cobbled streets; and, down below, the spacious, gracious part – squares and avenues of the 18th/19th centuries. The concrete fangs of the Soviet era make a desolate outer ring. Strelsau's rock is less dramatic than Edinburgh's sinking ship – more the shape of a heaped-up sand-castle, with the dome of the royal palace and the spire of the Gothic cathedral sticking out of the top. Still, any tourist would feel he was getting his money's worth of the picturesque, especially with an exchange-rate of 500 kR (Ruritanian krunas) to the pound and still inflating at about 100% per annum. Below the rock – roughly where the railway runs in Edinburgh – between the gracious part and the cobbled part, flows the river Volzer (or Wloczr, depending on your ethnic preference), with several bridges. The river looks fine from the bridges or the banks, but don't try swimming in it, as I did later – the fish all died of chemicals years ago.

My hotel, previously 'The Lenin', now 'The Astoria', was in one of the gracious squares. My room was small and high up, but clean. There was no proper table to work on, but Colonel Danzing had arranged for me to write my business articles in the offices of a German-language magazine called *Augen* which had computer and fax facilities.

Not many of the other rooms in my hotel were occupied – the place had been used under the communists, Vladek said, mainly for minor party functionaries attending rubber-stamp conferences and hadn't yet been face-lifted for Western tourists. But we shared the slow, creaking lift as far as the floor below mine with a petite white-faced, black-haired girl, dressed in black and white, who stared resolutely at the lift-buttons and wouldn't even give me a glance. Vladek, accompanying me to my room, said she looked like trouble, but I thought she might be trouble worth taking and asked him why she was so frosty.

'We were speaking German, you see. She is Slav.'

'The ethnic split is that bad?'

'Not ethnic so much as historical-political. We are all the same race, but sometimes we have been part of the German world, sometimes Slav, divided by religion, divided by power. Throughout our history, not just the history of this century, it has been a see-saw.'

Obviously I had been brought in as ballast for the German end of the see-saw. Danzing, Grabenau and Tarlenheim were all German names, though Vladek's first name suggested some Slav connection. Of course I spoke German not Ruritanian (a Slav language) and, since most of the leading Slavs had been communists, it was clearly their turn to lose weight. All the same, I didn't like the idea of being an exclusively German candidate. I would have to rely on my immediate sponsors until I knew more about the place, but the sooner I added a few Slav acquaintances to my quiver the better; and why not start on the floor below? The girl, I have to say, wasn't especially good-looking, though she had a good body. I've trained myself over the years not to be too fussy about women's faces or indeed their looks in general. The ones who are born beautiful are too much effort to get close to and often not worth it when you do; whereas the others don't expect much and occasionally have a lot to offer. It's the law of life, really: backing the favourite is a waste of everybody's time and trouble, you only stand to make a serious profit on outsiders.

Vladek left me to unpack and relax. He and Grabenau were to call round later and take me out to a restaurant for supper, but meanwhile it was early evening. The hotel bar was empty except for the barman and a mean-looking stubble-bearded man in a grey tweed jacket, dark trousers and white polo-neck sweater. He was drinking mineral water and had his back against the bar so as to face the entrance-hall. Correctly assuming he was American, I introduced myself by my false name and asked him in English what brought him to Strelsau.

'Why do you ask?'

'I'm here to explore business possibilities for my newspaper and wondered if you'd found any.'

'I'm a churchman not a businessman.'

'Which church?'

'I don't know that we have a community in your country.'

I was afraid he'd ask me to start one, but he wasn't the usual proselytising type. In fact he was distinctly cagey and this provoked me to press him further.

'Considering they've got Catholics and Russian Orthodox here already, is there much scope for alternative religion?'

The whites of his eyes showed above his green pupils.

'The true religion of this country,' he said, 'is primitive Christianity. Bohemia produced the Hussites, but they were little more than a protest against the worst aspects of Papism. In this country some folk went right back to basics and that tradition – for all the other churches tried to stamp it out with every kind of atrocity – has never completely died out.'

'So you're here to revive it?'

'I'm here to study it, Mr Fenton. In case there should be an opportunity for reciprocal arrangements with our own folk.'

The idea depressed me – it was clearly open season for mountebanks in Ruritania and maybe they needed a king even less than they needed a few spare religions. Also the word 'folk' always irritates me.

'Are you primitives too?'

'You're being offensive, Mr Fenton.'

'You used the word yourself.'

'Primitive Christianity was the term I used. That is a very different concept. It aims at truth and authenticity, whereas you seem to be implying something from the stone-age.'

'Sorry.'

'O.K.'

'Have another drink, Mr . . .!'

'Thanks, but I have to go. Fisher John.'

He pronounced it 'Jarn'. We shook hands. Suddenly the little white-faced girl from the lift appeared in the entrance-hall and Fisher John bounced off the bar to intercept her. They spoke briefly, then turned together towards the street door. I saw I had to seize my chance and caught them up on the pavement. A cab was waiting with its engine running.

'Excuse me, Fisher,' I said, not sure whether it was his first name or the primitive Christian substitute for 'pastor' or 'reverend', 'I wouldn't like you to go away with the impression that I'm just a yob . . .'

Saying this I managed to catch the eye of the girl and smiled encouragingly. She didn't smile back, but she didn't look away.

'Religion matters a lot to me,' I said without a trace of irony, 'but I don't find it something easy to talk about in the first instance.'

He gave me a very sharp and puzzled look.

'I can't talk now,' he said. 'Maybe later.'

We shook hands again and he gave me a card from his breast pocket before following the girl into the cab. The card was printed in raised green letters: 'DISCIPLES OF THE FIRST INSTANCE', with his name and an address in Tulsa, Oklahoma. No wonder he looked puzzled by my random phrase.

The restaurant was in a basement in the gracious part of the city. It had an expensive Hollywood-Roman decor, but the food was mostly local – thick, spicy flavours, peasant cooking – nice, but completely at odds with the ambience. We were four at the table: myself, Vladek and Grabenau plus an elderly German who had only recently returned from a long exile in Switzerland to reclaim his ancestral estate. He was called Count Wenslaus von Wunklisch and claimed to be descended from an older dynasty of Ruritanian rulers than the Elphbergs.

'So we're nouveaux, are we?' I said. 'I thought the name sounded iffy.'

'I am not competing for your throne, don't worry!' he said in English, putting his prehensile brown-spotted fingers on my arm. 'On the contrary, I shall do all in my power to give you joy of it.'

My impression was that he represented any funds there might be behind the royalist party and also that, although he took to me immediately, he was on sticky terms with Grabenau and contemptuous of Vladek, who was deferential to him. The Count warmly invited me to stay in his castle.

'In the mountains, Charles, very very romantic, but remote.'

'His name is Karl,' said Grabenau in a prickly whisper across the table, 'but for the present, especially in public places, it would be better to call him Ed or at least Edwin.'

'I prefer Charles,' said the Count, again touching my arm. 'Edwin is ridiculous, Ed vulgar, and Karl only reminds me of that bearded monster from the British Museum who brought so much misery on mankind.'

'I was called after him,' I said.

'Oh dear!' said Wunklisch, with a long sharkish smile under his bristly grey moustache. 'But no one need be aware of that.'

'My second name too, I'm afraid.'

'What? Karl Marx Rassendyll?'

I nodded, hanging my head in mock shame, while he laughed happily and patted me on the shoulder.

'I take my hat off to your parents. They didn't do things by halves.' He raised his glass. 'To Karl Marx Rassendyll!'

I raised mine in return, but Grabenau and Vladek looked furious and alarmed and I saw that the pretty fair-haired waitress in a very tight short skirt and ephemeral blouse, who had just arrived at the table with some plates of meat balls, was staring at me.

'I'm hoping to see Rassendyll's waxwork in the Palace of Youth tomorrow,' I said, 'but I doubt if he'd be pleased to be shown off in a building intended for Marxist propaganda.'

The waitress put the plates down in front of us and went away, but I had the feeling she'd given me mine with particular deference. If so, it was the first I'd yet received and I distinctly fancied it. The others still looked tight-lipped, but the Count couldn't care less.

'Well played!' he said, eating with his fork in his left hand, since his right now rested permanently on my arm. 'But we cannot, no, we cannot in any circumstances crown you Karl Marx the First – or would it have to be Second? So I think Charles is altogether preferable, don't you?'

'Except that Charles the First sounds unlucky to an Englishman,' I said, 'and if I came on to begin with as Prince Charles, there might be some confusion.'

It was arranged before we parted that I should spend next weekend at the Count's castle.

'Expect no comforts, Karl Marx!' he said. 'It was turned into a prison by your namesake's Utopian followers and I have only just repossessed it. But the scenery is magnificent, there will be some rough shooting and plenty to eat and drink. We shall also be able to talk quite freely and call a king a king. My car will come for you on Friday morning. It will take much of the day to get there, I'm afraid, because the roads in our poor homeland would disgrace a colony of apes.'

Like the remark about talking freely, this was a parting jab at Grabenau. He certainly looked as if it put the finishing touch to a bad evening, but then his whole face and manner spoke of a life of bad evenings. In fact he reminded me slightly of Dad – not to look at, but because of the disillusionment he gave off like the smell of exhaust from a worn-out engine. No doubt he'd been a genuine socialist too in his day and that was why he couldn't see any fun at all in royalism.

The Palace of Youth, where I went next morning with Vladek, was a warehouse pretending to be a Greek temple, with pillars and long steps all round it. The exhibition devoted to my great-grandmother's life and times was on the first floor, sparsely attended, mostly by grannies. There were family photos of Flavia as a girl – chubby, then thinner and prettier as she got into her teens, then distinctly dishy at about the time she met my great-grandfather. There were pictures from *The Illustrated London News* of the Coronation at which he impersonated King Rudolf V; and nearby a small scale-model of the Castle of Zenda, in which you could see the real king sitting with his head in his hands and a chain attached to his ankle in his moat-level dungeon. An oil-portrait of the villainous, black-bearded Duke Michael in a blue uniform hung behind that and then there were photos and an official portrait of the restored King Rudolf and an artist's impression of his marriage to Flavia in the cathedral. But it was difficult to tell whether the king and his double really looked exactly alike, since the only photos of Rudolf Rassendyll were in family groups of the Burlesdons taken before he ever visited Ruritania, with a self-portrait or two as the artist-photographer Edwin Fenton, which were mostly hat and beard. Rupert of Hentzau never seemed to have had himself either photographed or painted – no time, I suppose, between screwing ladies and executing evil deeds. The best the exhibition could do to evoke him was a glass case containing a hussar's uniform and a pair of rapiers purporting to be those used by Hentzau and Rassendyll in their final duel. I wasn't surprised the exhibition hadn't switched on the customers – it was just adequate if you knew the story, but dead and distant if you didn't.

And then round a corner we came into a screened-off area which was all dark except for a rectangular box in the centre lit from the ceiling. We walked up to the railing round the box and found ourselves peering down through a sheet of glass at a man lying in an open coffin. He was dressed in black boots and a white military uniform with a red sash diagonally across the chest and although his eyes were closed he looked almost alive. It was my great-grandfather, Rudolf Rassendyll – or rather his waxwork – with thick, dark-red hair and a long nose. I could see we had points in common but I didn't mistake it for myself – perhaps it looked too noble and self-conscious, the face of somebody used to being looked at, like an actor's or a politician's. Vladek evidently saw things differently. He, of course, had had a hand in mounting the exhibition, so he wasn't surprised by the waxwork itself, but he kept looking from it to me and back and murmuring excitedly to himself.

'If it were not for the shaved head,' he said finally, 'you would be almost identical. The jaw, the cheek-bone, the temples, the upper-lip – the mouth is perhaps a little fuller and more pouting in your case – but even the ears are the same and, above all, the nose. I could almost believe in Reincarnation or – God forgive me! – Resurrection.'

His eyes damp, he seized my hand and, with a little dip of the knee, kissed it.

'I was a Doubting Thomas,' he said. 'Receiving you at the airport looking like a Nazi, driving in Grabenau's proletarian car, encountering so many mundane circumstances of our shabby life here, I was a supporter of monarchy, but not a real believer. Now I understand that Colonel Danzing made no mistake. We have found our rightful king.'

'Well, good,' I said. 'Thanks, Vladek. But the problem is whether anybody much wants their rightful king. The visitors to this exhibition would just about fill a minibus and most of them couldn't get into it without assistance.'

Two or three bunched-up old women came in at that moment and Vladek pulled me quickly into a corner. They stared down in silence at the coffin, then one of them crossed herself. As they hobbled out and before we had time to move, a girl in school uniform entered. She was perhaps fifteen or sixteen and seemed uncertain, even furtive, her hands clasped tensely behind her back. Not seeing us in our dark corner, she relaxed and brought her hands into view, revealing a small bunch of red roses – the tight sort favoured by Mr Kinnock and despised by Colonel Danzing, but at least they weren't wrapped in cellophane. She stared down for a while at the waxwork, then dropped the roses on the glass at the foot of the coffin and glancing round guiltily, spotted us. She froze, seemed about to faint with terror, then moved as if to pick up the flowers again.

'It's all right. Why not? He was a good man,' said Vladek soothingly. She left the flowers and hurried out past us, eyes down.

'You see, you see, Karl,' said Vladek eagerly, 'the feelings are there, but people are still half-ashamed of them.'

The rest of the exhibition dealt with Flavia's reign as Queen in her own right and was mostly photos of royal occasions before and after the First War. Apart from the very noticeable change in Flavia herself – turning after the death of Rudolf Rassendyll into a gaunt witch with staring eyes and hair tied up tightly in a scarf – it was routine footage of military parades, carriage processions, state visits and PR stunts with miners, factory-workers, villagers, municipal trees, etc. The final item was a large, badly-drawn painting of the queen going down under the Nazi tank in front of the royal palace. The scale was all wrong and it looked more like a bulldozer knocking down a telegraph-post (the oversize crown added to that impression). There was something familiar about the technique and I turned towards Vladek.

35

'Yes,' he said proudly, 'I am responsible. Of course there is no photographic record, but I found it quite easy to imagine.'

I searched for something neutral to say.

'What's the palace used for now?'

'The President lives there.'

'Can he be got out?'

'It's one of our problems, of course.'

'I hope it won't need tanks.'

Vladek laughed uneasily.

'The President is a philosopher,' he said. 'A professional philosopher, I mean. He has written serious books. He will not be so unwise as to hold on to his office if the country shows its desire for a king.'

And that, I thought, as we left the Palace of Youth and its dismal exhibition, was sheer fantasy. One schoolgirl with five tight red roses didn't make a restoration. As far as I could see, it would be tanks or nothing.

5

Sightseeing in Strelsau

Colonel Danzing had asked me to keep in touch with him regularly by coded letter. That seemed a bit childish, but since he was providing the stamps along with all my other living expenses plus the air-fare, I went along with it. He showed me how a simple book-code worked and asked me to choose any book I liked. *The Prince* seemed an appropriate title, though I'd never read it; the Colonel approved and told me to buy a copy in English translation to take with me to Ruritania. Rather than spend good drinking-money on a book I borrowed it from the local library.

After my visit to the exhibition in the Palace of Youth I thought I might as well open my secret correspondence with the Colonel by warning him that royalism in Ruritania wasn't flavour of the month, with the implicit message that quick results couldn't be expected and my expenses were likely to be open-ended. I shook off Vladek, therefore, returned to my hotel-room, composed a brief message and opened my copy of *The Prince* at random:

> Whether it be better to be beloved than feared, or feared than beloved? It is answered, both would be convenient, but because that is hard to attain, it is better and more secure, if one must be wanting, to be feared than beloved; for in the general men are ungrateful, inconstant, hypocritical, fearful of danger, and covetous of gain . . .

This was amazing stuff! The depression that had come over me after the exhibition lifted and for the first time I felt really encouraged. O.K., nobody badly wanted a king of Ruritania, but suppose they got one all the same! I was it. Nothing had changed in my situation, which was still a case of grasping at red roses. The change was in my attitude: red roses might come later, when the outsider crossed the line in front, but they were no part of the race, which was just man and horse. The man was me, in the Elphberg colours, and the horse . . .? As the man said, 'my kingdom for a horse', meaning presumably that if he could get his hands on a horse he'd keep his kingdom.

I scrubbed out my first message to Colonel Danzing – 'Not much joy so far, but the food is edible' – substituted 'Machiavelli is my favourite author' and coded it: '105 NWELOW: RAAOOCNKIW:, GUOMRWGML, U'. Then I signed it Karl Marx (DWUANWUP) to annoy him, addressed an envelope and went out to look for a post-office. Since I didn't want Vladek seeing that I was making secret reports to the Colonel I'd arranged to meet him again – though he warned me I wouldn't find it easy – at the cathedral, near the top of the old town. There was a post-office just over one of the bridges, but I very soon lost my way following a street that seemed to go up and then began twisting down again and fetched up, after trying to cut through side-streets, in a gloomy cul-de-sac of shuttered, crumbling houses with a stench of shit.

As I cursed aloud and turned to go back I saw two men coming towards me. They were about twenty yards away and it was very obvious from the way they fanned out as soon as I saw them that their only business in the street was with me. One of them was Sumo-size, with a boulder-shaped head and shortish hair, the other tall and narrow, with shoulder-length dark hair and a ferocious Tatar face. They gave me the shivers, but I kept walking towards them hoping I was mistaken in their intentions. I wasn't. The huge one stopped right in my path, while the thin one got hold of my arm and said in German:

'Give your Deutschmarks!'

'I don't have any.'

'Your dollars, then!'

'Sorry, no dollars either.'

The Sumo one trod on my right foot, the other produced a knife.

'Your pounds and credit-cards! Give!'

I played rugby at school, I took karate classes up to brown belt, second grade, but this was not a match I could win. Not being a credit-worthy person I had no plastic cards, but I gave him my pounds and when they'd checked my belt and pockets to make sure I hadn't kept any back, they let me go.

The money was no great loss – Colonel Danzing might have to top up the weekly allowance he'd arranged for me at a local bank – but the loss of self-esteem was serious. My great-grandfather would surely have sprung up a sheer wall or crippled one of his assailants with a fore-arm smash and dodged the other. I remembered one occasion in the book when he'd had to deal with no fewer than three assailants and made brilliant use of a small metal table. I definitely needed to be fitter and sharper.

Vladek was waiting for me in front of the cathedral. I didn't tell him I'd been mugged – he'd never have let me out of his sight again – but I asked him if the old town was as dangerous as it looked.

'More so!' he said. 'Tourists are advised never to go there alone, not even in a public bus, but to travel through in their own coaches or by taxi. Of course the taxi-driver might easily charge you all your hard currency anyway. You were lucky not to be troubled – perhaps because you looked like a robber yourself.'

'No police?'

'Police! They're so badly paid that many people say they go mugging as soon as they're off-duty. Who can live on Ruritanian krunas?'

'What about you?'

This was not a question he wanted to answer.

'I manage somehow. Shall we go inside?'

'Can you arrange for me to attend a gym, Vladek?'

'Very easily.'

I didn't fancy the cathedral. It was big, with plenty of space for large-scale TV opportunities such as coronations, but dark and very Catholic – cluttered with religious statues and those gruesome wooden booths, like mobile torture-chambers, they use for confessing. The Elphberg vault was round the back of the main altar, with the various tombs lined up behind a high iron railing. The whole area had been spruced up recently – there was new gold paint on the railing and a smart new royal flag, with red roses, a stag's head and a mailed fist, hanging from a horizontal pole in the wall behind. The tombs were inscribed to several Rudolfs, a Frederick or two and one Heinrich. The nearest and latest had been thoroughly cleaned up and read 'RUDOLFO Qui in hac civitate nuper regnavit in corde ipsius in aeternum regnat FLAVIA REGINA'. The translation is given in *Rupert of Hentzau*, but I couldn't remember the details, only that it was cleverly aimed at both Rudolfs: the king she was married to as well as the substitute she was in love with and who in fact wasn't actually dead at all at the time the inscription was made. This was where the waxwork had been and where they had recently re-buried the genuine corpse of Rudolf Rassendyll, my great-grandfather, after digging him up from the Harz Mountains and giving him a state funeral.

'So why is there no inscription to Flavia?' I asked.

'She's not here. After her killing in front of the palace the Nazis disposed of the body we don't know where.'

'No records?'

'None that we can trace.'

'If you could find her, you could have another state funeral.'

'Exactly.'

'The Nazis were Germans,' I said. 'Flavia was German, a relation of Kaiser Wilhelm even. Germans are very punctilious, correct people – surely they wouldn't just have chucked her on a rubbish-tip?'

'True, but they didn't want her remembered as a patriotic heroine and the communists after the war didn't want her remembered either, so it's probably too late to pick up the trail.'

I thought about this as we walked back through the cathedral. Vladek stopped to light a candle in front of a statue with a foot worn away where people had kissed it over several centuries. He did so himself after lighting his candle and sticking it beside a lot of others in a tray of vicious metal spikes. When he urged me to do the same, I shook my head. I'm squeamish about other people's saliva, even if I know them quite well. I never kiss my sister-in-law, for instance, although I like and even respect her.

'This is Our Lady of Wloczovar,' said Vladek, 'the old Slav name for Strelsau. In ancient times she was supposed to have saved our country many times: from the Poles, the Austrians, Bohemians, Moravians, Hungarians . . .'

'But not from the Germans or the Russians in modern times.'

'Not?' said Vladek. 'Where are the Russians and the Germans now? It's a Slav superstition, of course, and the Elphbergs discontinued the old custom of the monarch kissing Our Lady's foot after the Coronation, but that was in my opinion a political mistake – a slight to the Slavs among their subjects. A King of Ruritania must be seen to be Slav as well as German, especially now. What harm in making a prayer to Our Lady of Wloczovar with a candle and a kiss? You certainly need her help.'

I overcame my nausea and did as he suggested. I even breathed a prayer on to her eroded toe: 'Find me the horse, lady!' And whether it was her doing or not, I had a sudden inspiration as we left the cathedral:

'Vladek,' I said, 'has anybody tried the other grave?'

He looked confused.

'The real King Rudolf's grave in the cemetery at Zenda. Couldn't that be where the Nazis put Flavia after they'd scraped her off the palace square?'

The square was actually more or less a circle, with a big fountain in the middle. Three marble ladies, their drapes slipping provocatively, were swarming up a green-slimed rock towards an enormous naked man in bronze, who was blowing spray over them out of an ear-trumpet.

'The River Volzer,' said Vladek.

'And the ladies?'

'Zenda, the forest nymph; Plotla, nymph of the eastern plain; and Karapata, nymph of the mountains: the three provinces of Ruritania.'

'He must be fertilising them.'

'I think so.'

'It's a very explicit scene to have right under the royal windows.'

'The Elphbergs have seldom been undersexed. You yourself bear witness.'

The square sloped upwards and, beyond the fountain, on the very top of the hill, was the palace, a long, elegant building with a flattish dome and a pillared portico, above high, wide marble steps. I stared at it with mounting enthusiasm. This was an address worth killing for. The flag of the new Republic, dark green, light green and blue like Grabenau's deputy's badge, stirred lethargically on a tall pole over the portico. I recalled from my City days Collins's first law of the Euromarkets: 'Never lend money to a country with green in its flag!' There were a few people in the square, some cars parked in an official space near a police post to the side of the palace and a small party of tourists snapping the ceremonial soldiers in blue-and-gold uniforms standing in front of sentry-boxes at either side of the steps.

Suddenly the main doors at the top of the steps opened. Everybody in the square turned to look and the tourists abandoned the soldiers and began aiming their cameras upwards as about half a dozen men in suits emerged from the doors. They were followed by a camera crew walking backwards and then two smaller figures, a man and a woman, strolling casually, evidently talking together. The men in suits made a half circle round them, their heads swivelling jerkily as they scanned the steps and square for potential assassins.

'President Slovodjak,' said Vladek, as, like everyone else, we moved closer and formed a small crowd below the steps, deterred

41

from going any closer by the soldiers, who left their sentry-boxes and paced up and down beside the bottom step. But we were near enough now to see the faces of the group at the top.

'I know the woman,' I said.

'You do?'

'Not to speak to. I saw her on TV.'

The president, pink-cheeked and diminutive, with thick grey hair swept back off an impressive philosopher's brow, was now kissing the hand of his companion. Smiling, attractively flushed, with short cinnamon-coloured hair fashionably spiked, Clare Studebaker was dressed simply but expensively in a white bosom-hugging vest and pale green jacket and skirt. She was a bit short for my taste and would probably turn dumpy in a few years, but I had a momentary desire to run up the steps and introduce myself as the real owner of this stately home. Then she started down the steps, still smiling, accompanied by the camera crew, while the President remained standing among his security men at the top, one hand slightly raised, like a good host not shutting the door until his guests have disappeared from sight. I decided to act. Pushing Vladek and one or two other people around us aside, I ran back some twenty yards towards the fountain, chose a spot fully visible to the President and the descending Clare and, shouting 'Nil Quae Feci', stood on my head. Taking a rapid upside-down reconnaissance I could see that I'd succeeded in catching everybody's attention. The security men, one of them speaking urgently into a hand-radio, were closing round the President; the crowd's faces were turned my way; Vladek was standing stupefied; Clare had stopped halfway down the steps and her cameraman was raising his equipment to his shoulder. The two soldiers were unslinging their guns.

I regained my feet and bellowed in German:

'Mr President! Here Queen Flavia died for freedom. Where does she lie now – our country's heroine? I call for her body to be found and buried with honour in the royal vault!'

I made a deep bow and, as the President and his entourage retired rapidly into the palace and the doors closed behind them, knelt down with my head bent and my hands on my chest, as if my next trick might be a display of hara-kiri. The crowd kept its distance, but began to chatter excitedly, a police car entered the square with its siren squawking and other police on foot were running towards me. Vladek reached me first, but just behind him was Clare.

'Hold the police, if you can!' I said to Vladek. 'Tell them I'm just a mad Englishman with a passion for royalty!'

42

I got to my feet and looked urgently into Clare's blue eyes.

'I'm not mad,' I said in English, 'but somebody had to say it. Did you get the message?'

'More or less. You speak very good English. Are you Ruritanian?'

The police, intercepted by Vladek and deterred by their respect for the interviewer, were standing round us.

'English,' I said, 'but I feel very warmly towards Ruritanians and I was shocked to find that there was no memorial to this courageous woman who died resisting the Nazis. Must history always belong to men?'

I could see she was having difficulty digesting this, trying to match the acceptable sentiment to my unacceptable shaven head, as if she'd eaten a chocolate flavoured with fish.

'What was the first thing you said, before you addressed the President?'

'Latin,' I replied and smiled enigmatically, my main aim being to spin out the conversation and make sure she wouldn't forget me. But she sensed I was playing with her and started to turn away.

'If I were you,' she said patronisingly, 'I'd be more careful about getting involved in what is a very complicated situation here.'

'What were you talking to the President about?'

'Just that.'

She walked away with her camera crew, leaving me to be arrested and taken to a police-station near the river. But as I continued to point out – reiterating the Rassendyll motto in German ('ich habe nichts getan') – I'd done nothing. What could they charge me with? Disturbing the peace by standing on my head in a public place and addressing a naïve petition to the President? I wasn't armed, I hadn't threatened anybody, I'd just been carried away by my strong feelings after visiting the royal tombs in the cathedral. They murmured about a fine, but when I opened my wallet and showed them it was empty, they gave up and released me.

Vladek remained loyal and supportive throughout my interrogation but he was completely mystified by my behaviour.

'Straws in the wind, Vladek,' I said, as we drank whisky on Colonel Danzing's account back in my hotel bar. 'We need to make the monarchy an issue, not just a dim option. The chance of raising a little dust-cloud in front of both the President and the BBC was too good to miss.'

'But the tourists and the BBC were taking pictures. Is it sensible to make a public spectacle before we're ready?'

'No one will recognise me,' I said, 'because no one has the slightest idea I exist. And even if anyone did, consider the symbolism: the President standing at the top of the steps, the King at the bottom, upside-down. To whom does the palace rightfully belong?'

Vladek liked that idea and brooded on it.

'I will do a painting,' he said. 'But I hope Colonel Danzing hears nothing about it – or Mr Grabenau – they have no imagination.'

He returned to his studio to disfigure another canvas, while I went up to my room, lay on my bed and read Machiavelli:

> . . . it is better to be hot and precipitate than cautious and apprehensive; for fortune is a woman, and must be hectored to keep her under; and it is visible every day she suffers herself to be managed by those who are brisk and audacious rather than by those who are cold and phlegmatic in their motions, and therefore, like a woman, she is always a friend to those who are young, because being less circumspect they attack her with more security and boldness.

He had imagination for sure.

6

The River Volzer

Vladek finished his painting and was delighted with it, but I put off going to see it with the excuse that I needed to spend all my spare time in the gym he'd found for me. The instructor was an ex-soldier, not much older than me, called Andrzej. He wasn't particularly tall or muscle-bound, but you could see just by the way he stood and moved that if my two muggers had tangled with him they'd have got the equivalent of a metal table up their noses. I told him I wanted to be fighting fit and that was no figure of speech, and without asking any questions he put me on what he called 'a radical self-defence regime', which combined body-building exercises with a repertoire of kicks, locks and swipes guaranteed to cause radical, if not lethal damage to anything on two legs.

Nothing came out in public about my head-stand: no photos, no news-item in the local press, no report by Clare Studebaker for the BBC. It only went to prove the shortcomings of any kind of PR effort unless you cause actual bodily harm or the media are already focussed on the subject. Grabenau, however, had heard about it. Presumably he had contacts in the police. I was meeting him for lunch in the canteen of the parliament building, so that he could introduce me to some other deputies who might prove useful allies in the future. For the present my role was strictly that of a foreign journalist, with no hint of my real identity. Arriving at the entrance to the building to see me through the security checks, Grabenau looked even more dyspeptic than usual.

'What were you playing at?' he asked sourly as we walked down a corridor side-by-side.

I shrugged. People have been asking me that question all my life and it never expects or deserves an answer.

'Nothing I've seen of you convinces me you're a serious person,' he went on, still sounding like every schoolmaster I've ever had to do with. 'I'm beginning to regret being drawn into this pantomime of Danzing's.'

'Pantomime' annoyed me. I slowed down, let my arms hang loosely and wiggled my hands about as Andrzej had taught me: 'Relax into any encounter,' he advised.

'Mr Grabenau,' I said, very slowly and almost tonelessly, still following Andrzej's advice ('breathe deeply, speak slowly without emotion, ask a question so as to pass the tension to your adversary'). 'What can I do to gain your good opinion?'

'It's not *my* opinion that matters,' he said, 'but a whole people's.'

Sanctimonious bugger! I shook my arms gently downwards as if dropping water off my hands.

'Do you think people would have such a bad opinion if they knew who I really was?' I said. 'Given that it was my great-grandmother who died resisting the invaders and that it's her house – actually mine now – the President's treating as if he owned it.'

This was too much for Grabenau. He stopped dead and confronted me.

'What arrogance is this? The palace doesn't belong to you or your family, but to the people of Ruritania. At present and probably for a long time in the future they have an elected President and it's his right to occupy the palace.'

'Excuse me!' I said, rotating my shoulders first in turn and then both together, 'what right is that? Surely you're not still a communist, Mr Grabenau?'

People were pushing past us all the time, so we spoke in low voices with our faces close together, his at the level of my chin. I gave the word 'communist' extra volume, startling one or two passers-by and causing Grabenau to glance around apprehensively.

'Certainly not!' he said.

Gotcha! I put my hands on my hips and rose gently on my toes.

'But perhaps you *were* once and haven't quite shaken off your Marxist-Leninist reactions?'

He was looking winded now. I put my face very close to his and spoke in an urgent whisper:

'If Count von Wunklisch can float gently back from Switzerland and recover his family castle, why should I be locked out of my ancestral palace? I regard it as stolen property – stolen by Nazis from my family, stolen later on by communists and now occupied by Republican squatters who pretend to respect the laws of property.'

'This is not the place to talk about these things,' he said, trying to break the clinch and walk on down the corridor.

46

'Fair enough. But I think you have to make up your mind, Mr Grabenau. Are *you* a serious person? Whose side are you on?'

I surprised myself with my own vehemence and this easy victory. Perhaps I was at last shaping up to the ghost of my father, perhaps it was the influence of Machiavelli, undoubtedly it owed much to the admirable Andrzej. We walked in silence through several swing-doors which I insisted on holding open for Grabenau ('never let your adversary out of eyeshot – think of the eye not just as a visual receiver but as a laser'); then, as we joined a self-service queue in the crowded and noisy canteen, Grabenau muttered in my ear:

'No tricks here, please, unless you want to cause me severe embarrassment. I may be on your side when the time comes, but for the present our politics is not so much the art of the possible as of making the impossible possible.'

He nodded and smiled wearily at passing acquaintances as we edged towards the counter for a choice of goulash or salami salad and then, under cover of the clashing plates as a cook ladled out goulash, confided:

'Everyone here is uncertain. It's a question always of who can be trusted – who is strong, who is weak. It's not the time to take sides, but to explore opinions and tendencies.'

'O.K.,' I said, 'but it's different for me. I *am* one of the sides. Maybe that gives me a certain strength.'

We joined three deputies already seated with their lunches and beers at a table. They looked anxiously at my shaved head and I avoided smiling so as to keep them worried. The conversation was exclusively about business opportunities for foreign investors and I took notes. They talked as if this tinpot state – with its peasant-based agriculture and obsolete factories – must be a great prize to western moneybags simply because of its previous obscurity and present innocence. They were like a lumpish, unattractive girl imagining that every handsome capitalist wanted her just because she was a virgin. No doubt they were overdoing the optimism in front of someone they saw as a useful blurb-writer, but what really depressed me was their collective myopia and parochialism. If these were Grabenau's most promising allies, likely levers of my restoration, I'd be better off kissing Our Lady of Wloczovar's toe than their arses.

When I'd had more than I could stomach of the business opportunities, I put away my notebook, finished my beer, stretched my legs out and asked casually:

'Any worries about the military?'

They all looked as if I'd been sick on the table. Hans Grünberger,

47

a vast pudding in his mid-thirties, with another only slightly smaller pudding for his head, was the first to recover:

'Why should you think so?'

'Military people tend to be resistant to change. Yours might want to put the clock back to a command economy.'

'I think not,' said Grabenau. 'Our army is small and has never shown any desire to intervene in politics.'

'Well, you might say that – ' I conceded, smiling round at them all, 'or you might equally say that as an outstation of the Soviet military machine it was nothing *but* an intervention in politics.'

'That's all in the past,' said Hugo Maitek, smoothing down the skeins of hair that bridged his bald forehead. 'The Cossacks in Plotla will be returning to Ukraine next year and meanwhile there is even talk of integration with NATO.'

'One other thing . . .' I said. 'Investors are nervous people, particularly worried about instability in countries they don't know much about. I've heard people in London say that Ruritania looks stable, with a popular president and an elected coalition government, but that underneath there's a serious rift between Slavs and Germans. Could that become a problem?'

This was the big one. However, unlike the question about the army, they'd clearly expected it and exchanged knowing looks before the least talkative and least unimpressive of the group, a neat, dark, dandyish fellow called Misha Kurtinov, made his prepared reply:

'It *is* a problem and no one could deny it. I see that you've put your notebook away, so – off the record – I'll speak frankly. In the first place, of course, there's one point of complete agreement between Slavs and Germans: nothing must happen to deter potential investors. In the second place, on the other hand – I speak as a Slav myself – the country must not be allowed to become again, as it was for more than a century, a German bourgeoisie exploiting a Slav peasantry.'

'Or a Slav *nomenklatura* penalising a German underclass,' said Grünberger.

'It is for this reason,' said Kurtinov, carefully shifting his coffee-cup as if it might be concealing an underclass German, 'that many of us are anxious to encourage people from the English-speaking countries in particular to take shares in the Ruritanian economy.'

'You discourage Germans?'

'We discourage nobody – we are too poor and in any case no free country could discriminate in that way – but we would very much prefer investors from further afield. This is off the record, as I said, but please emphasize our desire for British and American investment.'

The others kept their eyes down during this statement and their disagreement was palpable. Kurtinov, as token Slav, had been picked to sell the party line of ethnic togetherness, but he couldn't help drawing attention to its danger-point: the more German money flowed into Ruritania the stronger the German faction would become and *vice versa*. Thinking it over afterwards as I sat in the visitors' gallery and watched the afternoon session of parliament, I concluded that Grabenau and his fellow-Germans only needed me if they couldn't get the upper hand by more conventional means; my best hope, therefore, was an improvement in Slav prospects and who would bet on that? There was something else from the conversation at lunch which I'd marked down as significant, but the beer I'd drunk had blotted it out.

The session I watched was all about education – sparsely attended and drearily detailed – and I had difficulty staying awake. I tried counting Slavs and Germans but it wasn't easy: there were about a dozen small parties in shifting alliances with one another and they didn't sit facing each other like the government and opposition in the British parliament but all together in an amphitheatre arrangement facing the Speaker and one or two government ministers on a platform. There was simultaneous translation over headphones between the two languages, but most of the deputies spoke in German whether they were Slavs or not. It looked as if Ruritanian, like Welsh or Irish, was a language on a life-support system.

Grabenau's manner towards me had changed noticeably. After lunch, as he led me to the visitors' gallery, he said:

'That was excellent, Edwin. You were quite serious and your questions made a good impression.'

'Even the one about the military?'

'I don't think we need fear them, even though they're predominantly Slav. The most senior officers associated with the old regime have been retired and their places taken by more reliable men. The younger ones, like everyone else, are more interested in sharing the good life of the West than playing politics. We have never been a militaristic country. Our army is more accustomed to ceremonial than fighting.'

But when he came back, still in a friendly mood, to fetch me from the gallery my woozy brain suddenly achieved link-up.

'Interesting about the Cossacks,' I said.

Instantly he became his old self, turning on me almost with a snarl:

'Why?'

I used my eyes as Andrezej recommended, but kept my voice cool and quiet:

'Out there in Plotla, twiddling their thumbs. Why didn't anybody mention them to me before?'

'They have no relevance to your situation or any situation. They will return shortly to Ukraine, as Maitek said.'

'Awkward if they don't, though.'

'It will happen.'

'You're quite sure?'

'Absolutely.'

I'd seen nothing since that first evening either of Fisher John or the small dark girl, but as I got back to the hotel after parting with Grabenau, I met her coming out. She was with a man in a black bomber-jacket and jeans, his face mostly hidden by the peak of his baseball cap and one arm round her waist. I nodded and smiled at her as we passed and was surprised by the way she looked at me, eyes wide open and looking straight into mine, lips slightly parted, as if she were going to say something. I paused for a second but she didn't speak and the man seemed to be steering her on impatiently, so I passed them and started up the steps to the hotel entrance. When I glanced back I caught her doing the same, but the man was muttering angrily to her as they turned left along the pavement. It was dark by now, but a street-lamp lit them from behind and something in the man's hand behind her back glittered for a moment. Surely it couldn't be a gun?

Even if it was, what could I do about it? Shout after them, go inside and tell the hotel staff, call the police? Or tell myself I hadn't really seen it – it was a trick of the light and anyway none of my business? Those were the reasonable options that went through my mind, but I didn't fancy them. I ran down the steps, jumped the man from behind and drove him against a parked car, knocking the girl to her knees. It wasn't a manoeuvre that would have earned me any praise from Andrzej – he was hot on elegance and control at all times, whereas the man and I were both sprawling and winded. Still, Andrzej might have approved of the way I kept the initiative by snapping the man's right arm over the car's outside mirror. He screamed with pain and the gun – it definitely was a gun – dropped under the car. But at this point the door on the far side of the car opened and the driver got out pointing a hand-gun of his own at me.

'Get inside the hotel!' I shouted to the girl, then kicking free of the first man, who was trying to get his head in my crutch, ducked

50

and ran along the pavement while his accomplice fired, missed and started after me.

The street emerged on to the river. Cars were whizzing along the embankment road between me and the river itself, but there was no cover and the man was still gaining ground while I hesitated. I took off just in front of an upcoming car. Its brakes squealed and it hooted angrily, but I made it. I was now beside the river. Unfortunately my pursuer was already halfway across the road and there was even less cover here than before. I started towards the nearest bridge, some two hundred metres ahead, and heard a shot. My pursuer was still gaining ground, but it wasn't he who'd fired. Another shot: this time the bullet passed beside my ear. It came from in front and now I could see someone aiming a serious-looking weapon at me from behind the parapet of the bridge. No time to consider options – I ducked through the railing and dived straight into the river below the embankment as a third shot pinged into the railing.

I don't, as I mentioned earlier, recommend swimming in the River Volzer at any time of the year. It was still early autumn – not particularly cold – and there'd been no rain since I arrived in Strelsau, so I was lucky enough not to have to contend with a strong current, but I swallowed a cocktail of noxious chemicals and already felt sick before I was forced to get my head under again by another shot from the bridge. I was in danger of flooding my lungs simply from panic, but I trod water in the shadow cast by the bridge and forced myself to calm down, then swam slowly downstream underwater, coming up for air when I had to, and finally clinging to the side of a barge moored several bridges further down.

By the time I got up on to the deck of the barge I was totally exhausted and shivering uncontrollably. I hoped the men with guns might believe they'd finished me off in the river, but I couldn't count on it and they might stay around the hotel waiting for me. There was nowhere else to go: Vladek lived miles out, even if I could find his particular tower, and I didn't know Grabenau's address. As for the police, I wasn't at all sure it wasn't some plain-clothes or off-duty squad of them that I'd been involved with – the sudden appearance of the sharpshooter on the bridge suggested this was a fairly sophisticated organisation with radio contact and no fear of authority. My best chance was to stay on the barge – preferably inside it. If I could hide out until the morning I might be safe walking around the busier streets until it was time for Count von Wunklisch's car to collect me at the hotel.

There were no lights on the barge, but parts of the deck were lit by the lamps along the embankment. Keeping to the shadows, I edged my way round to the door of the cabin at the back. The door was fastened and I began looking around for something to break a window with. But first – from a sort of absurd reluctance, I suppose, to break into someone's property if they were actually there – I knocked on the door. Silence. Or was there a slight scuffling sound? I knocked again and tried the handle again. Now there were definitely sounds inside and suddenly a nervous voice speaking German from the other side of the door:

'What do you want? Who is it?'

'I'm English,' I said. 'I've been in the river and I'm dying of cold. Can you help me?'

That seemed to cover my plight without at this stage introducing any suggestion of crime or danger to cause him further alarm. There were more sounds of movement inside, then quite a long pause. At last the door was unbolted and opened a crack, through which poked the barrel of a shot-gun. I held out my empty hands like a beggar and I must have looked as pathetic as I felt. The door opened wider and against the darkness inside a small, wizened-faced, white-haired man was revealed, with another face – a woman's – seemingly balanced on his right shoulder. They stared at me silently for a while, then the man, still pointing his gun at my chest, advanced a step and peered either side of the door, so as to check that I had no lurking accomplices.

'Speak English!' he said in English with a thick accent.

'My name is Edwin Fenton,' I said. 'I'm a journalist from London and I need help.'

'Let him come in!' said the woman in German. She was stout, nearly twice the size of the man, with grey hair in a bun and a round, brown, fleshy face.

'Come in!' said the man.

They retreated carefully from the doorway, down a little ladder, and I followed.

'Close the door behind you!' said the man.

I did so and threw the bolts. The windows were thickly curtained so that we were now in complete darkness for a moment until the woman lit an oil lamp on the table down one side of the cabin. The man continued to point his gun at me. They were both in their night clothes, with coats thrown over them. Shivering and dripping I sat down on the steps, with my arms folded tightly round my chest like the sleeves of a straitjacket. The woman now disappeared through a door at the far end of the cabin and reappeared almost immediately with a towel and blanket. She laid them near me on the end of a bench beside the table, then went to a cooker in the corner and put a kettle on. The man withdrew several paces and sat down on a chair, his gun on his knee, and pointed to the towel and blanket.

'Please!' he said.

I stripped off and dried myself and wrapped myself in the blanket.

'Please sit down!' he said, indicating the bench.

The woman picked up my wet clothes and hung them on a clothes horse, then brought me a mug of tea without milk and a piece of chocolate.

'How did you come to be in the river?' the man asked, as they both sat down at the far end of the table with their own mugs of tea.

I explained all the circumstances from the moment I'd seen the gun in the man's hand.

'You know nothing about these people?' asked the man.

'Nothing whatever. Would *you* have any idea?'

The man shrugged.

'We live in bad times,' said the woman, who had been staring at me with disconcerting concentration throughout my narrative. 'You are English and you speak perfect German. How is that?'

'My mother was German.'

'She's dead?'

I nodded sadly. I did feel very orphaned at this moment, even though she'd died several years ago.

'But not all Englishmen look alike?'

'No,' I said. 'No more than any other nation – in fact we're probably more mixed up than most.'

The woman nudged her husband and pointed at me.

'Just look!' she said.

The man suddenly seemed astounded. His eyes flickered rapidly to and fro between me and something beyond me.

'Yes,' he said, 'yes, it's him.'

I was sitting, as I said, on the end of the bench near the door. I was facing the curtained windows and mainly in profile to the old couple sitting at the inner end of the cabin. I'd bolted the door but suddenly had the nasty feeling that somebody must have come in – perhaps one of my pursuers. I turned my head nervously – nobody. Then I saw for the first time that there was a picture pinned to the wall beside the door: a page cut from some glossy magazine – a coloured photo in profile of the waxwork of Rudolf Rassendyll. I'd been posing right in front of it, well lit by the lamp on the table, for the past half hour.

'His hair would certainly be red, you can see,' said the woman.

'We are remarkably alike,' I said.

'There could be no mistake,' she said.

'Well, no,' I said, too tired to argue, 'but will you keep the secret?'

'What secret?' she said. Her husband had put his gun on the floor and seemed to have gone into a trance as he stared at me.

'He was my great-grandfather,' I said. 'My name is Rassendyll.'

'But did he have children?'

'Just one. My grandfather.'

'Who was the mother?'

'I can't say any more about it,' I said, 'Will you please keep my secret?'

She smiled, got up from where she was sitting and sat next to me.

'When I was a little girl,' she said, 'I saw the Queen.'

'Did you really?'

'I could never forget. Those were bad times when we lost our Queen.'

I nodded sympathetically, but I felt utterly finished and distinctly ill.

'Would you mind if I went to sleep?' I managed to say, then dropped my head on to my arms on the table and swam immediately into unconsciousness.

7

Previce Castle

I'm not a person that worries much. Maybe I inherited a relaxed temperament from my great-grandfather or maybe as a child I learnt to leave all the worrying to Mum and Dad who specialised in it. But I did worry through that night in the barge – or at least my feverish mind did. It had got hold, as feverish minds do, of the simple idea that my only hope was to be picked up by the Count's car and it kicked and pummelled this idea through every possible variation. So all night I was waiting for, missing, wildly pursuing vehicles of every description – Skodas, Porsches, 2CVs, a milk-float, a Nissan with a puncture, a Rolls with no engine, a bicycle rickshaw – until at last, aching and pouring with sweat, I opened my eyes to see daylight.

I was lying on a mattress on the floor with a blanket over me. My hosts were sitting at the table with mugs of tea, watching me steadily. Seeing my eyes open, the woman came and put her hand on my damp head.

'You want a drink?'

'Very much indeed. But I must be going.'

'No hurry,' she said, pouring me a mug of tea.

'I have to be at my hotel by half past nine.'

'What hotel?'

'The Astoria.'

'Astoria?' She turned to the man.

He shrugged.

'Or Lenin?' I tried.

'Ah, Lenin. Not so far.'

I looked at my watch, but though claiming to be 'water-resistant' it had failed to resist the toxic waters of the River Volzer.

'Do you know the time?'

'Nearly nine,' said the man.

'Then I must hurry.'

I started to get up, realised I was naked under the blanket and looked about for my clothes. They were still on the clothes-horse. I wrapped the blanket awkwardly round my waist and stood up shakily. The woman, meanwhile, had been putting food – rye bread and slices of sausage – on a plate and now she laid the plate on the table and patted the seat in front of it.

'Eat first!' she said.

'How long to the hotel?'

'Ten minutes.'

Getting myself on to the bench, I lost the blanket and glanced apologetically at the woman, who never stopped watching me.

'Only like your mother,' she said and gave me a motherish smile, though there was something flirtatious about it too.

'We saw you when we moved you,' she added. 'You will be a handsome man when you grow your hair.' She gestured towards the magazine-page on the wall: 'Just like your grandfather.'

I swallowed some of the food, then struggled into my still damp clothes. My real mother, I thought, would never have let me do that without an appalling fuss.

'Georg will show you the way,' she said, when I was ready.

'Thanks,' I said. 'You saved my life.'

'We are pleased you've come back,' she said. 'We will come to see you wear your crown.'

'You think I will?'

'Why not? We have always had kings. Ruritania without a king is like a man without the bulge.' She pointed at the crotch of my tight, wet trousers.

'I'll keep you seats in the front row of the cathedral,' I said and went over and kissed her on both brown cheeks.

Georg guided me with hardly a word all the way to the hotel. When it seemed clear that no one was lying in wait for me, he shook my hand warmly and left, while I went quickly to my room to change and re-pack my rucksack.

Vladek was in the hall when I came down and led me outside to the car I'd been dreaming about all night – one of the few I hadn't dreamt about, in fact – a Range Rover. As we were about to get in, the hotel receptionist appeared at the top of the steps waving an envelope.

'Mr Fenton?'

Vladek, to whom I'd already described my adventure of the night before, urged me into the front seat of the car before running up the steps and taking the letter.

56

'Were you afraid of a trap?' I asked, as he got in behind and closed the door.

'Your friends on the barge had the right idea,' he said. 'We should behave seriously and correctly. You should not be the one to fetch messages.'

The car's driver was a sturdy-looking fellow in a thick, khaki-green jersey matching the colour of the Rover. He had a rugby forward's head and his short fair hair was cut straight over his forehead. He glanced sideways at me as we drew away from the pavement.

'His Majesty's secret is safe with me,' he said solemnly.

I glanced back sharply at him, but he wasn't being humorous.

'This is Thomas,' said Vladek, 'the Count's chauffeur and body-guard.'

'Oh, yes,' said Thomas, 'I am from Switzerland, not Ruritania.' Meaning, I took it, that he was better manufactured and more reliable than the alternative.

I opened the envelope. Inside was a short note from the girl I'd rescued:

> *Thanks for your help. I got away. I only hope you did too. I don't know how they knew I was in that hotel. I am hiding now with friends, but I hope we meet again. The American sends greetings. Gerda.*

I gave the letter to Vladek.

'It makes no sense to me,' he said. 'Who is the American?'

I told him about Fisher John and his mission to make reciprocal arrangements with the folk in the mountains.

'There was a community there in the past,' he said, 'but they've not been active this century and I thought they'd been more or less wiped out by communism.'

'Mountains make madmen,' said Thomas from Switzerland.

I soon began to fall asleep and when Vladek noticed, he got Thomas to stop the car so that we could change places and I could lie on the back seat. I was woken – I don't know how many hours later – by the car's engine being switched off and the sound of voices. It was a road-block. Vladek and the driver wound down their windows and showed papers to soldiers with AK47s. The soldiers peered through the windows at me and I peered blearily back without raising my head. But they insisted on seeing my passport and searching the car,

57

so I had to sit up. We were among low wooded hills with a range of mountains on the horizon in front. There were quite a lot of troops about and a couple of armoured vehicles were parked either side of the road where it passed over a stone bridge. An officer was now examining my passport.

'You are a journalist, Mr Fenton?' he asked in passable English.

I nodded apathetically. I was beginning to feel nausea again.

'Answer please, Mr Fenton!'

'Yes,' I said, also in English, 'I'm a journalist.'

'What you make here?'

'Going to stay with a friend,' I said.

'Count von Wunklisch,' put in Vladek anxiously. 'He sent his car specially for Mr Fenton.'

The officer ignored him.

'In what newspaper you are writing?'

'Not a newspaper. A business magazine called *Open Sesame*.'

I could see he wasn't following this, so I repeated it in German.

'Are you a spy?'

'No way.'

'All English businessmen are spies.'

'The Count has invited him for a weekend's shooting,' put in Vladek again. It seemed the wrong thing to say in the circumstances.

'Shooting?' The officer patted his pistol-holster nervously as if he expected an outbreak any minute. 'We are not encouraging foreigners in the mountains for any purpose.'

'What's the problem?' I asked.

'It's dangerous.'

'Landslides? Bandits?'

'I cannot give you further information.'

At this point my nausea overcame me and, pushing head-first past the officer, I staggered out of the car just in time to throw up my breakfast-sausage on the road. The officer handed my passport to Vladek and withdrew angrily, stopping briefly to wipe the side of one boot on a tuft of grass.

'You proceed at your own risk,' he said over his shoulder as he signalled to the soldiers near the bridge to let us through.

I slept again for the rest of the journey and woke shivering to find we'd arrived at Previce Castle. We were in a large courtyard surrounded by a high wall and the building itself still looked more like a prison than a tourist attraction – a massive stone barrack with barred windows, although there were elegant pillars between them and architectural curlicues over the tops. However, the Count had domesticated a rocket-shaped tower at one end and I was helped inside, seated in front of a log fire and given a glass of brandy.

'I hope this is not some serious illness you've caught in your kingdom,' said the Count, occupying a leather armchair at the side of the fire.

Vladek asked about the reason for the military checkpoint.

'We will discuss that tomorrow when we can hope that Karl Marx will be feeling better.'

I finished the brandy and was shown by a pretty girl of about eighteen, wearing some ethnic costume, to my bedroom on the second floor of the tower. There, after retching feebly into the toilet-bowl in the en-suite bathroom, I undressed and collapsed into a luxurious nest of blankets and hot-water bottles and slept through the night and well into the next day.

It must have been afternoon by the time I got out of bed, weak in the limbs but no longer sick. The pretty maid had brought me a light breakfast and drawn the curtains. I dozed off and woke again when she came to remove the tray. I asked her name.

'Magda, sir.'

'Mine's Karl. I mean Edwin.'

'Sir.'

'Perhaps that's simplest. Can I have a hot bath, Magda?'

'I'll run it, sir.'

It had been running for ten minutes or so when I got out of bed and went to the window. The weather had changed while I was sleeping and the view was blotted out by a mist of rain. I moved away from the window to go and turn off the bathtaps, just as Magda came in at the door for the same purpose.

'Shall I turn off the bath for you, sir?' she asked, not seeming much embarrassed by my total nudity.

'I was just going to get into it,' I said and, deciding not to be embarrassed either, walked boldly past her into the bathroom and felt the water with my hand.

'It's fine,' I called out, turning off the hot and standing by the bath while the cold ran a bit longer. 'Thanks very much.'

She was standing now in the bathroom doorway.

'Does everybody in the mountains wear national costume?' I asked, waving my hand vaguely towards her embroidered blouse and ample flowered skirt over suede boots.

'No,' she said, 'but the Count prefers it.'

The bath was cool enough now and I got into it.

'Nice,' I said, lying back in the water and smiling at her, wondering if she was going to offer to loofah my back.

'Ring the bell, sir,' she said, pointing to a button in the wall beside the bath, 'if you need anything.'

Coming on top of my previous nude scene with the old woman in the barge, I was puzzled by Magda's behaviour and when I got downstairs again and was settled in front of the fire with the Count and Vladek, asked if all Ruritanian women were equally unabashed by naked male strangers.

'You misunderstand,' said the Count. 'You are not a stranger. In the person of the King you are every woman's father, brother, son or lover – an intimate part of their life and dreams. So your body is not a source of prurient shame but of interest, satisfaction and pride. I'm afraid you will have to get used to the complete absence of privacy, even for your private parts.'

'I think it suits me,' I said. 'Perhaps I'm a natural narcissist.'

'We must hope so,' said the Count. 'Royal persons who have not been sufficiently narcissistic have invariably come to grief. And by the same token extreme narcissists who were not royal, such as Napoleon Bonaparte and Adolf Hitler, have proved very successful rulers until their weakness for world domination instead of straightforward sex overcame them.'

'It may be balm to my narcissism,' I said, 'to be treated as if I were a royal person, but nothing I've seen so far in Ruritania suggests that the thing will go much beyond taking baths in front of maids in ethnic costume.'

'Your encounters with criminal elements in the streets and chemical elements in the river have made you severe and cynical,' said the Count.

'No,' I said, 'I meant my encounters with democratic elements in the royal palace and parliament. These people have created enough splinter-groups of their own without you and me and Colonel Danzing introducing another one from outside.'

'Ours is not another splinter,' said the Count, 'but the glue to stick all the splinters together.'

'You were going to tell us about the reason for the checkpoint,' said Vladek.

'There is some kind of disturbance, not in itself perhaps all that serious, but an American has disappeared – feared kidnapped or even murdered – and the government is no doubt afraid that other foreigners might be targeted.'

'An American missionary called Fisher John?' I asked.

'I don't know, but I understand there is a religious basis to the insurrection as well as a nationalist one.'

'An insurrection?' said Vladek. 'Do you mean these people are fighting the government?'

'I think so.'

'Then it's very serious.'

'Not necessarily. It depends how well armed they are and how well organised.'

'Slavs?' I asked.

'You can take it that all the mountain people – excepting one or two returned landowners like myself – are Slav. Likewise the people of Plotla, the province in the plain to the east. But numerically speaking they are perhaps less than half the population and mostly peasants. The real weight of the country – industrial, financial and intellectual – is concentrated in Strelsau and the mainly Germanic province of Zenda.'

'There seem to be a lot of Slav deputies in parliament,' I said.

'Those are mostly the ex-communists who now call themselves Liberal-Socialists or Socialist Democrats or Democratic-Unionists. But there are Germans among them too, such as our friend Anton Grabenau – people one might call all-weather amphibians, who adapt with impressive facility to any political climate.'

'What part does the President play?'

'Mainly ceremonial. He signs what Parliament decrees, but because Stepan Slobodjak is the man he is, he has more power than appears in the constitution. He was a leading protestor against Soviet imperialism in the Seventies and Eighties – a figure parallel to Walesa in Poland or Havel in Czechoslovakia. Slobodjak is the keeper of the Ruritanian conscience. He stands for principles and morality, he is the white knight of freedom, unsullied by compromise and cowardice.'

'A difficult act to follow.'

'Quite so.'

'Is he ambitious? I mean does he want more constitutional power?'

'Not at all. He has everything he wants already – an assiduous staff, an admiring wife, an adoring nation, a library.'

'Any weaknesses?'

'He is vain and intellectually conceited, also elderly and often tired, but there are no rumours of women, drink or corruption.'

'How could he be replaced with a King?'

'His health is not wonderful – he spent several years in prison under the communists – so he might conveniently die. Otherwise he would have to be willing to replace himself – to retire in favour of a King, thus bestowing all his moral authority on his successor.'

'Is that likely?'

'No. He is an enthusiastic republican.'

The Count watched me while I thought about this.

'Why do *you* want to replace him?' I asked.

The Count's eyes flickered towards Vladek, making it clear that the question couldn't be properly answered here and now.

'I'm not such a republican,' he said lightly.

'The problem with Slobodjak,' said Vladek, 'is that he's a genuine socialist – that's why the so-called socialists put him in prison – so when he interferes in politics it's always for the best moral reasons – public welfare, freedom, equality of opportunity – and just undermines what little authority the government has by showing up the compromises they've had to make with opposition factions.'

'Too good for this world,' said the Count, getting up from his chair and going to the window, as if he wanted to close the discussion.

'But if it was clear that the majority of the people wanted a King,' said Vladek, 'Slobodjak would surely agree to retire.'

'Surely,' said the Count, with open derision, which seemed to apply equally to the people, the president and the earnestly optimistic Vladek. 'But look, the mist is clearing! Are you fit to go out, Karl Marx?'

The mist had not cleared much, but it was less dense outside than it seemed through the windows. The castle stood on a cliff with open ground all round it and we followed the edge of the cliff for some way before the path went in amongst trees. There was a decaying wooden construction here – a kind of cabin on a high platform.

'A watch-tower,' said the Count.

He and I were walking behind Vladek and Thomas the body-guard/chauffeur, who was carrying a couple of shotguns, in case any game broke cover. The Count stopped, while the others entered the trees.

'They had a high wire fence all round this open part and watch-towers at each corner. This is the only one still surviving. Perhaps I'll restore it as a summer-house and twine it about with flowers, so that my guests can take tea here and experience a pleasant *frisson* at the thought of evil times now happily gone by.'

'A serious prison,' I said.

'Oh, yes, and our dear good president was once an inmate. You see, he naturally feels he has earned his beautiful palace and will not be happy to leave it, whatever the people say. And, of course, the people will not tell him to leave it – he knows that – because he is the one stable and believable element in all this unbelievably unwholesome place. Oh, yes, Karl Marx, if the river made you sick, I can tell you that's only the beginning. Ruritania is so sick that it really ought to die.'

'So why have you come back to it?'

'My homeland, dear boy!' He waved an arm theatrically back towards the castle: 'My ancestral hearth!'

I picked a bit of rotten timber off the steps leading up to the watch-tower and crumbled it slowly.

'I am reasonably rich,' he said, after watching me for a moment or two. 'I have lived in Switzerland in some comfort most of my life and I have bored myself for a good many years. So I hoped it might be amusing to try a new life in Ruritania. Until I came here and saw it would not be amusing at all, merely sickening, and I began to make plans to leave again. And then I visited London and Colonel Danzing told me about his mad idea for restoring the monarchy. All the same, I was intrigued when he told me a little about you . . .'

'He doesn't think much of me.'

'No, he was quite shocked by your unsuitability and so, you see, I began to wonder whether fate had not shuffled the cards again and given me a hand I could play. Because Colonel Danzing's Ruritania and Ruritania as it now is are not the same place. Therefore a King who would be unsuitable for the one might be highly suitable for the other. And when I actually met you I became quite sure that fate had dealt me a most interesting hand and now the problem is, how are we to play it? But I have an important question to put to you first, Karl Marx, and that is why I could not discuss this matter in front of our poor friend Vladek.'

He suddenly left me and walked round the watch-tower, evidently to make sure we were not being spied on. I was reminded of Colonel Danzing's antics in Regent's Park.

'It is quite plain to me as to you,' he said, returning and putting one arm round my shoulders, 'that nothing is to be looked for from parliament or the government. There is no faction or even combination of factions which could, even if it wished to, deliver you your throne. Hard currency, of course, will go some way and I have enough of it to make a start, but quite frankly those people are not even worth buying. You might as well buy the fishing rights in the River Volzer.'

'So?'

'So we come to my question and I must say that if you give me the wrong answer, I may have to go back to playing bridge in Switzerland after all.'

'Could I ask you a question first?'

'Dear boy, I know what your question is: what do I get out of it?'

'More or less.'

There were shouts in the distance.

'Tell them we're coming!' said the Count. 'I'm sure you can shout louder than I can.'

'Coming!' I bellowed into the trees and when they shouted again, so did I. The mist had lifted almost entirely and the sound came back to us like a boomerang from behind, where the cliff curved out into more forest the far side of the castle. We started to walk on into the trees.

'In the first place,' said the Count, 'I have always liked the idea of myself as an *eminence grise* – you know what that means?'

'The power behind the throne.'

'Exactly. Colonel Danzing told me you were pig ignorant, but I knew you'd had a paid education. In the second place, of course, thrones these days do not have power behind them, but in front, and it is there I would wish to be and there I think you would need me, since you may be street-wise but you are hardly power-wise. You will need a government and a minister to control it. That would be my role.'

'Then someone would have to elect you, wouldn't they?'

'Oh, I suppose so. But elections, you must know, are only a branch of PR and PR is mainly a question of money. I would not see those technical details as much of a problem, provided the package were attractive enough.' Shots sounded ahead of us.

'I'm sure you'd be a first-rate prime minister,' I said, 'but the whole thing seems to me extremely remote. I mean, it's one thing weaving fantasies of power from London, like Colonel Danzing, but when you're here it's all gritty real. I reckon even Mr Kinnock's cellophane rose had a better chance than my crimson climber.'

64

'Yes, but you are a realist and you come from a country that has real elections. This makes you a little narrow-minded perhaps. I am working round to my crucial question. Colonel Danzing said you knew no history at all.'

'He was right.'

'You'll forgive me, then, if I tell you how the Soviet Union came about?'

'Lenin, wasn't it?'

'So you do know some history.'

'That was the only kind Dad wanted us to know.'

'But he wouldn't have told you that Lenin cheated?'

'In what sense?'

'By seizing power from a minority position, without any mandate from the people. The mandate was discovered later, when the system had been reorganised.'

'Dad's view was that it was a weak position, but made strong by Lenin's courage and genius.'

'Ah, good! So there was no moral issue involved?'

'In Dad's eyes, all the morality was on Lenin's side.'

'Do you have *any* moral principles yourself, Karl?'

He had dropped his usual bantering tone. We were walking downhill now and fir-trees hemmed us in on steep slopes above and below. The banks beside the path were deep green moss, with various kinds of mushrooms in clumps under the trees. It was like an illustration from a fairytale – there should have been gnomes sitting on the mushrooms and an ogre striding round the bend of the path.

'What exactly do you mean?'

'Is there anything you wouldn't do or wouldn't wish to be done for you in pursuit of your aims?'

'The question hasn't really come up in the ordinary course of a layabout's life. I suppose I'd have had no qualms about cheating on Social Security if I'd wanted to moonlight, but I was too lazy.'

'I'm asking you to consider the question now.'

'I wouldn't actually kick anyone in the teeth for the hell of it. I mean, I don't have the skinhead mentality.'

'But if somebody was in your way and wouldn't get out of it voluntarily?'

'It would depend on his attitude and, of course, his size. If he really annoyed me and I thought he looked weedy enough, yes, I'd probably take a swipe at his teeth.'

'But if he was a kindly and polite old man, much loved by all, who had never done you any harm and intended you none, but still wouldn't allow you into your own house?'

'I'd prefer to argue it out with him and convince him he was being unhelpful.'

'And if he still wouldn't give way?'

I knew what he was really saying or trying to get me to say, but I was reluctant to give him a straight answer. Not so much because I cared a toss about the President, whom I didn't know, as because I didn't like the way the Count was trying to edge me into some scenario of his own.

'The family motto is *Nil Quae Feci.*'

'I don't follow.'

'I've done nothing, officer. No admission of guilt – past, present or future.'

'You surprise me, Karl Marx, and disappoint me. Is guilt a concept that registers with you?'

'I went to a public school of sorts, with a Christian ethic. The one thing they knew enough about to teach was guilt.'

'Of course. I should have known. You are not such a simple fellow. Well, I will think about it.'

We rounded the next bend and met a dead body in the middle of the path. It was Thomas the Swiss. He no longer had his shotguns with him and there was no sign whatever of Vladek.

8

Our Lady of Chostok

We didn't have to carry the body back to the castle ourselves. As well as the pretty maid, Magda, and a female cook, Count von Wunklisch had two or three male retainers and they were told off to mark the place carefully and lay Thomas in the garage. However the phone in the local police-station was continuously engaged, so the Count decided to take the corpse in the back of the Range Rover it had so recently chauffeured and put it personally under the noses of the police; and, of course, report Vladek's disappearance. I asked if I could go too and the Count reluctantly agreed when I said that otherwise I'd have to occupy myself searching the woods for traces of Vladek.

The mountain-town of Chostok was about half an hour away along twisting roads and it was quite dark when we arrived and parked in the yard of the police-station on the outskirts. There was a light inside, but the door was locked and the Count had to argue passionately with a voice over the entry-phone before bolts and chains were undone and we were admitted. There were only two policemen in the building. The Count being well-known as one of the richest people in the country, we got deference rather than the usual hassle I associate with police, but it hardly signified since they were in a state of near-panic and, far from investigating any crimes, were just hoping they wouldn't be the targets of the next one themselves.

Thomas, they were sure, had been the victim of marauding Slav nationalists; Vladek was either their prisoner or already dead too; and their earnest advice to us was to get back in the car and try to reach Strelsau – or at least the nearest regular army unit in the foot-hills. Chostok itself was quiet, but only because there was some religious ceremony going on in the centre. The rest of the police, including the captain, were supposed to be there controlling the crowd, but it was more likely they were really lying low in their own homes or had actually joined the nationalists. As for the corpse, they would

67

take a brief statement of the circumstances in which we'd found it, but the best thing for the present would be to drive it to the town hospital and lodge it in their morgue. If and when things returned to normal, it could then be examined.

'This is not some local peasant you can push under the carpet,' said the Count, 'but a Swiss citizen. There will be international repercussions.'

'Let the Swiss come and make an investigation!' said the senior of the two policemen. 'What can we do, when Karapata is at war with Strelsau?'

Very unwillingly, before he typed our statements on an iron-age machine, one of them came out with us to see the body for himself.

'You say he was carrying a shot-gun?'

'Two,' said the Count.

'This wound was not made by a shot-gun.'

'Of course it wasn't. Do you think he shot himself?'

'It would be simpler.'

'I'm not looking for simplicity,' said the Count very angrily, 'I'm looking for justice. Is this a civilised country with criminal laws or is it the Wild West?'

The policeman shrugged. The Count knew the answer to his own question.

The hospital was on the other side of Chostok. The policeman, handing us a chit for Thomas's admittance to cold storage, advised us to go through the back streets rather than the middle. But the Count didn't usually drive his own car and couldn't find the way. We were forced back to the centre by the hill-side into which the town was built.

The main square was packed with people round a huge bonfire. Beyond was the church, an elaborate iced-cake with both an onion dome and a spire, as if it couldn't make up its mind between East and West, and people were streaming in and out of its wide-open doors. The Count started to reverse when he saw there was no way of driving through the crowd, but the road behind was suddenly blocked by the arrival of an elderly lorry, which hooted and flashed its lights when the Count leaned out of his window to remonstrate. The open back of the lorry, we both saw at the same moment, was full of armed men in a motley collection of gear from some army-surplus store.

'I am not a demon driver,' said the Count, 'so it would be

foolish of me to try to race forward or back. If they are not completely drunk, they will probably take hard currency and let me go. But I am not sure about you, Karl Marx. It strikes me that foreigners are not finding a pleasant welcome here. I would suggest you mingle with the crowd and, whenever you can conveniently do so, make your way to the hospital, where I will wait for you if I can get there myself.'

'Fair enough!' I said, quite glad anyway to get clear of the company of Thomas for a while.

I opened the door and jumped out, just as the men on the back of the lorry began to jump down too and run towards the car. One or two came on after me, but I was already into the edge of the crowd and hidden by the darkness away from the street-lights, made blacker by the contrast of the blazing fire in the middle of the square. The whole population of Chostok must have been round it, bar perhaps the police, but although everybody was excited there was no sense of danger or any sign of violence. It was more like Guy Fawkes night on Highbury Fields, which Jennifer and Freddy and I attended one year. There were no fireworks, it's true, but there didn't need to be, with the fire as the principal source of attraction.

They weren't just burning a simple dummy but what looked like the whole contents of the church. As I pushed my way nearer I could see the flame-filled skeletons of several confession-boxes and, further up the pile, roughly sawn-up pieces of a carved wooden screen in some hard wood which were obviously going to stay alight a long time. The people coming out of the church were bringing new bits and pieces all the time – curtains, a carved lectern, prayer-books, more screen-work, crucifixes with writhing Christs on them, holy pictures and various statues of saints and mothers, most of them plaster, many damaged, some headless. Then there began to be articles of clothing – robes, little black hats with bobbles on top – the vandals had obviously just got into the priest's dressing-room.

A lot of the people were clearly shocked – there were audible gasps when the saints and mothers and especially the writhing Christs went on to the flames. But their shock was mixed with a sense of satisfaction at their own power over these things and their excitement was much more intense than the kind we got watching fireworks on Highbury Fields: these people were like children breaking up their own home or school – their elation was sharpened by their pain and anxiety. If I touched any of them too distinctly as I squeezed through to the inner circle round the fire, they jumped. There was a sort of collective electricity running through the whole crowd.

69

I pressed on round the fire and was about to join the stream of people going into the church when I noticed on both sides of the entrance a lot of men with guns wearing the same assorted military gear as the ones in the lorry. They weren't interfering with the people or taking part in dismantling the church, but were just hanging about in groups. Remembering my hairless head and that I was taller than most people, I got worried that I might be recognised by somebody from the lorry, so I edged my way back into the thicker crowd round the fire and there I had a bit of luck. Quite a lot of the older men in the crowd were wearing proletarian caps – not all that unlike the tweed variety worn by farmers and gardeners in England, but flatter, broader and made of some inferior material without any fuzz to it. Somebody had dropped his and I found myself kicking it. I picked it up and put it on and – hey presto! – if I hunched my shoulders a bit, I was any old soviet worker.

Now I had no worry about going into the church past the army-surplus brigade. In fact, the work inside the church was more or less completed – the place was virtually bare and the main interest centred on demolishing what was left of the stained-glass. The windows were high up and a group of middle-aged men was ineffectually trying to reach beyond the bottom panes of one window with a curtain-rod, while a second group – mostly younger men – was flinging prayer-books at another window, equally ineffectually. I was quite involved in the general atmosphere myself by now and I thought this showed a sad lack of initiative. The windows – repellently funereal without any sun shining through them – reminded me of our chapel-windows at school; besides, if the people of Chostok wanted a change of church windows, that was their decision. Anyway, I went outside and asked the nearest military type if I could borrow his Kalashnikov. He objected abusively, but when I explained that it was only needed for a little job in the church, he went inside with me. Between us and several of his mates, who came in to see what was happening, we disposed of all the remaining stained-glass as well as a couple of chandeliers which the pyromaniacs had missed.

I was now definitely one of the lads and, after we'd celebrated our success with some nips of local white spirit from a bottle one of them had inside his camouflage-jacket, we looked around for some other contribution we could make to the festivities. The altar, stripped of its coverings, was still standing in its usual place at the top of the church, but it was a huge slab of marble on four massive legs and would have taken a team with sledge-hammers or a bulldozer to dislodge; the same went for the pulpit. Then, in a dark railed-off

70

corner near the altar I saw a real prize: a life-size wooden statue of some female saint – perhaps the Virgin Mary, since she looked quite like the stone statue of Our Lady of Wloczovar whose toe I had kissed in Strelsau Cathedral. The railings, with gilded spikes on top, were too high to climb over easily, but there was a gate secured by a heavy chain and padlock. No doubt that was what had deterred the rest of the iconoclasts up to now. I pointed out the problem to my companions and after a good many dangerous ricochets – it wasn't as easy as they make it look on films – they shot open the padlock.

Quite a crowd had collected to watch this feat of modern firepower and there was a scatter of applause at our success. We bowed ceremoniously to our audience and then I started to unwind the chain from the railings. Several of the lads were forming a firing-squad aimed at the wooden lady, but I stopped them. This was obviously the church's prize exhibit and something everybody should enjoy. It was the guy for the top of the bonfire. I was still untying the chain when a small door in the side-wall opened and out bounded Fisher John.

'Nein!' he said, speaking German with a strong American twang. 'This is reserved. Not for damage. Not for shooting.'

He pushed me roughly aside and stood across the railing-door as if he meant to defend it with his life. I was afraid it might come to that, since my military friends were irritated as much by his accent as his intervention.

'Why not? Who says? Get out of the light, goddam Americanski!'

They crowded up on him, poking their weapons at him in a very menacing way, while the audience behind watched with huge interest and total neutrality. I was wondering whether I ought to risk taking his side against my own party or if it would be more sensible to melt immediately out of the limelight – Fisher John hadn't recognised me – when he produced his ace:

'Maria says so,' he said in a loud resonant voice, the voice of a practised preacher. 'Our Lady of Chostok says so.'

The soldiers looked uncertain, but the audience gave a huge mob sigh and some of them even went down on their knees.

'She will appear before you,' continued Fisher John, 'now that the church is cleansed of Satan's furniture, but you must all leave the building and she has given strict orders that this image alone – because it is her own image – must be spared destruction.'

The soldiers shuffled uncomfortably and the crowd remained completely silent and motionless while he spoke. He stepped firmly away from the railing, as if he had no further fear for the statue,

71

and addressed the soldiers brusquely, sounding more like their commander than near-victim:

'Clear the church now!'

They did as he said, obviously glad to have their status once more clearly defined, and the people gave them no trouble, eagerly hurrying out ahead of them. I had missed my chance of mingling with the crowd and I obviously wasn't a soldier, so I was left alone with Fisher John.

'You too – out!' he said fiercely, pointing at the far end of the church, still full of exiting people and shepherding soldiers, with his whole arm extended histrionically.

'What was all that about?' I said in English.

He got such a shock that I thought it might turn into a seizure. Probably his confrontation with the men with guns had wound him up to the point where a mouse running out from behind the altar would have given him palpitations.

'Ed Fenton,' I said, 'from the Hotel Astoria,' and I raised my cap to show him my stubble. 'And you're Fisher John of First Instance, Oklahoma.'

He pulled himself together, though he was still trembling.

'This situation is dynamite, Ed,' he said. 'Much worse than the one you got Gerda out of – for which I congratulate and thank you. You're a tough customer, Ed, but I wouldn't underestimate what's going on here.'

'I don't,' I said. 'A man I knew was murdered this afternoon.'

'A lot more people are going to go the same way before this day's commencement reaches its conclusion,' he said portentously.

'What's this about Our Lady of Chostok?' I asked. 'Are you going to raise her? Or . . .' indicating the wooden statue, '. . . bring her to life?'

Except for us, the church was now completely empty. Through the open doors we could see the top of the fire and hear the noise of the crowd rising as they got the news from the people who had just emerged.

'I very seriously advise you, Ed, to get the hell out, unless you want to be the kind of war correspondent who gets a posthumous citation but no marked grave.'

'Is this an uprising and are you leading it?'

'It's war, boy. I am certainly not leading it and I had no intention of getting involved in it, but I mean to get out alive if I can and to take that with me.'

He nodded at the statue, then the whites of his eyes showed above the pupils as I remembered they did before when he was agitated.

'You don't happen to know anywhere it could be hidden?'

'I'm a stranger here myself,' I said. 'Why do you want to hide it?'

'That figure of the Virgin,' he said, 'is the single most valuable thing in the whole of Ruritania.'

'Do you mean spiritually?'

'Maybe that too, but it's a unique masterpiece of wood-carving – 12th or 13th century in almost perfect condition – and it's survived every bloody upheaval in Eastern Europe until now.'

'I thought you were a churchman,' I said, 'not an art-historian.'

'I am a churchman. Does that mean I'm a philistine?'

'The philistines seem to have had a field-day here,' I said, looking round the ruined church.

'This was all *kitsch* – Papist rubbish,' he said. 'But that figure was made by a truly religious man and a great artist.'

The little side-door began opening and he suddenly became tense again.

'I have to go, Ed. Get the hell out now!'

He turned towards the little door.

'You could try Previce Castle,' I suggested. 'Count von Wunklisch's place. That's big enough to hide Nelson's Column.'

'O.K., thanks. Now, for the love of God, lose yourself!'

He went to the little door, saying in his transatlantic German to whoever was behind it:

'It's clear. I think we should start.'

There was nowhere left to conceal me in the church, so I made my way to the open doors and slid round one of them without attracting too much attention. They saw me, of course, because they were all concentrated on the church interior with their backs to the fire and were very quiet and expectant. The people in the front row asked me if 'she' was coming now. I shrugged to show I knew no more than they did and inserted myself inconspicuously into the third or fourth row back. It was probably time I went looking for the hospital and the Count, but I couldn't miss whatever spectacle was promised next.

It was surprisingly low-key. After about ten minutes the crowd stopped even whispering and went completely silent – so that only the crackling of the fire could be heard – as a group of about twenty people could be seen approaching down the inside of the church. Half of them were armed men in camouflage, more professional-looking and better kitted-out than the ones in the square; the other half were dressed in plain black cassocks – men and women. But the central

73

figure was the one that drew everybody's attention: a woman, taller than average, dressed in a white robe and small white soft shoes, with a simple white band round her head and long fair hair down to her shoulders. As the group reached the doors they fanned out on the top step, with the woman in white at the centre, the people in black cassocks either side of her and the soldiers on the wings. None of them was Fisher John – perhaps he was busy packing up the statue. The crowd went down on its knees. One or two of the armed men round the steps did so too – awkwardly and uncertainly – but most of them came to some sort of ragged attention. No one seemed to have given them any clear instructions.

The woman in white started to speak. Her face was beautiful in a plain, scrubbed sort of way, very regular, longish oval, with distinct cheek-bones, large eyes and quite a small mouth. She wore no make-up. Her voice was high and very clear and strong, so that even the back of the crowd, beyond the fire, would have heard every word – and it was, quite frankly, thrilling. Whether she really was what she claimed to be and the meaning of what she said hardly mattered. Joan of Arc probably had the same sort of instinctual effect. Kneeling with the rest, I felt like her slave and ready to remain so for the rest of my life or at least until she stopped speaking. But she didn't speak for long, even though her address came in two languages, each sentence first in Ruritanian and then German.

'The day is dawning. This is the last night of your darkness. The light shines again. It shines through me. I will be with you and lead you – as I was with you and led you in many dark times past – until all Ruritania is one in the one true faith of Jesus my son. There will be no more ignorance of the truth, no more obscurity, no more corrupt practices and false priests, whether from East or West. All will be plain and simple, as it was when my son first walked the earth and I taught him the love of God and he taught the world.'

She waited for a moment, straight and still, her face looking calmly out over the crowd, her arms at her sides – she made no gestures at all, but she didn't stand stiffly like a statue. Her body inside the plain white robe touched different parts of the material as the breeze blew or as she breathed or swayed infinitesimally. She was as relaxed as an actress or a model.

'But when this work is done and Ruritania is one in the true faith, I shall leave you again. Do not be sad and think of me as dead then. I shall not be dead, I shall be alive, as I always was, in Heaven, watching over you. But you must believe and believe nothing else except the true faith and do nothing else except what will establish the true

74

faith in Ruritania. In the name of my son, for ever and ever, Amen.'

When they had all fervently repeated 'Amen', she stood there in silence just as before, for up to a minute. Then she walked along the line of her supporters, held out her hand to one of the soldiers on the right flank and led him back to the centre. The soldier, in his camouflage, with an automatic rifle slung over one shoulder and a plain black beret on his head, was hardly taller than her. He had a round, plebeian face, clean-shaven, but with blackish jowls, and a beaky nose. His eyes also seemed to be black and were close together. He never smiled, though he had a sort of fleeting sneer which perhaps did duty for a smile, and he looked discontented and mean.

'This is my servant Michael,' she said. 'Listen to him!'

She went and stood behind him, like a guardian angel, while he gestured irritably to the crowd to get off its knees. He made no attempt to speak Ruritanian, although German certainly wasn't his native language. He looked southern – perhaps he came from Georgia or Romania.

'I am a soldier, not a speech-maker,' he began unpromisingly, his voice sounding like a crow's after hers, 'and I am only here to say that what we have begun we will finish, that Ruritania will be one country again for the good of all its people, that we will drive out all gangsters and corrupt politicians and Western infiltrators and that in all churches, like this one, we will restore the purity of the true faith. No one who joins our cause will be harmed by us, but all those who oppose it will be thrown aside. Ruritania in the true faith!'

He unslung his gun and raised it above his head, at which some of his armed followers round the steps actually fired theirs into the air, causing the front rows of the crowd to step back hastily against the rows behind and the whole mass of people to heave and jostle dangerously. Michael spoke angrily to his troops and they stopped firing, but it was obvious that, even if this uprising had divine assistance, it badly lacked discipline and training and its leader – frightening as he appeared – had no public charisma.

The crowd had lost its concentration and was beginning to shift around and talk among itself. Michael waved his gun again and shouted over the rising noise:

'Go to your homes now, everyone! But tomorrow morning all men who are fit and less than thirty-five years old must come to this square and be ready to join us on the march to Bilavice, our next objective. Ruritania in the true faith!'

The people obeyed him immediately and began to disperse, but it seemed to me that the powerful stimulus of the bonfire and the genuine holy awe created by the woman in white had been dissipated by this clumsy bandit chieftain and that if I had been one of their fit men under thirty-five I'd have found a hole in the ground and stayed there until after they'd left for their next objective. Thinking this and watching to see what the party on stage would do next – would the woman float over the crowd or suddenly vanish? – I entirely forgot that to all intents and purposes I *was* one of their fit men under thirty-five. The crowd round me had drained away and I was standing there exposed as the soldiers began to move into the now vacant space in front of the fire. The ones I had been leading inside the church immediately recognised me and took hold of my arms with excited camaraderie:

'You're the one! You must come with us. We'll need you at Bilavice, the church is much bigger there . . . etc. etc.'

As I stood there bemused, wondering whether to make a dash for one of the streets, try to outdistance them and hide somewhere until I could safely search for the hospital, a soldier I hadn't met before, a big fellow with a thick Stalin moustache and some sort of special arm-band, came over to see what the fuss was about. My friends told him all about my brilliant exploits in the church – now that things had calmed down I was beginning anyway to regret departing so far from the family motto – and urged him to recruit me immediately for greater glory at Bilavice. I hoped he'd say that he'd look for me in the square in the morning, but he probably noticed my reluctance. The upshot was that I was enrolled there and then.

Together with several other likely young men, some enthusiastic, some distinctly press-ganged, who had been part of the crowd, I was led to a lorry and invited to climb into the back. As I did so I looked round at the church and saw that Our Lady of Chostok and her party had disappeared. Some of the soldiers seemed to be preparing to spend the night in the square, but they were taking no chances with new recruits. In a convoy of lorries which had been parked in side-streets, we drove out of town and down a lot of hairpin bends to a farm. There we spent the night, sleeping as best we could, on bales of hay inside a barn. It wasn't specially cold, but I thought miserably of my room with the en-suite bathroom and Magda in her flowered blouse and, most of all, of what might have come out of the Count's kitchen for my now ravenous appetite. My only comfort was that at least, unlike Thomas in his ice-tray, I still had an appetite.

9

Mountain Air

We got some kind of porridge to eat, with tea to drink, at dawn. Afterwards we were given time to wash and shave in a cold-water sink and then the new boys were lined up in the farm-yard so that the Ruritanian Army of the True Faith – that was what we had joined – could assess what it had picked up. The big man with the Stalin moustache and the arm-band, who seemed to be the sergeant-major, came along the line followed by a runt of a man carrying a clipboard – they looked like Laurel and Hardy. Each recruit in turn was asked a few personal questions and then told to do some physical task – running round the yard, lifting a ploughshare, scrambling over a stable door, climbing a rope – to test their stamina and speed of reaction. Most of them were very young and healthy, but clumsy and slow in the uptake. The big man amused himself making mock of their efforts and promising them they wouldn't know themselves in a week – they'd either be fit or dead.

While Laurel and Hardy made their way up the line – I was near the far end of it – I was considering what answers I'd give. Obviously I was going to stand out as totally un-local, even if I managed to conceal the fact that I wasn't even Ruritanian. I also had to have yet another name. The questions so far had been perfunctory, but they might be less so in my case.

The boy on my right was about sixteen and extremely nervous – he'd probably never spent a night away from his home and mother before. His name sounded like Tishkon Yavelets and he was a real Ruritanian-speaker. He knew some school German, but it was a completely foreign language to him. He had three sisters and two elder brothers and came from a farm, smaller than this one, in another valley nearby. He had once been to Bilavice, but never beyond the borders of Karapata and the only town he really knew was Chostok. He could shoot and run up hills, he said – even catch a rabbit with his bare hands if it was far enough away from its burrow. His head

77

only came up to my shoulder, but he was well-built and presumably nimble when he wasn't nervous. As it was, the sergeant-major told him to jump over the horse-trough and he caught his foot and fell painfully across it. I was too busy inventing my *curriculum vitae* to join in the general laughter and the sergeant-major waited for the bedraggled and confused boy to limp back into the line before he moved on to me.

'You don't find that funny, Shorty?' I was the tallest person in the line.

'No,' I said, trying to sound neither truculent nor obsequious.

'Go and do the same – only better!'

The horse-trough wasn't very high off the ground and I made a reasonably graceful job of it.

'Now run three times round the yard as fast as you're able.'

The others – those who had been made to run at all – had only been set one circuit. My patience was being tested. I took it at a good loping pace, but not as fast as if my life depended on it. When I finished, panting a bit, I could see my tormentor debating with himself whether to make me do it again faster. He decided that would be too boring and – probably irritated by the flat cap I was still sporting – snapped instead:

'Stand on your head!'

This wasn't a smooth, even surface like the cobbles in the palace square at Strelsau and I missed it the first time. The sergeant-major looked delighted. At the second attempt I got it and held it. It was he who tired first:

'Stand in line!'

I resumed my cap and did so, while he turned to the rest of the recruits:

'This man with the ugly bald head is pleased with himself. He can do simple tasks quickly and correctly. But although I like soldiers who take pride in their abilities, I do not like cocky recruits. I will ask this man to lick my boots to teach him his place.'

He placed one foot just in front of me. I stared straight into the distance.

'Lick my boot, piece of shit!'

'Captain!' I said. 'I am a free man, ready to fight for my country and learn what you have to teach me. You have no reason to insult me.'

'Lick my boot!'

'You're asking too much.'

'Lick my boot!'

He didn't like this *impasse* any more than I did – in other circumstances he was probably a kind family man not a bully – but he couldn't see any way out that wouldn't look like weakness. I let him wait for a little, until I could see sweat round his hairline, then I licked my index finger, bent down and rubbed the toe of his boot with the spittle and straightened up again. He considered this for a moment or two, decided it was an acceptable compromise not a further provocation and withdrew his boot as if he was completely satisfied.

'Name?'

'Berg.'

'German?'

'Ruritanian.'

'First name?'

'Karl.'

'Patronymic?'

'Marx.'

'Marx! Karl Marx! Are you making a fool of me?'

He was all ready to start the boot-licking episode over again.

'That's my name, Captain. My father was a very dedicated Marxist and he thought I couldn't have a better name than his hero's.'

'Where are you from?'

'Strelsau.'

'Occupation?'

'Teacher of English.'

'An intellectual? What are you doing here?'

'I met some soldiers in Chostok. They told me I should join the Ruritanian Army of the True Faith.'

'Yes, I remember some of them admired you for your hooligan behaviour in the church.'

'I am new to the true faith. When I saw they wanted to clear the church of its contents, I thought I could help.'

'What were you doing in Chostok?'

This was the tricky bit. I had decided to be as truthful as possible, since any other story could very easily be blown apart by my total ignorance of the area.

'I was staying with a relative near Chostok and we came on a sightseeing visit.'

'Name of your relative?'

'Count von Wunklisch.'

'That millionaire! He must be a supporter of the Strelsau government.'

'I don't think so. He only returned to live in Ruritania recently and it's quite possible he feels as I do, that the government in Strelsau is ruining the country.'

The runtish assistant with the clipboard was already well down his second sheet of paper with my replies and the sergeant-major obviously felt my interrogation was becoming too complicated. He abruptly moved on to the next man, but then looked back at me again:

'Have you any particular skills, Herr Berg, other than teaching English and standing on your head?'

'I can sometimes shoot straight,' I said, 'I can swim . . . that's about it.'

'And you can talk like a lawyer and you are related to a millionaire.'

His heavy, expressionless face was momentarily improved by a smile.

'But for all your advantages you have learnt something today.'

'Not to be too pleased with myself, Captain.'

'I am a corporal, not a captain.'

He began questioning the man on my left.

We didn't move on for some time. The commander's boast about going straight on to Bilavice was only a manner of speaking. The Chostok affair had been the rebel army's first major public appearance – up till then it had been little more than a few guerrilla groups operating round different villages in the most inaccessible parts of the mountains. There was a nucleus of trained soldiers like our Corporal Radichev – drop-outs or deserters from the regular Ruritanian Army – but most of us were young peasants from the mountains who were still under the age for compulsory military service or had been allowed to postpone it because they were eldest sons and needed on the farms. Our military gear – issued to us after that first parade – was so motley that I was allowed to keep my flat cap, but there were plenty of reasonably new automatic rifles and quantities of ammunition from the arsenals of the ex-Warsaw Pact. I saw no sign of anything heavier, such as rockets or grenades, let alone artillery or armoured vehicles, but those might have been reserved for more established units.

After a few days in which they acted as demonstrators and sheep-dogs to the new flock, the 'trained' soldiers moved to some other base and more recruits took their places. We were taught only the rudiments of our new trade: firing, moving under cover, making simple assaults and keeping more or less in step on the march. All this took me back to my teens in the school cadet force and when Corporal Radichev, who had become quite friendly after our first encounter, saw that I knew roughly what I was supposed to be doing, he put me in charge of one section of the recruits. There seemed to be no one senior to him at the farm and I asked him why, with at least fifty men and boys now under his command, he remained a corporal. He explained that this army was proud of having almost no ranks at all. There were a few other corporals and the odd sergeant, but even the commander-in-chief, the dreaded Michael of the beaky nose and close-together eyes, only called himself 'Captain'.

'It is the opposite to our currency,' he said. 'We don't want inflation in our army. Officers are for offices.'

But somebody was organising this army, however minimally. The runtish man from our first parade was in charge of communications and had dealings with headquarters somewhere by radio and phone. Lorries turned up at the farm with more weapons and supplies as well as more recruits. We were clothed and we were adequately fed.

The main question for me, once I was trusted enough to take my section out for exercises in the valley, was whether I should simply dive into the undergrowth and find my way to Previce Castle. I decided not to for several reasons: the weather was turning cold and wet, the terrain was mountainous and completely unknown to me, the Count had probably fled back to Strelsau by now, and I was unexpectedly enjoying myself. And there was another reason, which I hardly admitted to myself: the hope that when we did move on to our next objective I might see Our Lady of Chostok again.

We'd been at the farm for two or three weeks – the farmer, incidentally, continued to milk his few cows, graze his sheep and plough his steep fields with some help from the recruits – when we got our first reminder that this wasn't just an outward-bound course. We were a mile or two above the farm, crossing the river where it came down through a thickly-wooded ravine over a series of small waterfalls; my section was supposed to secure the crossing while the Corporal and the rest of the force waited in cover further back. I had sent two men over and was just going across myself with five or six more when we heard the frenetic chugging of a helicopter. I knew the sound well. My siestas in my brother's pretence of a garden in Hackney had often been disturbed by a police helicopter making wide circles overhead as it observed the traffic or a football crowd or escaping bank-robbers or whatever police helicopters do.

This one was also circling and in a moment we saw it over the crest of the hill on our right. It was much larger and fatter than the police helicopter over Hackney and was khaki-green instead of white.

There was little we could do to avoid being seen – it was hardly likely to be one of ours – since we were nearly up to our thighs in fast water, with loose boulders underfoot. I shouted to my companions to keep moving and concentrate on not falling in. The helicopter circled round again and came lower – now it had certainly spotted us – and on the next circle I could even see the helmeted faces of the crew peering down at us. Reaching shallower water, I placed each foot carefully on a steady rock, straightened up and gave them a two-finger sign. That seemed to discourage them – at any rate they rose over the trees and chugged away out of earshot. I learnt afterwards that they had been taking pictures and much later – when a lot of water had flowed down that river – the image of me with my flat cap and two-finger sign, which was interpreted to mean 'victory' not, as I had intended it, 'up-yours', became famous.

Because there was no shortage of fire-arms and ammunition, we got a lot of practice at shooting and it wasn't the rarefied kind they have in regular cadet-forces and armies, with special ranges and targets and a lot of safety-precautions. We just stood or lay at one side of a field and banged off at a gate or tree or boulder or even a bird. We also shot rabbits and pigeons to improve our meals. Of course you don't have to be specially accurate with a Kalashnikov – you can just spray bullets in the general direction of the target as if you were using a hose – but if you're fighting someone with the same weapon it gives you the edge to be spot on straight off. Several of the lads became quite good at hitting the mark first time and so did I. The best of us all was the boy called Tishkon who had fallen foul of the horse-trough. He was brighter than he'd first appeared and in the evenings when we mostly played cards or just talked I helped him improve his German. But his real ambition was to learn English so that he could go West and make his fortune and when I began to teach him a few phrases, others wanted to learn them too. So most evenings when we weren't out on night exercises, I found myself giving regular English lessons to a class of about a dozen and continuing the lessons even more informally as we crept about the landscape on manoeuvres. At the same time I was picking up a useful smattering of Ruritanian, especially from Tishkon.

Corporal Radichev was not one of my regular pupils, but he liked to try a few English phrases himself when he occasionally took me into the farmhouse for a drink of schnapps with the farmer. The farmer was a weather-beaten veteran of the outdoor life and a passionate Slav nationalist; his wife was younger and less rugged-looking. She smiled sweetly and served us, but she never sat down with us or spoke more than a few words. Their daughter worked in a shop in Chostok and their son had been with one of the first guerrilla groups and was now driving the Captain's car.

'What sort of car does the Captain have?' I asked on one of these occasions.

'A very good car,' said the farmer. 'Made in England.'

'You'll see it tomorrow,' said Radichev, 'when the Captain comes to inspect our readiness.'

Early the next morning we formed up in three lines in the farm-yard to receive the Captain. He kept us waiting, but the Corporal wouldn't allow us to fall out – he was evidently afraid of the Captain's temper – so we remained there in a light drizzle for about half an hour. I was glad of my cap. The car that eventually rounded the corner of the farmhouse and drew up near its door was Count von Wunklisch's Range Rover. The farmer's son leapt out of the driving-seat and opened the other front door for Michael, while the Corporal brought us to attention. Michael, who wore no badge of rank at all, was followed by a man wearing an armband like the Corporal's, but blue instead of black. All three walked rapidly along the lines, more as a matter of form than to make any proper inspec-tion. My cap brought them up short for a moment – everyone else had got woollen caps or, in a few cases, forage-caps – but Michael said nothing and moved on.

When he had finished, the Corporal stood us at ease and the Captain addressed us, with the same irritable and menacing awk-wardness he had shown in the square at Chostok. First he introduced his companion as Sergeant Vakisch, who was second only to himself in the rebel army and responsible for all matters of supply and logis-tics. Then he told us the Corporal was satisfied with our progress, that the time for training was now over and that we must consider ourselves real soldiers and behave accordingly, obeying orders with-out question, doing no unnecessary damage to anywhere we might pass through – since it was all friendly country, our own country and our own people – but eliminating, if we had to, anyone that resisted. No prisoners were to be taken, since there was nowhere to put them except underground. He sneered wanly. Our immediate objective, he continued, was Bilavice, but we would pause there only to regroup. Before winter set in properly we needed to be in control of most of the province – certainly all the mountains – so that the enemy could not hem us in, cut off our supplies and starve us into surrender. His own hope was that we might even reach the airfield at Kapitsa in the foothills and either seize it for ourselves or at least prevent its use by the enemy.

With that, we were dismissed for a break, after which we were to demonstrate how well we could shoot and mount an attack. The Captain and his logistical expert went into the farmhouse with the Corporal. After a few minutes the Corporal appeared again and summoned me inside. There was no sign of the farmer or his wife. The Captain and the Sergeant – a tall, intelligent-looking fellow with thick wavy hair who looked as if he might have been a headmaster or a hospital consultant before becoming a guerrilla – were seated at the kitchen table, the Corporal sat down a little apart and I was told to stand in front of the table and remove my cap.

'You call yourself Karl Marx Berg?' asked Michael.

'Sir.'

'But your real name is Edwin Fenton – a British journalist.'

'That is correct.'

'Are you spying or just trying to get a good story for your paper?'

'Neither. It's been a series of accidents. I was visiting Count von Wunklisch – his driver was killed . . .

'I know all that.'

'Where is the Count now, sir?

'I ask the questions.'

'Another friend of mine also disappeared,' I said, 'an artist called Vladek Tarlenheim.'

'You are in danger of disappearing yourself,' said Michael, with his half sneer, 'if you don't shut your mouth except when you're told to open it.'

'Either I'm a soldier in your army,' I said, 'in which case I'll do as you say, or I'm a British journalist, in which case I'm as much entitled to ask questions as you are and I'd like a chair.'

'You have a nerve, Herr Fenton. There's nothing to stop me having you shot. The Ruritanian government would shoot me in any case if they could catch me, so it is quite irrelevant to them what I choose to do with you.'

He stared at me maliciously, then scratched his head.

'You remind me of somebody.' He looked at the Sergeant, who nodded slightly and looked puzzled. 'Have you ever had your photo in the paper? Have you been on television? Are you a *famous* journalist?'

'Not at all,' I said. 'I'm not even a journalist in any real sense. I'm just here to write articles for a business magazine about Western business opportunities in Ruritania.'

This amused Michael. He laughed very briefly – it could have been a cough.

'We have interesting opportunities for arms-dealers at present. Do you wish to return home, Herr Fenton?'

'To London?'

'Isn't that your home?'

This was a strange thought and, as I soon realised, an unwelcome one. Fond as I was of Freddy and Jennifer, the idea of finding myself back in Hackney with the usual round of nothing to do filled me with despair. *Nil Quae Feci* was the story of my life in London.

'No,' I said. 'Absolutely not.'

They both looked surprised.

'So what do you wish to do?' asked the Sergeant.

This was more difficult to answer. The purpose I had originally come for could not be mentioned and, in any case, seemed quite remote at present. Perhaps I had assumed too many different identities recently and could no longer be quite sure who I was or what I wanted. And if I asked to go back to Strelsau I'd either be thrown back on the tortuous soundings and shufflings of Grabenau and the deputies or, most likely, repatriated to England anyway.

'I was hoping to visit Bilavice,' I said.

'You want to get a scoop for your magazine?' said Michael.

'As a soldier,' I said.

'You want to exchange fire with the Ruritanian Army? It may come to fighting in Bilavice.'

'It seems a pity to waste all this training you've given me.'

'We are going to kill people,' said Michael. 'And some of us will be killed. That cannot be avoided. If the enemy captures you, you may be shot as a mercenary. So you would never get back home to London.'

'Need they know who I am?'

'You are very recognisable,' said the Sergeant, 'at least without your cap.'

'I'll take the risk.'

They consulted together in low voices. It was odd how the argument had switched. Instead of being the prisoner who might be beneficently released, I had become the soldier anxious not to be discharged.

'Corporal Radichev is pleased with your conduct and abilities,' said Michael. 'He had intended you to command one platoon during

85

the advance on Bilavice and would regret losing your services. I am willing to believe that I never saw you without your cap and that you are a Ruritanian national called Karl Marx Berg. Is that what you want, Herr Berg?'

'Sir! Thank you.' I clicked my heels and put on my cap.

'Dismiss!'

I turned to go. This army didn't hold with saluting.

'Your friend the Count is alive and well. He is under house arrest in his Castle, but, as you know, it is quite a comfortable place and I am looking after his car for him. Your friend Herr Tarlenheim is also alive, but less comfortable. He was injured at the time of his capture, but is now recovering in Chostok hospital.'

I went to the door.

'Don't prove a disappointment to us, Herr Fenton, above all not a traitor, or I will personally pull out your eyes as in the play by your national poet.'

10

The Battle of Bilavice

We saw Michael again a few days later. The lorry we were travelling in towards Bilavice crested a range of hills and started a long descent down a road designed like a bolt of lightning. Parked on a passing-space just before the first bend was the Count's Range Rover with an open map flapping under stones on its bonnet. There were three people in military clothes standing near the car. Michael, with another soldier beside him, was staring down into the valley through binoculars, while his driver – the farmer's son – watched the road and waved to us as if we were all out on a picnic. I had just time before our lorry took the bend to notice that there was a fourth person, inside the car. She wasn't wearing white, but as her face turned towards us I was nearly certain it was Our Lady of Chostok.

Of course it was obvious when I thought about it that she must be Michael's woman as well as his guardian angel. Yet on the church steps they'd appeared to belong to such different worlds that their common purpose seemed coincidental. And she'd fetched him across the stage with such theatrical aplomb that I'd somehow accepted their relationship as theatrical too. This new idea that it was quite real and just what you'd expect – their common purpose came *from* their relationship – depressed me. It wasn't that I'd actually believed she was a higher being, but I had thought of her as separate. I hadn't given her a private life apart from her role as Joan of Arc.

Our lorry decanted us into an orchard on the outskirts of Bilavice and went back to fetch Corporal Radichev and the rest of our group. As we lay or reclined in weak sunshine under the trees gorging ourselves on apples, Tishkon told me about the True Faith we were theoretically fighting for. Our training hadn't included any kind of indoctrination, religious or political; it was simply assumed that we were all Slav nationalists with a natural dislike for any existing or recent authority – the government in Strelsau, the Catholic and

Orthodox churches, Soviet communism. Most of our men's religion probably went no further than a vague notion of being Christian with a lot of ancestral superstition. Tishkon was exceptional. His family, he said, had belonged for generations – even discreetly during the communist period – to the Community of the True Faith, an ancient and fiercely independent sect of radical protestants which rejected the Old Testament as Jewish Nationalism with a particularly repulsive god and every Christian doctrine since the Gospels as inauthentic. Knowing as little as I did about the Bible, let alone church history, I wasn't sure what this meant.

'We just believe in Jesus,' he said, 'and his Father and Mother and that they are three people, not one.'

'His father being God not Joseph the carpenter?'

'Joseph was not the real father of Jesus.'

Tishkon, who was usually timid and deferential, suddenly became confident and authoritative on this subject.

'But is the lady in white we saw in Chostok really Jesus's mother?' I asked.

'Oh yes.'

'How come? She looked quite human to me.'

'Of course she's human. Wasn't she human in the Gospel?'

'Yes, but humans generally disappear when they die. She must have died a long time ago.'

Tishkon went silent. I thought I had mortally offended him, but he was probably just struggling to find the right German words.

'She became a god,' he said finally. 'Gods don't die.'

'She's human *and* a god?'

'That's right. If Jesus and his mother could be humans once, why not again? Whenever they choose. That's what we believe.'

'So from time to time they drop down from Heaven to give you a helping hand?'

'If we ask them properly and if they think we deserve their help.'

'But why you particularly? Why don't they drop down to help all mankind?'

This made him think hard again. He pulled his nose and crinkled his forehead as he wrestled with this thorny theological problem in a foreign language.

'Maybe they do. How would we know? Maybe they only come to us because we are the only people who ask them.'

'What do they do when they come down? Do they make things go the way you want them?'

'No. They might do a few healing miracles, but mostly they

inspire us with courage and resolve and remind us of what is right and what isn't. I told you, when they are on earth they are only human, just as they were in the Gospels.'

'So they could be killed?'

'Oh yes.'

'But that wouldn't stop them coming back another time?'

'Why should it? You can see from the Gospels they are not afraid of pain or even being killed.'

'So the fact that Our Lady of Chostok is inspiring our army doesn't mean we'll necessarily win?'

'No.' He smiled at my simplicity. 'Otherwise we would have conquered the world by now, wouldn't we?'

'But if God made the world, doesn't he want you – his special people – to conquer it?'

'I don't think so. Anyone that reads the Gospels can tell that he's more interested in how people behave than in what they have.'

That was a bit too naive. I might have asked him why he was prepared to kill to have something he didn't have – control of Bilavice, for instance – if behaviour was all that mattered. In my experience people behave better when they have what they want. Instead I asked him another cynical question:

'Wouldn't it be a temptation to men – or women – who wanted people to admire them or give them things, to pretend they were Jesus or Mary when they weren't?'

'Yes, but *we* have to decide if they're pretending or not.'

He threw his apple-core at a bird in the tree above us and just missed it. The bird flew away in a fright, dropping a white blob on my cap.

'We have to decide that about most people anyway,' said Tishkon severely.

It seemed a reasonable and foolproof faith, if you thought it necessary to believe in gods at all. Of course, if this faith became widespread, there would be mountebanks claiming to be Jesus and Mary all over the world's television channels, but since there were already any number of them claiming to be scientists, professors, statesmen, singers, artists, millionaires, prophets, economic experts and at least one proposing to be king of a country he'd never visited until now, that was just the human scene as we knew it. As I went round the edges of the orchard to check that our sentries were alert, I imagined myself being crowned in Strelsau Cathedral by Our Lady of Chostok herself, while the confession-boxes and the rest of the contents of the building blazed merrily in the square outside. But perhaps if she really was what Tishkon thought she was, she wouldn't.

The night was chilly and we had no proper camping equipment – the Sergeant's logistics didn't run to that. We did have an assortment of coats and ground-sheets, carried, like our personal belongings, in an assortment of kitbags and backpacks, but we weren't allowed to light a fire. There was a shed with open sides for sorting the fruit from the orchard, but between cold and nervousness about what might happen tomorrow, it wasn't easy to sleep anywhere for more than an hour or two. Corporal Radichev and his lorry-load arrived towards evening and we ate bread and sausage and chocolate with more apples, but the main incentive for taking Bilavice began to seem the prospect of hot dinners afterwards.

We were to enter the suburbs on foot at first light and simply make for the centre, while the other groups of nationalists did the same from all round the side nearest the mountains. There was known to be some force of enemy troops in the town and it was hoped we would simply drive them in front of us out of town. The road towards the foot-hills had been left open deliberately to encourage them to leave. We no more wanted to kill a lot of them, who were after all our countrymen even if on the wrong side, than to lose a lot of us. I asked the Corporal if Michael – or whoever had drawn up this simple plan – had considered that the enemy might use their free exit as a free entrance for reinforcements – on the principle that if you want to get into a cinema free, it's always worth trying the exit doors first. The Corporal said that the exit road would be mined and blown up if necessary and anyway that reinforcements were unlikely, given the inadequacy of the Ruritanian Army.

'But supposing they come at us from the air?'

'They have a small air-force, of course, but they wouldn't want to use it against Bilavice – that would be bad propaganda – and they are altogether very confused. They have not yet admitted the existence of the Ruritanian Army of the True Faith, but are talking of a few troublemakers in the mountains. They don't want even to speak of fighting a war. This is how we hope to get to Kapitsa before winter – by flowing quickly through the mountains while they are still biting their fingernails.'

'And what's our objective after that? To flow through the whole country – to end up in Strelsau?'

'I don't know. I don't think we have the capacity for that. Maybe the Captain wants to be able to bargain for some sort of Slav autonomy in Karapata.'

That seemed a retrograde goal – to break yet one more fraction off a small country which was hardly viable as it was. On the other hand it was in my personal interest to weaken the current regime in Strelsau. I rubbed my head vigorously – the reappearing hair was itching – and knelt down on the floor in a corner of the shed to pore over a street-map of Bilavice by the light of the Corporal's torch.

'Tell me about Our Lady of Chostok,' I said, when we had memorised our route to the centre and worked out which junctions and open areas might be especially risky. The Corporal's friendliness vanished instantly; it was as if we were back in the farm-yard with his boot between us.

'Why do you ask?' he snapped.

'She made an extraordinary impression on me.'

'Of course. Why not?'

'Where does she come from?' I persisted in a tone of innocent interest, ignoring his hostility. 'Is she a local girl?'

'A local girl! You . . . you . . .'

He became inarticulate with anger, snatched up the town plan and started to walk away.

'You are just a journalist after all,' he said and switching off the torch, stumped away into the darkness of the orchard.

His reaction was so violent and instinctive that I could only think he really believed, like Tishkon, that she came directly from Heaven; or at least he didn't want to consider any alternative. I wondered where she would be during the assault on Bilavice – presumably waiting in some hide-out until a message brought her to the church to change into her white costume for another propaganda exercise. My feelings about her now were distinctly bitchy – Radichev had probably detected them under my faux-naiveté – all because of that fleeting glimpse of her sitting in the back of the Range Rover like any ordinary mortal.

The assault was a doddle to begin with. We walked steadily in a spaced-out line along a road which soon began to be built-up. There was the odd example of cheap, Soviet-style architecture – a cooperative milk depot, a block of flats that looked empty, a locked and shuttered police-station – but mostly it was thick whitewashed walls with small window-boxes. Some of them still had bright flower-displays, though it was so late in the year.

When we came to street-corners we treated them like rivers, sending a couple of men across first to cover the blind side while the rest of us crossed. My section of twenty men was the advance party

91

– Corporal Radichev and the rest followed after a short interval. The Corporal hadn't spoken to me again since last night's incident, except to say 'Move!' when we were all ready to leave the orchard.

We soon reached taller houses with gables facing a small park beside the river. Bilavice was not built into a hill-side like Chostok, but on a broad plateau between the highest range of mountains we'd just left and the lower range which gradually dwindled into foot-hills. The river here was broad and fast and there was an old stone bridge crossing it perhaps half a mile ahead on our right, at the far edge of the park, with a road that led straight from the bridge to the centre of town. That was the entry-route for another group of our army – ours went down a street immediately to our left, turned right again further on and arrived at the central square from behind the church.

So far we hadn't seen another human being. It was incredibly early, of course, and hardly even light – the sky was covered with a low mat of grey cloud – but everyone in the district must have been aware that the rebels were closing in, since we'd been treating the whole landscape as if we owned it, so they'd probably be keeping out of sight until the trouble was over.

Turning left into our side street, we walked steadily, almost nonchalantly down it, toting our Kalashnikovs in front of us like huge penises looking for a poke. There'd been no sign of any rival invaders on the bridge and I was hoping we might be first into the square and sitting smugly on the church steps by the time Michael and his veterans arrived. Suddenly there was a terrific engine-noise and a small tank came out of the right-hand turning in front of us and stopped, blocking our way. We'd had no training with tanks – actually this was more of an armoured-scout-car or armoured personnel carrier, running on wheels not tracks – and the only exercise we'd done that was remotely comparable was an assault on a haystack. That had been a case of keeping the haystack pre-occupied with covering fire from one flank, while rushing it from the front. Here we didn't have flank cover and this steel-plated haystack was just now levelling its machine-gun so as to hose the whole section away down the street. Our own guns were useless unless somebody chose to put his head out of the top.

'Get back!' I shouted. 'Back round the corner!' and ran myself, stooping and weaving as the armoured-vehicle's machine-gun opened up. It made an appalling noise in the narrow street, but whether deliberately or because the gunner hadn't quite adjusted his sights yet, the first burst was well overhead. The second was lower, but by that time we were round the corner, all but the slowest mover, a genial, flat-footed, flat-faced simpleton called Krabik whose skull was shattered from behind and who must have been dead well before he hit the road. This was bad, but not nearly as bad as it could have been. The problem was what to do now. For anything we had to give it in return, the armoured-vehicle could just keep following us straight down the road we'd come in by and run us literally out of town.

I signalled to Radichev further back down the entrance-road to get into cover, but there wasn't much offered – houses along one side and the park along the other. The park contained the odd tree and bench and a children's playground with swings and slides, but it was otherwise just open lawn and paths. The river beyond that might not be as polluted as the Volzer, but it was swollen and dangerous even for good swimmers. I stood there hating Michael for dropping us into this horrible heap of shit. What was the use of training us to fight in the mountains when he wanted us to capture a town? How come nobody ever mentioned armoured-vehicles or told us what we were supposed to do about them?

My section, sweating and trembling, were looking at me with pitiful, panic-stricken expressions and there were only seconds to decide what order to give them. The armoured-vehicle was approaching our end of the street and must now be just about straddling Krabik in the entrance. The houses to our left abutted directly on the pavement, but across the street we had just escaped from, on the corner facing us, there was a house set back inside some sort of enclosure, a yard or garden. The wall was high, but not impossible. If we could get in there we'd have a breathing-space, we might even be able to outflank the steel monster altogether and penetrate to the town centre through or between the houses. But the monster was between us and safety.

When I panted out this desperate scheme to my section they looked unbelieving. Run away *towards* the enemy? But at that moment the armoured-vehicle appeared and turned towards us, jerking its gun downwards as it did so, ready to mow us down point-blank as we huddled in a tight group against the wall. I seized the nearest man – it was Tishkon – by his arm, put my head down and raced straight under the gun, the length of the car, and reached the enclosure on the far corner. The others were close behind us. The gun opened up, but too late. We were already helping each other over the wall and, as the turret swivelled round on to its new target, we were over and safe inside. The gun fired anyway, but its rounds only shattered a few windows well above our heads.

My men weren't looking as happy as they might have been after

93

such a miraculous escape and there was a bad smell. What with all the fruit they'd consumed in the orchard and the terror of being under fire for the first time, several had shitted themselves. But I felt exhilarated, extremely pleased with myself – maybe I could become a professional mercenary if I failed to make King of Ruritania. I counted heads and found fifteen, including my own. Four, the others said, had preferred to run the other way, back towards the Corporal. The armoured-vehicle, meanwhile, was still in the entrance to the street, just the other side of the wall, probably debating with itself whether to go after Radichev's section or hold the street in case we emerged again. I considered that course – to get behind the vehicle and race for the centre by our original route – but it seemed too risky and I doubted if any of the others would follow me.

The tight space we were in, at the back of a house, was a yard used for keeping chickens. There were coops of them all round the walls and they looked even more frightened than we did. I thought I had a glimpse of somebody peeping down at us from an upstairs window with broken panes, but we didn't need to trouble our hosts further: there was a high wooden door in one corner of the yard and it wasn't locked. I pushed it cautiously and peered round. An alley beside the house led into a narrow cobbled lane. As I crept stealthily forwards to see further, a white cat on a low wall sat and stared at me from a half-crouched position, with its shoulders projecting, as if it thought I might be bad or mad but was giving me the benefit of the doubt. I put one finger out towards it and it allowed me to rub its head and pull its ear, then immediately rolled over to have its belly tickled. When I went back to the yard it followed me with its tail in the air, but took fright when it saw fourteen more of me and jumped up on the wall we'd just come over. There it sat coolly observing both sides of somebody else's quarrel, the interlopers in the yard and the armoured-vehicle still immobile with its engine running in the entrance to the street.

'Our Lady is with us,' I said to my section, indicating the white cat, which might have been a Tom, and led them out into the cobbled lane.

The lane twisted a bit, but was obviously making for the centre. The engine of the armoured-vehicle was still threateningly audible, but there was no other sound at all and no sign of life in the houses we passed. I wondered what had happened to the rest of the Army of the True Faith – perhaps they'd already been routed in the approaches to the town and we were the forlorn hope. The lane led us into a street which I calculated must be the one we'd been aiming for all along. It

94

was empty and, very warily indeed, we turned to the right along it. The far end seemed to be blocked by a high, sheer wall, but as we got nearer we could see that it was set back and was in fact the rear of the church, with a narrow railed space round which our street turned both left and right to reach the central square at the front of the church. Just as we reached this point we heard gunfire. It didn't seem to come from the armoured-vehicle behind us but from more to the right, towards the bridge.

I chose the slightly longer, left-hand route round the church – there were some cars parked on the street here which provided cover – and we approached the square one car at a time like boys playing Prisoners' Base, until we were almost level with the portico in front of the church. Still in the lead and holding my gun in my left hand while I used my right to signal to the others – come on, keep back, space out! – I suddenly noticed a soldier leaning on one of the pillars under the portico. He was wearing a helmet, so he clearly wasn't one of ours, and catching sight of me at the same moment, he was in the act of levelling his gun at me. I jumped aside as he fired and ran behind a parked car so as to fire back, but Tishkon, just behind me, had fired already and punched his arms in the air like a successful footballer as the enemy soldier flopped backwards.

'Get down!' I shouted and took off my cap and flapped it at them to reinforce the message, just as the cars around us started to ping and clang. The dead man's comrades in the portico, kneeling or lying behind the pillars, were raking our position. Then there was a new burst of fire straight down the street: another soldier in a helmet was half round the corner of the building opposite the portico. I had a go at him and forced him temporarily back out of sight, but our position was unpleasant, not least because we had no idea whether we were dealing with a few odd snipers or the outposts of a regiment. What I could see of the square seemed to be completely empty, but they would hardly be drawn up on parade. If we rushed the portico we'd be exposed to the man or men round the corner, and vice versa. Either way we might find ourselves confronting hopelessly superior numbers.

But Our Lady of Chostok was still watching over us: the car I was sheltering behind had its key in the ignition. It was a medium-sized beige Lada, as square as a tank but not so well plated. Four of us got into it, leaving the others to keep the portico covered. I started the engine, found first gear and roared straight for the square, while my passengers on the right wound down their windows and gave a broadside to the portico. Tishkon was in the back directly behind me

95

– his window was already shattered – and as we turned the corner he treated its blind side to a sustained sweep of fire at waist-level. There were four or five soldiers there and at least two of them dropped immediately. The others were probably hurt – at any rate they gave us no further trouble as I veered round in a steep curve – the car handled like a farm-cart – and accelerated towards the front of the church. As I did so I saw another armoured-vehicle. It was half-way down the broad street leading to the bridge and was firing vigorously in the direction of the bridge. We were now speeding alongside the length of the portico and I braked as smoothly as I could to allow our right-hand broadside, which Tishkon had left his side to join, full scope. The enemy in the portico – perhaps half a dozen – were now exposed to fire from two sides and they crumpled. When I turned full circle to give them a second dose from Tishkon's window the two or three mobile ones were scurrying towards the safer end of the portico. They didn't make it. Leaving our boys on foot to occupy the portico, I paused with the engine still running to survey the square. It looked to be clear.

Then from another street which left the square opposite the church but at a sharp angle so that we couldn't see down it, appeared our third armoured-vehicle to date. It wasn't coming very fast and it wasn't about to destroy us with its gun – it was travelling backwards, retreating from some unseen threat further down its street. It backed into the square and seemed temporarily uncertain what to do next, as a strange contraption heaved up beyond it. It was a lorry disguised as a shed. A huge sheet of corrugated iron stretched right across the front of the bonnet and rose almost level with the roof of the cab, so that the driver must have been able to see out only by sitting on a huge pile of cushions; another sheet of corrugated iron protected the back of the lorry, from which every so often an arm appeared and lobbed some sort of grenade towards the armoured-vehicle. No wonder it was retreating as these things – which may have been as home-made as the armoured lorry – bounced off its plating and exploded near its wheels.

I was wondering if there was anything I could do to make things worse for the armoured-vehicle, when Tishkon pointed out a new hazard. Soldiers in helmets were pouring out of a stately building – the town-hall, in fact – at right angles to the church, and clearly deploying for a counter-assault on the portico, where my section was still busy appropriating helmets and weapons from the dead. Guns blazing, we drove straight at the assault party where it was thickest and, as they scattered, chased one of them and ran him down. This was a mistake. The impact slowed us almost to a halt and the enemy now had an easy target. Tishkon was hit and so was I. We scrambled out of the car on the covered side and prepared to die for the cause with our guns in our hands, but we had already lost Tishkon's accuracy. He made it out of the car, but he was humped down on his knees staring at the paving-stones and pouring blood all over them.

But while we had been evacuating our Lada, the corrugated-iron lorry had rammed the armoured-vehicle. Men from the lorry were jumping on to the car to get at its occupants, but others – a mass of them, who must have been moving up behind the lorry – were surging towards our attackers. At the same time there was an explosion behind us – the armoured-vehicle guarding the approach from the bridge was in flames. Our attackers were now fleeing for their lives, which many of them lost there and then, and the square was ours.

The cost to me was heavy. I really liked Tishkon and he'd obviously had it. We laid him on the ground, told him we'd taken Bilavice and he must live to enjoy the victory, but his eyes only flickered and blood continued to pour out of his clothes. We got the jacket off and pushed it against the hole in his side where a bullet had gone in, but it didn't make him feel better. My sight was blurred with tears when I looked up to find a half-circle of our rescuers round us.

'He was the best,' I said miserably to the nearest figure in camouflage, a medium-sized, rather slim fellow in a forage-cap, who seemed to be their leader.

'What was his name?' he said in a low, controlled voice which sounded odd after all the loud, harsh voices I'd got used to.

'Tishkon Yavelets,' I said.

'And yours?'

Exhausted and overstrained with excitement and grief – and my left arm had started to hurt abominably – I couldn't immediately answer. For half a minute at least I couldn't recall which name I was currently under.

'Don't you remember?' said the unusual voice.

I wiped the tears out of my eyes with the back of my hand, then took off my cap and scratched my head. That did the trick.

'Karl Marx Berg,' I said, looking at the soldier's face clearly for the first time.

There could be no doubt about it. Tishkon pegged out at about that moment, but I hope he also recognised our Lady of Chostok with her long hair pushed up under her forage-cap and an AK47 tucked comfortably under one armpit.

11

Ruritanian Made Easy

Bilavice belonged to us. The armoured vehicle which had so nearly done for us had been destroyed, like the one on the road to the bridge, by a hand-launched rocket belonging to Michael's group. Why hadn't we been issued with one? Weren't we expected to meet any armour or didn't we matter – cannon-fodder – only intended to create a diversion? The inside of Bilavice's church was scoured out like Chostok's and the same kind of performance laid on afterwards, but I took no part in any of it. Tishkon's death had spoilt my sense of achievement and I shouldn't have enjoyed it; in any case I was being operated on. My wound wasn't as bad as it might have been – the bullet had entered my upper arm and missed the elbow – but I had ceased to be a combatant.

Bilavice Hospital was a relatively comfortable place, certainly after so many weeks in a barn. The place seemed to be clean, the surgeon competent, nurses always warm the cockles of my heart and if I hadn't had to lie in one position with my injured arm held up in a sling arrangement, I might have been able to sleep better. As it was I felt more depressed than grateful. Corporal Radichev came to visit me the next day, bringing my old civilian clothes from their temporary storage in the orchard sorting-shed, and told me about the victory celebrations. The people, he said, had been less wholehearted than those in Chostok about the destruction of their church interior and only a few of them had knelt to Our Lady of Chostok. His own attitude had changed a bit too: he seemed to have been infected by Bilavice's lack of enthusiasm, not to the point of denying her special power for those of the true faith, but so that he could at least understand the reservations of others. This was probably why he'd taken the trouble to visit me – he didn't refer directly to our falling-out and he warmly praised my 'brave conduct' – but he was basically a kindly and reasonable man and, just as in the matter of the boot, he must have felt he'd gone over the top.

When he'd finished telling me about the celebrations I'd missed he had nothing much more to say. Tired and gloomy, I hardly spoke. But he stayed sitting there in silence for some time and at last he said:

'There was a woman asking after you.'

'That's nice!'

'She knew who you really were.'

'Oh yes?' I wondered which real me she meant.

He looked carefully round the ward – there were several casualties from yesterday, including enemy soldiers.

'She knew you're really a British journalist,' he said in a powerful whisper which could certainly have been heard by the patients in the beds on either side of mine if they'd been aware of anything but their own pain.

'What did she look like?'

'Quite small. Dark.'

I could only think of Our Lady of Chostok and the Count's Magda – evidently this wasn't either of them.

'Did you give her my address?'

'I told her you were in hospital.'

I began to feel sleepy and closed my eyes.

'We shall bury Tishkon this afternoon,' said the Corporal, 'with the others.'

'Say a prayer for him for me! Whatever he would approve of – nothing from the Old Testament. How many others?'

'Only about ten – of ours. More of the enemy.'

Twenty-plus dead to make Michael master of Bilavice – it didn't seem a worthwhile cause – but of course I was depressed and death had come even closer to me this time than it had with Thomas's corpse. But since the dead don't know what they're missing it's really very silly to get worked up about what they might have felt if they'd known they were going to be missing it. People who fight for their own or other people's causes don't expect to come out dead. They take that risk, of course, but the odds they're really considering are what advantage it might give them on the presumption of staying alive.

The corporal left at last, shaking my good right arm vigorously and hoping I'd be back with the group before long.

'Good-bye, Mis-ter Fen-ton!' he said in spaced-out English.

'Svidani, Kaprel!' I said in svelter Ruritanian.

I had my next visitor a day later, when I was feeling better. It was Gerda, the girl from the Astoria hotel, but she looked quite different

99

because, I realised, I'd never seen her smiling. When she'd thanked me effusively for my gallantry outside the hotel and I'd muttered *Nil Quae Feci* or words to that effect, I told her that if she'd smiled at me like that in the first place I'd never have let her go out with a man from the mafia.

'Not mafia,' she said, '*Corpus* – Secret Police.'

'You still have secret police in the democratic republic of Ruritania?'

'Not the same Secret Police, of course, as we had under communism – it was called *Komsec* then – but the same people. It was very brave of you to attack such terrible people.'

'I had no idea. If they'd worn a badge saying Secret Police I'd have left you to your fate. I thought they were just common thugs.'

'They are, but they work for the state.'

'For the government, you mean? The present government?'

'Of course.'

'For good President Slobodjak?'

'Not for him personally. He probably hates them, but what can he do? When you move into a house which is rotten all through and full of rats, you have to live in it if you have no other.'

'You could repair the house and poison the rats.'

'Not if the house is ready to fall down and the workmen are more afraid of the rats than the owner.'

We talked for some time about the evils of Ruritania and Eastern Europe in general and then Gerda – sitting on the chair at my bedside occupied the day before by Corporal Radichev – suddenly said:

'You are growing your hair, Mr Fenton.'

'I'm tired of being a skinhead. People see me in the wrong light.'

'That's true.'

'We skinheads only crave a little understanding.'

'I have been sitting here looking at you in a different light for quite a long time.'

'I'm sorry. Are you bored?'

'Did you see the exhibition in the Palace of Youth in Strelsau?'

'I did drop in. Very interesting in its way if you're keen on history.'

'You *are* the man in the coffin.'

'What? Do I look so ill?'

'The husband of Queen Flavia – I forget his name – the Englishman with the red hair and long nose.'

'I thought he was a waxwork.'

'You wouldn't have looked like him if he'd been a skeleton, would you?'

100

'Somebody told me there was a resemblance.'

'Your hair is the same colour, your nose also long and straight, your whole face similar. Lying down like that with your hair beginning to grow you look *exactly* like him.'

'Gerda . . .' I said, '. . . may I call you that?'

'Of course. But what am I to call you? You see, I am trained to look and I have a good memory. I don't go round exhibitions with my eyes closed and my mind switched off, I read the information and study the exhibits. My memory fails me now for the real name of the man in the coffin – the Queen's husband – but I remember his false name very well – the name he took when he was pretending to be a photographer in a beard. That name was Edwin Fenton, Mr Fenton.'

'Are you secret police yourself, Gerda?'

'I am not secret police, no, but I was student resistance in the last years of communism and we were not less observant or dedicated to our task than the secret police, though much less vicious.'

'And who are you working for now?'

'For Slav Nationalism, of course. Didn't you know that? You have been fighting for Slav Nationalism, you were instrumental in saving one of their key agents in Strelsau, you helped to capture Bilavice . . . Are you just Clint Eastwood or a knight in shining armour from a mediaeval romance who happened to be riding through Ruritania looking for good deeds to do? Or did you come here with some purpose in mind?'

'What would you think if I did?'

'What would I think? I don't know. It never occurred to me till now. Did Queen Flavia and her English husband have any children?'

'Actually they did. A son.'

'And who was he?'

'Very briefly a school bursar. My grandfather.'

She sat there looking at me for a long time with an extremely serious expression. I had the feeling of being interviewed for a job – in fact I *was* once interviewed in my palmy days in the City by just such a small, sharp woman in charge of somebody's investment department. That one turned me down, this one looked as if she might too. At last she crossed her legs – she had very nice legs indeed – and rested her small chin on her small hand.

'It's something I had never thought of at all. Nobody has, I'm sure, among those I know. It's almost ridiculous. But why not? Nobody has thought of a better way to solve so many problems.'

101

'The President seems to be a good man,' I said, as devil's advocate.

'The President is old and losing control. The Slavs no longer believe he can help them, although they respect him and he might wish to. His day is past. He has carried us out of the communist nightmare, but he cannot carry us further. He is Moses, who led the slaves out of Egypt, but could not himself reach the promised land.'

I was feeling tired again.

'It's all quite complex and alien to a simple Englishman,' I said, and I yawned and scratched my head, jerking my damaged arm in its sling painfully as I did so. The yawn turned to a yelp. She stood up at once.

'I'm sorry, I shouldn't have stayed so long. I never meant to, but how was I to know that I'd discover something so extraordinary? Will you tell me your real name? You can save me going back to the exhibition and finding out for myself.'

'I wonder if I won't just go quietly back to London,' I said.

'I don't think so,' she said. 'And it would be a pity.'

'Karl Rassendyll,' I said and held out my hand.

'Now I remember,' she said, taking my hand. 'Thank you, Karl.'

She didn't let my hand go at once, looking at me with the same intense expression as before. Then she suddenly smiled and let my hand go.

'We couldn't have a better-looking one,' she said, and quickly turned and went out.

She came again next day, when I was out of bed and had my arm in a more convenient sling round my neck.

'I cannot return to Strelsau for the moment,' she said, 'for the reasons you know, so I am helping the new administration in Bilavice to enjoy its new status as capital of Ruritania Slavonitsa.'

'Is this a new country already?'

'No, but a more distinct and self-confident region which is almost ready to discuss its future role in the country as a whole.'

'And who is running the new administration?'

'The same people as before, of course, but with a fresh sense of their priorities.'

'Like the secret police.'

'Four-and-a-half million population, Karl! Ruritania doesn't have enough educated and trained people to keep in a cupboard as spares like your left wing in England. It must always be a question of recycling.'

'Well,' I said, 'I suppose I'm part of the same trend towards conservation.'

'You are really a wonderful survival, Karl,' she said, 'and I'm beginning to think that fortune may be smiling on us at last.'

She was smiling herself and her enthusiasm lit up her whole face and took away all the unattractive severity it had had in the lift when I first saw her.

'The idea is so good and so unexpected that I think it must work,' she said. 'That's to say, I think we must make it work. Nothing can be done until Michael has finished this campaign – he will have to be told who you are, of course, and he may not like the idea at all. In that case, I'm afraid we could do nothing.'

I began to be irritated. I'd had enough of Michael ruling my destiny.

'Is Michael confident of capturing the airfield at Kapitsa now?'

She looked round significantly at the rest of the ward and spoke in such a hushed voice that I could only just make out what she said.

'Please, Karl . . . this is not a topic we can discuss.'

'But my secret is?' I said, putting my mouth almost into her ear and hissing like a snake.

'They are not secrets of the same order,' she said, not noticing any sarcasm in my approach. 'Many lives might be put at risk, whereas in your case . . .'

'Only one,' I said aloud and stood up and walked to the window. Outside there were a few trees and some scrubby grass between our ward and another hospital building opposite. The trees were losing their leaves – winter was close.

'I'm sorry,' she said, coming to stand beside me, 'I didn't mean it to sound like that. I didn't mean to make you angry.'

'It's all right,' I said, 'I'm not angry about that. I don't know what I am angry about. Maybe I'm not angry at all.'

But I was and it was something to do with Michael. He used people – used some of them up altogether and didn't mind if they blundered into tanks in the process – and he might be so condescending as to use me further, but I really didn't like him. Could it be just because the only time I'd met him I'd called him 'sir' and not been offered a chair? Was I so petty about my dignity?

Gerda kept coming and after a few days we went for a walk into the town. It's strange being a sightseer in a place you first knew as just a playing-field for a game of life and death. From the hospital

we crossed the old stone bridge and looked down at the river we'd
surely have drowned in if I'd decided to run that way and we'd got
so far. It was a bright warm day and the mountains we'd come
down from to capture Bilavice were hazy and distant. Nostalgia was
something new to me – perhaps I'd occasionally felt it for my Lotus
days in the Eighties, but not as a sense of real loss, since I always
assumed I'd do better than a Lotus one day. This feeling now was a
genuine pain. It wasn't just for Tishkon, though I remembered him
most days, but for the whole training episode, the whole group. Yet
I've never much cared to be part of a group – neither at school nor
in the City.

'Tush, pish!' I said aloud and startled Gerda, leaning over the
parapet with her trimmed and disciplined black hair a little tousled
for once.

'What's the matter, Karl?'

'I'm getting old,' I said. 'I shall be thirty before I'm much older.'

She took my good arm and we walked on towards the square.

'You look younger when you don't wear that awful cap,' she said.

'I shall continue to wear it,' I said, 'until I'm not afraid to
be recognised for looking like my great-grandfather the waxwork.'

'That might be a very long time.'

'Well, I shall be able to discard it when my hair turns white.'

Another difference from the Bilavice I'd seen before was that
it contained people – ordinary people strolling about, talking in
groups, going in and out of shops – where before there were
only killers in helmets. Quite a lot of people were in the square,
enjoying the Indian summer. The church had its doors closed, as
it had when I last saw it, and showed no sign from the front of
having been vandalised. The town-hall had notices on a large new
board outside it. Some were printed, some written by hand, but all
were in two languages.

'Do you speak Ruritanian?' I asked Gerda.

'Of course.'

'You learnt it at your mother's knee?'

'I learnt it.'

'Isn't it a bit unnecessary – a bit pious – to keep up this double
language fiction? I mean who really speaks it? Out of a population,
you say, of four-and-a-half million? A few thousand?'

She didn't answer for some time, but let go of my arm. She
was furious, standing very close, virtually spitting at the point of
my chin:

'You have so much to learn! You feel so superior to us from your safe, well-organised country with your important language and your hard currency and your proud history of progress and freedom and being protected from what happens in the rest of this cold, hard, brutal world. I know what you feel like. I can understand you, even if you can't understand me. I have never been to England or America, no, but I know your complacency. We hear and see it every day on our news broadcasts and yours. This little language of ours which you so much despise is not some nice souvenir for tourists, some charming old-world survival from the pretty mountain scenery, it is our identity. I learnt Ruritanian because I wanted to belong to my country. Well, your German is perfect – that is a start – but do you imagine anyone could rule over Ruritania without speaking our language?'

'I never got the impression the Elphbergs bothered with Ruritanian,' I said, backing away from her outburst.

'No, probably not. But that was another world. That was a world of many peoples and many kings – many different peoples, but all the kings were German.'

'Not our British kings.'

'Yes, yours too. How badly educated you are!'

'Well,' I said, 'point taken. But as a matter of fact I did learn some Ruritanian from my friend Tishkon Yavelets.'

I walked away across the corner of the square and sat on the church steps leading up to the portico we'd broadsided in our moment of glory. Staring vaguely at the cars parked just where they'd been when we were using them for cover, I was astounded to see that the one at the end of the line was a beige Lada.

'That's odd!' I said to Gerda, who had come and sat beside me. I pointed to the Lada.

'*You* are odd,' she said. 'What were you trained for? Is there anything you take seriously?'

'I'm seriously intrigued by that car,' I said and walked over to have a closer look. There were plastic bags stuck with tape over the missing windows and bullet-holes here and there in the bodywork. I looked at the ignition – no key.

'Perhaps you were trained to repair worn-out cars,' said Gerda at my elbow.

'That's not a worn-out car,' I said. 'That's a heroic car. But the driver's learned his lesson.'

The sight of the battered but still useable Lada drove away my depression and nostalgia.

'Gerda,' I said, 'I am still under thirty, my faculties are mainly

unimpaired, my mind still razor-sharp – will you teach me Ruritanian?'

'I will,' she said.

I put my good arm round her and we were friends again.

She had a room in a house along the street the corrugated lorry
had appeared from. The whole town went down a slope on this
side, so one had a view from her window of orchards and fields
and farms beyond. It was a nice place for our lessons and we mixed
them with a lot of sex of a fairly athletic kind – it would have been
more athletic without the hindrance of my arm, but Gerda made up
for my comparative stasis with extra activity of her own. I've already
mentioned her legs. Her body – when she took off her black trousers,
black jacket and white basics – was quite French in style, with a tight,
jutting bottom, just visible spine and ribs and small round breasts.
Her stomach was almost flat and the hair between her legs sparse. I
was like a beached Spanish galleon with my mast in the air and she
like a fleet of Drake's small ships, attacking from all angles.

'Your hair down here is much brighter red,' she said, switching
my belly with her black hair.

'Less exposed to the weather,' I said.

I didn't leave all the action to her. My left arm was still painful,
but if I got my right round her middle I could turn her over quite
easily or pull her up off the floor on to the bed and vice versa.
We didn't let these encounters interrupt our work on Ruritanian
vocabulary:

'This is entitled what?'

'No, Karl. "What is this called?" '

'What is this called, Gerda?'

'This is called . . . you want the rude name or the medical name?'

'As many names as possible, please!'

'Vlug . . .'

'Vlug? You can't be serious!'

'I am laughing so much I can't say it.'

Even to this day there are serious gaps in my command of
idiomatic Ruritanian, but I am totally fluent when it comes to
the parts of the body.

We didn't spend all day and every day in Gerda's room. She
was extremely busy in the local museum and the town-hall next

door to it, where she was organising an exhibition and a series of concerts. And when I left the hospital a day or two after we started our honeymoon/language classes, she found me a room of my own:

'It would not be respectable here, Karl, whatever it might be in London or Strelsau, to share a room.'

She also arranged for me to take language classes of my own, in the town-hall most evenings, so that the citizens of Bulavice could acquire a smattering of English.

'My classes will be terribly dull compared to yours, Gerda.'

'I hope so. But you need friends and the people need to learn your important world language.'

I also gave her a hand with the exhibition, which was a display of local crafts with a strident nationalist message. One of my jobs was to help make the labels and since this propaganda element didn't appeal to me at all I was always trying to tone it down.

'Do we have to tell them yet again that this cock's head is a traditional Ruritanian Slav motif? I mean, the person that carved it probably couldn't care less.'

'You must please leave it as it is! The purpose of this exhibition is to show the essential solidarity of our people. Even in small ways, which they were perhaps not conscious of, they were all the time reinforcing their common identity.'

'He probably took the idea off an English beer-mat.'

'You are so crude and arrogant!'

I tried a more oblique form of disruption:

'What about this lovely plate? It looks very plain and we haven't found any political content in it so far. But consider the wavy pattern round the edge! Some connection with a cock's comb? A traditional Ruritanian Slav motif?'

'Good. Very good, Karl. Put that in!'

'It was a joke.'

'I know, but I believe you are quite correct.'

'You've been brainwashed,' I said. 'Your communist education has made you see the whole of life as a Party message.'

'The exact opposite. I want everything to do with this terrible totalitarian philosophy to be stripped away and the real identity of the people, which it tried to obliterate, rediscovered and revealed.'

I gave up trying to argue: why spoil a very good physical relationship for an ideological impasse? Gerda without her clothes on was never a bore.

107

The concert-programme at the town-hall was equally spiked with propaganda. Gerda had been trained as a musician until she switched to political activism, which had not allowed her time to practise her viola. Ruritanian Slavs, she told me, were exceptionally musical: Bilavice possessed a band, a small orchestra, a string quartet and several pianists.

'It's a pity we can't use the church for our concerts,' said Gerda. 'It would have given us a better acoustic, but without any windows it would be too cold at this time of year.'

'Why not repair the windows?'

'It's expensive and there is an argument about who should pay. The town council think the army should pay, but we think they should, since they have received their freedom for nothing. It would have been best not to damage the windows in the first place, in my view – they were fine windows – but the soldiers insisted on shooting them all out. They said it was their custom.'

I've never been particularly musical myself. Still, I obviously had to attend at least the opening concert in Gerda's programme and it turned out to be more interesting than I'd expected. There was a large audience of Bilavice's leading citizens, of whom I knew a good many from my English classes.

'Still wearing your cap, Mr Berg?' one of them called out from a row or two back as I reached my seat in the front row next to Gerda.

'I go nowhere without it,' I called back in English.

'I am going to London,' called out another, also in English, repeating a phrase we'd been practising in one of the lessons.

'Ve are going to London,' called out another.

'Ven ve haf ze munnee,' said several in chorus.

'Is this what you teach them?' muttered Gerda disapprovingly, 'these conventional tourist aspirations?'

'We get on to Slav Nationalism in the next lesson,' I said, sitting down with a cheery wave to my pupils.

The first item was an overture by Ruritania's most admired composer, Rustivan Carol. He was hardly known outside the country, but the programme-note – written by Gerda – said he was a pupil of Smetana and might easily have rivalled his master if only the German cultural establishment which dominated 19th-century Ruritania and listened exclusively to Beethoven, Brahms and Wagner, had ever given any encouragement to their native composers. The overture would have made a pleasant background to a TV travel slot, with shots of mountains and rivers and smiling peasants round wooden

108

tables, but was thin on its own. Gerda's programme-note assured me that Carol's use of bird-song was extremely innovative for its time and went to the root of the people's instinctive love for their landscape, but I missed the bird-song altogether. Looking round the hall to keep myself attentive, I noticed three latecomers standing at the back: Fisher John, Count von Wunklisch and Vladek Tarlenheim. They found seats before the next item, a symphony by Dvořák. After that there was a break and we all met up in the improvised bar in the town-hall's lobby.

'You have been through the wars, Karl Marx,' said the Count, 'but did you know who you were fighting for?'

Vladek had been wounded in the leg and suffered a cracked skull during the ambush in which Thomas had been killed, but had quite recovered except for a slight limp. He was sharing the Count's home imprisonment at Previce Castle while the Ruritanian Army of the True Faith consolidated its grip on Karapata. Fisher John's position was less easy to determine. It was he who had arranged this excursion in a taxi from Chostok, though at the Count's expense. He was certainly allied in some way to the True Faith and considered reliable enough to be responsible for the prisoners, but Gerda didn't strike me as too friendly to him and I thought he seemed ill at ease. Perhaps he didn't like music. Gerda and the Count were open enemies.

'I hope Michael Jagdanovitch will remember to service my car,' said the Count. 'These Bulgarians are very careless about such things.'

'He is not Bulgarian,' said Gerda.

'Forgive me! Perhaps I meant Serbian or Ruthenian.'

'His mother is from Ruritania.'

'Ah. I thought she was Hungarian,' said the Count in his suavest manner.

'She was born in our country.'

'That certainly makes him native – by a thread.'

'We are not so obsessed with pure blood as Germans are. It's a question for us of where your heart lies.'

'When I hear any Slav – or would-be Slav – talk about the heart, I check my wallet and my passport.'

Vladek and I drew away from this acid-slinging.

'Who is this fierce lady, Karl?'

'She organised the concert.'

'Is she organising you?'

'In a sense.'

'Is that good?'

'Very good on some scores.'

109

'What are you going to do now, Karl? Do you hope to lead the Slavs against Strelsau?'

'They already have a leader.'

'He is just a bandit. Don't trust him!'

'I'm more interested in his woman – Our Lady of Chostok.'

'Is she his woman?'

'I thought you'd be able to tell me.'

'No one has ever heard of her before,' said Vladek. 'The people in the high mountains believe she is supernatural, but you have seen her, what do you think?'

'She rides in the back of the Count's car and she wears military kit and carries a Kalashnikov, which I would guess she also uses.'

'Just another bandit, then!'

The second half of the concert consisted of a complete performance of Smetana's *My Country*. Some parts were better than others, but my attention wandered. The Count had whispered to me just before we went back in:

'What do you know about this American missionary?'

'He seems to be a friend of the nationalists, at least the True Faith part of them.'

'He is interested in money.'

'You mean he wanted a bribe to let you escape?'

'Not exactly. He thinks I will be free again anyway in a month or so when the present campaign is over. But he wants to go shares with me in a business opportunity. He has something very marketable, he says. If I will arrange for it to leave the country, he will give me a small percentage of its price. This expedition today is part of the process of softening me up. What can it be? Has he discovered the Ruritanian Crown Jewels?'

I didn't tell the Count what I thought – knew – it must be. Fisher John was waiting for us at the entrance and looking suspicious of our whispered conversation; besides, something made me keep the knowledge to myself. Sailing merrily down the Moldau, Vltava, or whichever river it was, with old Smetana, I was thinking hard about 'my country'. Was it really mine or was it Gerda's, or Michael's, or the Count's, or Corporal Radichev's, or the Secret Police's, or President Slobodjak's or all these confused Bilaviceans'? I came to no definite or immediate conclusion – except that it certainly wasn't Fisher John's and it would be a pity if he got home to Oklahoma with any part of it.

12

Fallen Leaves

The first snow fell and we had no news of Michael's success or otherwise. The national radio and television services still didn't suggest that the government was facing anything but a little local banditry; however, they admitted that civilian flights to Kapitsa might be suspended without notice and advised people travelling to Karapata by road or rail to consult the authorities first. There was apparently still a train-service between Kapitsa and Bilavice, though the checks and searches made by both sides were said to be extremely stringent and ruinously expensive in bribes. I didn't meet anyone who had risked the journey personally and goods got through only fitfully. Bilavice was well supplied with local produce, but the amenities of modern life started to peter out. Chocolate, paper, batteries, soap-powder, light-bulbs, tinned food became first over-priced and then unobtainable. Petrol was short and few people used their cars. There was still electricity, because Karapata's power-stations were mainly supplied from a huge hydro-electric scheme built by the communists in the mountains. All the same, the atmosphere in Bilavice was generally pessimistic and jittery. Judging by the people who turned up in increasing numbers at my English classes, the population was more or less evenly divided between those who hoped for a resounding nationalist victory and those who just wanted an end to hostilities either way.

The concerts continued; so did my Ruritanian lessons, but more sporadically since a person of Gerda's energy and political passion was obviously wasted on mere culture. She was sitting on more and more committees connected with the general administration of the town and when it was announced that she'd been co-opted to the council itself as 'special representative for Slav national interests', I asked her if this was a one-woman coup.

'The Council is a democratic body, Karl,' she said wearily. 'One day somebody will have to explain to you what real democracy means.'

'In our country,' I said, 'it means the rule of the most assertive.'
The mayor, a bag-eyed, bald father of six, who ran a saw-mill and
sometimes attended my classes, approached the subject with careful
ambiguity:

'We have a saying, Mr Berg, "If the woman wants to cut down
the tree, sharpen the axe".'

'What does that mean?' I asked. 'That you should cut it down
for her? Or that she needs a sharper axe than a man?'

'I've always taken it to mean that you should let her cut down
the tree, but not let her sharpen the axe. The axe being, of course,
much more valuable to the woodcutter than any single tree, it could
be ruined by inexpert sharpening.'

'So you let her have her way in the short term, but keep a
grip on the instruments of power?'

'That would be reading too much into a simple piece of folk
wisdom.'

Deprived of Gerda's private lessons more often than I liked and with
little else to do in the daytime, I attended the local gym, swam and
even jogged – becoming a fitness freak of the kind I used to despise
in London. Also, twice a week, I paraded with the local militia –
mostly older men who were supposed to be holding Bilavice for the
Ruritanian Army of the True Faith while it was in the field. As a
distinguished veteran of the glorious battle of Bilavice I was made a
temporary corporal – with a black armband – and expected to pass on
my expertise in infantry training. In the light of my own experience
I suggested to the commander of the militia – a temporary sergeant
called Brobek, that we ought to concentrate on street-fighting and lay
our hands on heavier weapons. If the regular army tried to recapture
Bilavice, I said, they'd probably use tanks and even artillery – wasn't
there something we could do about that?

Sergeant Brobek, who had himself done military service in the
artillery and now ran a transport company, many of whose lorries had
been commandeered by Michael's army, thought there was nothing.
He had a long face and a permanently gloomy outlook and was one
of those conscientious types who always say 'no' to every suggestion
and then ruin their health proving it can be done after all.

The upshot was that we brought the surviving armoured-car
back into service – though we couldn't afford the petrol to take it
out much – and with the help of the local foundry, a garage and a
quarry company constructed a quantity of home-made grenades and

mortars. We practised using these things round an abandoned factory outside the town and also attended the local rifle-club to bring our sharp-shooting up to a higher standard. The twenty or so best shots in the militia were then formed into an elite squad of snipers and spent a lot of their spare time enthusiastically investigating people's top floors and roofs and arguing about the best spots for ambushes. The rest of us concentrated on the rougher business of handling explosives and projecting them by one means or another.

Meanwhile, as Gerda had become less and less available, I had discovered an alternative source of Ruritanian lessons. The room Gerda had found for me was on the opposite side of the town from the way I had first entered it and near the edge. In fact the back garden, which was mostly a vegetable plot, gave directly on to a large wood. The house was newer than most in Bilavice – part of an estate added to the town in the Sixties or so when some communist five-year-plan had been trying to turn mountain peasants into factory-workers. Hoping no doubt to make the peasants feel less alienated, the authorities had built them a street of houses in the traditional style – though they were smaller, cheaper imitations – instead of blocks of flats. The house was lived in by a childless couple in their late thirties. The husband, Mikos, was an electrician and a member of the town council. He was one of the ultra-nationalists, an eager supporter of Gerda's new regime and I thought a fairly nasty piece of work, resentful and spiteful, with a sharp bad-tempered face. I never saw him smile, let alone laugh, and he was a puny size too: he looked like a stoat. He was civil to me, however, since I was Gerda's protégé, and I took care to cross his path as seldom as possible.

His wife, Susha, worked at the power-station, mostly night-shifts. Electricity had probably brought them together, but now kept them mostly apart. It was not surprising they had no children since he was not often at home in the daytime and she only occasionally at night. Their personalities had nothing in common. She was a cheerful, well-built extrovert who had no interest whatever in politics and occupied her spare time and energy gossiping with a large circle of women-friends and acting as courtesy aunt to their children. She seemed perfectly happy with this arrangement and never spoke as if she missed having children of her own. Nor did she give any sign of distress at being saddled with such a miserable husband: she seemed to accept his moans and complaints about the food, the other people on the council, the stupidity of his customers, the indiscipline of other people's children, as if an unattractive husband was simply a natural misfortune like bad weather or old age.

In the early days when I spent a lot of my time across the town with Gerda, I saw as little of Susha as I did of her husband. I liked her a lot more, of course, but I thought of her as older than she actually was and as simply a pleasant peasant. We got to know each other better after I'd been to church one Sunday, a week or two before the snow fell. I'm not sure why I went that particular day – I was probably at a loose end, with Gerda busy at the town-hall on some emergency committee – but it had been at the back of my mind for some time to see what the True Faith got up to in an empty church.

The windows had been temporarily boarded up and, although it was quite bright outside, it was extremely dark inside, lit by two or three naked light-bulbs hanging straight from flexes where the chandeliers must have been. There was a congregation of about fifty people and we sat in the body of the church on plain upright chairs in a rough circle, ignoring the raised bit with the altar. It was more like a séance, I suppose – though I've never attended one – than the services in our school chapel. A man and woman in long black robes, like the ones I'd seen escorting Our Lady of Chostok, sat in the inner ring of the circle and moved the proceedings along if they seemed to be flagging, but mostly people just stood up and recited passages from the Gospels – which they knew by heart – or said prayers or delivered little sermons of their own. There was no singing and the worshippers tended to recite in Ruritanian but speak in German. They all seemed very dedicated and concentrated, but when I got tired of testing my Ruritanian comprehension on the Gospel texts, I started to think about sliding out.

Then the man in black robes got up and began to speak about the Virgin Mother. Some people were worried, he said, about her being associated with violence and bloodshed, since she never had been in the Gospels. He found this a problem himself. On the other hand, it was a tradition in the True Faith that she had appeared in the past and given her blessing to uprisings at times of great stress and hardship. Since the True Faith believed in always sticking strictly to the Gospels and allowing no later accretions of doctrine, these episodes had not been recorded or even much discussed among believers, but many would certainly like to believe they had really happened. He would like to believe that himself. He didn't think that all violence was entirely against the spirit of the Gospels – Jesus had undoubtedly been rough with the moneychangers in the temple and had treated the Jewish religious establishment with open contempt. Every worshipper, in the end, had to decide for him- or herself what was right and true and what wasn't. In his own view, they could most

114

safely and correctly wait on events. If Our Lady of Chostok led the True Faith to Strelsau and even beyond, that would be wonderful. If she didn't, well, they might have been mistaken about her, but the Gospels remained and nothing could take them away or destroy their eternal message of hope, truth and faith.

I was looking round the congregation to see what effect this jesuitical approach was having on them, when I noticed my landlady. From where I sat she'd been directly behind someone else, but now she was leaning forward staring intently at the man in the black robe. In profile, with her straight brown hair held back in a scarf and the jaw stretched, her round pale face looked younger, her rather blobby nose gained length and outline and her mouth was more sensual. But I think it was mainly the intentness that changed both what she looked like and my attitude towards her. She was full of some strong emotion – presumably religious – and I found that exciting. I moved my chair a little so as to be able to observe her even when she'd sat back in her chair and I had no further thoughts of leaving the church.

I was among the first to go out at the end, quickly putting my cap on as usual when in public – I had sat at the back and in the darkest part of the circle – and hung around waiting for her. She greeted me with surprise and pleasure at my having attended the service and we walked back to her house together. What was her own view about our Lady, I asked – genuine or not?

'Of course it must be her.'

'Why are you so certain? The pastor seemed uncertain.'

'I saw her.'

'I know, but didn't everybody?'

'I saw her just now – as the pastor was speaking – standing behind him.'

'Are you sure? Close behind him?'

'No. Further back. Behind the pulpit.'

'Was she wearing white?'

'No, blue.'

This sounded less interesting: a genuine hallucination.

'Like in the pictures of her?'

'No,' she said, after thinking for a moment, 'Not like a picture.'

'Did you recognise her face?'

'I didn't notice her face particularly. More her expression. It was so calm and forgiving. She knows what it's like to be human.'

When we got back to the house, her husband was there. I refused the offer of a meal and went to my room to correct some written tests I'd given my English classes. But I was restless and as soon as I heard the front door slam and looked out to see Mikos walking away down the street I went downstairs to the kitchen to ask for a cup of tea – coffee by now was only for the very rich and even tea was a luxury. Susha was at the sink in a plastic apron with a pattern of large orange flowers, but she had finished washing up and was staring out of the window.

'A fox – in the edge of the wood – look!'

I stood beside her and saw the fox, which seemed to be staring back at us.

'You're seeing a lot of things today, Susha.'

'I saw her as plainly as I see that fox.'

'I believe you.'

The fox suddenly made off.

'What's fox in Ruritanian?'

'Lish. Why do you want to know?'

I undid the bow tying her apron at the back, drew it carefully over her head and threw it towards a chair.

'I'm trying to learn Ruritanian. Will you give me lessons?'

'Chasti!' she said in Ruritanian and then in German: 'Happily!'

She smiled and did look very happy. We started by sitting on the sofa together with the Gospels in front of us, but I said I needed something more everyday.

'What about a walk in the wood?' I suggested. 'You can tell me the names of everything we see.'

That idea pleased her too. We put on scarves and went out through the vegetable plot into the wood. It wasn't fir-trees, but the kind that lose their leaves in winter and most of the branches were bare. This was an advantage by the time the Ruritanian lesson was wearing thin and we were both warm from walking and unbearably randy. She was just as ready for sex as I was, her pale face flushed, her lips parted, her prominent brown eyes almost out on stalks.

There was no one else about. We found a dell well-padded with newly fallen leaves and took off our scarves and our lower clothes – it was too crisp to strip completely. She was big all over – especially after Gerda – big thighs, big buttocks, big belly. Her breasts were not very visible on this occasion, but I could feel under her jersey that they were made on the same generous principle as the rest. Gerda always protected herself, but Susha didn't. There wasn't much foreplay, since we neither of us felt like wasting any more time. She lay down on the leaves, drew up her legs, pulled me down and we were away. I never had a better three minutes in my life.

After that we sometimes walked in the wood together, but always went home when we wanted to lie down. It was really too late in the year for outdoor sex and besides we had a sort of tacit agreement not to spoil such a memorable beginning by trying to repeat it. Indoors we always used my room, since she clearly wanted to keep the marital bed inviolate, perhaps simply on practical grounds, so that the stoat wouldn't notice anything amiss. I asked her, when we'd been lovers for a week or two and there were no secrets between us except my real identity, if she didn't have any moral qualms, considering she was a practising member of the True Faith. The question surprised and upset her:

'You think I'm behaving badly?'

'From my point of view you're behaving like an angel.'

'This wouldn't have happened with anyone else.'

'I'm sure not.'

'I wouldn't think – I never thought before – of adultery with any man in the world. It would be against my husband and against my religion.'

'I'm honoured you make one exception.'

She was not satisfied with my flip replies and continued very seriously to try to make me understand.

'I do it with you because of who you are.'

'And who am I?'

'I don't know who you are, Karl.'

'Who do you *think* I am?'

'I don't think. You came to me on the day I saw the Virgin in the church. Perhaps I don't want to know who you are. Perhaps the Virgin didn't want to know when the angel came to her.'

'Susha, I am not anyone of that kind. Really not.'

'Why do we talk about it? I don't think we want to talk about it.'

And that was all we did talk about it. Maybe she really believed I was a supernatural visitant, maybe it suited her to pretend she did. Either way it suited me and when the snow came and before the bad news followed it, Susha and I snuggled down most days in my narrow bed and forgot altogether about Slav nationalism and even about improving my Ruritanian.

The bad news came in the form of much fuller news from the national broadcasting station. A serious attack by 'bandits' on Kapitsa Airport had been frustrated, we were told, and the 'terrorists' driven off with heavy losses. Their cause, we were assured, was now doomed and the government would soon be able to make all areas of the country, including the bandits' 'last strongholds' in the mountains safe for law-abiding citizens. President Slobodjak praised the courageous and patriotic conduct of the army, which had resisted all efforts on the part of the terrorists to divide it on ethnic grounds and had earned the gratitude of the whole country. From now on Slavs and Germans would be able to work together to restore prosperity to all parts of the community.

'What exactly has happened?' I asked Gerda, as I emerged from my English class on the evening this broadcast was made and met her in the lobby of the town-hall. Most of my pupils had seemed relieved at the news, but Gerda's face was tight and she was shivering with tension.

'The bastards used bombs and rockets,' she said. 'This will only make our cause more resistant to any compromise.'

She was speaking, of course, in front of the people leaving my class. I walked her home, supporting her more and more as her shivering became more violent. When we got into her room she collapsed completely, burst into tears and sobbed in my arms.

'It's completely finished. We shall be back where we started, but worse because the people will not trust us a second time.'

She had spoken on the phone to Michael's logistics chief, the tall sergeant who had been present at my interview in the farmhouse. The rebels had been in the neighbourhood of Kapitsa for some time, but unable to prevent the army using the airport or to mount a credible attack against the better-equipped forces defending it. Then they had succeeded in downing an incoming aircraft, but this was their undoing, because it contained civilian as well as military passengers and the government was finally driven to act decisively. In spite of the danger to the town of Kapitsa itself and the damage and loss of life which must have resulted, the army was ordered to use artillery and tanks and given air support for a full-scale attack. The nationalists had been decimated and routed and were now dispersed in small groups making for the safety of the high mountains.

'Where was the sergeant speaking from?'

'From a village on the direct road to Chostok.'

'Is he coming to Bilavice?'

Gerda looked at me as if I hadn't understood anything she'd said.

'No one is coming to Bilavice except the army.'

'The regular army?'

'*We* have no army any more.'

'Are we supposed to defend Bilavice?'

118

'What with?'

'We've made a few preparations.'

'Preparations for suicide.'

'What about you?'

'I am completely finished too.'

This total abdication seemed to revive her energy. She disentangled herself from me and began throwing her few clothes and belongings into a rucksack.

'What is the town council doing?'

'Waiting.'

'Do they know all this?'

'Not yet. They know it's bad, but not how bad.'

'Shouldn't you tell them?'

'I am no longer a member of the town council. They are already deciding to be loyal Ruritanians again. If I tell them everything I know they will arrest me and give me to the army.'

'Where are you going? To Chostok?'

'Where else?'

'How?'

'Mr Brobek is arranging transport – a coach – for all who would be shot by the army if they catch us.'

'As bad as that?'

'Certainly. And you will have to come too, of course.'

I wondered about that. I didn't like the idea of spending the winter ring-fenced in Chostok in the sole company of the last-ditch nationalists. Gerda turned round from her packing when I made no reply.

'You should not be in any doubt of that, Karl. You are very well known in Bilavice now – as a fighter for the nationalists and as a friend of mine.'

'The army will know nothing about me, except that I'm a foreign national.'

'The people of Bilavice will tell them.'

'I don't think I've made any enemies here.' The stoat perhaps, if he knew about my relationship with his wife, but I was sure he didn't.

'In this situation, Karl, you don't need enemies, you only need friends who are afraid for themselves. From tomorrow there will not be one person in Bilavice who ever had a good word to say for Slav Nationalism. Please understand that! It is not brave, it is not pleasant, but it is completely normal.'

'Are we not to try out a single grenade or a single home-made mortar? What about our snipers and all their carefully laid plans?'

Gerda looked at me and shook her head. She almost smiled.

'Go and get your things now, Karl, from your own room. Brobek's coach will leave his place at half past eleven. You must be there or you will be left behind. If you are left behind, you will have to do your grenade-throwing and your sniping all by yourself. Or you can just go into the square, like Queen Flavia, and stand in front of the tanks with your ugly cap on your head.'

13

Another Haircut

I didn't deliberately *not* go to Brobek's place to join the coach-party to Chostok. When I got back to Susha's house they were both there, she and her husband. It was one of her nights off from the power-station and he, of course, as a prominent nationalist, had left the council meeting in panic. I heard them in the kitchen as I let myself in with my own key, but they didn't hear me because he was shouting. The burden of it was that he was going in Brobek's coach and she was going with him. I knew why she didn't want to – she thought I might be staying behind – but he didn't know that and she couldn't tell him. In between his shouts I could hear her trying to head him off. She wasn't used to arguing with him or even questioning any of his dictats and this lack of practice, together with the fact that her reasons for not going had to be invented, put her in a very weak position. She produced too many reasons: her essential work at the power-station, her friends, nowhere to live in Chostok and nothing to live on, better for him to go on his own and for her to look after the house and so on. She obviously didn't have a chance of changing his mind.

At this point I opened the front door again and shut it with a bang, then went into the kitchen. Mikos was standing like a scrawny, frantically worked-up cockerel – symbol of Slav nationalism – in the middle of the floor, while beautiful Susha – she was beautiful these days – was backed against the sink looking sick.

'It seems we've got to get out,' I said into the sudden silence.

'Are you also leaving Bilavice, Mr Berg?' asked Mikos.

'Gerda tells me I've got no choice,' I said. 'I'm to meet her at Brobek's place at half past eleven.'

'We too,' said Mikos. 'I've just been telling my wife. She doesn't think it's necessary. You tell her!'

I looked at Susha with a surprised expression.

'For anyone connected with the True Faith I should think it's essential,' I said.

Susha said nothing, but it was obvious she was completely convinced.

I went to my room to pack and I could hear them doing the same – only of course they had very much more to pack than I did, so I was through while they were still agonising over what to take.

'I'll see you at Brobek's,' I called out from the hall, with my pack on my shoulder.

'See you!' called out Mikos from the bedroom, sounding almost friendly. Susha appeared in the kitchen doorway. She didn't say anything for fear of being heard by Mikos – it was a cheaply-built house, as I mentioned – just smiled.

'Goodbye, Susha,' I said. 'Thanks for having me. It was lovely.'

She didn't speak or move, but continued to smile. I went out and shut the door behind me.

I suppose I still intended – as I walked away down the street – to catch the coach. It's hard to say. I was already fairly sure I didn't *want* to catch it, but I certainly wasn't considering any alternative. Brobek's place was over the bridge, near the hospital, and I had nearly an hour in hand, so I simply proposed to get a drink and something to eat before what would surely be an arduous and freezing journey in an antique vehicle up corkscrew roads probably blocked with snow.

The best place to eat and drink quickly in Bilavice at this stage of the evening – night-life was more or less non-existent at the best of times – was the bar in the railway-station. So there, through an inch or so of slushy snow on the pavements, I went, like King Wenceslaus homing for his supper after the good deed done with the winter fuel. I was very conscious of Susha's happiness and pleased with myself for being the cause of it. When and if anyone comes to write my biography, he will probably – or she certainly – conclude that it was the prospect of being cooped up through the winter in Chostok, with both Gerda and Susha at loose ends and probably in cramped accommodation, that made me behave so shoddily and walk out on them rather than risk damaging my self-esteem. It wasn't like that at all. I daresay my self-esteem would indeed have been damaged, but I liked them both too much to give them any pain on purpose.

What happened was that I got to the station, had a schnapps and a couple of beers – there was nothing to eat but some very grey sausage which I didn't fancy – and discovered a train leaving for Kapitsa. That seemed such a civilised form of transport compared to a clapped-out coach climbing snowbound mountains that I immediately bought a ticket, without thinking too distinctly about the change of destination. The main thing was to get out of Bilavice. True, Kapitsa was in the opposite direction from Chostok and was in the hands of the Ruritanian Army, but I'd signed no contract with the Army of the True Faith, I wasn't a fanatical Slav nationalist and I owed them nothing – if anything, they owed me. As for my reception in Kapitsa, I saw no problem. My problem, as Gerda pointed out, was Bilavice. In Kapitsa I could simply phone the British Embassy in Strelsau and give them the glad news that, if they'd been missing him, Ed Fenton was alive and free.

The train was waiting at buffers beside a platform – the line didn't go beyond Bilavice. It was scheduled to leave at eleven and as I climbed up into an enormous old-fashioned carriage with a corridor, I had a momentary qualm about the coach. What if they waited for me when I didn't turn up? Or went round the town looking for me and then left it too late to escape the incoming enemy? There were still five minutes in hand. I left my bag in an empty compartment and rushed to a public phone. Brobek's number was engaged. I tried again several times and finally got his transport company's answerphone:

'Karl Berg,' I told it. 'Unforeseen circumstances. Don't wait for me! Love to Gerda!' I regretted that as soon as I said it, but you can't erase messages on answerphones, so I quickly added: 'Respects and thanks to Mikos and Susha. Goodbye, good journey, see you!'

I came away from the phone to find my train on the point of leaving. The stationmaster had his whistle to his mouth and his flag raised. I raced for the nearest door and got it open as the whistle blew, the flag fell and the train jerked. But as I got my foot on the step and turned to close the door, I saw that there was another latecomer running on to the platform: a girl in denims with a rucksack on her back. I leant out, holding on to the door with my left hand and extending my right to the girl. She ran alongside and caught my hand as the train began to gather speed. For a few moments I thought I wasn't strong enough and we'd both end up in a heap on the platform. But all my training and gym-classes and practice at hurling grenades had toughened my muscles and I hauled her off her feet and fought my way back up the steps with her and finally sat down with a bump on the passage floor to see what I'd caught.

'I hope this was the train you wanted,' I said.

'There's only one line out of Bilavice,' she said, dusting her knees, straightening her clothes and resetting her denim cap.

She wore a complete denim outfit – jeans, jacket and cap all in blue to match her pale blue eyes – and looked as if she might have been directing, or possibly starring in, a film. But I knew, of course, that she hadn't. She was Our Lady of Chostok. She didn't thank me for my action and behaved quite distantly and coolly, as if she took it for granted that any man who happened to be standing in the doorway of a train she was about to miss would make sure to drag her on to it. Still, she came and sat in the same compartment as me and I took that as thanks enough.

'How long have you been in Bilavice?' I asked.

'Off and on.'

At that rate she could have been the figure in blue in the church who had such a powerful effect on Susha.

'What happened at Kapitsa?'

'What do you mean?'

'It sounds as if there was some sort of disaster.'

'I wasn't there.'

'I assumed you'd be on your way to Chostok with Michael and the others.'

She didn't answer – it was obvious she wasn't.

'We last met,' I said, 'in the square at Bilavice.'

I sounded, even to myself, as if I was desperately trying to claim acquaintance with somebody I'd once met at a crowded party.

'I remember the cap,' she said.

After that I gave up for a while and we sat silently staring out of the window into the darkess as the train descended a series of long loops down from the Bilavice plateau. The snow on the banks of the line reflected the lights of the train, but nothing was visible beyond. We had more or less finished with the steepest part and were entering the hill-country below when the guard came in and clipped our tickets.

'Change at Kapitsa!' he said, handing her back her ticket.

'I thought this was a through train,' she said.

'All trains stop at Kapitsa until further notice.'

'Are you going on to Strelsau?' I asked, when the man had gone, thinking I might do the same.

'No. Vlod.'

She got up and pulled down the blinds over the door and windows on to the corridor.

'Where's that?'

'In Plotla,' she said.

'Is that where you come from? Your home town?'

'No.'

'What takes you to Vlod, then?' was my next line, but I hadn't the heart to say it. It was like talking to the recorded voice on a telephone information service. Her tone wasn't rude or even dismissive, just efficient and automatic. After pulling down the blinds she sat down again and unzipped a side-pocket on her rucksack.

'I have a favour to ask,' she said.

'Go ahead!' I said, expecting to be told to stop asking silly questions.

Instead she drew a pair of scissors out of the side-pocket and held them out to me.

'Will you please cut my hair!'

Completely thrown, I simply stared at her.

'I know you are not a hairdresser – I presume you are not. You only have to cut it off.'

'If that's what you want.'

She gave me the scissors and with the other hand took off her denim cap. Her long blonde hair was piled up under it and secured with pins. She pulled out the pins with a few quick movements and the hair fell down to her shoulders. We passed through a village station without stopping. She hadn't drawn the blinds down over the outside windows and I wondered if any gaping peasant on the platform had had this sudden vision of Our Lady's head and shoulders framed in a shower of pale gold hair whisking past inside the night-train to Kapitsa. If so they might also have seen the half-crazed face of the man in the flat cap opposite her, gripping the closed scissors in his palm as if he was about to stab her.

'As short as you can,' she said, and drew her finger round the back of her head at roughly the level of the earlobes.

'It's a terrible thing to do,' I said.

'I'm sorry to ask you, but it's not easy to do it myself.'

'I meant, it's such beautiful hair,' I said.

'Are you sentimental? It will grow again.'

'True. But it ought to be cut properly. I shall make a butcher's job of it.'

'You think I should make an appointment with the hairdresser in Kapitsa?'

'Or Vlod,' I said, so distressed at the thought of what I had to do that I missed her irony.

'Vlod would be too late,' she said. 'Cut please!'

I stood up, put my fingers into the scissor-handles and snipped the air a few times to test the blades' resistance. Then I sat down on the seat beside her and gathered her hair in my left hand.

125

'No! Wait a moment!'

I let go of her hair, relieved to think she was having second thoughts about this vandal act.

'Have you got a newspaper?'

'Sorry, no.'

'Or a towel? Something to cover the seat so that we leave no traces.'

I took a damp, grubby towel out of my bag and she stood up while I laid it over the seat. Then we both sat down again and I started to cut. I soon found it necessary to kneel on the seat, with my side braced against the back and my knees touching her bottom, but I was too concentrated on the job in hand to be sexually aroused and besides she was as relaxed and unconcerned as if I really was a hairdresser. I'm not turned on by being made to feel subordinate – whips and bonds and women in boots do nothing for me – and she was certainly not turned on by me. Hairdressers, however, have one perk – they're allowed to talk to their customers.

'You know my name, but I don't know yours.'

She made no reply immediately, but turned her face more towards the window to make my task easier as I worked round to the back of her head. My right knee slipped on the pile of fallen hair and I butted her by mistake at the base of the spine.

'Sorry!' I said.

'Yelena,' she said.

'I've always had to think of you up to now as just Our Lady of Chostok.'

Our eyes met in the reflection in the train window and since she didn't look away and I didn't either, there was a hiatus in the haircutting. It was a battle of wills and she clearly wasn't used to losing such battles. It was beginning to become ridiculous when she spoke:

'Why don't you go on?'

'Turn your head a bit more, please!'

She did so and broke the eye contact in the window.

'What do you expect to happen when we reach Kapitsa?' I asked.

'What do you mean?'

'Will it be like crossing a frontier – passports and customs?'

I remembered then that I had no passport. It was still at Previce Castle with the rest of the things I'd brought from Strelsau, including my copy – Hackney Library's copy – of Machiavelli.

'Why ask me?'

'I suppose I thought you'd know.'

I was getting increasingly irritated by this persistent stonewalling.

She exacted services from me but gave nothing in return except the privilege of serving.

'Are you Ruritanian?' she asked.

'Yes – no – sort of.'

'Then you will know better than me. I am not even a sort of Ruritanian.'

'Where from?'

'From Ukraine.'

I had finished all but the far side of her hair.

'Would you mind changing places now?' I said. 'So that I can do the last bit.'

She moved up and I knelt on the seat next to the window. And now I was aroused. Perhaps this profile looked more vulnerable than the other, perhaps I was that much closer. Her high-boned cheek, the deep arc of her jaw and the longish neck were extremely near and intimate as I held the hair away from her ear. There was a mole just under where the hair dwindled into down in front of her ear. The eyebrow was thick and straight over the inner corner of her eye, but curved up from the centre before fading away over the outer edge. That shallow saucer of tight skin between the cheekbone and the temple was within nine inches of my long Rassendyll/Elphberg nose. I put my knee deliberately against her bottom. She moved a few inches away. I edged it forward again.

'Finish cutting please!' she commanded.

'Tiring work,' I said.

'You are strong.'

'My left arm is still weak from a wound in Bilavice.'

'But you are using the right arm.'

'That's weak from lifting you on to the train.'

She suddenly stood up and almost in the same movement pulled the scissors off my fingers.

'I can finish it now myself.'

She went to the door and opened it a little, peered out cautiously for a moment to check that the corridor was clear, stepped delicately through the gap and closed the door behind her. I was left kneeling on the seat with huge quantities of pale gold hair and a hot flush of frustration, betrayal and injustice. What a bitch! What a cock-teaser! What an egotistical Ukrainian narcissist!

I returned to my own seat and glared belligerently at the pile of hair on the opposite seat. Then I suddenly felt very hungry. Her rucksack was still lying on the seat and I wondered if it contained any food. Even if it did, of course, she'd never give any of it to me.

Generosity was not in her nature. I returned to my angry contempla-
tion of the fallen hair, then after some time got up, undid the flap and
the string at the top of her rucksack and pulled it open. It seemed to
be mostly clothes, neatly packed, with a book in Russian on top and
directly below that an immaculate pale blue towel. She had a towel
of her own all the time! Bloody hell! I slid one hand down the back
of the rucksack to see if there was anything edible. The door clicked
and I looked up to see her half through it.

'What are you doing? Are you a thief?'

She'd finished off her hair and tidied up the part I'd done.
It didn't look *soigné*, but it certainly didn't spoil her looks.

'I'm incredibly hungry,' I said.

'You're incredibly bad-mannered,' she said.

Coming from her that annoyed me.

'Bad manners are catching,' I said.

'You think I owe you something?'

'Give as well as take,' I said.

She went to the rucksack and did it up again, put the scissors
away in their side pocket, zipped it up and unzipped another below
it. She extracted a small bar of chocolate and held it out to me.

'That's all I have. I have nothing else to give you, unless
you want money.'

'Thanks,' I said, 'I don't eat money.' I took the bar, broke
it in half and held out one half to her.

She paid no attention, but started gathering up the loose hair
in my towel and carefully adding stray bits from the floor and the
back of the seat. I ate my half of the chocolate bar and again held
out the other.

'Won't you go halves?'

'Your payment,' she said. 'I don't want it.'

I ate it, while she picked up the towel and its contents in
a bundle in both arms.

'Do you want to keep this dirty towel?'

'I half choked on my chocolate.

'Not if it's any use to you.'

'Open the window please!'

Being an old-fashioned carriage it had the kind of window you
could actually open. I pulled down the top and she stood on the
seat and lifted her bundle to breast height. She wore her breasts flat.
The wind rushing in from outside caught a few small bunches of hair
and blew them on to the floor. I picked them up as she dropped the
whole bundle out of the window. I was about to reach up and send

128

the stray hair after it, when I had a better idea. I closed the window – the air was bitter – and put the pinch of hair in the top pocket of my shirt.

'Why did you do that?'

'The rest of my payment,' I said. 'You gave me a bar of chocolate, Our Lady of Chostok gave me a relic.'

She almost smiled, then picked up her rucksack and went to the door.

'Goodbye,' she said.

I must have looked completely crestfallen.

'It would be best if we were not together when we reach Kapitsa,' she said.

'You think I might give you away?'

'Or I might give you away. Not deliberately. But it's easier to make one story for yourself alone. With two people they can set up traps.'

'The ticket-collector saw us together in the same compartment.'

'I can say that I came into the compartment after you helped me catch the train, but had to go to another because you started to annoy me.'

'Annoy you? I'm cast as the lusting brute?'

'But not miscast, surely? Anyway, men don't consider that disgraceful. On the contrary.'

'And suppose I mention the hair?'

'You can easily destroy me, if you wish. And I you, after your exploits in Bilavice. We must each act as we think right and best.'

She went out and closed the door.

I spent the rest of the journey obsessively spotting and disposing of odd hairs, but it never occurred to me that, although I was wearing my original jeans and sweater, with an anorak bought in Bilavice against the cold weather and, of course, my faithful cap, the bag beside me contained almost nothing but spare underwear, a khaki shirt or two, and the camouflage jacket and trousers I had worn as a soldier of the Ruritanian Army of the True Faith.

The train's brakes wailed as we slowed towards Kapitsa.

14

The Prisoner of Kapitsa

All my protests in loud English and pretence that I knew only a few words of German did no good at all. Offering money – I had no hard currency, just a small amount of Ruritanian krunas earned from my English lessons – was worse than useless. It simply confirmed, what my wretched bag already told them, that I was a nationalist on the run. I was taken straight from the train, which had been searched end to end by about twenty-five armed soldiers, in the back of a van, to an army barracks and dumped in a cell to await further questioning. With me and into adjoining cells went three of my former comrades from the Bilavice defence group, who had been on the same train. We didn't speak and could hardly meet each other's eyes in the van: where was all our braggardly sniping and grenade-throwing now?

Our Lady of Chostok – Yelena – was nowhere to be seen. Perhaps her Ukrainian passport had passed her through to Vlod, perhaps she was being reserved for special treatment, gentler or nastier than ours. My main occupation, as I sat alone on the bed in my cell waiting for further developments, was thinking of all the questions I should have asked her in the train: why aren't you with Michael any more? when you made that speech in front of the church in Chostok, did you believe what you said? if I told you who I really am, would you still treat me as just a serviceable slob? are you a Lesbian? I also speculated on what her replies might have been, but of course I knew perfectly well there wouldn't have been any, which was why I hadn't asked the questions in the first place.

It was unpleasant and extremely boring being in the cell, but I wasn't really worried because I was sure that once I got interviewed by somebody higher up than the soldiers who'd arrested me, I'd be able to pull my status as a foreign national and get help from the British Embassy or Grabenau or the Count, who might by now or surely would soon be free of his own imprisonment.

After a day or two of solitary confinement, during which I

saw only the guard who brought me food twice a day and seemed to be a deaf mute – of course I was still pretending to speak only English – I was marched to a small bare room containing a table and two chairs and interviewed by a lieutenant of about nineteen. Thin-lipped, shaven-headed, wearing glasses with thin silver rims, he looked as if he hoped to be running a death-camp when he grew up. He spoke good English.

'Mr Edwin Fenton?'

'Yes.'

He consulted papers in front of him.

'If we are to prove your identity we need passport or other documents.'

'All my things, including my passport, are at Previce Castle.'

'Previce Castle is not yet liberated.'

'Could you phone the British Embassy in Strelsau?'

'That is not necessary.'

'Of course it's necessary. I'm a British citizen and I'm being kept in prison on charges I don't understand. I wish to phone the British Embassy.'

'The British Embassy will be informed when investigations are completed.'

'But how can you complete your investigations until you've established my identity?'

'I understand you are British. That is clear.'

'Good! So I have a right to speak to my Embassy.'

'No, no right. Mercenaries have no rights.'

'I am not a mercenary.'

'You were a combatant with terrorists.'

'What's your evidence for that?'

'You were carrying military clothing and you travelled from Bilavice which was in the hands of terrorists.'

'I was a journalist observing events in the front line and I wore the clothes as some protection from being seen and shot by mistake.'

I wasn't sure whether war correspondents wore camouflage on the job, but it seemed a credible idea. The teenage Himmler sighed.

'Journalists must have papers, must have identification, must be accredited to war zones. No journalists have been accredited to these terrorists.'

'I happened to be visiting my friend Count von Wunklisch at Previce Castle and became involved with the terrorists by accident. It was too late then to ask for my accreditation.'

'You only speak English, Mr Fenton?'

131

'A little German.'

'I think you did not understand very well the position you were in.'

'I understood very well that a war had broken out and I thought that as a journalist it was my duty to see and report what I could.'

Himmler shook his head and wagged his finger with infuriating complacency.

'No journalist,' he said. 'We have no identification for a journalist, so we have to agree a mercenary, but a mercenary not fully understanding what he is doing.'

I controlled my urgent need to pick him up by a leg and an arm and hurl him at the guard standing to attention by the door.

'Can I please speak to the British Embassy or to Count von Wunklisch or to a parliamentary deputy called Anton Grabenau?'

'This is not necessary.'

'Not necessary! That's a completely stupid thing to say! You're holding me in prison and accusing me of being a mercenary. This must be illegal.'

This time he nodded his head in little quick jerks like a car mascot, patiently humouring my outburst.

'Normal laws do not apply. This is a military emergency. Not understanding is best, Mr Fenton.'

I stood up and banged my chair on the floor.

'I demand to be put in touch with the British Embassy!'

He compressed his lips so tightly that he seemed to have a sewn-up scar where his mouth should be and signed to the guard. I was marched back to my cell.

Two or three more days went by and I began to get seriously depressed. I was used by now to the foul smell of the toilet-bowl in the corner; and the food – porridge in the morning and a thin soup with a piece of bread at night – kept me alive, though violently hungry. I was not let out even for exercise, so I spent much of my time walking round and round the cell, running on the spot, standing on my head, jumping, swinging my arms, practising lethal blows against an invisible enemy whose face I envisaged with thin lips and thin-rimmed glasses. I tried to remember all the Ruritanian words and phrases I had ever learnt, but since almost every one conjured up an image of the circumstances I'd learnt them in with either Gerda or Susha, I soon found this too painful.

I thought hard about escape, of course. The cell was not a custom-built dungeon, but simply a small room in a kind of barrack-building: the barred window looked out on a bare tarmac space surrounded with other one-storey buildings. People, mostly soldiers, crossed the space from time to time, hurrying through what was evidently a cold wind, though there was no snow here yet. The walls were not particularly thick. I could hear the guard coming down the corridor and faint sounds from the cells on either side – coughing, the flush of a toilet, doors slammed. The walls went right up to the ceiling, which was about twelve feet high – I could just touch it if I stood on the bed or leapt in the air. But the only way out of this place for a prisoner without any kind of weapon or instrument was to pull the bars off the window with his bare hands or rush the guard when he opened the door to slide porridge or soup in along the floor. Since he always peered through the grille in the door and ordered me to stand at the far side of the cell before he would open up, it would have to be some rush. I made a few practice runs and decided he'd get the door closed and have time to spit in my food for good measure without even trying.

My depression was less to do with any real worry about my ultimate release – I was sure that at some stage I'd get access to someone with more authority and broader ideas than the Himmler youth. What depressed me was the emptiness of my own barrel. I didn't know any books or long poems – or even short ones – by heart; my thoughts hardly went beyond food; sex in this utterly sexless place seemed a bad joke and even the bunch of pale gold hair in my top pocket failed to stir me: basically I found my own company completely lacking in style or content. I began to take much the same view of myself as Yelena obviously had – a strong right arm to get on to a train with and a haircutter in an emergency – but of no conceivable interest personally or intellectually. Would my great-grandfather, I asked myself, have lost interest in himself in the same circumstances? Of course, he never made the mistake, so far as I could remember, of getting himself jailed. But his double, King Rudolf V, my distant cousin and great-grand-stepfather, did, in the dungeon of Zenda Castle, and it broke him up completely. Perhaps I was going the same way and would emerge like him as a chronic alcoholic. I only wished somebody would offer me a drink and start me off.

It occurred to me, of course, that prisoners traditionally keep themselves sane or plot escapes by tapping out messages to each other along the pipes. There were pipes in my cell, running close to the floor under the window and straight through to the cells on either side, but I didn't know morse code. Probably one could have shouted through the walls, but if my neighbours were still the ex-Home Guard

133

of Bilavice I didn't feel I had much to shout to them except 'sorry it didn't work out'. Altogether, by the time I was marched out of my cell again, I had decided that of all the experiences on this earth, my own sole company was the pits and I was really looking forward to another interview, even with the lipless boy.

I found myself, after waiting half an hour or so in an antechamber with a silent guard, in a large room containing about ten people. There were three officers in military uniform sitting behind a long table; an elderly woman and a young man in civilian clothes taking notes at side tables; a saturnine, hook-nosed officer in his mid-thirties seated facing the long table, with a sort of lectern in front of him; and on my side of the room, also seated behind a similar lectern, young Himmler. He, it turned out, was not only my defence counsel before this military court but also my interpreter, so that unless I cared to give away my knowledge of German my case had to be filtered exclusively through him. The whole thing was Kafkaesque. I've never read Kafka, but you don't have to have been to hell to know what hellish means.

The prosecutor put some papers on his lectern and kicked off with a brief statement of the charges against me: I was a British mercenary – identity not firmly established, but certainly English-speaking and claiming to be a British citizen called Edwin Fenton – who had been a combatant with the so-called Ruritanian Army of the True Faith against the Republic of Ruritania and therefore a terrorist. He offered no proof, called no witnesses, sat down and left the floor to his esteemed colleague, Second-Lieutenant Schutz. My baby-faced defender now stood up nervously, put his papers on his lectern and began by agreeing fervently with the prosecutor's summary of the probable facts. However, he said, given that his client spoke virtually no German, he would ask the court to take a lenient view of his crime. There was no doubt, of course, that he knew he was among terrorists, but he misunderstood his own position and thought he was not so much fighting as observing. There was no evidence that he was a professional journalist but he might well have hoped to be able to make some money when he went back to his own country by selling his story to a newspaper. He was also probably very confused about the issues and was essentially unaware that he was actually fighting against the legitimate forces of the Republic of Ruritania and therefore open to a charge of State Treason. He sat down.

'What is going on?' I said loudly in English. 'I don't understand a thing. Is this a court? Where are my rights? I wish to speak to the British Embassy in Strelsau. Bitte, Britisher Embassee!'

134

The judges consulted together and my defender was told to give me a brief version of what had been said. Meanwhile the prosecutor was sitting twisting one of his very large ears with impatience and as soon as the translation was finished he was on his feet again.

'Second-Lieutenant Schutz's account of the prisoner's misapprehensions might be more credible,' he declared in a voice creamy with satisfaction, 'if we did not have incontrovertible evidence to the contrary. Please put on your cap, Mr Fenton!'

I looked blank.

'Put on his cap!' he said sharply to my guards and one of them did so.

'Observe his appearance, Colonel!' he said to the judge at the centre of the table and paused, while the colonel – a pink, pudgy-faced buffer of about fifty with bristly white hair and a yellowing moustache carefully separated from his nose by a shaved trench – stared at me. So did his two flanking judges. I set my jaw and stared back from under my cap with what I hoped was rugged British insolence.

'Now compare this!' said the prosecutor and with a melodramatic gesture produced from among the papers on his lectern an enlarged photograph and held it up. He walked the few steps to the judges' table and laid the photograph in front of the colonel. All three judges looked at it carefully, looked up at me, looked back at the photograph.

'Second-Lieutenant Schutz!' said the colonel.

My defence counsel hastily crossed to the table and was shown the photograph. When he too had compared it with me he seemed completely unnerved.

'Show it to the prisoner and ask him if he has anything to say!'

His face white, hand shaking, the poor boy showed me an excellent aerial shot of myself in my flat cap and shoulder-slung Kalashnikov standing ahead of my section in a mountain-stream and making a two-finger sign at the camera. The face was mostly hidden, but the nose poked out sufficiently to be unmistakable. I felt more sorry for the boy than for myself. It looked as if he had been set up for this forensic disaster, encouraged to make his lame excuse about misunderstandings so that the prosecutor could achieve maximum effect when he produced the ace in his hand. Surely prosecutors were supposed to present their evidence first? The judges must have colluded in bending the rules.

Standing there in my cap, unquestionably the same person as the rude guerrilla in the photograph, what could I do? I adopted more or less the same pose and gave the judges two fingers.

'There is no victory for you,' said the colonel, stretching the sides of his mouth to show his teeth as if he meant to brush them.

'It doesn't mean victory,' I said in English, 'it means up yours.'

Second-Lieutenant Schutz was unable or unwilling to translate this and I didn't see either of the note-takers write it down, so that misunderstanding persisted.

But although the argument might have been said to be over, the prosecutor had three more aces in his hand and wanted to show them. He retrieved the photograph from the cowed Schutz and asked the judges if he might now call his witnesses. They were called and they were my three old comrades from Bilavice. Each in turn, never catching my eye, described me as the leading light in the planned defence of Bilavice against the Ruritanian Army, the energetic corporal who, wounded in the original assault on the town, had enthusiastically organised the manufacture of grenades and mortars, supervised the selection of an elite band of snipers, suggested and approved points of ambush and counter-attack. My name, they all agreed, was Karl Berg and I not only spoke German like a native, but also made a very decent shot at Ruritanian. I was pleased to hear that. Schutz was asked to sit down – he was no longer in any state to stand up and made no attempt to question the witnesses or cast doubt on their evidence – and the colonel dealt directly with me.

'Mr Berg,' he said, 'Can you deny any part of this evidence?'

'My name is not Berg,' I replied in German, 'and I am a British citizen. Otherwise it's broadly correct.'

'May we know why you chose to fight with such enthusiasm for our enemies?'

Put like that it did sound bad. Why had I? It all started with vandalising the church-windows. Yet at no point did I feel any particular animosity towards the Ruritanian Army – except perhaps when they were trying to annihilate me in Bilavice – nor any great sympathy with the nationalist cause. I'd actually grown to dislike the nationalists' leader.

'No reply, Mr Berg?'

'I think,' I said, 'that I wasn't so much fighting *against* enemies as *with* friends.'

'It's a pity for you that you chose such friends!' said the colonel, flashing his teeth again. 'Have you any further points to make, Second-Lieutenant Schutz?'

Schutz stood up like a puppet, moved his head as if it was attached to tight wires and spoke with difficulty:

'No, sir.'

Schutz sat down, the three judges put their heads together and everyone else was preternaturally silent.

'What is your real name, Mr Berg?' the colonel said suddenly.

'The name on my passport is Edwin Fenton,' I said, 'and several Ruritanian citizens, including Count von Wunklisch, the parliamentary deputy Anton Grabenau, the artist Vladek Tarlenheim and the Ruritanian Ambassador in London, Colonel Danzing, can vouch for my identity.'

'I simply do not understand your motives, Mr Fenton,' said the colonel. 'These are all well known and loyal Ruritanians. What possessed you to betray their friendship for these other "friends"?'

I shrugged. There seemed no easy answer. But thinking about the question afterwards, I realised how loaded it was, as those sort of questions fired at one by angry and baffled schoolmasters always were. 'Loyal' to what?

The court's verdict was that I was a mercenary guilty of fighting for terrorists and that that constituted State Treason for which the prescribed sentence was death by firing-squad. Under the emergency regulations there was no necessity to inform the British Embassy until after the sentence had been carried out, but the court would consider whether or not it might be advisable in the circumstances.

15

A New Taste For Opera

Am I writing these memoirs in my cell – like Alec Guinness in the film where he murders all his relations for a title – the night before they take me out at dawn? It did occur to me to pull title, to send a note to the colonel asking him if he was really prepared to eliminate the great-grandson of their last monarch, the nearest thing to a king they had. But he'd have bared his teeth and torn the note up, of course, thinking it was yet another of Mr Fenton's inexplicable idiocies. In any case, I suddenly remembered that I wasn't the only possible king on offer: there was still Freddy waiting in the wings and I couldn't help thinking that, offered the prospect of being Queen Jennifer, my sister-in-law – fond as we were of each other – would not have stood in the way of my execution. She would have seen it as a moral imperative, the inevitable outcome of a misspent life, better for everyone, especially myself. Freddy didn't know Ruritanian, of course, but his German was nearly as good as mine and he'd undoubtedly be 'loyal' to anything they asked him to be loyal to. His loyalty to Hackney Council proved that.

No, I am not writing in that cell, but in a room larger and more comfortable, though nearly as empty, in less nerve-wracking circumstances. My nerves *were* wracked in the days that followed the court's verdict, chiefly, I believe, because of that teasing hope of survival, supposing that the court in its wisdom chose to inform the British Embassy of my plight *before* sentence was carried out. If there'd been no let-out clause I would surely have been calmer and happier. Perhaps I would have asked for pen and paper and sat down to write these memoirs up to this point, ending with the pious reflection that I had now bored myself so silly that it would be a relief to be shot of myself.

While I'm in this introspective vein I should emphasize that although I can almost recall what it was like to be ready to lose my own company for ever, its only lasting effect has been to make me detest solitude. I have not seen the point of Buddhism or turned to Jesus or embraced the soppy humanism which was buried somewhere under my father's dour socialism or even learnt to love prisoners. I have had no moral conversion at all nor improved my character, but merely reverted to my old arrogant, selfish self, with the extra determination never to be forced to contemplate it at such close quarters again, but to let it hum away unexamined like the engine of a really good car that never goes wrong as long as you don't tinker with it. Having looked into the heart of darkness and seen my own face, I'm grateful that most of the time it's other people that have to look at it.

There were no sounds now from the neighbouring cells. My comrades had probably purchased their freedom and returned to Bilavice. I hoped so. I bore them no grudge for dropping me in it: on the contrary they'd relieved me of any lingering shame. I'd encouraged them to think of me and themselves as heroes and then we'd all four scarpered. Of course it would have been suicide, as Gerda said, to try to defend Bilavice without any help from our own side, but we'd not made a tactical retreat to rejoin our own side at Chostok, we'd simply run. And if the man with the armband runs, you're entitled to shoot him in the back.

I continued to exercise in my cell, but less frenetically. I spent long hours lying on the bed staring at the ceiling: it was difficult to sleep. My meals had improved, perhaps because my captors felt some pity for me, more likely because they now had three fewer mouths to feed. There was some grisly stew one night, an antique chicken-leg in a spiced sauce another, cabbage and potato most nights with the soup. And now that I could admit to knowing German I was able to speak to my guard. He was usually the same fellow, though he had the odd day or night off. I asked him if I could get my clothes washed. There was a tiny washbasin in the cell, in which I might have washed my shirt an arm at a time, but nowhere to hang anything up to dry. He brought me a pair of pink-striped pyjamas and an army greatcoat and took away all my clothes. But just as he was tramping away down the corridor I remembered what I'd left in the pocket of my shirt and urgently called out to him through the grille. When I told him the reason, he was delighted, re-opened the door and allowed me to remove my bunch of Yelena's hair while the door stood ajar between us.

This was my moment, if ever there was one, to fight for life – what had I to lose if he shot me down in the corridor? But I made no attempt to escape, took the hair, held it up to show him and stowed it in the breast pocket of my borrowed pyjamas, while he stood in the open doorway beaming like Father Christmas – his face was that sort of shape anyway.

Perhaps my spirit was flickering low by then, my will to survive atrophied by lack of food and fresh air and poisoned by self-dislike. I don't think so. I think I know instinctively when a moment is good or not, when the wind is behind me or in my face, when it's fate that opens a door and when it's only the guard. Next day he brought me back my clothes, washed and ironed, but he too had evidently thought about that lapse of security with the door and he pushed the little pile of clean clothes in along the floor like my food.

'Did you do this?' I asked when he had closed the door and while he remained outside watching through the grille for my reaction.

'My wife.'

'Please thank her!'

'Look in the pocket!' he said.

I put my fingers inside the shirt-pocket and drew out a little rectangle of thin card. It was a mass-produced picture of the Virgin Mary in her standard blue robe – a typical Catholic product in soft focus, with 'Ave Maria' printed underneath.

'Please thank your wife,' I said, 'I'm very touched.'

I found it less touching than uncanny, in view of the claims made by the owner of the hair it had replaced.

'She prays for you every day,' said the guard, 'and she lit a candle for you in the church on Sunday.'

Did I believe I was actually going to be stood up against a wall and filled with bullets? Not wholly. Although we're supposed to be the only animal that has a sense of past and future, it's a very embryonic sense, decaying into nostalgia and frozen snapshots of the past, projecting the future mostly in the form of fears or hopes of a two-dimensional kind: yes or no, with a slot for 'don't know' like a pollster's question-form and just as unable to cope with variables and shades of yes-ness and no-ness which falsify the projection almost from the start. I did think about the actual moment, the bullets hitting me, and comforted myself with the fact that I'd already experienced that in a mild form and it wasn't so terrible at the moment it happened. The pain came afterwards and I assumed I'd be missing that phase on this occasion. The worst would be the time just before – the waiting outside the headmaster's study or in the dentist's chair while the instruments were prepared and one had no active role.

140

The mind being the main problem, then, the simplest solution would be to slosh it so full of alcohol that it wouldn't know whether it was going to be shot to pieces or awarded the Nobel Peace Prize. Having no alcohol I decided the next best thing would be to get so heavily into fantasy that my mind would be confused anyway. I lay on my bed and tried to let my imagination rip. It started, of course, poor ill-nourished thing, with an Indian restaurant in Islington where Freddy and Jennifer and I had celebrated their third wedding anniversary; and then, gathering strength, found a better restaurant near Covent Garden where I used to take girls in the Eighties. But meals, however good, only demonstrate the human predicament at its most extreme: they are nothing at all in retrospect, meaningless in the future, good only in immediate expectation and fulfilment. Next I tried sex – not much different. Money, then? That was better grist for fantasy because of being a vaguer entity with a larger range of pleasures attached, some of them purely intellectual, such as obtaining a personal interview with my stroppy bank-manager so as to hand him a cheque for five million to cover my £50 overdraft and telling him to transfer the balance to another bank. But what to do with my limitless fantasy money? Meals and sex had already proved unsuitable. What about houses, cars, travel? As soon as they became freely available, of course, they lost their appeal. But suppose I gave most of my billions, in my father's memory, to the Labour Party on the sole condition that they changed their red rose to a black spanner? What pleasures would I buy myself with the small change – two million or so?

I yawned and fell asleep – pleasure enough in my circumstances – and dreamed vividly of a huge sheet of calm water, a lake among mountains where I was waterskiing behind a speed-boat. Was this my chosen slice of the rich man's life? I have never waterskied in reality. From time to time I would fall over, deliberately it seemed, because I wanted the boat to come nearer so that I could identify its occupants. Michael was surely the one sitting in the stern, but his arm obscured his face. Was the driver Yelena, with her hair either cut short or pinned up under a yachting-cap? I never found out – I was now in a church, perhaps the cathedral in Strelsau, since I seemed to be kissing the toe of Our Lady of Wloczovar – or was it the wooden statue stolen by Fisher John? – and suddenly they were shooting at the windows from outside, so that glass slivers or bullets were falling all round me. I was lying down, feeling no pain, but one wouldn't feel pain, would one, after the execution was over?

I woke up in a bad temper. Had they bungled it? Surely I

shouldn't still be conscious? I was lying on my bed in the cell, but very cold, in a draught. Part of the window was broken, there were pieces of glass all over the floor and among them the stone that must have done the damage. Round it, secured by a rubber-band, was a piece of roughly-torn paper. I quickly got off the bed and picked it up, glancing first out of the window and then at the grille in the door to see if I was being watched. The space outside the window was completely empty and since it was the middle of the afternoon, two or three hours short of my supper, the guard had probably got his feet up somewhere and hadn't heard the window being smashed. There was a brief message in capitals on the paper, in Ruritanian:

HAVE FAITH, CORPORAL, UNTIL THE END

I read this in disbelief. I tried to make the Ruritanian mean something else, but what else could it mean? Whoever threw the stone must have gone to some trouble, taken some risk to deliver this piece of tawdry uplift. Couldn't they have wrapped it round a file while they were about it? Perhaps it was in code, but how was I supposed to puzzle it out? I tried to make anagrams out of the Ruritanian words, but would they be words in Ruritanian or German or English? I juggled about with all three and got nothing but nonsense. I turned the paper over and found a single word, also in capitals:

TOSCA

A name? A Ruritanian word whose meaning I didn't know? Or the famous opera, which I'd never heard or seen and whose story I didn't know? As darkness began to fall outside I abandoned all this mental effort, flushed the paper down the loo, used the rubber-band to make a more handy bundle of Yelena's hair and put it back in my shirt pocket with the picture of the Virgin Mary. I didn't really want to keep that, but I hesitated to throw it down the loo out of respect for the guard's wife rather than the superstition it represented. Then I sat on the hot pipes to one side of the window to try to neutralise the icy draught coming through the hole.

When the guard arrived with my supper and peered through the grille, I pointed at the broken window and the stone on the floor and said:

'Can you do something about this? It's very cold.'

His face disappeared immediately and a moment later I heard an alarm bell, followed by running feet. A face I didn't know looked

142

apprehensively through the grille and then the door was unlocked and two guards came in pointing guns at me. Behind was my familiar guard and a sergeant. When they'd searched the cell, tested the bars and found nothing suspicious except the stone, my guard was sent to fetch an officer, while I was locked in again and the others waited outside in the corridor. All this while I'd sat quietly on the pipes – except when I was being body-searched – and said nothing beyond explaining that I'd been asleep when the stone arrived and hadn't seen who threw it. But as I sat I was still turning over the message in my mind, trying to find some secret key. It occurred to me after some time that it could just be read not as a last religious up-yours to a person without religion, but as an exhortation to keep hoping right up to the end. That still didn't explain the name or word on the back, but perhaps 'Tosca' had nothing to do with my message, just happened to have been written on the piece of paper already.

A fattish captain with thick eyebrows, small eyes and hairs protruding from his nose was now let into my cell, while the soldiers with guns came in too to cover me with their weapons. The captain searched the place for himself, examined the damaged window and the stone, tried the bars, questioned me closely and finally gave orders for me to be moved into the next cell.

'Captain!' I said, as he was about to leave, 'Can you tell me whether they've informed the British Embassy?'

'I can't tell you,' he said, 'But you won't have to wait much longer.'

'Wait for what?'

He didn't care to answer that, but rubbed the channel below his hairy nose several times.

'You will be informed,' he said and turned to go again.

'Captain!' I said, 'I think I know what you mean. Is it possible to make a last request?'

He said nothing, but waited.

'The hardest thing,' I said, 'is never to hear music again. I'm very fond of music. Would it be possible for me to listen to my favourite opera once more before . . .?'

'How would that be possible?'

'If somebody would lend me cassettes and a player . . .'

'What is your favourite opera?'

'*Tosca*,' I said.

'Composer?'

I stood and gaped at him.

'I don't know what's happening to my memory, Captain. My favourite music in the whole world . . . I'll forget my own name . . .'

I hung my head.

'*Tosca!*' he said. 'Is that Puccini?'

'I fancy it is.'

'Don't count on it!' he said as he went out.

The next cell was warmer, of course, but the loo stank worse than mine.

The following morning my plate of porridge came accompanied by a small portable cassette-player with earphones and a boxed set of the tapes of *Tosca*, complete with libretto in Italian and German translation. When I'd played the whole thing through, I played it again and many times more until I could hum the tunes and had acquired my life-long addiction to opera. And a longer life it promised to be, since now I knew what the message meant and roughly what I was to be prepared for.

All the same it was not much to cling to when the guard handed me a letter the morning after that. The attention of the British Embassy *would be* drawn, it said, to my case at the appropriate time and the Embassy would no doubt inform my relatives as well as Colonel Danzing, the former Ruritanian Ambassador in London, of the measures found necessary to protect the Republic in such a dangerous emergency. It had not been found possible to contact either Count von Wunklisch or Herr Tarlenheim, but they too would be informed as soon as convenient. Herr Grabenau had already been informed and had expressed his deep sorrow at the outcome, while finding it hard to believe that such a promising and well-connected young man had descended to a crime against the State for which unfortunately there was the clearest possible first-hand evidence. The sentence of the court, the letter went on, would be carried out at dawn tomorrow, but not before I had been visited by Father Roddich, the chaplain, and offered spiritual consolation and preparation. The letter was signed 'with regrets' by Colonel Maggerling, officer commanding the 2nd Regiment of Infantry, Kapitsa.

I played *Tosca* several times more and wondered why Colonel Danzing had retired or been replaced. Was it connected with me or just old age? Grabenau's response was quite consistent with every-thing I knew about him – I liked that 'well-connected', a masterly marker put down for the future in case anybody should ever accuse him of allowing the heir to the throne to be shot in ignorance. I was glad that at least I hadn't stayed in Strelsau waiting for him to discern through his fog of factions no clear political consensus for the restoration of the monarchy.

Father Roddich, the military chaplain, was a young, tall, black-haired peasant from the countryside round Zenda, who had shown more aptitude for school lessons than the rest of his large family and been sent to a seminary to ease the pressure on the limited resources of his father's farm. We talked more about his own circumstances than the prospects for my soul, since I told him I didn't possess one. He looked mildly shocked and assured me I would be proved wrong.

'What form will the proof take?' I asked.

He was unwilling to say. His brief was probably to comfort and calm the condemned man, not threaten him with hell-fire and he tried to nudge the discussion back on to standard lines: that dying was a stage everyone had to go through and that the important thing was to set my mind on the better world I would soon be entering.

'What can you tell me about that better world, Father?'

Very little, of course. Priests have even vaguer ideas of what they're promising than politicians.

'I used to work in the City of London,' I said. 'We would never have advised our clients to invest even a worthless Ruritanian kruna on the basis of such an inadequate prospectus.'

'You must have faith,' he said.

We left it there. I asked him how he came to have faith himself and discovered that he too was more of an investment in this world than the next. I declined to confess my sins, but allowed him to say a brief prayer for me and then, as he raised his hand to bless me, the guard at the grille must have raised his to someone further down the corridor. Marching feet halted at my door, it was opened wide and I was led out by two armed soldiers to find two more and the fat captain with the hairy nose in the corridor with my usual guard. I shook his hand and asked him to give my respects to his wife – there were tears in his eyes – and thanked the captain warmly for the loan of *Tosca*. Then we marched away down the corridor, the captain in front, the chaplain behind, the four guards and me in a close phalanx in the middle.

'*E lucevan le stelle . . .*' I hummed half aloud and '*E non ho amato mai tanto la vita!*'. *Tosca* was now certainly my last hope, but I had no great faith in it at this appalling moment, especially when

I considered that the heroine's belief that her lover would only have to face a firing-squad using blanks was false and that the bullets fired at him were real.

16

A Change of Life

We emerged from the corridor into a concrete car-park with a vicious wind swirling round it. It wasn't an ordinary car-park, since the only vehicles parked there were half a dozen armoured ones. It seemed appropriate that I should be seen into oblivion by this fleet of my old enemies from Bilavice. The building on the right was a large hangar with its sliding doors closed. The captain led our little procession towards it and then round and behind to a yard about the size of six tennis-courts, surrounded with a high wall topped with barbed wire. Piled up on three sides was scrap of various kinds, mostly bits and pieces of vehicles. That seemed appropriate too, a kind of last reproof from my father about the vanity of everything on wheels. The fourth side of this dump, the back wall of the hangar, was partly clear and obviously reserved for my own demolition.

Ten armed soldiers, lined up at attention as if waiting to be inspected, stood with their backs to the piles of scrap and faced the blank wall of the hangar, while in the middle of the yard was a group of three officers, whose faces turned towards us as we marched round the side of the building and halted in the broad gateway. One of the officers was the colonel from the military court, the second was the younger of the two who had sat with him at the table – the adjutant of the regiment – but the third I hadn't seen before. He was a good-looking, fair-haired youth with a turned-up nose and a sprinkling of acne along his jaw – he reminded me of my brother Freddy – and he seemed to be having an argument with the colonel. Our arrival put a stop to it and the colonel, with the adjutant following him as if they were wired together, turned and walked aside, proclaiming in a choleric voice for all to hear:

'Proceed, then, Lieutenant, but it is completely irregular and I shall see you and Lieutenant Grauner as soon as this affair is over!'

The lieutenant saluted and marched forward to meet our group.

147

I was now feeling weak in the legs and sick in the stomach. I would have liked to sit down just where I was or at least lean on one of my guards. My nose was running from the cold wind and rather than sniff I kept wiping it with my sleeve and tipping my head backwards. The sky was full of large racing clouds, high up, and it was barely light. The sun wasn't visible at all. Three large birds with long necks flew over from right to left – swans, geese, storks, cranes? My ignorance was lamentable, but what did it matter when the few things I had managed to store in my head – including all that intimately acquired Ruritanian vocabulary – were going to be wiped clean anyway? I tried to whistle the tune from *Tosca* – 'I never loved life so much' – but it sounded more like the wind under the door in a horror-film. I certainly had no hope at all that those ten soldiers had blanks in their guns – the presence of Colonel Maggerling and his side-kick from the court precluded that.

The young lieutenant and the captain in front of our group spoke briefly and the captain indicated the middle of the empty wall and ordered my four guards to take me there. I caught his eye for a moment and he bit his lip. He and Father Roddich remained together near the entrance, while the soldiers and I went forward to the wall. Then they withdrew towards the captain and I was standing alone. The lieutenant looked nervously at his watch.

'Get on with it, Lieutenant!' shouted the colonel.

Several things happened at once: the lieutenant gave an order to the soldiers facing me and they raised their weapons; the captain started forward with one hand up towards the soldiers and the other pulling a handkerchief out of his pocket, as he called out that he'd forgotten the blindfold; and on the far side of the hangar there was suddenly a tremendous noise of engines starting. The colonel's mouth opened and he made a step forward, the lieutenant seemed to be temporarily at a loss, but then he drew his revolver from the holster at his side and almost leaping in the air with the effort to be heard above the engines, screamed:

'Fire!'

I sat down abruptly. The muscles simply folded my legs independently, as if I'd been banged behind the knees. The captain – halfway over to me with his handkerchief – threw himself on the ground. The soldiers facing me fired, but not at me. The burst went to my right, over the captain and the heads of Father Roddich and the four guards, who all also dived to the ground. The lieutenant went straight up to the colonel and his adjutant and pointed his

148

revolver at them, shouting to the soldiers in a voice almost falsetto with excitement:

'Disarm the guards!'

The fallen captain and I were left detached, while the soldiers surrounded Father Roddich and the guards and the lieutenant backed his two superior officers, with their hands in the air, towards the same group. I saw the captain put his hand to his revolver holster, but he didn't even unbutton it. That gesture of impotence made my spirits surge up through me again as if I'd just stepped from a cold bathroom into a hot bath. I got up, still shaking with shock, and went over to him.

'You were right, Captain,' I said, 'it was Puccini.'

He looked bewildered.

'*Tosca*,' I said. 'But this time it worked.'

His handkerchief was still fluttering in his hand. I stuffed it back in his pocket, then opened his holster and removed the revolver.

'Better join the party!' I said.

He stood up slowly, still dazed, and I swivelled him round and escorted him towards the group near the gate. At that moment an armoured vehicle rolled into the gateway and stopped. I looked wildly round to see where I could run, but its machine-gun remained pointed in the air and a soldier's head and shoulders rose out of the top. He had a smile on his face and raised two fingers. The lieutenant gave him two fingers back and then, as I urged my prisoner on towards the group, turned and saluted me.

'Sir!' he said.

The mutiny of the 2nd Regiment of Infantry had been planned for a week or two later, when there was to be a visit of inspection by a senior general from Strelsau. He and his staff would have been held as hostages to reinforce the mutineers' demands for a full inquiry into the so-called 'Kapitsa Atrocity' – the attack on the rebels during which parts of the town had been damaged and many civilian lives lost. Based on the border of the province of Karapata, the 2nd Regiment consisted mostly of Slav soldiers, officered by a mixture of Slavs and Germans, with the senior posts held by Germans. It had played no significant part in the 'Kapitsa Atrocity', which was carried out by the predominantly German airforce and artillery, and its uncertain loyalty to the Strelsau government had been the reason why so little had been done earlier to contain the rebels in the mountains.

I almost got the impression that by downing a civilian aircraft over the Kapitsa airfield Michael had deliberately provoked the Kapitsa Atrocity so as to split the enemy forces, but no one would admit as much.

I received this information in a confused form in the officers' mess, where the victorious mutineers – mostly lieutenants with a captain or two – gathered briefly to toast their success in schnapps and vodka. While our own drama was taking place in the scrapyard, the other armoured vehicles had been deployed at strategic points and the rest of the barracks seized piecemeal by Slav soldiers under Slav subalterns. Standing beside a blazing fire, surrounded by leather armchairs and exhilarated, flushed young officers, with old photographs of Warsaw Pact parades and exercises on the walls, I discovered a pleasure I had not even fantasised about in my cell. In the space of three minutes, from collapsing in front of the firing-squad to being saluted by Lieutenant Voleski, I had been transformed from a piece of human scrap to a prince. They knew my real identity because Gerda had revealed it to Michael and the mutineers had had secret contact with rebel headquarters. The date of the mutiny was brought forward solely on my account.

Now everything that had told against me in front of the court was in my favour. I was no longer a foolish and disloyal mercenary, but a hero of Slav self-determination. The new description fitted me no better than the old, but I much preferred it. No one seemed to hold my rash flight from Bilavice against me – Bilavice itself, incidentally, had not yet even been approached by the Ruritanian army, so our panic was premature. All that mattered now was that I had abandoned my German connections to side with Slavs and had risked my life – very nearly paid it – for their cause. So here I stood clinking glasses with my admirers while the colonel and his fellow Germans nursed their humiliation in the cell-block I had just vacated. My own particular saviour, Lieutenant Voleski, told me that the worst moment was when the colonel nearly countermanded the whole execution because of finding the wrong subaltern on parade. The lieutenant detailed for the job was, of course, a reliable German, but the conspirators had gone into his room the night before, held him down and poured alcohol into him until he was incapable. Voleski's perhaps too flippant explanation that his colleague had drunk too much the night before even to be able to stand up, let alone conduct an execution, had put the colonel into a passion. It looked as if his rage might throw out the timing arranged for the mutiny with the other participants round the barracks, but Voleski had finally persuaded him that it would be inhuman and perhaps even an international war crime to make the condemned man go through it all again another day.

'And the soldiers in the firing-squad?' I asked.

'There were some substitutions the day before, but most of the soldiers in this regiment are of our way of thinking.'

'Forgive me asking,' I said, 'it may seem ungrateful after such a brilliant *coup*, but why did it have to be left to the last moment? Couldn't you have seized the colonel in his bed or his office and released me earlier?'

We considered that,' said Voleski, 'but it would have been more difficult to be sure of success with the colonel close to a telephone and alarm system and protected by his German sympathisers. There would certainly have been bloodshed in those circumstances. As it is, there was none at all.'

'No,' I said, 'not even mine.'

'We knew you had the courage to bear it,' said Voleski, tapping my heart enthusiastically, 'And everything had to be decided in a great hurry, because of you.'

'Who threw the stone through my window?'

'That was me.'

'So are you the leader of the mutiny?'

'Me? No, certainly not.'

But he failed to tell me who was and when one of the captains, in a voice already slurred from drinking too much so early in the morning, announced that it was time to 'dishcush' their next moves, I began to wonder if they had any distinct leader at all or if they hoped to sustain their mutiny with democratic conferences. If so, it was surely doomed. They would still be arguing when German-commanded tanks surrounded their barracks.

'One larsht toasht,' called out the captain, refilling his glass and raising it: 'Our distinguished and courageoush comrad, Karl Berg! May he one day remember, if hizh deshtiny should be to rule our country, that hizh life wazh shaved by the Shecond Regiment of Infantry, Kapitsha!'

'Berg! Berg!' they all called out, filling and raising glasses so hastily that the carpet and chairs were drenched in spirits.

'No! *Elph*berg!' shouted Voleski, his voice going falsetto with excitement again as it had in the scrapyard.

'Elphberg, Elphberg!' they echoed, downing their drinks and flinging the glasses in a salvo at the back of the fire. I thought of my dream and my cell window.

'Was *Tosca* your idea?' I asked Voleski.

151

'*Tosca?* No.' He laughed. 'That meant nothing to me.'

'Then it wasn't your message or your plan?'

'I just carried it out,' he said, embraced me and went through with the others to an adjoining room.

I'd been briefly afraid during the toast that they might be proposing to elect me their leader and, seeing no glorious future for myself as the democratic colonel of a mutinous regiment, was wondering how to refuse without offence. But they had other plans for me. I was considered too precious an asset to the Slav cause to be put to further risk and was conducted outside to the colonel's 4×4.

'Where are we going?' I asked the soldier in the driver's seat. 'To Chostok?'

'No, sir. Sebrikov.'

Sebrikov was not a town or even a village, but the name of the huge lake and hydro-electric plant that supplied most of Karapata with electricity. My driver, who came from Kapitsa, had no idea why we were going there and wasn't sure we'd make it through the snow, but he had a radio and there was a corporal in the back of the car who came from the area and told us that if we got stuck we'd soon be rescued from the nearest farm or village.

'These are not bare mountains,' he said reassuringly, 'but full of my relations.'

The journey took many hours and – except for a couple of times when I had to get out to help dislodge the car from a drift – I slept. The back of the seat made a hard pillow and the vehicle was constantly twisting and turning and sometimes sliding, but the heating was reasonably powerful and nothing short of actual pursuit by the enemy could have kept me awake. I was knackered, I was half drunk and I was alive when I'd expected to be dead. It was sleep that went nearer to being ecstatic than merely therapeutic. By the time we got out of the second drift – with the help of a tractor supplied by one of the corporal's relations – we were nearing Sebrikov. I closed my eyes and was dozing off again when the corporal behind me, proud of his local scenery and disappointed that I'd missed most of it so far, touched my shoulder.

'Sebrikov dam, sir!'

It was high above us still, but filled the windscreen: a vast, smooth black collar across the gap between snow-covered mountain-shoulders. We climbed to the right and it disappeared for a while, but every so often as we circled up we caught glimpses and finally rose above it and could see part of the huge sheet of water it contained. The further shore, the far end of the dam, must have been nearly a mile away.

Now I began to wonder what we were heading for in this black and white landscape: a bandit hideout? another barn in a farmyard? a cave? I thought hopefully of Previce Castle, with Magda waiting to loofah my back in a hot bath, but although I've never been good at geography I knew that Chostok was a long way off somewhere to our right and the Count's castle beyond that.

We hadn't been running along above the lake for more than about half a mile when the corporal, who had been having a crackling conversation with someone over the radio, warned the driver to slow down and soon afterwards we turned left down a track – it was probably a drive, but the snow made it look rough – and stopped at closed wrought-iron gates set into a high concrete wall. The corporal spoke into the radio again and in a few minutes the gates were opened by a man in rubber boots, fur hat and a heavy belted coat with big pockets and a fur collar. He looked more like a hunter than a guerrilla. After we'd passed through the gates and he'd closed them again, he followed us in a small truck.

At the end of the track, which wound through a wood of fir-trees, was a two-storied wooden chalet close to the edge of the lake. The corporal said it was a holiday house built for the former Secretary of the Ruritanian Communist Party. He was now in exile in one of the ex-Soviet states ending in -stan and the parliament in Strelsau was still bickering about whether they could afford to keep the place on as a retreat for the current prime-minister. Meanwhile it seemed to have fallen into other hands. The man in rubber-boots, politely shocked that I had no luggage of any kind, opened the front door for me, but then disappeared with the corporal and the driver somewhere round the back.

The large room I found myself in took up most of the ground-floor and suggested a hunting-lodge, with antlered heads on the walls, a big log-fire and a gallery all round at first-floor level, reached by a narrow right-angled staircase in one corner. Sliding windows on the side looking over the lake led to a covered verandah; beyond that a slope of snow went down to a jetty with a boathouse nearby. The place appeared to be completely empty. I warmed myself in front of the fire under the largest stag's head, walked to the window and stared out at the lake, then climbed the staircase and creaked round the gallery. There were doors leading off it on three sides; the fourth had more sliding windows opening on to a balcony overlooking the

153

lake and forming the roof of the verandah below. I tried a door in search of a loo. It was a bedroom with a view of the far end of the dam; the near end was obscured by the wooded mountain-side. We had seen the sun for a while as we got higher up the mountains, but now it was growing dark and a little snow was falling. The bed, with a soft green cover, looked inviting. I lay down, closed my eyes and went back to sleep.

I don't think I slept for long – my bladder was beginning to make urgent demands. I lay there for a while disputing with it, but finally opened my eyes, sat up and swung my legs off the bed. Yelena was sitting in an armchair near the window watching me. She was between me and what little light was left outside, but I recognised her at once, though her cropped hair had been tidied up since I'd last seen her in the train to Kapitsa. She was wearing a thick white jersey with a floppy polo-neck and a narrow blue skirt of some heavy material.

'You managed to find a proper hairdresser, then?' I said.

'Why didn't you tell me you were Karl *Elph*berg?' she said.

'What difference would that have made?'

'A great deal. Now, without your cap, it's obvious.'

I only remembered then that I'd left my faithful cap in my cell. The colonel or one of his colleagues would have it now – a reproachful reminder of the whirligig of fate. I stood up.

'I need a pee.'

'First door to the right.'

The next pleasure in store for me was a meal, but although it came with Hungarian wine and in three courses plus cheese I ate it alone, at a small table in the main room, served by a short dark peasant-woman, who was also the cook. She was middle-aged to elderly, had a slight squint and only spoke, with a thick accent, to acknowledge my remarks:

'Did you make this soup?'

'Yes.'

'Delicious! Who shot the stags?'

'I don't know.'

'When is Yelena coming back?'

'I don't know.'

'Are you from these parts?'

'No.'

'Where from?'

'Rovereto.'

'Sounds like Italy?'

'Is Italia.'

154

Her German was vestigial and I didn't try very hard because I was chiefly interested in the food, still exhausted, and also irritated by Yelena's behaviour. She was downstairs when I came out of the loo and called up that we'd talk tomorrow when I'd eaten and slept, before disappearing into the back of the house. I didn't see her again that night. I felt I'd exchanged one kind of solitary confinement for another, even if my status and the comforts attached to it had improved significantly.

After the meal I settled down with my coffee to watch TV – there was a set in the corner of the room, under the stairs. Watching TV is not my idea of an occupation for adults younger than sixty or eighty but I used to be driven to it in London by the need to divide up the day a bit. The programmes here were if anything directed at a deeper level of disadvantage even than the British ones, but I sat courageously through a comedy slot in which a Ruritanian version of Rowan Atkinson tried to nurture a boa-constrictor in his mother-in-law's bathroom without her noticing, followed by a chat-show mainly devoted to a sentimental folk-group from Kapitsa. That seemed ill-timed in view of the news bulletin that followed it.

The government was admitting to army 'unrest' in Kapitsa and blaming it on 'foreign troublemakers' who were trying to destabilise the country and stir up 'ethnic tension'. A government minister was interviewed and assured his viewers that there was no question at present of 'a violent response'. Rather, a mediator would be sent with a brief to listen to the soldiers' grievances and to try to remedy them, since the root of the trouble seemed to be a feeling that there was some 'imbalance' in 'promotion prospects' and the minister certainly wished to correct this – or at least the impression of it, since he didn't admit it was actually true.

The general who was interviewed next thought quite differently: he saw little scope for mediation in 'a military context', in which 'the first duty of soldiers was to obey orders'. However 'this is a demo-cratic country now', he said sarcastically and 'straightforward military solutions are not always practicable in peacetime situations'. He had a large cube-shaped head set on squared-off shoulders which filled half the screen and questions about what he really meant bounced off him like air-gun pellets off a lump of granite, but his meaning was perfectly clear: the sooner we were into a wartime situation and he could blitz the hell out of the Second Regiment of Infantry and possibly parliament too, the sooner normality would be restored to a world gone mad.

The news passed on to other matters – fears about deteriorating

155

nuclear stockpiles in Russia, the latest complications in the Balkans, some minor border dispute with Slovakia, doubts expressed in parliament about whether Ukraine would stick to its agreed schedule for repatriating the Cossacks in Plotla, a change of government in Poland, a mafia shoot-out in Strelsau. I switched off. Ruritania may lag behind Britain in all sorts of important ways, but its news service is the same acupuncture by a thousand needles of anxiety. I sat staring at the blank screen, satiated, relaxed, thinking about the person whose reflection I could dimly see, as he was 24 hours earlier. What if he had been able then to look forward as I was now looking back? Then life would be much the same as opera and we'd have to enjoy it more for the tunes than the story. I hummed the tune from *Tosca* and wished I still had the cassettes. But perhaps there was music in this place – I had got out of the habit of expecting independent diversions. I walked round my new luxury cell, but there was no sign even of a loudspeaker. Disappointed I flopped down in another chair and turned over the magazines on a small table next to it. They were mostly old copies of *Ogonyok* and *Der Spiegel*. If Yelena was really Ukrainian she presumably spoke Russian as well as German and Ruritanian. Did she also speak Italian to her cook?

Underneath the other magazines was one of a quite different sort, thinner, on matt paper without a glossy cover, its contents starting straight off on the front page under a title in big green letters: 'FIRST INSTANCE NEWS'. Under that, in smaller green print: 'Disciples of the First Instance, Tulsa, Oklahoma' and the date – a month or two earlier – in black. The front-page article was a tract about fund-raising, arguing that it should be seen not as a pact with mammon but as the conquest of mammon, turning mammon's own weapon – money – into the ploughshare of God. I flipped the page and found a headline reading 'OUR FISHER IN RURITANIA' and a large photograph of Fisher John.

The article below the photo clarified immediately what had puzzled me before: the nature of Fisher John's relationship with the rebels. He was turning mammon's weapon collected from the faithful of the First Instance in Tulsa, Oklahoma, into God's ploughshare for the True Faith in the lovely mountains of Karapata. In other words, if Count von Wunklisch represented the funds behind restoring a German monarchy in Ruritania, Fisher John represented the funds behind Ruritanian Slav nationalism. The reason we'd never been short of small arms and ammunition was that mammon's-weapon-turned-God's-ploughshare fetched up as Michael's AK47s and rocket-launchers.

17

Biology and Theology

I was woken at eight next morning by a brisk knock on my door. I was sleeping in the bed with the green cover, since no one had suggested anywhere different. The door opened and Yelena put her head round it.

'Time to get up,' she said and immediately disappeared, shutting the door.

Her peremptory, schoolmistress tone was annoying and inclined me to turn over and go back to sleep; but contradictorily I wanted to see more of her, so I got up and had a shower. When I came downstairs I saw that the small table had been moved to the window looking out on the lake and was laid for breakfast, with one place. It was petty, no doubt, after being given a holiday chalet in exchange for a death-cell, but I was irritated still more by this further evidence of being deliberately isolated and when the Italian cook came in with muesli, coffee and a boiled egg, I took it out on her:

'Why am I eating alone again? Where is Yelena?'

'Please!'

I was standing away from the table to show my displeasure and she put the things down and indicated the chair.

'Maria is coming,' she said.

'Maria?'

She nodded and went out before I could ask any more questions which she either couldn't understand or didn't want to answer. I kept my stand-off protest going a little longer, but my appetite was too much for me and I sat down and polished off the muesli. The sun was shining directly through the window and I moved my chair sideways to avoid it before tackling the egg. As I did so, I saw that Yelena was standing in the middle of the room. My irritation increased by another notch. Was she always trying to pretend she'd *materialised*?

'Who is Maria?'

'I am Maria.'

'You told me you were Yelena.'

'I have more than one name, like you.'

'So which am I to call you?'

'As you like.'

'Why do I always have to eat by myself?'

'I never take any breakfast.'

'Or supper?'

'I was out last night.'

She brought an upright chair, put it near my table and sat down. I kept an eye on her while I finished my egg, in case she tried to dematerialise. Then I put the egg aside and reached for another piece of toast, all the while glancing at her frequently and slightly raising my eyebrows, as if to say 'Still here? Surely you have better things to do?' The duel of silence, if it was a duel, finished with her speaking first:

'You like attention paid to you. Aren't you getting enough?'

'Not really. I've been living alone for too long and I'm not a natural hermit.'

'Conditions are better, though?'

'No comparison. All I lack is human company.'

She watched me silently again, while I spread the toast with butter and jam and sipped my coffee. Her bony, scrubbed face, in the bright light from the sun and snow, looked severe, even hostile. She sat bolt upright, legs close together, hands loosely clasped in her lap. She was much better-looking, but she reminded me depressingly of my sister-in-law on one of her regular disciplinary outings.

'You're very selfish in the use you make of human company,' she said.

'What makes you say that?'

'At least female company.'

'I give as good as I get. I would have thought that in your case I gave more than I got.'

'You helped me on to the train, you cut my hair and you wanted to rape me.'

'Rape you? For Heaven's sake! You attracted me and I showed it. Is that rape? I thought it was just sex. Or do you think men shouldn't be *allowed* to have sex with women?'

I wondered suddenly if she was actually a nun. But nuns should stick to their cloisters and not wear pale blue denim outfits or ask men to cut their hair if they want to retain their apartheid. She smiled.

'It depends. For the man's purpose only? Or for the purpose of both man and woman? In the case of Susha I think you behaved badly, don't you?'

'Yes, I probably did. But I don't see what that's got to do with you.'

'I believe she was very unhappy when you failed to go to Chostok.'

'I'm sorry to hear that, but if I *had* gone to Chostok, you would have missed your train.'

'I could have caught another. I was not running away from Bilavice like you.'

I felt this was unfair. Was I running away or was I just leaving Bilavice?

'Weren't you also running away?' I said.

'No.'

'So why the sudden need to get rid of your hair?'

'I am known to the government authorities by photographs with long hair. I didn't wish to be recognised.'

'Did they let you go on to Vlod?'

'I bought a ticket to Vlod, but I wasn't going there. I was going to see some officers of the Second Regiment in Kapitsa.'

She watched me steadily while I thought about this.

'You were involved with the mutiny?'

'It was my initiative, though I left most of the details to them.'

'And you also left me to be arrested and taken out to be shot.'

'You weren't apparently a very important person, were you?'

I stirred my coffee as calmly as I could and looked at her with all the contempt I've always felt for snobs.

'Completely expendable,' I said.

'I also thought that since you were really an English journalist you'd be released in a few days. Also that you deserved to suffer a little.'

I drank my coffee and pushed my chair back.

'Yelena,' I said, 'or should I call you Maria? It was very kind of you to entertain me here and remind me of my failings, but I think you've fully repaid any obligation you owe me for my help in the train, and I'll be on my way. Is there transport or shall I walk?'

I stood up and put my hands in my pockets in case I was tempted to strangle her. She was close to laughing and her face was so attractive when her small mouth spread across it, that I wasn't really as keen to leave as I pretended.

'Where do you want to go?'

'I don't mind. Kapitsa's out of bounds, I suppose, but Chostok or Previce Castle or even Strelsau would suit me fine.'

'Susha is back in Bilavice,' she said.

159

'Make it Bilavice, then! I can offer her my apologies or my company, whichever she prefers.'

'You'll find Gerda there too.'

She was laughing openly and I felt my face going red with a mixture of anger and confusion.

'Where's my coat?'

I remembered throwing it over a chair as I came in the night before and I started to go round the room looking for it.

'Anna hung it up for you. But enough of this! You don't have to go.'

'But I certainly do,' I said, making for the door into the kitchen. 'You've fed me and rested me and told me I'm a rapist and a shit and I think we've had as much of each other as we can stand.'

'Possibly that's true,' she said, suddenly serious again. 'But it's not really a personal matter. You are not just Edwin Fenton and I'm not just Yelena Lopotska. I am also, for one thing, Tosca.'

'*You* sent the message?'

'I wrote it and advised them what to do. Perhaps you still don't understand the risk we took by changing our plan at the last moment. Now they have only a colonel to bargain with instead of an important general. This was a decision I had to take and I'm still not certain it was the right one. Do you think I would even have considered risking the lives of perhaps 500 men for an English journalist who had been playing soldiers and playing with women? Your value as Karl Rassendyll is still not established – maybe you have no value and we have bought a bad horse – but we have paid a lot for you, believe me! It was not at all for your wonderful character and abilities – perhaps a little for your handsome face so like your great-grandfather's and King Rudolf V's – but mostly for your name and your pedigree.'

It was hard to know how to respond to this. Gratitude seemed inappropriate, since I'd been rescued not for myself but my ancestry. Much more than Colonel Danzing, this beautiful but impossibly self-satisfied manageress and moral tutor made me feel uncomfortable, totally miscast. Maybe after all I wasn't so different from my great-grandfather: his famous code of honour, his gentlemanly refusal to go on pretending he was king was probably just a cover for the same sense of unsuitability. He, after all, had a private income to go back to. On the other hand, who – come to think of it – wouldn't feel unsuitable for a job like that? Hereditary top-dog? Almost every monarch I'd ever heard of could take *Nil Quae Feci* as his family motto.

I was standing near the bottom of the stairs while this went through my mind and now I sat down on the second or third step

160

and looked across at Yelena without replying at all. She stood up as I sat down, then walked across and sat on the arm of a chair facing me.

'For myself,' she said, 'I think the horse is not as bad as all that, but I'm still wondering how best to use it. Maybe you have some ideas yourself?' She looked at her watch. 'I'm expecting Michael in about an hour, which is why I got you up so early and in such a bad temper. I thought we should understand one another first.'

The atmosphere was suddenly lighter. She too had probably been in a bad temper or nervous about something.

'I'm still very unclear about a lot of things,' I said. 'When I first saw you in front of the church at Chostok, you were making an extraordinary speech. It was not only the way you made it – though that had a very extraordinary effect on me. What I thought you actually said seems so incredible now that I probably imagined the whole thing . . .'

I tailed off. I was trying to avoid making the question I wanted to ask sound like a criticism. Women are easy to provoke and this one especially so and the fireworks can be amusing, but I wasn't aiming for another scoring match – not even to equalise the one I'd just lost – so much as a straight answer. Her face was quite relaxed and expressionless, as if she wasn't bothered, but she kept her eyes on me all the time in an intimidating way. That made me determine not to be intimidated.

'Did you believe what you said?'

'I never say what I don't believe.'

'No, I'm sure that's right. So you did – you still do – actually claim to be the Virgin Mary?'

'Will you listen seriously and carefully and try to understand?'

'I will.' I smiled encouragingly.

'You're not a serious person.'

'I can be when I try.'

'Then try harder!'

We both smiled at the same moment and I would have been quite happy for that moment to go on indefinitely, but she resolutely suppressed her smile and I followed suit.

'People are not paintings or antiques,' she said. 'They cannot be verified as genuine articles or fakes. What a person is, is what she feels herself to be and what she achieves. I know that I was born Yelena Lopotska, an ordinary Soviet child, only daughter of engineers working in the nuclear industry. But when I came to live here in Karapata with my husband – who was a water engineer attached to this Sebrikov hydro-electric project – I discovered the True Faith and began to understand my true purpose: to be a vehicle, a container for the person I felt myself to be.'

'How did your husband react?'

'My husband had leukaemia. We were both very young. It was because of what was happening to him that I first looked for help from the True Faith. Our Marxist/Leninist education offered nothing to a young man who was dying or to his wife. This simple faith consoled us both, it gave us what we so much wanted, another world, another life to meet in, but I wonder if we really believed it then. It seemed a little too simple. Then, after my husband died, I thought more deeply. Why not simple? Why do religions so often try to complicate things, to make mysteries? Of course, it's to give power to their priests. There is nothing complicated or mysterious about Jesus. He tells people how best to live their lives in his own time. Does he ever say his mother is a virgin impregnated by God or anything but a human mother, the wife of a carpenter? Yes, he does say he is the son of God. But is this some biological pedigree like yours? What a primitive idea! Isn't that the first absurdity which leads to all the others: the impossible virgin mother who bears the biological son of God, the son who is magically present in bread and wine, the popes and priests with special powers conferred on them by hierarchies and ceremonies instead of by their own merits? How do these churches with their fantastic doctrines and rigid power-structures differ essentially from Marxism/Leninism? But the True Faith is only faith in the authenticity of Jesus as he appears in the New Testament. No, I do not claim to be the Virgin Mary – there never was such a person. Or that I am not a human being, born Yelena Lopotska near Kiev. Jesus and his mother were also humans as long as they were on earth. If God created the world, then He is the father and mother of all living creatures at all times and all places. The existence of the world and its creatures is sufficient mystery and miracle and already contains God. Why should He change the laws of physics, which are His own laws? Gods only come to earth as gods in human myths and stories. All I claim is to be an empty computer which fills up with the disk put into it. You can call the disk Mary, mother of Jesus – call it what you like – its programme is the same as you find in the New Testament, directed to a new time and place.'

'I know hardly anything about the New Testament,' I said, 'but the one thing I remember from school is the non-violent bit, turning the other cheek instead of punching back. That always seemed to me a clever idea, but quite unrealistic. Violence doesn't seem to bother you.'

162

'It's not very important. Jesus was often quite aggressive towards authoritarian, conventional or corrupt people – nevertheless, the revolution he led was specifically non-violent. This was a tactical decision on his part, not an inflexible rule for all times and all places. All living creatures die. Death is not an issue, then, since it's universal, inevitable. Of course, the *fear* of death may be an issue for creatures without understanding and for humans who reject understanding – but what's that to us? We have enemies, as Jesus did, and we cannot ignore or walk round them. It's no great step – no fundamental alteration of principle – to go from throwing moneychangers out of the temple or abusing Pharisees to taking the lives or threatening the lives of violent enemies. Of course it should never be done for any purpose but the advancement of the True Faith, nor with cruelty or for pleasure, but if the time and situation demand it, then violence may be necessary.'

She delivered this arrant cant with complete conviction, sitting on the arm of the chair with one leg crossed neatly over the other and her weight on one arm resting on the chair's back, as if she was coaching me in the answer to an exam question. Her determined, intense face was that of the engineers' daughter from Kiev and she had no doubt once recited her Marxist/Leninist lessons with the same earnestness. I transferred my attention to her breasts, a little more evident now under her jersey than they had been in the train. Silence fell. I continued to stare in a relaxed, unfocussed way at her softer parts.

'I see that you are really not a serious person,' she said, in a mild, kind voice, implying that she didn't blame me personally, 'and I begin to wonder if there is any use we can make of you.'

I raised my eyes and looked steadily into hers.

'Where does Fisher John fit into all this?' I asked innocently.

'Why do you ask?'

'Does he call you Maria or Yelena?'

'I've told you, it makes no difference. You, of all people, should be able to understand that Edwin Fenton can be Karl Rassendyll and Karl Rassendyll can be King Karl – or King Karel, as I would prefer it in its Slav form – according to circumstances.'

'But if he understands that Maria inhabits Yelena – if that's the right way to put it – what about the folk back in Tulsa? Do they know what their money is being used for?'

She jumped up off the chair as if I'd hit her.

'What do you mean? You think this is some kind of cheat? Some kind of mafia corruption? You think we just want something for ourselves?'

163

I was fairly sure Fisher John did, but also sure this wasn't the moment to say so. Yelena stood over me, rather as she had in the square at Bilavice, but this time she looked as if she regretted not having her machine-gun with her.

'I'm sorry,' I said. 'What I meant was that your motives are perfectly clear, but I still find Fisher John's fuzzy . . .'

She was still furious and I held up both my hands, palm outwards, to show my harmless intentions and keep her at bay.

'And also how I fit in. If you're leading this religious movement, if you're Joan of Arc . . . as it were,' I added hastily, seeing this was only pouring paraffin on an already blazing fire, '. . . you don't seem to need yet another outsider, a person with what you quite rightly term a primitive biological pedigree. Fisher John may be contributing something you do need – I make no allegations – but what do you think I can contribute?'

She stood there for a while swallowing her anger – it really was a physical thing which made her whole body shiver, her nose sniff and her hand go up to rub the back of her neck; then she turned and walked rapidly right round the room before stopping in front of the fire to warm her hands.

'There are four elements,' she said, resuming her calm, tutorial tone. 'The True Faith itself – that is my responsibility. The Ruritanian Army of the True Faith – that is Michael's. The support of well-wishers outside our country – that is Fisher's. And, lastly, the political system which we would have to establish in our country to consolidate and protect our spiritual achievements. The True Faith itself has no political structure, of course, and the country's political structure as it exists – the President and the Republic – probably could not be reconciled with it. This has been a problem for us all along and when I learnt of the possibility of a restored monarchy, it seemed to me perhaps a providential solution. But I was thinking only in the abstract, forgetting that a monarchy depends on a particular monarch and that the authentic blood-line is no guarantee of quality.'

'I'm not what you hoped for?' I said, joining her beside the fire.

'You are a very dubious asset.'

'The story of my life,' I said.

'We shall discuss it with Michael and hope to resolve the whole question.'

'Shall I have any say in the discussion?'

'Of course. But if you can only be provocative, it will be a foregone conclusion. Michael does not take a light view of anything.'

'But you do?'

'No, I don't either.'

She moved away towards the door into the kitchen.

'But I can make some small allowance for a man with certain good points among so many inadequacies. Michael will make no such allowance.'

She went into the kitchen before I could ask her what she thought my good points were; and a moment or two later Anna emerged and began clearing the breakfast things.

18

Footwork

I located my anorak, got Anna to unlock the windows and walked down the slope of snow in front of the house to the jetty. I could see between the planks of the boathouse that there was a boat in there and, since the lake was free of ice, thought about borrowing it. But the boathouse was padlocked and in good repair. I walked to the end of the jetty and from here I could see that further round this side of the lake, beyond the wood that grew down the hill and enclosed the chalet, was a settlement of one-storey wooden huts. Smoke was rising from several chimneys and a row of lorries was parked to one side. Among them was Colonel Maggerling's 4×4 and, recalling my journey to Sebrikov and the events that led up to it, I also recalled the dream I'd had in my cell of waterskiing on a lake with two people who might have been Yelena and Michael. Or was it on that occasion I'd had the dream? The mind is full of double bluffs: maybe it was last night, after I'd seen the lake and Yelena had told me Michael was going to join us here.

I returned to the chalet and walked round the back, where the track continued through the trees to the camp I'd just seen. The surface had been pressed down by the passage of vehicles, though it was mushy on top. That didn't bother me too much – my canvas trainers were already sodden – and I picked my way along towards the camp without much difficulty. There was a small hut and a barrier at the entrance and as soon as I appeared a man in a military greatcoat came out to stop me.

'Just taking a walk,' I said defensively. 'I'm staying at the house.' We recognised each other at the same moment. He was Petra, one of the boys from my section – he'd been just visible to one side of me in the aerial photo of the mountain-stream episode and he'd been with me in Bilavice too. I went forward to embrace him Slav-style, but he stepped back and stood to attention, with his rifle, which he'd been pointing vaguely at me, held in parade position against his side.

'What's the matter?' I said. 'I'm Karl Berg. Don't you recognise me?'

'Yes,' he said, 'but now we know who you really are.'

Apparently the two regular soldiers who brought me to Sebrikov had told everyone about my rescue and the reason for it. When Petra had explained this and we'd embraced anyway, he went inside his guard-hut and spoke on the telephone. The effect was extraordinary. As I stood by the barrier waiting for him to come out again, a door opened in one of the nearer huts and two or three guerrilla soldiers emerged, then other doors opened and more appeared, then more and more, all moving towards us. Suddenly the whole camp was full of men in motley military coats with guns slung over their shoulders, swarming in my direction. They seemed more curious than threatening – like a herd of cows in a field on a country-walk. Within a few minutes there must have been a hundred and fifty to two hundred men coalescing into a kind of phalanx between me and the huts and more still emerging in the distance.

'What's happening?' I said to Petra, as he came out of his guard-hut. 'What do they want?'

The cohort had stopped now about twenty yards away and the men at the back were coming round the sides, so that I was facing a long line two or three deep. Did there need to be quite so many to investigate one unarmed interloper? Or was this something to do with me personally? I began to think hastily back over my past conduct to see if I'd committed some unpardonable offence – adultery with Susha? taking the train to Kapitsa instead of the coach to Chostok? – did they know about these things, would it matter so much if they did? Petra looked surprised, but not alarmed. In answer to my question he only shrugged. Then among the vanguard I recognised Corporal Radichev, with his black armband and Stalin moustache. I started forward immediately to greet him:

'Corporal! Corporal Radichev! You remember me?'

He came forward too, smiling.

'Berg!' he said, 'Karl Marx Berg!' and then in his stilted English 'Mee-ster Fen-ton!'

Then he raised both arms in the air with clenched fists and, half-turning towards the crowd behind him, bellowed in his parade-ground voice:

'King Karel!'

I shook my head, partly in embarrassment, partly because I didn't feel I was entitled yet to this fresh change of persona, and we embraced enthusiastically. As we did so, the whole mass of them raised their arms with clenched fists and shouted:

167

'King Karel!'

It was an enormous sound that echoed off the rocks and seemed to hang in the cold air with the cloud of steam that rose from so many open mouths. Still holding the Corporal by the shoulders and peering round his ear at the ranks of shouting, gesticulating men – among whom I now recognised several of my old friends as well as the driver who'd brought me from Kapitsa – I was wondering how to acknowledge such a reception, when I heard the sound of a car's engine behind me. I turned to see a muddy Range Rover pulling up in front of the barrier. Petra went to raise the barrier for it, but the car doors were already opening and Michael and Sergeant Vakisch were getting out. My first reaction was to wonder why they'd exchanged the Count's brand-new car for something that looked as if it had been written off after a pile-up, but then my attention was caught by Michael's face. He was beside himself with fury.

'What are you doing here? What have you been saying to them?'

He spoke in quite a low voice which sounded all the more vicious for being contained, like a dog reserving most of its energy for biting not barking, and he was crunching feverishly towards me through the snow with his hands pushed out in front of him. I let go of the Corporal and took a step towards Michael. If this was going to be bare-hand stuff I had the advantage of height and the very sight and sound of him made me feel nearly as angry as he looked. I didn't bother to answer his question, but just smiled contemptuously down at him and measured by eye the distance from my right fist to his jaw. It was a real disappointment when Sergeant Vakisch, following closely behind, took the immediate heat out of the situation by laying his hand on Michael's shoulder.

'It's done anyway, Captain. Why not make the best of it?'

Michael paused, glanced at the Corporal behind me and the crowd further back, punched his left palm with his right fist as though it was too late to stop it punching something, and held it out to me.

'Mr Fenton!' he said with a gruesome sneer.

I took his hand and held it just long enough to show I was doing him as much of a favour as he was doing me.

'Good to see you, Captain!' I said insincerely.

He patted me on the arm and I was wondering how long we'd have to keep up this exchange of false pleasantries for the benefit of our audience, when Sergeant Vakisch came to the rescue again and ordered the men to form up for inspection.

The programme originally planned had been for Michael to inspect

168

his troops and their living-quarters before attending the conference at the house and they'd been waiting to turn out for him when Petra's phone-call had made them turn out for me instead. So Michael was left with no alternative but to take me round on the inspection with him and the pleasure I got from performing this first royal duty was at least doubled by the pleasure he didn't get from it. All three of us – Michael, Vakisch and I – then returned to the house in the Count's ruined car in a silence icier than the landscape. The car, Vakisch told me as we went into the house, had skidded into a rock during the retreat from Kapitsa.

Yelena was waiting for us in the main room of the chalet. Michael, having entered first, while I was talking to Vakisch, had evidently given her the gist of the disaster – from his point of view – in the camp and was now ready to relieve himself of his pent-up rage. Yelena forestalled him:

'Why did you do this, Karl?'

'I just went for a walk,' I said. 'You told me nothing about this barracks full of my old comrades and I had no idea they were going to make the sort of demonstration they did.'

'I heard it even from here,' she said, 'though I couldn't make out the words.'

'This man is a liability,' said Michael. 'He cannot be trusted, nothing he says can be taken at face value, nothing he does is for anyone's advantage but his own.'

I opened my mouth to say he shouldn't judge others by himself, but instead sat down – a neat demonstration of how our relative positions had changed since our first encounter in the farmhouse near Chostok – and took off my shoes and socks. Then I held out my legs and toasted my wet feet in front of the fire, while Michael turned his wrath on Yelena:

'You asked us here to talk about strategy – to consider using this man as a political figurehead. I say no. Absolutely no, from the beginning. As far as I'm concerned, there's nothing to talk about.'

Yelena didn't seem much put out. She looked at me briefly, neither smiling nor frowning, seeming to suggest that sitting there quietly and attending to my feet was just what she wanted me to do, then smiled at Vakisch, who was still near the door.

'Is that your opinion too, Vatslav?'

'I understand Michael's anger, of course,' said Vakisch. 'It would have been better for us to introduce Mr Berg to the men as a claimant to the throne than have him introduce himself, but this was surely not his fault and, as it's turned out, not such a disadvantage. On the contrary. If we'd come to a decision here and they'd received it with doubt or indifference, we should have been in a hole. As it is, if we do take such a decision, we know we can count on their spontaneous enthusiasm.'

Yelena looked at Michael. I had the feeling that there'd been many scenes of this sort in the past, with Michael neighing and stamping, Vakisch making soothing noises and Yelena bringing the horse's head round in the direction she wanted to go.

'But if we don't want to decide that way?' said Michael. 'What then? We're being forced into something that could turn out very badly.'

'Shall we discuss it, at least?' said Yelena.

She pointed with a charming, almost shy gesture at the chair just behind Michael and he sat down. Her other hand remained at her side, but one finger flickered momentarily at Vakisch and he too found a chair. She walked to the window and looked out as if to make sure no one was spying on us, then circled back past my chair and, as she passed me, very lightly brushed the top of my ear, without either Michael or Vakisch noticing. Then she sat down near Michael. I don't know whether it would have made any difference to my attitude if I'd been better educated and known what the Count told me much later, that ear-pulling was a favourite ploy of Napoleon's; as it was, I wriggled my toes, basked in the warmth of the fire and left most of the discussion to them.

It didn't in any case require much input from me. I was, as it were, the flag of convenience which they might or might not sail under and it was taken for granted that the flag itself would make no objection to being sailed under. I kept my main reservation – was it sensible to be associated exclusively with the Slav nationalists? – to myself, since the whole question of whether I actually became king still seemed very abstract and I was, after all, as much the prisoner – though a better treated one – of these people as I had been of the Ruritanian Army in Kapitsa. Michael, of course, had no wish to see me king – he'd much rather see me dead. On the other hand it was clear he couldn't be king himself or hope on his own to control all the nationalist forces. If more of the regular army followed the Second Regiment over to our side they certainly wouldn't accept the warlord of Karapata as overall commander; but, if the response of the Second Regiment was anything to go by, it did look as if the Slav elements of the army might be willing to unite with the guerrillas under my flag.

170

So it soon became a question of what was the maximum reward Michael could extract in exchange for putting up with me, rather than whether he would have me at all. And I saw now that the original roles played by Michael and Yelena on the steps of Chostok church faithfully reflected the reality: she was the driving force behind the nationalist rebellion and he only the instrument, 'my servant Michael' as she'd actually referred to him. The purpose of this conference was not to discuss strategy but simply to bring a second instrument – 'my servant Karel' as she might, but never did call me – into action without upsetting the first.

The real surprise came after we'd settled that the nationalists would aim to restore the monarchy and Yelena asked me very casually what form I thought the monarchy might take. I was stretched out almost horizontally in my chair by now and wondering if I could edge another log on to the fire with my foot or would have to get up and do it by hand.

'Mainly ceremonial, I suppose,' I said and, thinking of the British version which seemed mainly to consist of handing out medals, supporting good causes and shaking hands, added 'but I'd be glad of a few minimal powers, so that it wouldn't get completely boring.'

There was a pause. Feeling I might have said the wrong thing, I heaved myself out of the chair and tossed a couple of logs on the fire.

'That isn't how I see it,' said Yelena.

'How, then?' I said, watching the flames catch the bark of the new logs.

'Most powers would be yours.'

We all looked at her, none of us quite understanding what she meant.

'What is the point of a ceremonial king?' she said. 'We have such a figure already. There's nothing wrong with the president personally. What is wrong is the government and the fact that the president has no power to make it govern. I have no faith in democracy. It may be a workable system for Americans and British, though I think their systems could more accurately be called plutocracy and oligarchy, but it is not a workable system for us. We are accustomed to centralised power. The king should rule and his ministers carry out his wishes.'

Vakisch looked astounded.

'No parliament?' he said. 'No elections?'

'Both. But the role of parliament would be to legislate, to enable, to advise, perhaps to modify, definitely not to govern.'

'And the ministers?' asked Michael suspiciously. He had already demanded – though by no means been promised – the Ministry of Defence in return for his part in restoring the monarchy.

'The ministers would be chosen by the king, not elected. The king and his ministers together would compose the executive, but the ministers would be responsible for their actions to the people's representatives in parliament.'

'And the king?' asked Vakisch, seeming more and more during this discussion like a headmaster or senior manager than a guerrilla chief. 'To whom would he be responsible?'

'To God,' said Yelena.

We were all silent. This indeed was a party, faction or person we hadn't considered at all so far, but if the guerrillas were fighting in the name of the True Faith and if I was their candidate for secular power, then God could hardly be left out and Yelena was unquestionably his spokesperson.

'A king without a sense of responsibility to God is only a president by another name,' said Yelena. 'The mistake in this new age is to strip rulers of their sanctity, to make them too easily replaceable, so that they can be discarded every five years like old cars. People are fickle, easily swayed by conflicting opinions, lacking nerve and stamina. Choice is a great burden to most people. You can see it everywhere, not only in the old Soviet Empire. Let a king rule, that's his job!'

'But if he rules badly?' I said.

'If he loses his respect for God, he loses the respect of his people and loses his throne. Reality always breaks through eventually, even in the Soviet Empire, though it took seventy years. Reality has already broken through our new democracy and shown it to be at best a flock of sheep, at worst a pack of German wolves.'

This unexpected view of what we might be aiming for had an odd effect on Michael. He became more friendly and amenable, as if the prospect of *greater* power for me was preferable to whatever he'd originally envisaged. Perhaps it was simply that I'd been transformed from an annoying competitor in his own Slav enclave to a potential patron beyond it. But in any case neither he nor Vakisch saw this fresh prospect as anything much to do with me. Nor, for that matter, did I. It was Yelena's kingdom we were considering, just as it was Yelena's nationalist uprising which might lead us into it.

When she saw that none of us had anything more to say for the moment, Yelena opened the kitchen door and spoke to Anna, who brought in a tray of glasses and a bottle of Russian bubbly. We drank to the new kingdom of Ruritania, its king, its ministers (Vakisch had asked for nothing for himself, but surely he would be one of them) and its . . . what? How could Yelena's function be described? Was she the kingdom's patron, its donor, its sponsor?

'And you, Yelena . . .' I said, raising my glass to her, 'what will you be?'

They all three seemed to think this an awkward and unnecessary thing to say.

'I will be what I am,' she said, 'and then nothing.'

'Nothing?'

'Nothing nothing!' she said vehemently, annoyed at my persistence.

'To Yelena Nothing, then!' I said and drank off my glass.

The other two looked even more awkward, staring at their glasses but not joining the toast.

A meal was served and then Michael and Vakisch returned to Chostok. There was still an hour or two of daylight and although the house was now in the shadow of the mountain behind it there was still sunlight out on the lake. I asked Yelena if anyone ever used the boat.

'We can go for a ride, if you like,' she said.

It was a small cabin-cruiser which the former Party Secretary had used for fishing. It started without too much difficulty and, when I'd untied it and unbolted the lakeside door she steered it out a little uncertainly into open water.

'Do you want to drive, Karl? I'm not an expert.'

'No, you drive,' I said, 'and I'll look at the scenery.'

The lake was very much larger than appeared from the house and stretched away almost out of sight at the far end from the dam. The mountains there were very steep and sharp. It was a wild and overwhelming place, with everything on the same massive scale as the dam itself, but scenery never does much for me. On this occasion I was in quite a distracted state, both because of the driver and because I was still coming to terms with the events of the past two days: the acceptance of my claim to be king of Ruritania first by the young officers of the Second Regiment, then by the rebels in the camp and finally, just now, even by Michael and Vakisch.

We chugged along close to the dam for a while and then turned back up the lake. The sun had almost vanished in a yellow sky behind the mountains, but its light was still reflected off the water and the snow. Yelena steered the boat with the concentration she gave to everything, but she didn't need to – there were no islands, no hazards of any sort, no other boats and enough space to manoeuvre a fleet of battleships. She'd changed into white trousers, short brown boots and a white leather jacket with a fur collar, turned up to meet her short hair. It was quite warm in the cabin with the door and windows closed and she'd removed her fur gloves. Her hands were long, like her neck and her face, in which all the features balanced and proportioned each other almost mathematically. Her eyes were half closed against the glare from the water, but she seldom opened them very wide – with her distinct cheek-bones they gave her a faintly Oriental, perhaps Tatar look. There was a little colour in her face, possibly from the warmth of the cabin, but her skin was very pale. Beautiful as she was, I had no great desire at that moment to do more than look at her – she was too formidable, too self-contained. Of course if she'd cared to make the first move, shown any physical response to me, let alone touched my ear again, I'd have been ready and willing for anything and we could have safely let the boat drift.

'Do you really think,' I asked, after we'd been going for some time without a word spoken, 'that I can be that sort of king? I've had no training, no experience, never even had power over a dog.'

'People never know what they can do until they do it.'

'I could see myself as the ceremonial sort of king,' I said, 'because it would be mostly doing what I've always done, but with a better wage: playing around, dressing up, driving cars, chatting to people, drinking and dining . . .'

'You have so little sense of reality,' she said. 'Imagine what it would be like occupying this empty shell every waking moment of your life! You'd go mad.'

'True. But power maddens people too.'

'We have the winter ahead of us,' she said. 'Nothing much can be done to advance our cause in the military way until spring. Equally we have little to fear from the enemy until then. It's even possible that by the spring they'll be still more divided and confused than they are now.'

She paused, staring up at the triple peaks, like the middle fingers of a hand, dominating the far end of the lake. They were being invaded, quite quickly, by thick cloud.

'It's going to snow.'

She suddenly swung the wheel and the boat right round to head back the way we'd come.

'Your ignorance, your inexperience, your lack of training are probably advantages,' she said.

174

'Thanks.'

'*Tabula rasa.*'

'Meaning?'

'A clean slate. Ready for anything.'

'I often get criticised for that.'

The snow cloud was racing faster than we were and overtook us with thick driving flakes and a blasting wind that immediately churned up the water. It turned very dark and the boat, which had a feeble engine, was pulling, sliding and bucking, trying to slew round into the full force of the gale as Yelena continually fought it back on to its course. Then suddenly the engine cut out, the wheel became useless and we were being tossed violently from side to side as the boat drifted sideways into the waves. Yelena looked frightened. She tried to restart the motor, failed and, clinging to the wheel, shouted:

'Do something!'

I fell rather than walked across the cabin and took hold of the wheel, so that for a moment I had my arms round her and my body pressed against her back, with my mouth on her head. I felt much more exhilarated than afraid.

'Can you swim?' I said.

She escaped from my arms and slid on to the bench round the side of the cabin.

'Don't be a fool! No one could swim in this temperature.'

'We'll have to keep her afloat, then,' I said encouragingly, without the slightest idea of how that might be done. The whole boat shuddered and lurched and seemed to have taken the opposite decision. I looked hopefully at the dials, but they showed nothing because after trying to restart it Yelena had switched the engine off.

'Perhaps we've run out of fuel?'

'So what?'

Her fear had turned into anger at my inability to work a mechanical miracle.

'There might be a reserve tank.'

'Where?'

'Good question. I'm afraid I'm as ignorant of boats as . . .'

The boat gave another sickening lurch and tipped so far to one side that Yelena huddled in her corner was below my feet. I looked round the cabin in search of at least a lifebelt, spotted one hanging beside the steps behind and, as the boat tipped the other way and Yelena appeared above me, unhooked it and staggered up towards her with it. She pushed it away.

'Can't you do anything to the engine?'

I pushed the lifebelt back at her, even tried to slip it over her head, but between us it fell on the floor and slid to the opposite side of the cabin with the next lurch. As it went I saw that it had the boat's name on it: 'LENIN' – what else?

'We must just have faith in the good ship Lenin,' I said, 'and hope she doesn't turn right over.'

'Lenin?' she shouted, 'What are you talking about?'

I struggled back to the wheel and, seeing nothing else I could pretend to be busy with, turned the key in the ignition. The engine started. I looked at Yelena as I started to manipulate the wheel and get the boat under control again. Her expression was between fear and relief – she didn't yet quite believe what she could see and hear.

'You see,' I said, 'Lenin is still a name to conjure with.'

She said nothing, only looked at me sourly. Perhaps she just hated to hear that name or perhaps she wasn't pleased to have shown ordinary panic. I concentrated on steering – we weren't out of the storm yet – and used as little power as possible in case it was overstraining which had made it cut out. Gradually we made headway towards the shore and soon we began to see the lights of the house and then of the camp beyond it. Yelena ceased to look sour and came to stand beside me when I pointed to the lights.

'I'm sorry!' she said. 'It can get dangerous very suddenly. I should have been more wary. Luckily we hadn't gone too far up the lake.'

'I enjoyed it,' I said.

'You have an odd idea of enjoyment.'

I couldn't tell her that what I enjoyed was not the danger but its effect on her and that I was only not afraid myself because she was. Instead I called up another old memory from my patchy Christian education:

'You said Jesus never claimed to be a god, but what about the time he walked on the water. That sounds a bit of a miracle.'

We were close to the shore now and the waves were less choppy.

'The essence of all the miracles in the New Testament is faith. Jesus was not trying to prove himself a god but to show that one must have faith that there is a God and that He cares about humans. Personally I find the walking on water story uncharacteristic – too much like showing off.'

'Could you walk on the water?'

'What purpose could it serve other than to entertain people with primitive ideas?'

'It would have been an alternative to swimming if the boat had sunk.'

'Give me the wheel now! You're going too fast.'

She took the wheel and put the boat briefly into reverse to slow down, then let it drift gently towards the jetty.

'Even if we had been in real danger I would not have asked God for a miracle to save my own life.'

'Nor mine?'

'As I tried to explain before, individual lives are of no importance.'

'Silly me!' I said, 'I thought we couldn't be in real danger because I didn't see you praying. But now you tell me you wouldn't have prayed anyway. I shall be afraid to go out in a boat with you again.'

'The disadvantage of a clean slate,' she said, 'is that everything is of equal value to it: it can't distinguish between what's serious and what isn't.'

'Not much to be done about that, I'm afraid.'

'I think there is. It can be written on.'

The boat nosed into the boathouse, scraping the entrance first on one side, then the other.

'We've got the winter for that,' she said.

19

A Clean Slate

The poverty of my education couldn't be relieved in four or five months, but at least I wasn't studying some huge abstract subject like philosophy or geography. My course of study was more limited and technical – like plumbing, electrical engineering or business management – and I had the advantage of individual tuition from a dedicated and inspiring teacher. Also it wasn't a matter of trying to squeeze me roughly into something ready-made: we were tailoring the job to the wearer as well as the other way round.

History was our theoretical basis, but very selective history: the successes and mistakes of rulers from Pericles and Nero through Louis XIV and XVI to Nicholas II and Gorbachov. Predatory psychopaths like Napoleon, Hitler and Stalin we mostly left out of account, since I wasn't contemplating conquering Europe, or even Poland. Even so, the majority of our examples ruled big states and didn't provide very close models for the potential ruler of a tiny land-locked kingdom which would always be dependent on its big neighbours for most of the necessities of modern life – oil and computers, cars and Kalashnikovs. The trouble was that the lesser fry mostly got left out of the books – or at least the German books borrowed or stolen from various Ruritanian libraries by Yelena's contacts. Machiavelli, who was mainly a little ruler man, was naturally one of our prime texts and I wondered aloud if Yelena found it hard to reconcile his teaching with that of Jesus.

' "Render unto Caesar that which is Caesar's" covers it,' she said very off-handedly, as if it was something she didn't wish to discuss.

'Yes, but if you represent the interests of Jesus and I represent Caesar's,' I said, 'how would this work in practice?'

'Explain!'

'Suppose I promise the job of Minister of Defence to Michael in return for making me king and then give it to Lieutenant Voleski in return for getting rid of Michael! Would you and the True Faith simply stand aside and carry on worshipping, on the principle you quoted, or would you denounce me as wicked and unfit to rule and preach civil disobedience?'

'Machiavelli wrote mainly for princes,' she said, 'Jesus mainly spoke to non-princes. They are not addressing the same questions, but I would like to think that in the circumstances of Ruritania in the 1990s, which are not at all those of Palestine in the 0020s or Italy in the 1520s, there will be no contradiction between the actions of King Karel the First and the beliefs of the True Faith.'

'You mean I'd have to do as you tell me.'

'No. But what you believed to be best in the light of your training.'

'You intend to wash my brain and fill it with correct thoughts?'

'Your brain doesn't need to be washed, it's *tabula rasa*.'

'I may not have many ideas of my own, but I'm very resistant to other people's, especially when they have an ideological content.'

'To return to your specific example: the problem, I think, will hardly arise in that form because you will be a very poor pupil of mine if you don't understand that making rash promises leads to the downfall of rulers. The only condition for promising the Ministry of Defence to either Michael or Lieutenant Voleski should be that they perform the job successfully. I doubt if either of them could fulfil that condition.'

This wasn't the only hint I got that Michael had a strictly limited part to play in Yelena's plans.

These theoretical lessons occupied the first few weeks of my course. Most of my time was taken up with reading, but Yelena had other things to do. Often she knew the stuff already – otherwise she relied on me to give her the gist of what I'd read and pick out the salient points. We had tutorials two or three days a week and over meals in the evenings, if she was at home. Many days she was away and would tell me nothing about where she went or what she did. She was very severe if she felt I'd read something too superficially or hadn't read enough, but on the whole I surprised myself with my own diligence: reading for a practical purpose was very different from any reading I'd done in the past, for exams or in desperation when there was nothing better to do.

I kept fit by walking and running in the snow and by spending an hour a day in the rudimentary gym in the barracks. I also gave English lessons to the soldiers and received Ruritanian lessons in

179

return and on the days when Yelena was away I would usually eat in the barracks. But she discouraged me from joining their military exercises:

'That's not your job, Karel, and will only waste your time.'

I pleaded to be allowed to improve my marksmanship on the improvised firing-range behind the barracks and she agreed to that, mainly because she was in favour of my remaining on familiar terms with the soldiers;

'These will be your praetorian guard, Karel.'

And she quoted Machiavelli on the necessity for a prince to have forces of his own and not depend on mercenaries and auxiliaries. I saw this as further evidence of Michael's decline in the scheme of things.

The next stage in my education was acting lessons. Yelena brought an old, retired actor called David Devinsky from Bilavice and had him stay in the chalet for a fortnight teaching me how to stand, walk, speak and gesture both for stage and screen. I practised interviews and speeches, which he recorded on tape or video so that we could study the results and correct my errors. It all seemed a bit ludicrous at first, especially since Devinsky, who had been mainly a classical actor in supporting roles, seemed such an old ham himself. He was a smallish, pasty-faced, fussy person, quite nervous when he first arrived and full of baroque gestures and banal small-talk uttered in ringing tones, as if he were trying to disguise a bad script; but as he admitted when we got to know each other better:

'I was never a good actor myself, Sir (he always called me 'Sir', not by any of my names), but I know very well how it should be done and I am absolutely brilliant at picking holes in everyone else's performances.'

I was worried about losing my natural charm under this professional showbiz veneer.

'I shall not have you long enough to make a bad actor of you, Sir. You will forget most of what I tell you, but retain a few useful little tricks of the trade. For instance, you must never never clasp your hands together, either behind or before, unless you deliberately wish to convey that you are ill at ease.'

'Would I ever wish to convey that?'

'In your profession I should think not. The appearance of ease is an important part of our mystery, but I should say it is the heart and soul of yours, Sir.'

'Did you give lessons to Yelena before she began to appear as the holy mother?'

He looked round apprehensively, though she was not even in the house.

'This is not a question I can answer, Sir, forgive me! Nor shall I answer it in future if anyone were to ask the same question about you.'

'Then you should find another way of not answering it,' I said.

'How would you suggest, Sir?'

'What about "No"?'

'Would you think that the right answer to make in your case, Sir?'

'Anything else would give the impression that I was just playing a part.'

He looked unhappy.

'The business of acting is concerned with illusion, but not dishonesty.'

'I should think any idea of illusion would be fatal to my business,' I said. 'Even dishonesty would be preferable; so I might have to settle for the illusion of honesty. But I'll put the question to Yelena herself. I'm sure her reply will be "No".'

In fact I didn't ask her. I had virtually no secrets from her, while she had many from me, including the story of how she got from being the water-engineer's grieving widow to the True Faith's reincarnation of the mother of Jesus. The simplified version she'd offered me had little to do with the living icon who'd first presented herself to the people of Chostok and I suspected she must have put herself through the same sort of programme as I was following now. But if I kept my suspicion to myself that would be one secret on my side. In other words, I was beginning to learn lessons from my teacher which she didn't necessarily mean to teach.

By the time Devinsky left it was getting near Christmas and my training entered a new phase. Yelena began to take me about with her on excursions to the more accessible villages. We travelled in the Colonel's 4×4, which she'd retained, together with its driver and the useful corporal with local connections, as her private transport.

In each village we would meet and talk with the people and usually take part in a religious meeting similar to the one I'd attended in Bilavice. Yelena's status was somewhere between a church elder and a film-star. She behaved and was treated in a superficially ordinary way, drinking tea, discussing local problems, giving advice, smiling and setting people at their ease; but she was always addressed as Maria and I noticed that most people wanted to touch her and that when she spoke they never disputed her statements, only put deferential questions for clarification.

My own status was more nebulous: I was part of her retinue, introduced always just as 'Karel', with no further explanation, but never required to do more than observe, sit on the sidelines, make small-talk and be friendly. People looked at me curiously, were pleased to shake my hand and talk to me and answer questions about themselves and their families, but never questioned me. They seemed to have been prepared in advance on how I was to be treated, just as Yelena had given me strict instructions never to be off my guard, never to allow myself to be drawn into controversy or even into expressing a provocative opinion. In some ways I felt like a Denis Thatcher or Prince Philip character, the shadowy consort of the queen bee, and wondered if the people perhaps thought of me as Yelena's husband or lover; on the other hand, she didn't treat me that way herself, but more like a distinguished colleague, a foreign dignitary, as it were, a king bee in my own right. The word 'king', however, was never uttered by anybody.

All this was possible because we moved in very limited circles, church circles. There were certainly people living in and around these villages who weren't even fair-weather believers in the True Faith, but we didn't usually meet them. On one occasion we had just come out of a village church and were pausing in front of the door with a small crowd round us while our car waited nearby – Yelena never stayed very long anywhere nor allowed any individual to monopolise her for more than a few minutes – her technique was hit-and-run. I was separated from her by several people pressing to get near her and by a few fans of my own, when a short man wearing glasses, with a small pointed grey beard and moustache and a pot-belly edged up to me and said:

'I'm surprised at you.'

'Mr . . .?' I said politely holding out my hand.

'Dr Moritz,' he said, taking my hand briefly. 'I'm surprised at you lending yourself to this caper. It's got no future, no future at all. You'll only compromise yourself by trailing round behind this charlatan.'

'Are you a local man, Dr Moritz?' I asked blandly, 'Or just passing through?'

'I'm visiting my mother,' he said, 'but I live and work in Chostok. I helped to patch up Tarlenheim and I'm well acquainted with Count von Wunklisch.'

'Will you give them both my best wishes,' I said. 'If they're still at Previce Castle and we happen to be anywhere near it, I'll try to call on them.'

'They are still at the Castle,' he said, 'and not at all pleased at the way the greater part of it has been taken over as winter quarters by the nationalist rebels. They would hardly welcome a visit from you in your present company, I should think.'

'Well, we're all looking forward to the spring, of course.'

'You must realise,' he said angrily, 'that as soon as the snow melts, so will this snow queen and her absurd pretensions. We are not all gullible peasants in Karapata, you know.'

'I'd very much like to make contact with the Count again,' I said, 'but at present I'm no more a free agent than he is.'

I looked him in the eyes, so far as I could see them through his dizzyingly thick lenses, and he nodded his head and changed his tone completely.

'Understood. Well understood. I'm glad I managed to get a word with you.'

We'd been speaking in low voices and I'd been nodding and smiling at other people round us all the while, but Yelena had noticed who I was talking to. Easily and fluently she moved to my side, put her arm through mine and, with a melting smile for the doctor, led me all in the same movement, to the car. She gave no one other than Moritz the sense that she was dispensing too abruptly with their company. On the contrary, they all stood there deeply contented, full of happiness and gratitude for her visit, as I held the car door open for her and then got in beside her, turning to wave to them with a gesture polished by Devinsky. They all waved as we drove off, except Dr Moritz who was walking briskly away in the opposite direction.

Yelena didn't refer to the incident in front of the driver and the corporal, but waited until we were sharing our evening meal back at the chalet.

'Dr Moritz is a Catholic. What was he doing there?'

'He told me he was visiting his mother.'

'What did he say to you?'

'He told me my old friends were still at Previce Castle. I said I hoped to see them again soon.'

'Did he give you any message from them?'

'No.'

'Or take any from you?'

'I sent them my best wishes.'

I glanced at her innocently and twirled my spaghetti with theatrical panache. She watched me carefully, considering whether to interrogate me further, then started to cut up her own. She was a very neat feeder.

'You should avoid talking to such people. Dr Moritz works at the hospital in Chostok – he's in government employment – his interest lies with the *status quo*.'

This raised a question we'd skirted round until now.

'Shouldn't we make any overtures to the other side?'

'No.'

'Why not?'

'They're very worried, but they're still in a strong position. Making overtures from weakness to strength would only improve their morale.'

'But how far shall we get by fighting? Not, surely, as far as Strelsau?'

'It depends on the attitude of the Army.'

'You think they won't want to fight or that enough of them might actually join us?'

'If the government is forced to start an inquiry into the Kapitsa Atrocity, that will probably cause the resignation of the Minister of Defence as well as the Chief of Staff and other hard-line generals. Then we shall be in a very strong position.'

She told me that the Second Regiment was still holding out in its barracks in Kapitsa, while the government havered, as well it might, between the dangers of submitting to the demands of the mutineers and of allowing their own high command to commit a further atrocity and perhaps start a full-scale civil war. The main approaches to the Second Regiment's barracks were guarded by tanks and temporary barriers, but it was a half-hearted cordon and easy to get in and out of.

'So Colonel Maggerling and his senior officers are still locked up?'

'Oh yes.'

'I hope they're being treated more humanely than I was – allowed some exercise, conversation, reading-matter, better food.'

'Of course, but if the food supplies to the barracks were stopped they would be the first to suffer.'

'And heating?'

'Yes, they'd get very cold if heating oil weren't allowed in.'

'Our friends have got the government by the short hairs, haven't they?'

After the meal we moved with our coffee to chairs by the fire. Yelena sat with her legs folded under her.

'A useful exercise for you, Karel: suppose it was your government in this dilemma, what would you do?'

I sat and looked at her in silence.

'Come on, Karel, concentrate! Think!'

I was tired and she distracted me sitting like that and looking so available. She probably wasn't much older than me, yet our relationship from her point of view seemed to be mother and adolescent son – with the big difference, of course, that most adolescent sons aren't overtly keen to go to bed with their mothers.

'How old are you, Yelena?'

'What would you do about the Second Regiment?'

She was using my frustrated desire for her as a source of energy. It was a form of hydro-electrics: dammed-up water into electricity, dammed-up sex into the will for power. I knew nothing whatever about Joan of Arc, except that she'd somehow keyed up the effete French Dauphin to thrash the rude crude English, but surely Yelena must have studied her methods and had no doubt first tried them out on Michael.

'Do you think Joan of Arc ever had sex with the Dauphin? I'm sure he must have asked her.'

'Answer, please, Karel! Don't be lazy!'

'Answer my question and I'll answer yours!'

'No, she didn't.'

'What makes you so sure?'

'He didn't appeal to her. Now your answer!'

I gave a Machiavellian solution: a treaty with the Second Regiment under which they would surrender their prisoners in return for an inquiry; then, when the prisoners were free, cancellation of the inquiry, assault on the barracks and execution of the mutineers.

'This would split the army and the whole country.'

'Not if I got rid of the general or politician who'd made and broken the treaty – had his car blown up perhaps – and attributed it to Slav retaliation. Then I could hold the inquiry after all, blame the dead man for everything and unite the army and the country under my own benevolent, even-handed rule.'

I lay back in my chair, stared into the fire with a stern, patriarchal expression and enjoyed the sense of being stared at by her.

'You're giving me Borgia's or Stalin's solution. What's yours?' she said at last, with, I thought, a trace of anxiety.

185

'Tell me how old you are,' I said, 'and I'll think of another solution.'

But she wouldn't and I wouldn't and finally she retired to bed in a bad temper, leaving me, I felt, master of the field. I played myself one of the operas she'd brought me, together with a cheap compact-disc-player, from Bilavice. I think it was *Turandot*. She appeared then in the gallery, wearing a short white towelling dressing-gown like a boxer's, and asked me to turn it down. Her long bare legs, which she'd never shown me before, were visible through the gallery railing. I turned the music off immediately and ran up the stairs. She fled into her room and bolted the door. I went to the door but didn't touch it.

'Yelena!' I said, 'Yelena!'

I waited some time and then walked round the gallery several times, but there was no response at all and in the end I went to bed alone under my green cover.

In the morning there was no sign of Yelena, but I found an envelope beside my plate at breakfast. Inside was a letter in very careful handwriting, almost like print, the letters mostly not joined up. German, of course, was not her native language, though she spoke it fluently:

> *Dear Karel, I know that you think a woman's role is only to be made love to by men and that she should be eternally grateful if you personally find her sufficiently attractive to make the effort to pursue her. But please understand that I do not want you as a lover and will not have you under any circumstances. This is partly for personal reasons – I am a person, you know, not an object – but mainly because of the purpose to which my life is dedicated.*
>
> *I know you think nothing of my mission and imagine it's just a game I'm playing or that I'm deceiving myself. This is not so. Try to look at it from your own point of view, since you're not very good at putting yourself inside other people. You did not at first take your own position very seriously, but now I think you're beginning to understand that the strange chance of your birth gives you responsibilities as well as privileges beyond yourself. I am the same. Nobody actually told me face to face, as they did you, that I was more than I thought I was, but it was just as if somebody had. And because*

186

my summons came to me inwardly, instead of through any human agency, and because I was always a serious person and very seriously affected – as I think you never have been – by the loss of someone I loved, I responded quite differently from you. I threw myself into the task of being what I was asked to be, I accepted that this was the purpose of my life and nothing else.

You have not accepted any such thing. You are still drifting along in any current that catches you – for the moment it is some silly woman who has taken it into her head to make you king of Ruritania. Well, you think, why not? And since you also find the silly woman sexually attractive, why not sleep with her too – it's part of the offer, isn't it, with the free food and lodging, the opera recordings, the excursions and the general adulation for your wonderful person?

I'm afraid you are still just a consumer, Karel, with the mentality of your privileged class and country – the mentality, no doubt, of your distinguished great-grandfather, but not of your still more distinguished great-grandmother. The difference between them was not courage in the face of physical danger – they both had that – but courage of conviction. She knew she had to serve her country, but he couldn't be sure it was his country or that he could commit himself to it and preferred photography. Of course, he would have been happy to die for Ruritania, because in the short term he was brave and generous, but because he was also conventional and cowardly in the long term, he refused to live for it.

Consider this carefully, Karel, and if you believe you can only emulate Rudolf Rassendyll and not Flavia Elphberg, I will try to arrange for you to leave Karapata and return to Strelsau, from where I'm sure your country's embassy will easily be able to repatriate you. Otherwise, I make this condition of your staying: you must dedicate yourself to your preparations and treat me as what I am: not yours, never to be yours, Yelena.

This was not the best news to get over breakfast. When Anna brought my fresh toast, I asked if Yelena was still in.

'Is out.'

'When does she get back?'

Anna shrugged. I sat and stared at the lake, with a light wind ruffling its surface, and wondered what had been so special about the water engineer from Kiev that had turned his beautiful widow into a nun.

'Is hard,' said Anna, still standing behind me.

I looked round in surprise – she'd never volunteered any remark to me before.

'You know what's in this letter?' I asked, waving it towards her.

'You write,' she said, making the movements of writing, 'then Maria come back.'

'What does she want – a written contract?'

Anna shrugged again, then turned and clattered out into the kitchen – she always wore hard-soled shoes. I started to re-read the letter, then heard her returning. I took no notice, assuming she'd come to clear something, but when she remained standing beside the table, I looked up.

'La mano.'

She pointed to my left hand lying on the table while I held the letter with my right. I looked at my hand and turned it over, not understanding what she meant, thinking perhaps she wanted to read the lines and tell my fortune. She quickly put her closed right hand in my palm, opened and withdrew it. Lying on my palm were the crumpled picture of the Virgin and the little bunch of Yelena's hair in its rubber-band which I'd had in my shirt-pocket on the day of my near-execution. The shirt had been washed several times since then and other clothes provided for me and I'd assumed the tokens had been thrown away or disappeared in the wash.

'Thank you, Anna.'

'Is good,' she said. 'L'amore. Don't worry!'

She smiled and clattered out. Did she mean Yelena might really love me in spite of her letter? Or that I should persist in loving her? Or that she thought the hair combined with the picture implied a higher, religious sort of love of which she approved? At any rate I felt cheered by her sympathy and followed her advice:

Dear Yelena, Sorry! I don't doubt your mission, but, unlike you, I have never had a great love and thought I might have found one. Silly me to be turned on by a serious person. With a frivolous background like mine you should pity me and try to make allowances and if you ever look in a mirror you surely can't blame me? I would much prefer, of course, to dedicate myself to you than to regaining my paltry inheritance, but you give me no alternative. I shall emulate Flavia and put my country first. Onwards and upwards, then, and never until you say so yours, Karel.

I left the letter on the breakfast table and went out for a run, then, after a shower, settled down on my bed to read a disapproving German account of King Charles I, a man both serious and silly, religious and unreliable, dedicated and inept. I dozed off for a while and when I came yawning downstairs in the early afternoon in search of something to eat, saw a pair of man's legs stretched out towards the fire from one of the chairs. The owner was hidden behind a newspaper.

'Hello!'

It was Fisher John. He jumped up and shook my hand warmly.

'The news (nooz) is very good,' he said. 'It looks as if there will be an inquiry into the Kapitsa Atrocity. The government is sending a minister to talk with the Second Regiment and they hope to agree details and free up the hostages in time for Christmas.'

'Is Yelena back?'

'No. That's partly why I came – to let you know Maria would be away for a while. She's in retreat.'

'If it's anything to do with me,' I said, 'I've written her a letter.'

'I have your letter, Karl, and I'll deliver it to her.'

'You'll be seeing her in retreat?'

'Oh yes.'

'Why is she in retreat?'

'To prepare for Christmas. This will be a big event in our programme, of course, and, given the latest news from Kapitsa . . .' he flourished the newspaper, '. . . I should say a turning-point.'

'When will she be back?'

'I'd guess after Christmas, but we shall all meet up in Chostok on that day.'

'And what am I supposed to do meanwhile?'

'That depends on you, Karl. Maria seems a little uncertain where you stand. But *if* you're still going along with our programme, she asked me to tell you not to let up on your studies.'

'You mean I'm just to go on reading by myself? That's a bit fruitless – I need her to keep me up to the mark.'

'Two points there, Karl. First, she wants a change of emphasis.'

'How do you mean?'

'She thinks you've had enough historical orientation – she wants you to fill in on sociological, psychological, human problems.'

I looked at him suspiciously. This sounded like the punishment cell.

'How am I supposed to approach these problems?'

'I've brought a pile of books for you.'

'Thanks.'

'And the second point is that I'm here to help you through them.'

It *was* the punishment cell. I looked at him with undisguised horror. He looked back with a steady eye and an expression of deep concern.

'To a Republican like myself, Karl, the idea of a king in the modern world is very alien. Having thought about it, though, I believe it could be a great idea and could even catch on in relatively small and backward countries like this. But if we're going to make the experiment and back it with our own organisation, we need to know we've got the right material to work with – the right man in the starring role. That's where I come in. Social psychology and related studies are my area of expertise and I want to pass some of it on to you.'

I had a strong urge to demand my letter back. It wasn't in the contract that I had to swop tutors. On the other hand, Christmas wasn't all that far away, I had no desire to spend it with Freddy and Jennifer, and I thought I might just hold out.

Fisher John moved into the chalet and set to work on his corner of the clean slate.

20

The Three Kings

I couldn't make anything of Fisher John's pile of books. That's to say, I could have done if I'd wanted to, but their earnest tone and convoluted jargon and worst of all their stench of cheap moral perfume made me so angry that I threw several out of my bedroom window, where they sank pleasingly into the snow. My discussions with Fisher himself were no better. The ostensible subjects weren't the issue at all. He was there to brainwash me, to give me what he called 'a moral dimension', to replace my 'random reactions' with a 'thought-through agenda'. It wasn't just cussedness that made me reject this completely. His 'agenda' was a mixture of simple Christianity with Middle American social problems and I couldn't see it as any more relevant to Ruritania than my own brand of English consumerism. If Fisher was meant to be Yelena's counterweight to Machiavelli, she couldn't have done more to raise the old cynic in my esteem.

I looked forward to Christmas and the end of this abysmal servitude to my contract with passionate longing – only to discover that the True Faith celebrated Christmas – like the Orthodox Church – on January 6th. I had to survive twelve more days of Fisher John's tuition. I must say the man had patience. I never managed to make him lose his temper, even though when I'd first met him in the bar of the Astoria Hotel he'd seemed easy to annoy. But of course he saw me now not as a nosey outsider but a key element in the 'programme' and was determined somehow to discharge his role as my teacher and turn me into a good Disciple of the First Instance.

I pressed this patient determination of his to every limit I could think of. He would come out on runs with me, when I would deliberately go extra miles or lose the way and land us in snowdrifts, and still, bedraggled and exhausted – he was older and a lot less fit than me – he would try to talk about my relationship with my father, my sexual experiences at school, my resentment towards authority, my feelings about race, gender and colour. He wasn't a fool, he didn't take the responses I gave at face value, he was just trying to 'find my wavelength'. Then he would accompany me to the bar in the barracks and toy steadfastly with a glass of orange-juice while I knocked back beer and schnapps. After he'd helped me home a few times he gave up coming, having twigged that I only drank too much when he was with me.

I'd feel more ashamed of this whole episode – I do feel slightly ashamed – if it had been in any way my fault. Fisher – and certainly Yelena – should have known better. But of course fanatics, however worldly in some ways, never do: they would cease to be fanatics and lose all their purpose in life if they didn't believe that somewhere round the corner every Saul is bound to fall off his horse on the way to Damascus. But I had another particular reason for resisting Fisher's 'agenda': I suspected his own 'moral dimension' of being phoney.

I kept quiet about what the Count had told me during the concert at Bilavice until just before our mutual torment was due to end. We were jogging towards the dam and passed through a small wood of trees without leaves. One of them was dead, a stump more or less my height, and as I drew level with it – Fisher was struggling along about fifty yards behind – I paused, running on the spot, for him to catch up.

'Strange tree!' I said.

'Yeah?'

He was very short of breath, but continued manfully treading the snow beside me.

'Looks human.'

'Maybe.'

'Reminds me of carving.',

'What?'

'Thing in church.'

'Church?'

'Our Lady of Chostok – remember?'

He looked very wary.

'Uh-huh!' Some cowboy sound like that, as we kept treading.

'Did you save it?'

'Uh-huh!'

I started forward again, slowly so that he could keep up.

'Where is it now?'

There was no reply that I could hear.

'Did you try Previce Castle?'

Still no reply.

192

We came to a small road leading to the end of the dam. There was a guard-post here, manned now by two of the guerrillas. I waved as we approached and the soldiers came out smiling and put their right hands on their hearts. This had become the soldiers' own special salute to me, something between friendship and deference, and I returned the compliment as I ran past. At the point where the dam left the shore there was a kind of embrasure with a magnificent view along the dam itself, back up the lake to the triple peaks and down the sheer wall of the dam to the river and the hydro-electric plant directly under us. We stopped here, still jogging gently, to take in the view, as we often did before returning to the chalet.

'Those soldiers think a lot of you,' said Fisher, still breathing very heavily.

I nodded, waiting for the catch. Fisher never paid me a compliment except as a sweetener for some moral pill to follow.

'But there's always a danger in taking these things too personally.'

'It might make me vain?'

'You've got a very high opinion of yourself already, Karl. You know that, I know that. We've talked about your superiority complex.'

He meant he'd told me I had one.

'So what's the danger?'

'The danger is using other people . . .'

I reproduce the panting delivery of this sermon:

'. . . for your own . . . purposes, when your real role . . . is a conduit . . . Look at this dam! It's . . . a mighty thing . . . a breath-taking spectacle . . . but if the dam . . . thought it was here just for its own purpose . . . to be admired and saluted . . . for its beauty and size . . . wouldn't we have to tell it . . . that was false? . . . It's only here as part of a whole system . . . as a conduit . . . for electricity . . . to the whole community.'

He was still vaguely stamping his feet, but had stopped jumping up and down in his anxiety to get his message across.

'Keep moving, Fisher!' I said, 'You'll get chilled, your muscles will seize up.'

'What we want you to do, Karl, what Maria and I want you to do, is declare yourself . . . for Jesus. Show everyone that you *do* accept your power and responsibilities in the name of a greater than yourself.'

'I don't see it matters what the dam thinks,' I said, 'Whether it's just here to impress people or is a conduit for electricity. Or even whether it declares itself for Jesus. So long as it doesn't crack and does its job. It could easily imagine, for instance, that it's really meant to be a bridge across to the other side.'

I climbed up on the wall of the embrasure, beside a locked iron gate which led down steps to the top of the dam. It was possible to jump down from here and I did.

'What are you doing, Karl?'

'Seeing how it responds as a bridge,' I said and started to walk along the top of the dam.

The thing was several feet wide and the water on the lake side a foot or two below it, so that in summer it would have been easy to walk along. Now, of course, it was covered in snow, which made it a bit treacherous, and there was also the nerve-wracking drop into a whole different landscape on my left. I was doing it, I suppose, partly to get away from Fisher, partly to show off, mainly because having mentioned the bridge idea I felt challenged to try it. I turned, unsteadily, to look back at Fisher. He was leaning on the parapet looking very worried indeed.

'That's an incredibly foolhardy thing to do,' he said, 'it's irresponsible, Karl. You're giving me kittens.'

'The view's terrific,' I said.

I turned and went on, but as I looked down at the view I slipped and almost lost my footing.

'Please, Karl, please!'

'Come and try it!'

I had no thought that he would, but he jumped down and advanced a few steps along the dam, then stopped.

'I want you to come back, Karl. I'm pleading with you to come back.'

'In a minute,' I said. 'I'm enjoying myself.'

Do I only ever enjoy myself provoking other people? It's probably a tribute to my stint with Fisher that I ask myself such a question at all, but I reject it all the same. Making other people sweat is by no means my only enjoyment. I picked my way on along the dam.

'Karl!'

'Yes, Fisher?'

I didn't turn round. We were having to shout now anyway.

'I believe this is an evil impulse in you. Please stop!'

I did stop and stood with my feet apart looking down at the river far below in the valley. A light wind blew off the lake against my back and I stretched my arms out like wings and felt the chill starting to freeze the sweat on my torso. Then I turned my head towards Fisher. He had retreated a few steps and was leaning against the wall of the embrasure.

'The evil impulse is telling me to jump,' I called out, 'but I'm resisting it.'

He made no reply and I lowered my arms and walked slowly back towards him. When I was a yard or two away, I said:

'It was a temptation.'

'I could see that. I prayed for you.'

'Would an angel have held me up?'

'No, Karl.'

'Then what were you praying for?'

'That you wouldn't be a damn' fool and start dancing or waving your arms about.'

'What about Our Lady of Chostok?' I said. 'The wooden one. Is it at Previce Castle or has it left the country?'

'What do you mean, left the country?'

'I know you considered it very valuable.'

'I'd never do that, Karl.'

'Never do what?'

'Take it out of the country.'

Pressed against the wall he looked and sounded like a small crook being interrogated by a bigger one.

'Where is it now?' I asked.

'It's safe. It's quite safe for the present.'

'At Previce Castle?'

'I don't think . . .'

I started a slow dance where I stood, a sort of Highland fling, with my feet weaving and my arms curved over my head. He was right, it was very foolish. I hoped I wouldn't have to go on for long.

'It is at Previce, yes.'

I stopped dancing.

'That's good. Does the Count know it is?'

'Karl, it's getting very cold. We should start for home.'

'You climb up, I'll follow.'

It wasn't so easy to get up as to jump down and Fisher was nervous about making the sort of upward leap that was needed, in case he landed on the roof of the hydro-electric plant some hundreds of feet down.

'Shall I go first?' I said, 'then I can give you a hand.'

He pressed himself to one side while I jumped at the wall a couple of times and at the third attempt got my hands over the top and hauled myself up.

'You can rest easy now,' I said, straddling the parapet of the embrasure, 'at least your valuable pupil is safe. But before we go any

195

further I really want to know more about that statue. It means something to me. I nearly destroyed it that day in the church and then you kindly mentioned that it was a valuable part of my country's heritage. You're always urging me to think of the community and not myself and every time you say it I have this nagging memory of somebody telling me you wanted to get that statue out to the West.'

'It's not true, Karl. You've been misinformed.'

'I'm relieved,' I said, getting behind the parapet and leaning over, with one hand dangling towards him, 'but I still want more details. Does the Count know what it is, does he know where it is?'

By the time I'd pulled him up the wall to safety he was shivering uncontrollably. The wind had strengthened and it was certainly very cold. We warmed up again running home, but we were probably lucky not to catch pneumonia. According to Fisher, he'd visited the Count and suggested the export deal solely so as to look over the castle and see if there was a suitable hiding-place. Then he'd arranged the trip for the Count and Vladek to the concert at Bilavice and at the same time organised a visit to the cinema in Chostok for all the staff at the castle, while two trusty members of the True Faith had hidden the statue for him. So no one at the Castle had any knowledge of it and he very much hoped I wouldn't tell them.

'Its safety is all I mind about,' I said. 'But is Yelena in the secret?'

'No,' he said. 'That kind of thing doesn't bother her. She wouldn't consider it an issue.'

So I thought it a good day's work: I had another secret from Yelena and for the last day of my studies with Fisher I was altogether excused any more of his 'agenda'. He had a bad cold and mostly stayed in bed. When we met at lunch we talked about the news on television. The government had promised an inquiry into the Kapitsa Atrocity, the colonel and my other persecutors at Kapitsa were being released this very day and fresh senior officers were to be appointed to command the Second Regiment and bring it back into the fold of the Ruritanian Army.

'Doesn't this mean,' I asked, 'that we've lost some valuable allies?'

'I don't think so,' said Fisher, blowing his nose and looking very bleary-eyed. 'What it means is that the hard-liners will be out and the government will be more ready to come to some accommodation with us.'

'And where do I come in?'

'You'll surely be part of that accommodation.'

With his blocked nose it sounded like 'combination' and I began to have doubts about whether the news was all that good from my point of view. But I had no doubts whatever that if Fisher had any say in the matter I would be no part of anybody's combination. I had purchased the secret of the statue at the price of his total antagonism.

Most of the Christmas (Twelfth Night) service in Chostok church was just as dreary as all the others I'd attended and much the same. I suppose it's true that the more spiritual people are, the less they want all the glossy trappings, their eyes being turned inwards and upwards. But it's hard for non-spiritual people mixed up in these sessions because they miss all the inwardness and get left with nothing to look at – the windows were plain glass now, the chandeliers were naked light-bulbs and even the altar and pulpit had been removed – and nothing to listen to except the same old passages from the New Testament and devout statements which on the surface just sound trite.

Fisher and I had arrived early to join five or six black-robed people – the inner-circle of the True Faith – in the church vestry. A lot of the guerrillas were in town too, their lorries parked in the streets round the square, themselves gathering – in a more disciplined way than on the night of the bonfire – in the square itself. About three-quarters of the men from our own barracks by the lake had accompanied us to Chostok. Everyone was in high spirits because of the news of the government climb-down and the hope that they might not after all have to fight again in the spring, but could return to their farms and families.

We waited in the vestry in silence. Fisher and I had nothing more to say to one another and the black-robed people no more wanted to exchange small talk with me than I did with them. Immediately before the service was due to start Yelena joined us, escorted by Michael. She was wearing her white robe and headband and soft shoes, but her hair, of course, was still quite short. Her eyes looked tired and the skin over her cheek-bones tauter than usual – perhaps she had been fasting and praying all night. The black robes bowed to her and Fisher took her hand and kissed it. I was at the back of the group and wondered if I should do the same, but I didn't want to copy Fisher and my feelings for Yelena were mixed: she had put me through my punishment course on the 'moral dimension' and I wasn't sure I forgave her. So as she turned towards me I nodded in a neutral way and said:

'Hello!'

Yelena came straight towards me, holding out both hands. She took me by the upper arms, embraced me and kissed me on each cheek and then once more. I stood back in a daze when this was over, but not so much of a daze that I missed the expressions on Michael's and Fisher's faces. They hadn't expected this any more than I had and hated it. Yelena didn't smile – her face was very solemn – but her pale blue eyes were still looking steadily at mine as she stepped back. I wondered if she was trying to hypnotise me or if, not having communicated with Fisher, she assumed he'd accomplished his task and brought me to a holier frame of mind than she'd left me in. She made a sign to Fisher, who opened the vestry door – the little door he'd emerged from to save the statue all those months ago – and went through, followed by the black robes. We heard a collective sigh of anticipation from the people inside the church. Michael went next, with another unfriendly glance at me, then Yelena took my hand and led me through into the church.

'I may speak of you, Karel,' she said, very quietly, 'if the moment is right. Be ready!'

Holding her hand – child or lover, I hardly minded which – I was ready for anything, even Heaven.

As we appeared hand-in-hand behind the little procession of Fisher, the black robes and Michael, the whole church-full, with a scraping of chairs, went on its knees. Yelena gestured for them to sit again and we took the empty seats reserved for us at the centre of the congregation. Then the service proceeded in its desultory, improvised way and I kept myself alert by observing faces – there was nothing else to look at. Yelena had instructed me once on the importance of reading faces and trying to determine not so much their immediate thoughts as their general character – reliable, obstinate, timid, rash, conceited, frivolous (I'd bowed in acknowledgment of those last three), etc. In this company I tried to decide what the proportion was of true believers to time-servers and reckoned it was about ten percent. But some of the time my attention lapsed and I just thought lazily of the woman beside me.

After an hour or more, when a great many believers had had their say and the gaps between people standing up were growing longer, with some shuffling and coughing in the outer circles, two or three of the black robes said their pieces and then there was complete silence for a minute or so. Yelena stood up and the congregation knelt again. This time they stayed kneeling and she began to speak in short sentences, Ruritanian repeated in German, just as on the first occasion I'd seen her. She talked first, as most of them had, about the birth of Jesus in a stable and pointed out its significant simplicity and poverty in a world organised by and for the great people; but she didn't talk for long and soon reached her conclusion:

'. . . As well as cows and donkeys and sheep and shepherds and the carpenter Joseph, there were also kings at the birth of Jesus. These were the wise kings, the kings with knowledge and foresight, the kings who were good shepherds to their flocks. How many such kings do we have today, even if we call them presidents or prime ministers? How many kings who kneel at the cradle of Jesus in true humility and true faith? Dear people, we have such a king today in Karapata. I name him here before you all tonight in Chostok . . .'

She turned and put both her hands on my head.

'I name him Karel Rassendyll Elphberg, descendant in the direct line of Rudolf and Flavia, King-to-be of Ruritania.'

Her hands on my head induced such a tingling glow of pleasure that I closed my eyes and wanted to fall asleep. When she took her hands away and I opened my eyes again I saw that many of the congregation were weeping, others staring at me with open mouths and expressions of awful devotion, and a few – forgetting they had abandoned Catholicism or Orthodoxy – were even crossing themselves. But now Yelena sat down and as she did so brushed my ear with her hand and whispered:

'Speak, Karel! You must!'

I glanced at Michael and Fisher, both of them staring grimly at the floor. With Michael it was obviously a simple case of envy, but I felt almost sorry for Fisher, surreptitiously mopping his nose with his handkerchief. Clearly his brief had been to prepare me for this – not to coach me in exactly what I should say, but to bring me to the point where I would rise spontaneously and declare myself for Jesus. He had failed miserably. Still, it was worse for me. What on earth was I to say? I rose slowly from my knees, as slowly as I dared, while my mind raced. I stood and looked round the whole congregation, waiting for inspiration in the total silence that had fallen. The open doors were packed too, with the soldiers from the square pressing to see first Yelena and now me. I gained more time by gesturing to everybody to get off their knees and sit down. When the noise had finally subsided and I could think of no more delaying tactics, I began to speak, using German and as much Ruritanian as I could muster:

'People tell me I look exactly like a waxwork. I feel like one too. Wax in the hands of . . .'

I made an expressive, Devinsky-style gesture towards Yelena, stroking my hand upwards in the air to imply both her and her heavenly sponsors.

'But I've no wish to speak of myself. There were three kings at the cradle of Jesus and there are three kings in Chostok tonight. The gift I bring is nothing but the blood of Queen Flavia. The gift Michael brings is more dependable and more necessary: the victorious Army of the True Faith . . .'

I made a sweeping gesture from Michael – caught off-guard by the mention of his name and rapidly adjusting his expression to a friendly sneer – to the soldiers at the door.

'And the gift Fisher brings is perhaps the most precious of all: the encouragement and still more the support of his own folk in the West . . .'

Fisher, with his eyes watering, his nose running and his sodden handkerchief in his hand, looked like a rabbit crouched under a headlight, but he was more accustomed to public presentation than Michael and managed a more convincing smile.

'And I want to tell you something else about Fisher. On the night this church was cleared of its Catholic ornaments there were those who made no distinction between one object and another. That wonderful statue of Our Lady of Chostok, which should not be seen as a religious icon worthy of destruction but as a work of art made by a great Ruritanian artist, was in danger of going on the fire. Fisher knew better. He saved Chostok's greatest treasure at the risk of his own life. And he has kept it safely all this while against the day when it can be restored to Chostok. Not to the church, of course, where it would be out of place, but to the local museum, perhaps, where it will surely attract thousands of visitors from all over the world and help to ensure the future prosperity of this beautiful town. This is a kingly gift indeed.'

Fisher's attempt to keep his smile going for the benefit of the congregation, while trying to strike me dead with his eyes, told me clearly that he'd still hoped to outwit me and smuggle the statue out of the country. I turned and held out my hands to Michael and Fisher, made them rise to their feet, and stood between them with my arms round their shoulders.

'Three kings in the service of the mother of Jesus . . .' I said, knelt at Yelena's feet, kissed her hand and passed the buck to her.

21

Cobwebs and Dry Rot

My speech didn't make my number with the truly faithful. It wasn't devotional enough. On the other hand, it went down very well with the majority of the citizens of Chostok and also pleased Michael and the soldiers, who received us with enthusiasm when we came out on the steps of the church after the service. Fisher was hostile, of course, but he had been before. As we returned from our reception in the square through the now empty church, he muttered in my ear:

'Unforgivable!'

Unforgivable that he'd exchanged mere earthly riches for the gratitude of a whole community? Moralising is not my style, so I simply said:

'You should have prayed to the angel to give me a push.'

Yelena's attitude I couldn't quite gauge. She said nothing but she didn't seem annoyed with me. She was probably famished and exhausted and needed to recuperate after whatever harsh regime she'd imposed on herself in her retreat.

We were going now, it turned out, not back to the chalet but to Previce Castle, where the main body of guerrillas was based. Fisher insisted on travelling in the 4×4 with Yelena, no doubt so as to give her a bad report on my studies. Michael, whose favour I had temporarily gained even if I'd permanently forfeited Fisher's, offered me a place in the Range Rover. But I was reluctant to arrive back at the castle in the same car as I'd left, not from superstition, but to spare the Count's feelings. I couldn't avoid appearing to be on the wrong side as far as he was concerned, but I thought that sitting in the back of his stolen and damaged car with Michael would be a long-term error of image. So I accepted a lift in a lorry with Corporal Radichev and in this way I arrived, somewhat after the Range Rover, at the head of a convoy of guerrillas. As we all drew up in the courtyard of the castle and the soldiers spilled out round me, shaking my hand and patting me on the back, I glanced up at the tower and saw the Count and Vladek at a window on the first floor. I waved cheerily and the Count raised one finger in acknowledgment.

The guerrillas were quartered in the main block of the castle, which was still essentially a prison, though the cell doors were open and the cells themselves partly domesticated into soldiers' sleeping-quarters. They still had bars on the windows, but there were no bars on the windows of the suite of three large reception-rooms on the first-floor overlooking the cliff. They had been used as offices and rest-rooms for the prison-staff and were now the communal dining- and living-quarters of the guerrillas. Long trestle-tables were laid through all three rooms for a Christmas feast for several hundred. It wasn't a sophisticated affair. The rooms were bare and dilapidated, their eighteenth-century proportions ruined by false ceilings cutting off the tops of the once-elegant pilasters, their cheap brown paint peeling, their grand marble fireplaces chipped and grimy, their folding double-doors sagging at the hinges. The food, with bottles of wine and beer and schnapps, was all plonked on the table anyhow and everybody helped themselves greedily in the Slav style. There was no particular seating-plan. Yelena (the only woman present) and I sat together in the third room, with our backs to the windows, and I had the regular army corporal from Kapitsa on my other side. Corporal Radichev and several of the guerrillas from the Sebrikov contingent were opposite me, but Michael and Fisher and Vakisch were in other rooms.

Yelena ate a little and drank tea, but she was evidently almost at the end of her energy.

'Fisher thinks we should have nothing more to do with you,' she said.

'He gave me a hard time,' I said.

'He was meant to.'

'I think he suffered a bit himself.'

'A teacher expects to with a difficult pupil. We were both aware of your problems, but we didn't imagine you were also a bully.'

That seemed unjust. He had been put in to bully me, surely, but I had got the better of him.

'You probably regret laying your hands on my head in the church,' I said. 'You should have had a word with Fisher first.'

'Meaning?'

'He'd have told you I didn't make the grade in social psychology, you wouldn't have made me stand up and speak and Fischer would have been spared my revelation about the statue.'

'He never mentioned the statue. He just thought you weren't up to the job.'

I told her then the whole story of the statue. She wasn't – Fisher had been right about that – at all interested in where it might be now or even whether it was of any value, but she still tried to resist seeing Fisher in any but the best light and clung to his explanation of the deal he'd suggested to the Count. It came out in the course of her defence of him – probably only because she was tired and off-guard – that her 'retreat' had been in a house rented by Fisher near Chostok and she 'knew him too well to believe him capable of any selfish motive'.

'How long have you known him?'

'Some years.'

'So this isn't his first visit to Ruritania?'

'Of course not.'

I saw now – or thought I saw – a great light on the origins of Our Lady of Chostok – the one sitting beside me, not the statue. But I didn't press her any further, I thought it better to let her marinade for a while in doubts about Fisher. Instead I changed the subject and asked what her plans were. Would she, I asked hopefully, resume my education in the chalet beside the lake?

'We'll talk about that tomorrow,' she said.

It sounded like a rebuke and I wondered if Fisher had already done me more damage in her eyes than I could do him. At this point the corporal on my right, who had been busy so far piling into food and drink, leant across me and said to Yelena:

'We've got to go back to Kapitsa now, you know.'

'Now?'

'Not now now,' he said, 'not tonight, but tomorrow or the day after at the latest.'

She looked very put out.

'But I rely on you, corporal. You and driver Orlin and the car.'

'I understand that,' he said. 'But now that the mutiny's over we'll be posted deserters if we don't get back to barracks with the jeep.'

'I see. I never thought of that.'

She became silent and withdrawn. I pressed her to eat more or at least try a glass of wine.

'No thank you, Karel.'

'I've never seen you depressed,' I said. 'Is it my fault?'

'Always thinking of yourself,' she said. 'No, it's many things, of which you are only one small part.'

'Smaller than the loss of the colonel's jeep?'

'About the same.'

'You rate an unsuitable king about the same as a temporary transport problem?'

'You're not an unsuitable king, Karel. On the contrary.'

She put her hand on my arm.

'This will only increase your self-love, I'm afraid, but if one criticises one should also praise. When you stood up in the church between Michael and Fisher, it was obvious to everyone who was the real king. I regret your weaknesses – but at least you know what they are. Fisher is quite wrong in saying you're not up to the job. If you never come to do it, that will be one of the many wrong turnings of history.'

She removed her hand. Forgetting my contract entirely, I put my arm round her shoulder and clumsily kissed her cheek. She didn't fight me off, as I half expected, but received the kiss stoically and then gently removed my arm.

'I must go now,' she said and got to her feet.

Corporal Radichev and his companions across the table, who had watched me put my arm round her and kiss her and raised their glasses encouragingly, also got to theirs, begging her not to go. I rose too and the effect rippled down all the tables in all three rooms, so that the whole company stood up, not knowing why, with their glasses in their hands.

'I'm tired,' said Yelena to the men opposite and she looked as if she could hardly stay on her feet.

I put my arm round her again, this time to support her, but she gently removed it for the second time and instead put her arm through mine and started to walk along between the windows and the backs of the chairs. We progressed up the first room and then the two others to the exit at the far end of the whole suite, while everyone stood and no one spoke. At the door Yelena withdrew her arm, turned briefly with a smile and a brief nod to the long lines of standing soldiers, and went out like a sleepwalker.

I returned to my seat as conversation began again and the banquet deteriorated into a drunken racket. Balalaikas and guitars were produced, the tables pushed back, songs sung, bottles knocked over, glasses smashed, and lines of dancers, stamping and leaping, shook the floors to their joists. It must have been extremely disturbing to our imprisoned landlord in his tower next door, but I didn't give much thought to him: I was singing, dancing and drinking with the best and stayed behind, when most had staggered away to their cell-beds below, with the hard core of revellers who finally sank down and slept on the spot.

I was not, however, as drunk as my comrades and when I'd dozed for an hour or two and the whole place was quiet, I got up and opened a window. The cold air eased my headache. When I was sure no one else was awake I pulled myself on to the sill and jumped down. It was a long drop, but the alcohol I'd consumed made me relaxed and I landed softly in the snow. It was snowing again now, which I was glad of. Fisher hadn't told me exactly where he'd hidden the statue, but I'd seen round the castle before the banquet and not noticed any likely hiding-places – unless it was in an attic or with the heating-system in the basement. It occurred to me, though, that while they were discussing the secret export deal, the Count might have taken Fisher for the same walk into the woods as he'd taken me. I wanted to check Fisher's assurance that the thing was still at Previce, but I didn't want to leave a row of footprints leading straight to the spot. The snow would cover my tracks by morning and save me taking a long way round now to disguise them.

There were no sentries this side of the castle. They were posted at the gates leading into the courtyard more for form's sake than anything, since there was no conceivable enemy to be feared and the count and Vladek had no transport and would hardly attempt to escape on foot. I walked as fast as I could through virgin snow to the watch-tower at the edge of the wood and climbed the rickety stairs on the outside. It was very dark inside – the windows were filthy – and I couldn't see what state the floor-boards were in, so I felt my way carefully round the edge, past each of the three windows, collecting cobwebs in my hair and clothes as I went and once putting my foot through a rotten board. Finally, just before I came round to the door again, I bumped into a hard object leaning against the wall. It was wrapped in sacking and tied with string. I felt it over. It was certainly a human form.

Then I heard a movement on the staircase outside. I remained completely still beside the sacking parcel. Whoever it was outside stopped moving too. We both waited like this for some time, but he got tired or his nerve cracked first.

'Karl?'

It was Fisher.

'Hello, Fisher! It's very late. How did you guess I'd want to check your facts?'

'That was not difficult to guess, Karl, since you were given the room next to mine to sleep in. When you didn't come down, I

205

went up to see if you'd passed out and found the window open and tracks in the snow. You've got an obsession about this thing, haven't you?'

'Your facts seem to be correct, Fisher,' I said, stepping round the statue towards the doorway, 'so I can lay my obsession to rest.'

'I'm glad, Karl,' he said.

He was standing about two steps down – snow falling thickly on his hair and half-length coat – and he put his foot on the next step up as he saw me appear in the doorway.

'Laying that obsession to rest is what I'm here for.'

He suddenly lunged at me with a large knife and would probably have spitted me straight through the stomach if the step hadn't caved in under his sudden pressure. The point of the knife grazed my right thigh, tearing the jeans. I leapt back inside the doorway as he recovered his balance and came on.

'I'm going to get you anyway, Karl, because quite apart from that obsession of yours I think you're very bad news.'

I went back behind the statue as he entered the doorway, his knife flashing momentarily as it caught the light from the snow outside. I had no weapon of any sort and although I was stronger I was reluctant to jump on him in case the floor gave way and broke my impetus as it just had his. On the other hand he was presumably using a knife instead of a gun because he didn't want to make any noise, whereas I had nothing to lose if the whole castle heard us. As he took a step towards me I pushed the Virgin at him. It toppled very slowly and he had time to push it aside with his free arm, so that it rolled across between us and fell towards the middle of the floor. There wasn't a lot of noise, because of the sacking, but its weight broke through part of the boards. The whole place must have been riddled with dry rot. At least I hoped it was. As he made his second lunge I jumped sideways and landed as heavily as I could beside the statue. The boards gave way comprehensively and with one bound I was free, lying shaken and bruised, but still mobile, in the snow under the watch-tower.

Did Fisher really mean to kill me? (I asked myself as I loped with a limp towards the castle) but what then? How could he have got away with it? Of course, he could have pitched the body over the cliff where it wouldn't be found until at least the spring, left the snow to cover the tracks, returned the knife to whatever kitchen-drawer he'd found it in and hey presto! Disappearance of the heir to the throne! 'A pity, but he wasn't really up to the job, was he?' And so back to the True Faith, unsullied by a person with an evil impulse and too much knowledge of Fisher's own evil impulse. Without me, he

206

might still have hoped to export the statue and persuade the people of Chostok that I'd been fantasising. What he didn't know was that I'd told the whole story to Yelena. Would she have missed me enough to investigate my disappearance more thoroughly or even suspect Fisher of being involved? That question I couldn't honestly answer.

I was now quite close to the castle. Fisher wasn't following – he couldn't run as fast as me, could he? But what would he do if I sent the guard for him? Claim it was me that attacked him and was wounded as he got the knife away from me? Run away into the snowbound forest? Bluff it out with some story about seeing a man making for the watch-tower and stabbing him in the darkness, not knowing it was me? He was probably putting the same options to himself at this moment.

There was no sign of anyone outside the castle. The watch-tower was too far away and the noise of the statue falling and the rotten board breaking too muffled to alarm the guard; if they'd heard anything they'd probably assumed it was a small avalanche of snow off the cliff or a tree falling. I decided to let Fisher off his own hook for the moment. Yelena wouldn't like having to choose between him and me; Michael would most likely stick by him if he was really the source of the guerrillas' funds; and if I appealed direct to Vakisch and the soldiers I'd be forcing them to make a choice of allegiance. Best to pretend nothing had happened, keep Fisher sweating until further notice and make sure he had no second chance. Of course, I'd have to choose a safer place to spend the rest of the night than the room next door to his, but I could easily doss down in any of the ex-cells where there would be friends and weapons to protect me. Then as I passed the tower I had a better idea. It was very unlikely Michael would allow me any kind of conference with the Count and Vladek, but if I could somehow get in there now I could have a working breakfast with them before anyone missed me.

The small windows of the tower were not barred, but none of the ground-floor ones were unlatched. The only door was round the inner side, opening on to the courtyard. There was, however, a small one-storey extension built out of one wall – the Count had needed extra space for his kitchen – with a flat sloping roof. I got up there by way of a window ledge and from there, through an unlatched window, into the bathroom I'd used on my previous visit.

I washed my wound – it was only a long scratch – and went through to the bedroom. It was too dark to see who was occupying the bed – probably Vladek. I took the blanket spread over the top of his duvet without waking him and went downstairs to the sitting-room, where there was the remains of a fire. Here I slept the rest of the night on the sofa under my blanket and was woken early in the morning by an astounded Magda.

22

The Borgia Solution

Magda not only patched up my scratch with plaster, brought me coffee and picked the cobwebs out of my hair, she found some stout thread and sewed up the rent in my jeans; meanwhile I lay on the sofa in my underpants and asked her how they had all been enjoying the winter at Previce. She and her mother, she said, had been free to come and go, but the Count and Vladek had been allowed out only under supervision: in consequence they were 'as angry as bees'. She gave me back my mended jeans, roused my hosts and made us all breakfast. Vladek was pleased to see me, but the Count extremely grumpy:

'I know you are a natural weathercock, Karl Marx, but you have been stuck too long in the bad wind from these terrorists. Dr Moritz told me you were under some duress, but he also told me you were not making too much effort to escape it. I must tell you that you will not be forgiven by the German interests in Strelsau and you have probably ruined your chances of ever becoming king. Colonel Danzing, for example, was so shocked by what he heard of your conduct that he resigned his post as ambassador in London.'

'A bit extreme,' I said.

'Not for a man of honour like him. He felt responsible for inflicting you on our country.'

I asked if by the 'German interests' he meant the German part of the population in general.

'I don't think they are aware of your existence and probably just as well.'

'Then it's only a few hard-liners who won't forgive me?'

'Hard-liners? I am talking about the people with the power.'

'Won't they have less power now if the government's given way over the Kapitsa affair?'

'Don't rely on that!'

'They've promised an inquiry and the inquiry will surely weaken the position of the hard-liners, if not actually destroy it.'

'You are too optimistic.'

He became more friendly when I told him about my feud with Fisher and its violent outcome in the watch-tower.

'It's a pity you didn't kill this snake instead of just breaking up my floorboards, but as soon as spring comes we'll round him up with the others and I hope he may be shot. It's very clear he's the prime mover of all the trouble in Karapata as well as its source of funds.'

I disagreed. Yelena was now the prime mover, I told him, though Fisher might have set her going in the first place. I also said that simply crushing the guerrillas would do no good at all, except to return the country to its previous state of ethnic division and leave the ground fertile for more unrest.

'Are you becoming a serious politician, Karl Marx, or is it just that you're under the spell of this witch of the mountains?'

'If *you* are a serious politician,' I said, 'I wonder why you should see the time I've spent with the nationalists as counter-productive. Bring over the moderate German interests, get rid of the hard-liners, and you'd have a ruler acceptable right across the ethnic divide.'

'Very easy,' said the Count, 'to win the hearts of outlaws grasping at any distant hope of power. But to win the hearts of those in power and persuade them to share it with you, that is next to impossible. They don't need you, Karl Marx, and I'm not rich enough to bribe them to believe they do.'

'What would make them need me?'

'Nothing but the prospect or fear of losing power.'

'So they only need to be sufficiently frightened?'

'You are clutching at straws, dear boy. Yes, I saw yesterday how popular you are with your ragamuffin terrorists, but you might as well lead a mob of mafia in the back streets of Strelsau. These people are only fit to scare mountain crows and they will be destroyed in the spring if not sooner.'

I turned to Vladek, who had taken no part in the discussion and looked very gaunt and nervy, as if he was suffering from permanent constipation or perhaps just from spending the winter closeted with the Count. They both gave the impression of living on the edge of each other's tolerance.

'What's your opinion, Vladek?' I said. 'Have you any ideas?'

'I'm just an artist, Karl. I can paint your portrait, I know journalists who might publish stories about you, but I have no influence with

210

important people. I always thought Wunklisch did, but it seems not enough.'

After all my recent encouragements over the past months this made me feel as sour as the Count looked. Was I really no further forward than when I'd first arrived in Strelsau? It seemed I was further back, since Grabenau had actually written me off for execution, while Vladek and the Count had obviously lost all enthusiasm for my cause. I wasn't allowing, of course, for the depressing effect on them of being shut up all this time in the tower together.

We returned to the subject of the statue.

'On this matter at least your terrorist friends and I can agree: the carving should be returned to Chostok, but to whom it will belong then is another thorny problem. I think you will find that once order is restored in Karapata this valuable antique as well as the building it comes from will be reclaimed by the Catholic Church.'

The Count walked over to the window as he said this and exclaimed:

'Look! Your friends are already taking action.'

Two soldiers, accompanied by several others, were carrying the statue, still in its sacking and looking like a corpse, across the broad expanse of snow from the watch-tower to the courtyard entrance. Snow had stopped falling some time in the night and it was a brilliant sunny day. Standing next to Vladek and watching the scene – which could have been a funeral procession from an art film, except that several of the men were laughing and talking in loud voices – I remembered a previous idea.

'We still haven't located Flavia's body,' I said. 'It's surely worth looking in King Rudolf's grave at Zenda? Then we can use the occasion of a state funeral for Flavia to reveal that she had descendants.'

'This is not a bad idea,' said the Count, 'except that we are in no position to pursue it.'

'Perhaps I might persuade my friends to set you free for this purpose,' I said.

'That would be most acceptable.'

The prospect made both of them more cheerful. It was agreed – very reluctantly on my part – that Vladek should take photos of me and use them as the basis for painting a series of portraits and selected scenes of my adventures in Ruritania, so that he could organise an exhibition in Strelsau.

'And, of course, Karl, I will include your head-stand in front of the palace, which is one of my masterpieces.'

I had grave doubts about the thought of those masterpieces being used as PR for me – they'd make even statues of Stalin and Lenin look friendly – but at least the real thing, if they ever saw it, could only be an improvement. Vladek fetched his camera and took several rolls of film, solo as well as in groups with the Count and himself and also Magda – dressed, of course, in her fetching ethnic costume and beaming with pleasure at being included.

'Magda is really photogenic,' said Vladek. 'I should think this may easily launch her on a career advertising trips by Air Ruritania to the ski-slopes of Karapata.'

'Our problems do seem trivial,' I said. 'All I'm really asking is to be Chairman of the Ruritanian tourist industry.'

'An excellent approach,' said the Count, 'which could be suggested very seriously to our moderate friends in governing circles. You may be a weathercock, Karl Marx, but you have glamour – not only your story and mysterious ancestry but even I must say – with your newly grown hair – your personal appearance. Take some more shots of Karl with Magda, Tarlenheim! What could be more attractive to tourists and therefore to investors than a small romantic kingdom with mountain scenery in a cheap currency area?'

'The Switzerland of the East!' said Vladek.

'The Norway of the South!' said the Count.

'But unless your German friends make it up with my friends the terrorists,' I said, 'the ski-resorts and mountain scenery will be unsafe for tourists.'

I returned to the other part of the castle to negotiate their release and found the whole place in turmoil over my disappearance. Fisher had come back, but said nothing about seeing me. His story was that, not being able to sleep, he'd heard a noise in the watch-tower, gone to investigate and found the statue fallen over and the floor disintegrating. This was why orders had been given to bring the statue into the castle. Obviously Fisher would have preferred not to reveal its whereabouts, but had settled for pre-empting any confrontation with me. Yelena was still sleeping and had not been disturbed; Michael and Vakisch questioned me about where I'd been. I admitted that I'd slipped away to talk to my friends in the tower and, before they could accuse me of double-dealing, broached my plan for releasing them so that they could try to discover Queen Flavia's body and start the process of softening up Strelsau for the restoration of the monarchy. Michael was suspicious, of course, but Vakisch immediately saw the advantages:

'We lose nothing by letting them go. Even if they fail to achieve anything positive, we at least can only gain by demonstrating our confidence and good-will in this way, ahead of the results of the inquiry at Kapitsa.'

I added, on the spur of the moment, that I thought if Michael would send them in the Range Rover to the nearest army check-point in the foothills, the Count would undertake to send the car and driver back and indeed make a permanent gift of the car to Michael. True, it was damaged goods and in practice he owned the thing already, but I had the feeling this would tip the scale and it did. Michael had probably never actually owned a decent car in his life and he couldn't conceal his greedy delight.

When Vakisch and I visited the tower to convey the good news and I mentioned my improvised bribe, the Count looked pained for a moment and then gave a huge smile:

'With all my heart!' he said. 'I would never care to be seen in such a badly used car, but we have found the perfect owner for it.'

Now Vakisch looked pained, but neither he nor I mentioned the Count's comment to Michael and early the next morning the car took Vladek and the Count away to freedom.

With the Count's approval, I moved into the tower and so did Yelena. She was not at all well. The guerrillas had one or two paramedics with minimal knowledge of first-aid and how to use a thermometer, but seriously ill soldiers were simply packed off back to their homes or to Chostok Hospital as civilians.

I visited Yelena, lying glassy-eyed and feverish in the Count's four-poster bed, but she hardly seemed aware of me. Magda brought her water and aspirin and tried to tempt her to eat without success. I told Michael she ought to be seen by a proper doctor, then rang the hospital at Chostok and asked to speak to Dr Moritz. He was unavailable but the telephonist said he'd ring back.

'Who shall I say rang?'

'Karl.'

'Karl who?'

'Just Karl – at Previce Castle. As urgently as possible.'

Dr Moritz rang back after about ten minutes and when he heard my voice said with heavy sarcasm:

'Sir! What can I do for you?'

I explained the problem, but he wasn't at all sympathetic.

213

'Tell her to come and see me, if she cares to!'

'Dr Moritz,' I said, 'I've arrange for our mutual friends here to return to Strelsau. They went early this morning in the Count's own car, so we are left without any comfortable form of transport. Won't you, please, come and see her here?'

'You must absolutely guarantee on your personal word of honour,' he said, 'that if I come I shall not have to meet any of the terrorists nor be detained by them nor under any circumstances have any of my property – neither car nor medical equipment – stolen.'

'You talk as if they were just bandits.'

'In my opinion they are.'

'I will guarantee all those things, of course.'

'Then I'll be with you in an hour or so.'

I went to tell Michael of the promises I'd made. Michael unwillingly agreed to have nothing to do with the doctor but warned me not to allow him to administer any medicine to Yelena.

'Then how is he to cure her?'

'Let him prescribe and we'll fetch the stuff ourself from Chostok.'

'You think he'd try to poison her?'

'This man is one of our worst enemies.'

It was perhaps the first time I'd realised quite how bitter the personal hatred was between the two sides – Englishmen tend to think this sort of thing only happens in Ireland or the Middle East.

Before Moritz arrived I had a visit from the regular army corporal and the driver of Colonel Maggerling's 4×4. They were ready to leave for Kapitsa but wanted to say goodbye to Yelena first. No one but Michael, Vakisch, Magda and presumably Fisher (whom I'd not set eyes on since he'd tried to murder me), had been told Yelena was ill, so I asked the two soldiers to wait.

The doctor arrived in an up-market Skoda and, after a moment's hesitation, consented to shake my hand.

'You did well to get our friends out. It was high time and just in time.'

'Just in time for what?'

'That is my conjecture. Where is the patient?'

He examined her and then joined me in the sitting-room for coffee.

'A schnapps?' I asked.

'No thank you.'

'It comes from the Count's own drinks-cabinet.'

'Then I will. The patient needs to be moved.'

'Moved where?'

'To hospital. It may be only anaemia, but it could be worse. She

214

needs tests and I'm afraid Chostok is not properly equipped to carry out such tests.'

'Bilavice?'

'No. It's possible they could do them in Kapitsa, but really I'd recommend Strelsau.'

'You know that's impossible.'

'The only alternatives, then, are Kapitsa or Vlod.'

'But how are we to get her there?'

'You have the full resources of the Ruritanian Army of the True Faith – isn't that what these bandits call themselves? I will write out an admission chit for her and you can pick up some medicine in Chostok to tide her over, but I'm afraid, Mr . . . Karl, you will either have to get her to one of those hospitals or put your trust in heavenly powers, which it must be said she shows little sign at present of possessing.'

He drank his schnapps and stood up.

'May I offer one further word of advice? Non-professional. If you could shake off your association with these people, I believe you'd find a lot of support. You might even have mine. We Catholics are natural royalists, but the bloody True Faith – that we can't stomach. As for your journey with her ladyship . . .' He waved his hand at the ceiling. 'She may or may not survive it, but she's unlikely to survive by staying here.'

After the doctor had gone I passed this grim message to Michael and Vakisch and when they'd visited Yelena and got some sort of consent – or at least not dissent – from her, they finally agreed to the journey. The two soldiers would have to take her in the colonel's 4×4 and since it was already late in the day they agreed to postpone leaving until first light. I offered to go too, but Michael wouldn't even consider the idea: they couldn't risk losing two of their major assets at once, he said. I was pleased he considered me a major asset, but, with or without his permission, I was determined to go.

The only reason I had for not leaving was Magda. She was a sweet girl and already devoted to me; and although I was, of course, very upset by Yelena's illness, the pleasure of sharing the nursing with Magda partly made up for it. We agreed to take turns sitting up with Yelena through that night. My turn was first, so that I could get some sleep before concealing myself, with the corporal's connivance, under the luggage at the back of the 4×4. But when Magda came to take over I was reluctant to leave her. It was a

215

long and large bed and Yelena's legs didn't reach all the way down. Magda and I sat either side at the foot of the bed and talked in low voices:

'I wish you were coming too, Magda.'

'Who would look after the castle?'

'Your mother.'

'She only knows how to cook.'

'You could shut the tower. The rest of the castle is being looked after anyway by the soldiers.'

'Looked after!' she was scandalized. 'What would happen if they got into the tower?'

'Can you keep them out, all on your own?'

'They don't frighten me. They're just farm-boys, dressed up.'

'I should think they fancy you.'

'They'll none of them have me.'

'Who will have you, Magda?'

'Whoever I choose.'

'What will he look like?'

She was silent.

'Fair or dark hair?'

She still said nothing, then giggled and quickly covered her mouth with her hand and glanced anxiously at Yelena.

'Come on!' I said, 'What colour hair?'

'Dark. Maybe red.'

She giggled again.

'You like red hair?'

'Some sorts.'

'Not very common round here.'

'Not common at all.'

'What colour eyes?'

She stared into mine, her lips tightly pressed together.

'Greenish, I should think.'

'Green*ish*. That doesn't sound very exciting. What about blue?'

She stared some more.

'No, not blue.'

I reached my hand across the duvet and touched hers. Yelena stirred slightly and her foot moved under the duvet near our hands.

'You're laughing at me, Magda.'

'No, I'm not.'

'I heard you.'

'I wasn't laughing at *you*.'

'Who were you laughing at?'

'Myself – because it's obvious who I meant.'

'Who did you mean? I can't guess.'

'You can.'

I edged my bottom further on to the bed and stretched across to touch her hair.

'I'll tell you the colours I like,' I said.

'Oh yes?'

'Fair hair and brown eyes. Can you guess who that is?'

'No. Not at all.'

'We're both very bad at guessing.'

I leant across and kissed her. She responded with enthusiasm, but as I moved closer still I sat on Yelena's foot. She groaned, opened her eyes and said something very confused:

'Your solution,' she said. 'Borgia's betrayal.'

Magda and I sprang apart and Magda stood up. I remained where I was – men are more inconvenienced than women on these occasions.

'What did you say, Yelena?' I asked. 'Did you mean Caesar Borgia?'

'We didn't mean any harm,' said Magda, very pink and flustered, pulling her blouse straight and smoothing down her long skirt.

Yelena's eyes closed again and she seemed to go back to sleep. Magda looked at me fiercely and I got up and went to the door. Magda joined me there.

'We shouldn't have done that,' she said.

'I'm not married to her,' I said. ' "Betrayal" is going too far. She doesn't even love me.'

'You love her, don't you? Or why are you going to Kapitsa with her?'

Good question, to which I had no answer, especially since I didn't want to discourage or hurt Magda. Instead I kissed her again, just outside the door, for a short minute or two, and then tore myself away:

'Goodnight, beautiful Magda! Wake me in four hours!'

We didn't reach Kapitsa the next night – the roads were too slow – but stayed in a farm-house with one of the corporal's legion of relations. Yelena slept most of the way on the back seat, her head on my lap after I'd emerged from my hiding-place among the luggage, and seemed better for the medicine we'd picked up when it was still barely light at Chostok Hospital.

217

We pushed on again the following morning well before sunrise –
I was afraid Michael might find some way of pursuing us when he
discovered me missing – and arrived in sight of Kapitsa more or less
at dawn. As we descended the last hill, with a view of the airfield,
we saw an aircraft take off, rise and circle. It was followed by a
second and a third, then all three disappeared in formation towards
the mountains.

'What's going on?' I asked the corporal.

He was staring up through the top of the windscreen at the
disappearing aircraft and didn't reply at once.

'Could be a training flight,' said the driver.

'At this hour?' said the corporal.

'Were they military aircraft?' I asked.

'They were,' he said. 'That must have been just about the whole
Kapitsan airforce we saw there – all of it that's operational.'

'Some sort of reconnaissance?'

'They were carrying bombs.'

'Bombs?'

We were in the outer streets of Kapitsa, heading towards the
hospital, which the corporal said was on the far side of the town,
near the barracks and the airfield, when there was an enormous noise
of firing – not hand-guns or even machine-guns, but big explosives.
Yelena sat up suddenly and looked around.

'It's what I dreamed. Your Borgia solution.'

'What do you mean, Yelena?'

'You told me how you'd solve the problem at Kapitsa and that's
what they're doing.'

The streets were empty and the town not all that large, so
we'd almost reached the neighbourhood of the hospital by the time
the first outbreak of firing was followed by a second. Then a sheet
of flame rose suddenly behind the buildings in front of us and as we
turned a corner the driver braked suddenly. Through a brown cloud
of foul-smelling exhaust we saw two tanks trundling along the broad
street that ran beside the perimeter fence of the Second Regiment's
barracks. Their turrets were turned away from us and gently rocking,
as the guns pumped shells into the burning and disintegrating huts
nearest to the fence. Beyond that we could hear explosions and see
flames shooting up from other parts of the barracks. Our driver took
us straight back round the corner in reverse.

On our way out of Kapitsa we ran into a company of infantry. Their column of lorries, led by an armoured personnel carrier, had stopped along a street leading to the barracks. The corporal thought they must be part of the force assigned to seize the barracks, but, because the infantry was mainly Slav, were being kept out of the way until the tanks and artillery, mostly manned by Germans, had done their worst. We passed most of the column without trouble but the last lorry was beside a parked car and blocking the road and we had to pull up while it manoeuvred to let us past. I pushed Yelena down on the floor and tried to look as much as possible like an officer in civilian dress; the driver and corporal made friendly gestures towards the sergeant who was standing in the road guiding the lorry and the one in front of it into new positions. As the road became free and we started to move again, this sergeant suddenly became suspicious or perhaps just officious and stooped down to peer at me.

'Thank you, sergeant,' I said in a lordly way, raising my hand to shield my face. 'Carry on!'

He looked puzzled and, as the driver accelerated away, began to wave and shout.

'He's only just noticed we've got Second Regiment flashes on the car,' said the corporal. 'What a dozy fellow! But he'll be wiser to keep quiet about it or they'll strip him of his stripes.'

The thought that we were so easily identifiable and that the next column we met might be more alert, made the driver cautious and at one point we stayed under a bridge for a good ten minutes while a helicopter circled overhead. Yelena was sitting up in the seat now, very white and tense, but conscious and composed.

'Are you feeling better?' I asked.

'How could I feel better? Unless it's better to know the worst than to dread it.'

'You really expected this to happen?'

'Ever since they released the prisoners at Christmas. You were right and I knew you were right. They should not have released them without the President's personal guarantee.'

'Didn't they have that?'

'Not in writing. They had a promise on the telephone.'

'I don't see what difference it makes. This was done by the President's government. He's ultimately responsible for what's happening.'

'It was I who advised them to release the prisoners against the promise on the telephone. I am responsible.'

We could still hear tank and artillery fire in the distance and imagining what it must be like for our friends in the barracks made us all silent and morose. It was certainly then, thinking about the young officers who had saved me from execution and received me so enthusiastically in their mess, desperately racking my brain for some way of getting back at the treacherous bastards pounding them into oblivion, that I decided my family motto had served me long enough.

'There must be something we can do,' I said.

'Just get the hell out,' said the corporal, 'unless you mean suicide.'

'Vlod is two or three hours away,' said the driver, 'and we've got about a gallon of fuel. We have to do something about that.'

We found a petrol station, but it was still early and although the whole town must have been woken by the bombardment, the people were staying indoors. The petrol-station looked completely deserted, but there were living-quarters above it. The corporal went round the side and hammered on a door and I thought I saw a curtain move.

'Shoot it open, corporal!' I shouted for the curtain to hear, 'or put a grenade through the letter-box!'

'I wish we had a grenade,' he said.

'Then at least pretend you have!'

I took his gun and fired a short burst in the air. A thin, terrified man with a coat wrapped round his pyjamas quickly came to the door and we got our fuel, but while the tank was being filled and I was pacing up and down near the office, I got something even more valuable: a fresh idea, or rather an old one in a new light.

Ruritania is still way behind western Europe in the matter of ads and this anyway was a repair garage with a couple of pumps rather than a filling-station with a shop in western style. But there was one small ad – more of a sticker – attached to a corner of the grimy office window. The ad showed a big black tyre against a red background and in big white letters across the bottom: 'COSSACK TYRES'.

Leaving the petrol-station we saw the three aircraft again, returning from the mountains; but we only discovered that evening, after we'd left Yelena at Vlod Hospital and found rooms for ourselves in the town, that the Ruritanian Army had not only gloriously recaptured the barracks of the mutinous Second Regiment in Kapitsa, but also destroyed the dam and hydro-electric plant at Sebrikov. The province of Karapata would have to survive the rest of the winter without power-supplies. Given the nature of the people we were up against I don't think anyone can blame me for taking the action I did.

23

Eastern and
Western Approaches

The province of Plotla is mostly flat – part of the northern European plain extending from Britain to the Urals. In theory you could take a telescope up to Highgate and pick out the mountain behind Ekaterinburg, where Lenin had the Tsar and his family murdered. In practice you'd only see a yellow cloud of bad air over the ex-Soviet empire.

The landscape round Vlod is a wasteland of industrial development. When the communists came to power in Strelsau after the Second War they looked at the ancient farming lands of Plotla, studied the methods of Stalin, the Great Leader, and drew up a series of plans for improving yields, providing modern machinery and housing the workers. Then they ordered factories built to manufacture tractors, cranes, harvesters, fertilisers and building materials and sat back to await spectacular results. Since everybody got paid simply for being employed and the only incentive to the managers was siphoning off funds for themselves and rising up the system by providing illusory productivity statistics, the results were indeed spectacular: comprehensive pollution, acres of shoddily-built, obsolete factories and housing blocks and the ruination of thousands of square miles of good agricultural land.

In post-communist Plotla the few remaining farmers continue to cultivate their fields with spades and hoes and hand-held ploughs and they carry their stunted crops in horse- or ox-drawn carts. Amongst all this desolation the only fully functional and up-to-date institution is Vlod Hospital. Financed by international aid, newly equipped and expanded by the post-communist democracy, visited by distinguished foreign specialists, this hospital is at the sharp end of modern research into the poisonous effects and experimental treatment of 'Soviet sickness'.

The first tests on Yelena were inconclusive, but she seemed so much recovered after a blood-transfusion that I wondered if she was

221

seriously ill at all. I found her in a ward crowded with the apathetic casualties of my namesake's vision of the future. She was propped up against the pillows reading a book in Russian.

'They asked me for your next-of-kin,' I said.

'I have an aunt in Kiev,' she said.

'I was tempted to say Jesus,' I said, 'but I thought you'd prefer to remain anonymous, so I just gave my own name.'

She put down her book and looked at me inscrutably for a while.

'It was kind of you to bring me all the way here, Karel.'

'Not at all. I came as a favour to myself.'

'You don't have to sit here and talk to me if you don't want to.'

'What else should I want?'

'It must be boring for you without somebody to play with on the bed.'

'I'm sorry. Magda and I thought you were asleep.'

'You have no obligations to me, as you said yourself.'

'It was insensitive, I realise that. I can only say I'm sorry.'

She pointed to my leg, pulled up sideways on the bed.

'Did she sew your trousers for you?'

I told her then about Fisher's attempt to knife me in the watch-tower. When I'd finished she was silent for some time, with her eyes lowered so that I thought she might be falling asleep.

'The statue anyway,' I said, 'is safe. I saw them bringing it into the castle next morning.'

She still said nothing and I switched to the subject of Kapitsa. The barracks, I told her, had been overrun, with many casualties, and the Second Regiment had finally surrendered. The surviving officers were awaiting trial. I saw then that she was crying.

'Yelena,' I said, 'I should never have told you this. It was completely stupid. Insensitive again. It was only because I'm used to thinking of you as so tough, as responsible for everything . . .'

'I am responsible, Karel. For everything, as you say. For believing in Fisher. For believing what he told me about myself and my mission. For telling people what was not true, for leading them into disaster. And for Kapitsa.'

'People have some responsibility for themselves,' I said. 'Or do you think they're just Gadarene pigs, ready to jump off any precipice if you tell them to? On the other hand, it's true you made me really believe I could be king of Ruritania.'

'That's one thing I can't take all the responsibility for.'

'I think you must,' I said, moving closer to her and taking her hand, which was wet with the tears she'd been wiping off her face.

222

'If I'd never met you I'm sure I'd have got discouraged and left the country long ago.'

'You'll have to do that now. What's the alternative? When the spring comes they'll easily drive Michael out of the mountains.'

'Unless we can surprise them.'

'Karel, you must be realistic. The Ruritanian Army may have only three squadrons of aircraft and perhaps ten tanks and a few howitzers, but that is more than enough against people with none of these things.'

'Supposing we found friends who did have these things?'

'British? Americans? French? Which of them would support Slavs against Germans in order to turn a democracy into a kingdom?'

'I was thinking of your own countrymen and our neighbours, the Ukrainians.'

She blew her nose with a handkerchief from under the pillow and slowly shook her head.

'They'd be mad to get involved and never would. They have troubles enough of their own.'

'Including their own soldiers. About ten miles from here there's a whole regiment of Cossacks waiting to go back to a country that doesn't want them, has nowhere to house them and nothing for them to do.'

She smiled, looked interested for a moment, then shook her head again.

'It's a clever thought, Karel, but . . .'

'Five or six hundred of them, according to the corporal, with up to sixty tanks and some artillery. They wouldn't have to fight, only move in the wrong direction – from the Ruritanian Army's point of view.'

'They couldn't do that without orders from Ukraine.'

'That depends, doesn't it? On what they think of their bosses and how bored they are with doing nothing and having nothing in prospect. Why not ask them, at least? Why don't *you* ask them – in their language? They only have to move west instead of east and if they wanted to stay – Ruritania may have more to offer them than Ukraine.'

'You remember what Machiavelli says about mercenaries and auxiliaries: "unprofitable and dangerous"?'

'Yes, but how does he define them? Those forces which are not the prince's own, neither his subjects, his citizens nor his servants. I think we should ask the Cossacks to become citizens of Ruritania.'

'This would be a terrible risk, Karel.'

She was looking tired again and didn't want to argue any more. I left the hospital and went to meet the corporal and driver for a drink and cheap meal. It threatened to be our last, since we were all out of cash and it looked as if we might have to flog the 4×4, which the others had spent the day repainting a violent yellow.

The news from Strelsau was mixed. After noisy scenes in parliament during which the Slav deputies demanded the sacking and trial of the generals responsible both for this latest atrocity and the previous one, the junior minister who had promised an inquiry resigned.

The prime minister, however, refused to be held responsible. The minister's promise, he claimed, had not been endorsed by the government, which regarded the Kapitsa mutiny as an army matter. No government, he said, could make such promises under duress and he had always maintained that the mutineers would have to release their hostages before there could be any talk of an inquiry. True, they *had* released them, but the government was still considering its response when the army decided to seize the barracks. This was a purely military decision and the generals had been quite within their rights: no army could make terms with mutineers. Regardless of the rights or wrongs of the mutineers' demands, mutiny had to be suppressed and punished or all army discipline would be at an end.

He conceded, however, that there was some confusion between the political and military aspects of this 'complicated case' and he proposed to start a fresh inquiry into the whole affair which would 'subsume under its remit' the original inquiry into the Kapitsa Atrocity. Meanwhile, the trial of the captured officers would be postponed and the prime minister hoped this would provide a breathing-space and a chance to draw back from 'unleashing ethnic hatred'. He meant, presumably, that there was a real danger of civil war or at least of Plotla and Karapata splitting off from Strelsau, as Slovakia had split off from the Czechs.

So the prime minister wriggled free and the hard-line generals remained in control of the army. The President stayed above it all. No one suggested that he had endorsed the handing-over of the hostages in return for an inquiry. When I visited Yelena next day I pressed her about the promise on the phone to the officers of the Second Regiment.

'Was this the man himself speaking or just somebody in his office?'

'It was Slobodjak himself. They demanded to speak to him personally and at last he did come to the phone and the officer recognised his voice. Otherwise I would never have advised them to release the hostages.'

'Then if this could be proved . . .'

'How could it?'

Yelena was so much recovered that she was out of bed and we were talking in a small visitors' lounge next to the ward. On the walls were coloured photographs of sunny Ruritania: Zenda Castle, a rural landscape from Plotla and the Sebrikov dam in the mountains of Karapata. We sat in plastic armchairs drawn up close together so as not to have to raise our voices. Yelena wore a long hospital nightdress – some cheap cotton material printed with small pink roses, but her dressing-gown was her own white one, which I'd last caught a glimpse of in the gallery of the Sebrikov chalet. Her shoes were the soft white ones she'd used for her appearances before the faithful in Chostok. The improvement in her health and these mixed reminders of the history of our relationship had a powerful effect on me. She was both the Yelena I'd known and a new one I wasn't yet sure of – somebody less authoritative, more approachable. Perhaps it was I that had changed. I wasn't the pupil now or part of an entourage. Our relationship was more equal.

'There's a money problem,' I said. 'We're going to have to sell the car to pay for our rooms and food.'

'I have a little money still,' she said, 'which I'll give you. But don't sell the car. I want to visit the Cossacks in a day or two.'

'Seriously?'

'The consultant here is a good friend of their Colonel and has promised me an introduction.'

'Am I to go too?'

'Not immediately. But I must have my own vehicle and driver and bodyguard before putting my head into this lions' den. It's a question of status. People who have escaped from the Soviet system are very conscious of status. Above all, if you should pay them a visit later, as King Karel, you don't want to turn up in a taxi.'

'I couldn't afford one. But I must warn you that Orlin and the corporal have painted the colonel's car yellow.'

'Yellow?'

'I'm afraid so. They said it was the cheapest colour they could get.'

'A good yellow?'

'Buttercup? Dandelion? I'm not good at colours. No, it's more the colour of the chemical cloud over Vlod.'

'Shall we call it "royal yellow"?' she said.

Yelena's money wasn't enough to last us more than a few days. However my original rucksack – which I'd rejoined at Previce Castle and brought to Vlod – contained not only Hackney Library's copy of *The Prince* but also Colonel Danzing's authorization for my weekly allowance from the bank in Strelsau. I tried it on the bank's branch in Vlod, but they said it had to be drawn in Strelsau. It was very likely, of course, that Colonel Danzing would have stopped the allowance altogether. On the other hand, he might not have bothered – I'd drawn nothing after the first week and the next he'd heard of me I'd been waiting to be shot. Failing the bank, I would have to find Vladek or the Count and borrow from them. There was some risk, of course, in going to Strelsau. I might run into Grabenau or one of the ex-hostages from Kapitsa and be recognised as the escaped terrorist Ed Fenton/Karl Berg. Still, the risk of running out of money completely was greater. I bought a cheap and nasty grey fur hat (synthetic, not an ex-cat) to disguise my hair and a train ticket to Strelsau and went.

Strelsau was under a cloud of black rain – 'Communist Five-Year-Plan rain' or 'Stalin's rain', as a student I met in the station bar called it. I asked him what he thought about events in Kapitsa and he told me it was no more than the next segment of the wheel of history.

'What's that?'

'The generals will take over now. After communism, democracy; after democracy, the junta.'

'And after that?'

'Dictatorship. The biggest general will seize power.'

'You really believe that?'

He shrugged. He didn't much care. He was cynical. He'd emerged from school, he said, in a cloud of euphoria at believing himself part of the free world, only to discover that his part of the free world was an impoverished slum and that if he really wanted to be free he'd have to cheat his way into the rich part.

Colonel Danzing hadn't cancelled my drawing-power at the bank, but I wasn't so foolish as to demand the whole sum available. In the first place I might be robbed and in the second place I didn't want the cashier consulting the manager and starting an investigation into my credentials. For the same reason I rejected my first idea of asking them to extend the drawing power to their branch in Vlod. I took the money mostly in dollars, since the kruna had devalued catastrophically since I'd last been in Strelsau.

After buying myself an umbrella against Stalin's rain and some new clothes and stationery, I found a cafe and settled down to compose a coded message from Machiavelli informing Colonel Danzing I was still alive. I congratulated him on resigning his embassy under a corrupt government but hoped he would soon resume it under a grateful king and I asked him to apologise on my behalf to *Open Sesame*, the business magazine to which I had so far sent no copy at all. Understanding business opportunities in Ruritania, I explained, required a lot of background knowledge, which I had been busy acquiring. The passage I chose for my code began on page 110:

> A prince, therefore, who is wise and prudent, cannot or ought not to keep his parole, when the keeping of it is to his prejudice, and the causes for which he promised removed. Were men all good this doctrine was not to be taught, but because they are wicked and not likely to be punctual with you, you are not obliged to any such strictness with them; nor was there ever any prince that wanted lawful pretence to justify his breach of promise . . . Let a prince, therefore, do what he can to preserve his life, and continue his supremacy, the means which he uses shall be thought honourable, and be commended by everybody; because the people are always taken with the appearance and event of things, and the greatest part of the world consists of the people . . .

When I'd finished I used the cafe's phone to ring the BBC's office in Strelsau and asked for Clare Studebaker.

'Who's speaking?'

'A friend of Ed Fenton, the English journalist.'

'She's not available at the moment. Have you any message?'

'She may or may not be aware that Fenton went missing in Karapata some months ago and I have some very hot news for her. I'll be waiting outside the Cathedral at half past three. She must not inform the police, but I've no objection if she brings a minder or two from your office to stay at a distance and keep an eye on the encounter.'

There was a risk, of course, that they might inform the police, but I thought it more likely Clare Studebaker would prefer a story to an arrest.

It was still raining as I waited on the cathedral steps. A few people went in and out and hurried through the square, but the weather was too dismal for there to be any other loiterers. I was beginning to stamp my feet and think about giving up, when a white Citroen stopped at the far side of the square. After a few minutes Clare Studebaker got out, put up her umbrella and walked fastidiously across the wet cobbles. She was dressed in a double-breasted black raincoat with black leggings and her umbrella was scarlet. I raised and lowered my own umbrella a few times to show I was the person she was looking for.

'Thanks for coming,' I said in English when she stopped at a cautious distance.

'I know your voice,' she said. 'Where have I seen you before?'

'At the President's Palace,' I said, 'upside-down. But I wasn't wearing a hat.'

'The message I got was from a journalist called Ed Fenton. I checked with the Embassy and they said there were rumours he was in Karapata with the rebels.'

'He was,' I said, 'but now he's standing in front of you.'

I pulled out my passport, flipped it open and showed her the photo with the shaven head. She still looked dubious and showed signs of bolting, less from fear that I might assault her than that I might be wasting her time. Her mouth was tight with self-importance and her eye hard with suspicion that I wasn't important enough.

'What do you want to tell me?'

'I can tell you a lot of things,' I said, 'but not now. The story I have for you – and it's quite free – is simply this: when the officers of the Second Regiment in Kapitsa handed over their hostages at Christmas, they did so only because they were promised by the President himself – on the phone – that there would be an immediate inquiry into the Kapitsa Atrocity and that the barracks would not be attacked. As you know, that promise was broken and no word has got out that the President personally made it.'

'What's your evidence?'

'My evidence comes directly from the officers themselves, but they're obviously in no position to substantiate it. The only other person who could do that would be the President. I'm suggesting you ask him.'

'What's your motive for telling me this?'

'Somebody's lying – or at least omitting to tell the truth,' I said. 'I'd hate to think it was the good and honourable President

228

Slobodjak. On the other hand, I've met these officers myself – in fact I owe my life to them – and if they say they spoke to the President, I'm inclined to believe them.'

'If he did make that promise,' she said, 'he's in dire trouble. I doubt if he could admit it.'

'But if he did, what then?'

'A constitutional crisis, I should think. Something would have to give: the government, the Minister of Defence, the Chief of Staff or the President himself – or the whole bunch of them.'

'So ask him and see! And if he denies it – you're a very distinguished and experienced journalist, Ms Studebaker – just take note of how he denies it and see if you believe him!'

With that I inclined my head, bobbed my umbrella and hurried away – paying her back for the way she'd walked off on me in the palace square, but more importantly, I hoped, leaving my message to fester in her mind, like a piece of shrapnel in a wound. I'd have liked to get to know her better over coffee or a drink, but I couldn't risk removing my hat, being recognised as a Rassendyll and giving her another story which I wasn't yet ready for the world to know.

24

The Cavalry

The original Cossacks came west with Genghis Khan. They were Tatars on horses. Until the Russian Revolution in 1917 they lived in self-governing communities called 'hosts' in Russia, Ukraine, Lithuania and Poland – the mutual borders of those countries came and went like ectoplasm – and contracted their military services to Polish kings or Russian Tsars or their enemies. The Cossack hosts operated a system of compulsory military service (starting at 18 and lasting twenty years) more Spartan than the Spartans'. In the 16th century the Polish kings invited them in as military colonists to protect their borders and in the 19th and early 20th centuries the Tsars used them to quell revolutions. Most Cossacks fought for the Whites in the civil war after the Russian Revolution and Lenin abolished all their privileges. Stalin first forcibly collectivised them and then allowed them to form cavalry divisions within the Soviet army. The deal I was proposing to offer this particular group of them was like every other deal they'd ever made in their long history of semi-independence within other people's territories.

Yelena gave me these facts when I got back from Strelsau. She'd driven in the pollution yellow 4×4 to their barracks outside Vlod, talked to Colonel Stavrilev and discovered that the whole regiment was infuriated by the events in Kapitsa. They sided, naturally, with the Slavs and couldn't understand why the Slav elements in the Ruritanian Army didn't beat the hell out of the German elements. They had not appreciated that the heavy weapons were all on the German side.

'Perhaps they could borrow yours,' Yelena said jokingly to the Colonel and told him of the guerrilla activities in Karapata. 'But they too only have small arms and will be lucky to survive beyond the spring.'

Stavrilev was sympathetic, but the mention of spring depressed him. That was the date fixed for his own regiment's return to

Ukraine and he thought that, bad as their conditions were in the run-down barracks near Vlod, they would be far worse off when they got home and had to crowd into barracks already occupied by other regiments. There would be resentment and hostility on both sides and for him personally life would be a perpetual misery of resolving quarrels, punishing his own men and alternately mollifying and trying to screw concessions out of the army bureaucracy above him.

Yelena shifted the discussion to history and listened to Stavrilev's account of Cossack heroism through the centuries before pitching in with a potted version of Ruritanian history, in particular the romantic story of how the kingdom was saved a century ago by a visiting Englishman who happened to be the King's distant cousin and double. Stavrilev was intrigued and wanted to know what happened to the Queen and her gentleman Englishman afterwards. Yelena told him and then revealed that Rudolf Rassendyll's great-grandson was even now in Ruritania to claim his great-grandmother's kingdom. Stavrilev liked that idea but assumed it would be equally unwelcome to democrats and Slavs. Yelena said he was partly right and partly wrong. The would-be King was indeed claiming a German inheritance, but he had actually fought in the ranks of the Slav guerrillas and been under sentence of death at Kapitsa before his identity was recognised and he was rescued. It was in fact this very rescue which had led to the latest atrocity. Furthermore, she said, she knew the man quite well and he was at present staying *incognito* in Vlod. Would the Colonel care to meet him?

The upshot was that I was invited to dinner in the officers' mess in a week's time. Yelena insisted, however, that I would be coming only as plain Mr Karel Berg, since it was vital that no rumour of my existence should seep out either to the Ruritanian government or the authorities in Ukraine. She made this stipulation, she told me, partly for the reasons of security she gave the Colonel, but partly also because she thought I lacked the clothes to be anything but *incognito*.

Yelena was back in bed, completely exhausted by her expedition to the Cossacks, but buoyed up by her success. She seemed to have forgotten any reservations she'd originally had about the risks. She was delighted by the sheer effrontery of the idea, its historical aptness – given the Cossacks' long history of riding in to the rescue of kings – and the revival, after near despair, of her own hopes for the Slav people of Ruritania. But she didn't mention either her mission for the True Faith or her illness. The two probably went together.

231

'I'm just tired,' she said, when I asked if she knew any more about what was wrong with her.

'But you're having more tests?'

'Of course. You can't stay in this hospital without having tests. It's their *raison d'être*.'

I kissed her forehead as I left. It was clammy. Her eyes looked deeper in their sockets, with dark patches underneath. The doctor told me he knew nothing for certain yet, but he hoped for the best and would be giving her another transfusion.

Clare Studebaker did me proud. She obtained a televised interview with the President to ask him about the minister's resignation and the crisis over Kapitsa; and when he'd served up some bland pudding to the same recipe as the prime minister's, she suddenly asked him point-blank if it was true that the mutineers had released their hostages only against his personal promise of an inquiry and no assault on the barracks.

This interview was not, of course, broadcast in Ruritania and I didn't discover its exact contents until later, when Clare showed me a transcript which left no doubt whatever that my bomb had exploded and blown off the great man's trousers. He admitted he'd spoken to an officer in the barracks, but denied making the promises attributed to him. Why, then, Clare pressed him, did the mutineers release the hostages? Perhaps they had misunderstood him, was the feeble reply.

'A fatal misunderstanding for them, Mr President, wasn't it?'

'It was unfortunate. But you should reserve some of your sympathy, Mrs Studebaker, for the officers they were holding hostage. Mutiny, you know, is a terrible crime which no state can be lenient to. I wonder how you think the British would have dealt with this affair? Would they have sent in the SAS?'

'Are you suggesting, Mr President, that even if you had made such a promise and not kept it, that would have been justified in the circumstances?'

'I am certainly saying no such thing.'

'To break a promise of that sort would be wrong in any circumstances?'

'Obviously. One doesn't have to be a philosopher to know that.'

'But should a philosopher of all people speak in such a confused way on such a crucial matter that he can be fatally misunderstood?'

What a terrier!

'I reject that adjective – "confused". I may be an old man, Mrs Studebaker, but I assure you I still have a very clear head. It's possible, of course, that over a long distance line, speaking to an officer understandably wrought up, my speech might be less clear.'

He was pressing every public sympathy button he could see – probably at this point rattling his false teeth.

'So it was a question of their not *hearing* what you said?'

'Not hearing it correctly, I suppose. Since I was not on the receiving end, I can hardly say what they did or did not hear. I'm afraid they must have leapt to unjustified conclusions.'

'But you gave them no firm promise?'

'I've already said so.'

'No promise of any sort?'

'I have answered your question, Mrs Studebaker.'

Although Ruritania in general was not permitted to see this interview, its contents filtered back immediately into parliament and the President's hitherto cast-iron feet began to turn to clay, at least so far as the Slav deputies were concerned. One of them actually suggested that the President seemed to be a hostage himself to German interests and the military high command.

For my appointment with the Cossacks I wore the new clothes I'd bought in Strelsau, a black polo-neck sweater and trousers with a vaguely English tweed jacket to offset the fascist impression. *Incognito* I may have been, but Colonel Stavrilev didn't let that cramp his style. Our pollution- (or royal-) yellow 4×4, with the corporal up front next to the driver and Yelena – restored by her latest transfusion – and me behind, no sooner appeared at the entrance to the camp than the gates were opened, the guards stamped and saluted, and we swept through into the barrack square to find the Colonel with his senior officers and a guard of honour awaiting us outside the mess. The Colonel himself was a handsome clean-shaven man, heavily-built and heavily-medalled, wearing one of those enormous Russian peaked caps designed to keep snow off the shoulders as well as the face, and spoke a little English. He had a loud, encouraging laugh and it was immediately obvious that if he might prove useful to me, I was his answer to prayer – a completely new and unexpected factor which suddenly introduced colour and space into the dreary grey perspective that boxed him in.

We drank quantities of vodka in the mess bar and were on back-slapping terms even before we filed in to dine at the head of a long table where all the regiment's officers were assembled. Yelena drank nothing and made hardly any personal contribution to the conversation. She seemed to see her role purely as that of interpreter. The officers treated her with deference and admiration, but only as a beautiful woman, not as a person possessing any power of her own. This was odd to me, not least because she herself seemed to accept completely their estimate of her as my side-kick. She was conserving her energy, no doubt, and she knew her countrymen better than I did. To them she was the engineer's daughter from Kiev, not the semi-divine leader of a holy war, and she wanted the Cossacks to be impressed by me without reference to her.

As we sat at the head of the table, on either side of Colonel Stavrilev, I looked across at her and couldn't help smiling with pleasure. Many of the officers down the table did the same from time to time – it was a kind of aesthetic and possessive pleasure – they were all happy to be in the company of this attractive person. For me, of course, it was much more. I had come with her, would go away with her, she was my friend and ally. Also, she smiled back at me in the same spirit, not like a teacher approving of the way I had learned my lessons nor even in polite acknowledgment of my smile, but openly, collusively, as if she too was genuinely happy to be sitting opposite me. Colonel Stavrilev intercepted this smile and put his own interpretation on it.

'Queen!' he said to me in English, putting his hand on my shoulder, 'I sink you have Ukrainian Queen.'

I could feel the blood flooding up into my face.

'King first,' I said. 'One step at a time.'

Colonel Stavrilev turned to Yelena and asked a question in their own language, putting his other hand on her shoulder as if he meant to draw us together into his substantial embrace. Yelena, amused by the way I'd blushed and not at all put out herself, made some throwaway answer. The Colonel laughed loudly and translated into English for my benefit.

'She sinks *exactly* same,' he said, 'One sing first.' Then he turned to Yelena and made some further remark in Ukrainian, ordering her, with mock severity, to translate it into German. She hesitated.

'Prosho, Yelena Andriyivna!' he said, pretending to be angry.

'When a man and a woman have exactly the same opinion,' she said, 'it means they are in love.'

She looked at me steadily with a straight face.

'I'm not sure whether this is folk wisdom,' she added, 'or the Colonel's own.'

'Yelena Andriyivna,' I said, and then in Ruritanian, 'I am certainly in love with you.'

'You've been in love with so many,' she said, 'especially in Ruritanian.'

'What is reply?' asked the Colonel in English, 'She takes you?'

'No,' I said, 'she thinks I'm not serious.'

'Not serious?' he said, shocked and, not quite sure if he'd understood the word, turned again to Yelena: 'Ne seryozno?'

Yelena, still smiling, shook her head.

'Tak, doozhe seryozno,' he said, and removing his hands from our shoulders banged himself violently on the chest with them like a cartoon gorilla. 'Ya znayoo!'

'He says he knows,' she translated into German, 'that you are very serious. But of course he doesn't know you as well as I do and I consider it's better he should think of you as very serious, so I will not correct him.'

We went on to talk about the Kapitsa affair and I told the Colonel that it seemed likely the President intended a peaceful resolution but was pre-empted by the military and now implicated in their action. Did this mean, the Colonel asked, that the country would split apart? I said I hoped not, since the majority of Germans were moderate and such a small country could hardly hope to survive by dividing itself. The main problem now, I suggested, was that the once cohesive influence of the President, with his impeccable background as opponent and former victim of the communists, was being eroded by his new attachment to the hard-liners. Ruritania needed a genuine national leader who would stand up to the extremists on both sides and attract loyalty from all the rest. Colonel Stavrilev nodded at Yelena to show this squared with what she'd already told him and then suddenly stood up with his glass in his hand. Everyone else stood up too, but the Colonel gently pushed me down again.

'Our distinguished guest!' he said. 'Karel Berg!'

They all drank to me and sat down.

'Now you,' said Yelena.

I rose and raised my glass.

'Cossacks!' I said, 'Colonel Stavrilev!'

But as I began to sit down again, Yelena said quietly:

'You must tell them now what you want. These are not ordinary soldiers. They are a community as well as a regiment. They make their decisions together, even though the Colonel is their leader.'

'Another improvised speech?' I said. 'You've done this to me before. And this time I've had too much to drink.'

'So have they. Just tell them what you want! There will be no better opportunity.'

I looked down the lines of bemedalled uniforms and the staring faces, mostly flushed, mostly young; many, but not all, with the characteristic Tatar cheekbones, some with thick moustaches, all with short-clipped hair. I had a sense of absurdity, even fear. What if they refused? That would be disappointing, perhaps humiliating, probably the end of my Ruritanian adventure. But what if they accepted? I would be declaring war on a state, I would be hijacking the troops and equipment of a major power, I would be leading the descendants of Genghis Khan's and Stalin's hordes westward again.

Up to now I had dived and shimmied, popped up and popped down again, skirted other people's quarrels and causes, put my crown on and taken it off again like an actor between the stage and the wings. But if they accepted, I was cast for ever as King Karel – most likely failed-King Karel or ex-King Karel or even dead King Karel – but undoubtedly serious King Karel. I glanced at Yelena and remembered her letter – what she'd said about the difference between Rudolf Rassendyll and Queen Flavia. *Of course* he'd slid away – what else could he do? – and of course I should do the same. I looked just like him, I was just like him, I felt at that moment as if I actually *was* him. Privileged, idle, detached Englishmen don't thrust themselves permanently into other people's squalid realities, they do their bit (*Nil Quae Feci*), retire gracefully, casually to their island and leave the natives to strangle themselves in their insoluble and incomprehensible feuds.

I started to sit down and glanced once more, with a deprecating look of apology, at Yelena. She had turned absolutely white and was leaning forward, staring at me with an expression I recognised from the train journey to Kapitsa – that moment when she'd come back to the compartment and found me searching her bag for something to eat. 'Are you a thief?' she'd said – or something like it – with angry contempt. That was more or less what she was saying now, a thousand times more contemptuously, without moving her lips but with the whole force of her personality directed – the laser effect recommended by my gym-instructor Andrzej – through her pale eyes: 'Are you a coward?'

Halfway between sitting down and standing up again I almost lost my balance and had to steady myself by grabbing the outsize shoulder-tab of the officer sitting on my right.

'I'm not completely drunk,' I said, 'even on your royal hospitality. I'll explain why I staggered when I've first told you a story.'

The story was that of Rudolf Rassendyll and Queen Flavia and his decision not to remain King. Then I told them how I'd discovered my own lineage and come to Ruritania for the first time. All this Yelena translated sentence by sentence, so I kept it short and simple.

'The reason I staggered,' I said, 'was this: I was torn between the ghosts of my ancestors rising up inside me. The ghost of Rudolf Rassendyll told me to make the same decision as he did: not to wear a false crown. But the ghost of Queen Flavia told me that my crown would be hers: the true one crushed by German tanks in 1940. And then, as I leant for support on this gentleman next to me, I realised that the decision was not mine at all. I shall never wear any crown – true or false – without your help. What German tanks destroyed only Cossack tanks can replace. And if that's what you decide to do, then your reward will be your own land and village in Ruritania and your own self-governing status subject only to the authority of the crown you restore.'

I sat down without even token applause. I thought, with relief, that I had junked my case, but Yelena told me afterwards that applause was out of place – this was business, not performance or ceremony. She herself showed no sign of relaxing after my speech as I did, pushing my chair back from the table and downing another glass of vodka. She leant her elbows on the table and fixed every subsequent speaker with her laser look, translating everything they said for my benefit, but often abbreviating verbose statements into a few salient points. It was a long session, in which every conceivable opinion for or against was expressed and in which Colonel Stavrilev hardly took part, except occasionally to quell an argument or lead a lost rambler back to base. Many of them put direct questions to me, especially about their degree of independence, their income and housing and their relationship to the Ruritanian Army. I improvised answers as best I could, explaining that my first job would be to re-draft the constitution and that since my power would rest on theirs we would be mutually supportive. I didn't bother to make very careful replies, since I was sure that Yelena, translating them, would re-phrase or even re-invent them as necessary.

At last, when the discussion had become tired and repetitive, the Colonel stood up and demanded a show of hands. There were five against, the odd abstention, but all the rest were in favour of restoring King Karel to his throne.

Only as we reeled away towards dawn, after emptying every

bottle in sight, to the rooms provided for us in the barracks, did Colonel Stavrilev murmur despondently:

'Very few of our tanks actually work, you know.'

25

The Ringmaster

The trouble with the Cossacks' tanks wasn't just that they were old, but that they were tanks at all. Tanks – because they're so heavy – break down and wear out extremely quickly. The best thing to do with a tank, the Colonel told me, is to keep it permanently in mothballs; the next best thing, if you absolutely have to take it about with you, is to carry it on a transporter. The guns on his tanks, he said, were excellent and in good condition, the armour-plating was fine, but the engines and tracks were rubbish. However, he reckoned that if I could give him until spring he might – by cannibalising the rest – have about thirty tanks operational. I asked him if he couldn't at least put the rest in the field.

'No, sir, the most we can put in the field, as I said, is thirty.'

'I meant,' I said, 'literally in the field – in *a* field – semi-camou- flaged, to hide their defects not their presence, a half regiment of threatening hulks. Then the mobile tanks can keep the Ruritanian Army busy – preferably knock it out altogether – while the troops who would have been manning the hulks if they'd been operational can seize the airfield and the town – on foot, if necessary.'

We were in the Colonel's office the day after the decision-taking dinner, all of us in a bad state of health. The Colonel and I had straightforward hangovers, Yelena was exhausted. When she translated my suggestion, the Colonel, shaking his large head and occasionally banging it with his palm to stimulate the cells, took some time to master its details; then his shoulder-tabs began to wobble, his eyes watered, his body shook spasmodically and he laughed so loud and long that the whole thin-walled barracks must have heard it.

'Ne seryozno!' he finally managed to say. 'Rozoomiyoo.'

He spoke at some length in Ukrainian to Yelena, who translated wearily and more briefly.

'The Colonel thinks he understand you now, Karel. You want

the Cossacks to frighten the Ruritanians to death, not shoot them. You want a Cossack circus instead of a battle.'

She changed her tone, became more intense, almost pleading:

'Is this what you really want, Karel?'

'I think it is.'

'You must be absolutely clear, because the Colonel says that if he prepares his troops for a circus he will not be able to make a change at the last moment and deliver a genuine crippling blow.'

The Colonel spoke again and she translated:

'On the other hand, he says he thinks you're probably right – a circus is what's needed. But he is worried about the airforce. He knows it's very weak, but he doesn't like the idea of a circus with no air cover at all. That could turn into a Roman circus, he says, with the Cossacks playing Christians.'

I said I would try to neutralise the airforce and opted for the circus, but the Colonel still saw a problem.

'He can give you a fine performance in Kapitsa,' she said, 'but he doesn't think the tricks would work again for Strelsau. So if the Ruritanian Army is still in good order, undaunted and operational after Kapitsa, you might end up with only half your kingdom.'

'I believe Kapitsa will be enough,' I said.

The end of winter was almost in sight and I left the Cossacks to prepare their circus and Yelena in hospital undergoing further tests, while I went back to Strelsau.

The political situation had become very tense, with a large group of deputies – moderate Germans as well as Slavs – now snapping daily at the government's heels. The inquiry was still being delayed with the excuse that it was difficult to find suitably unbiased people to conduct it. The truth was that the government wanted people biased their way but not generally known to be and there were no such people of sufficient standing.

But they were all still focussed on Kapitsa. Because Karapata was in the hands of the guerrillas and all communications with the rest of the country severed, the bombing of the Sebrikov dam was ignored. It seemed to me that, properly presented, this neglected hard-line atrocity might damage the government and the President far more than Kapitsa.

I phoned Clare Studebaker, introduced myself again as Ed Fenton – she was eager to take another story from him after the success of the first one – and suggested she ask for clearance to visit Bilavice.

I myself would accompany her and see she was well received there. But I warned her not to identify me as Ed Fenton: I could perhaps form part of her team as a spare cameraman or driver.

'But why should I go to Bilavice?'

'Because you'll find that the civilian population is suffering terrible privations as a result of the destruction of their power-supplies. These innocent people are being punished by the government for being hostages to the guerrillas. The Kapitsa scandal is really nothing compared to Sebrikov. There might be some argument for bombarding a mutinous barracks, but surely none at all for destroying a dam and making war on the civilian population. If they don't allow you into Karapata, you can say as much. If they do, you can get pictures and interviews and prove it.'

'What do you get out of this, Mr Fenton?'

'Truth. Justice. Silly things of that sort.'

Apart from any damage she might inflict on the government, I also wanted a meeting with Michael.

My next move was to make contact with the Count. I knew he stayed in a hotel whenever he was in Strelsau and there were only three with four stars: the 'Atena', the 'Frederik' and the 'Royal Elphberg'. I tried the last first and was told the Count was out but would be back later. I left a message with the receptionist that I'd wait for him in the foyer at six o'clock.

'Your name, sir?'

'Karl Marx.'

'As in . . .?'

'As in *Das Kapital*.'

'I will see he gets the message, sir.'

The receptionist's *sangfroid* was exactly what I'd have expected from a hotel patronised by the Count.

I was making these phone calls from Andrzej's gym. He hadn't recognised me when I first walked through his door in my awful fur hat and was even more astonished when I removed it. He'd known me, of course, only as a skinhead. Being a friend of Vladek's, he'd visited the exhibition in the Palace of Youth and been very impressed with the waxwork and the story and personality of Rudolf Rassendyll. He'd even kept a copy of the magazine, one of whose glossy pages I'd seen, on the night of my swim in the River Volzer, pinned to the cabin-wall of the barge; and he brought it out of his office to show me. I admitted the likeness, explained the relationship and swore him to secrecy. He was an arch-royalist – probably all gym-instructors are – and more than happy, indeed much honoured, he said, to have me use his office as a base and sleeping-quarters for as long as I cared to. He told me the Flavia/Rassendyll exhibition was finished but he thought Vladek was due to have an exhibition of his own work there in early spring.

I waited in the foyer of the 'Royal Elphberg' with my hat on until the Count appeared from the lift.

'You simply cannot wear that dead cat in here, Karl Marx. The hotel will lose one of its stars.'

I told him that without it I'd already been recognised once today.

'This is a problem, yes,' he said. 'We are pregnant but not quite ready to reveal our big secret to the world. Perhaps another haircut? We have a barber's shop on the premises.'

'No,' I said. 'I shall want all my hair quite soon now. You'll have to put up with my hat or else we can talk in the street or in some hotel with no stars to lose.'

'You are becoming *exigeant*, dear boy,' he said, ushering me into the bar and ordering whiskies. 'Does this mean you are beginning to feel confident of success?'

'Who commands the airforce?' I asked.

'General Rischenheim,' he said. 'He looks like a jockey, but his father flew for the Luftwaffe in the war and he belongs to an old family.'

'You once asked me,' I said, 'If there was anything I wouldn't want done in my name . . .'

'I remember the occasion well. You gave a very equivocal answer – to the effect that you would never break anybody's teeth for the fun of it. I had not asked you that.'

'The question now,' I said, 'is what exactly you are able to do in my name?'

'I begin to see the importance of your hat, dear boy. It is not a dead cat, but the magic Tarnhelm from Wagner's *Ring* and has made you change shape altogether.'

'I'll tell you what I need,' I said, 'and then you tell me how much of it you can supply. If it seems to be enough, then I'll show you my whole hand and we can judge whether the two hands together might make a grand slam.'

'You are a bridge-player?'

'Not a serious player, no.'

'I am a very serious player. What am I playing for, Karl Marx? I know your stake, but what is mine?'

I didn't have time to reply. A tall man in a striped suit with thin slicked-down black hair and a long fleshy face had stopped behind the Count's chair and was staring at me. I waited for him to go away, but he put his hand lightly on the Count's shoulder and said:

'Is this your bridge-partner, Count? Does he always wear his hat indoors in the best hotels? And the name you gave him is surely a witticism?'

He didn't smile. The heavy lines on his face all ran downwards, as if he never did. The Count seemed pleased to see him.

'Join us, Helmut, please!'

He gestured to the empty chair between us at our small table.

'Karl Marx, this is General Practsin who – I think we are allowed to say in these days of democracy and open government – is head of *Corpus*. You know of *Corpus*? That is our nice new human name for the security service.'

He summoned a waiter and ordered three more whiskies.

'Now there are three of us, we can play Cut-throat Bridge,' he said.

'You haven't introduced this gentleman in the hat,' said Practsin, still staring at me.

'He is not quite in society yet, Helmut,' said the Count. 'But Karl Marx is indeed and quite genuinely his name, if not his whole name.'

'I recognise his face and especially his nose pretty well,' said Practsin.

'Where, I wonder, have you seen it before?' said the Count lightly.

'I am searching my memory.'

'No need,' said the Count. 'I know everything about him, even to the reason for his hat, and what I know you shall know, Helmut, but not, please, on this occasion.'

Practsin seemed satisfied and was silent as the waiter delivered the drinks. We clinked glasses.

'This is a very lucky meeting,' said the Count. 'Are you dining here, Helmut? Will you join us?'

'I'm afraid not. I'm meeting somebody else. Why is it lucky?'

'Because Karl Marx here is in the secret of our plans for an exhumation in Zenda and I wonder how far we've got.' He turned to me: 'General Practsin has been so kind as to interest himself in the details on our behalf. His department, you will understand, can call on much experience and expertise in such matters, and it seemed to me a more productive way to go to work than by tedious routine applications through courts or local councils.'

'There's no difficulty,' said the General. 'It can be done whenever you like. But if there's no immediate rush we may as well wait until the ground is softer.'

The Count raised his eyebrows at me and I nodded.

'Good, good,' said the Count, 'when the flowers are all springing, then, Helmut.'

When he'd finished his whisky General Practsin shook hands with the Count, stared again at me and moved away with the ominous final remark,

'A hat or possibly a cap.'

The Count looked delighted with the encounter.

'A good person for you to meet, Karl Marx – especially informally. General Practsin is not a bundle of jokes – both his parents were murdered by the communists when he was still a boy and he has much to forgive. I shall have to give him a full account of your adventures in due course, probably quite soon, because we don't want him acting independently. But if you can persuade him, when the time comes, that not all Slavs are incarnate fiends, I think he will prove a reliable partner.'

He beckoned the waiter and asked for a menu.

'But before we were interrupted I asked you a question to which I require a most specific reply. What is my stake, Karl Marx?'

'I can't think of anyone I'd rather have as prime minister,' I said, 'but I don't fancy the kind that stands in front.'

The waiter brought two menus and a wine list.

'You *are* wearing the Tarnhelm. See what you would like for supper – this is the best restaurant so far east – you would have to go to the far side of Asia to find a better. The minister who stands in front, you know, is more of a protection and easier to get rid of. The *eminence grise* is protected by the throne and more likely to be a permanent feature.'

'I hope we shall both be permanent features.'

'Let us drink to that!'

'These Generals,' I said, 'are they all close confederates?'

'Which generals do you mean?'

'Rischenheim and Practsin in particular.'

'Not close, no.'

'It occurred to me that if Rischenheim fell foul of *Corpus*, it might be necessary for his whole staff and organisation to be drawn into the investigation. But who then would be able to deploy the airforce in an emergency?'

We had a long working dinner together. The food and wine were as good as I'd ever had and I said I was proud to have a first-class hotel named after me.

'How did you know? The name has been changed.'

'I mean my new, my future name.'

'Ah yes. But that was my little joke – as part-owner. Its previous name was the "Karl Marx". Of course, one can never make better jokes than history does all on its own.'

'I used to think history very boring.'

'That was because conventional people taught you to think of it as serious facts. But it's really only irony on a long time-scale. You are a prime example, dear boy: a joke played by time on Ruritania and I do really believe now, after all you tell me, that time means to give us the punch-line.'

Clare Studebaker put the government on the spot with her request to visit Bilavice. They couldn't admit they didn't currently control Bilavice, since they'd consistently played down in public the successes of the guerrillas; nor did they want an influential foreign journalist telling the world – and indeed Ruritania itself indirectly – what they'd done to the Sebrikov dam and the power-supplies of their own people; but they couldn't absolutely forbid her to go because that would look as if they didn't control Bilavice and had made war on their own people. So they tried hard to dissuade her – dwelling on the winter roads and the dangers of terrorist action – saying that these people were completely ruthless and unpredictable and would not respect her nationality or her credentials as a journalist or even her sex. They hinted – this was rich – that the last British journalist to go there had not been heard of since. Who was this? she asked them; they replied that it was an unconfirmed rumour and it would be wrong to alarm the man's relations until they had more information. Finally, when she rejected all discouragements, they gave her permission to travel to Bilavice by road – the train service was temporarily discontinued – but warned her that the army authorities on the border would make their own assessment of the situation and might have to turn her back for her own safety. In other words, she could drive to a check-point and drive back again.

All this obstacle-making, of course, only made Clare the keener to go and, since the Ruritanian Army was too small to guard every possible crossing-point, it wasn't that difficult. To avoid any of the obvious bridges over the Volzer we only had to leave Strelsau from the other side of the river and take a circuitous route along minor roads. This made the trip much longer but, travelling in the first of our two Japanese 4×4s with Clare, that didn't bother me. She treated me now with more respect and I spent much of the journey telling her in English – the rest of our party were Ruritanians and only spoke German – about my early adventures with the Ruritanian Army of the True Faith, up to the point at which I narrowly escaped execution as a mercenary.

'And you escaped,' she said, 'because that just happened to be the day the Second Regiment chose to mutiny?'

'More or less.'

'If it had been more or less by even a few minutes,' she said, 'you'd surely be dead.'

I grunted vaguely. It was too soon yet to go into my later identity. Clare asked me about the True Faith. What did these people actually believe? I explained that it was a very basic form of Christianity.

'Not fanatics, then?'

'No. Except about church furniture.'

'I've heard that they believe Christ or his mother returns to earth from time to time.'

'They do, but it's a strictly human form of reincarnation. No miracles, for instance.'

'I've even heard that the Virgin Mary has made appearances in Karapata.'

'You can ask them about that when you see them.'

The foot-hills were now completely clear of snow and there were snowdrops and other small early spring flowers beginning to show in sheltered places. The people we passed on farms or in occasional villages stopped what they were doing and stared after us. We parked beside the road at the top of a rise and paced about in the cold wind, eating sandwiches and drinking cans of beer while we stretched our legs. We had brought enough rations for the six of us for two days in case we were really going to a starving town. Perhaps we should have brought an aid convoy, but the people in the villages looked healthy enough. It was sunny as well as cold and there was a spectacular view of the mountains ahead. The country here was mostly open – crops and pasture, with sheep and cows grazing.

'This place could be a tourist paradise,' said Clare, 'if people knew about it. It's so unspoiled.'

Wearing an expensive black leather outfit, but with sensible flat shoes, she looked, as she sounded, the quintessential townee out for a weekend in the country and didn't seem to be aware of the fatal contradiction in what she'd said. She asked me what had brought me to Ruritania in the first place. I told her I was here to tell the readers of *Open Sesame* about business opportunities.

'They must be really dragging the pond,' she said in her most arrogant voice. 'The only businessmen who'd look for opportunities in this place would be those who couldn't make it in Hungary or Poland or Prague. Ruritania is the back of beyond.'

'What brought you here, then?'

'They asked me to go to Dresden,' she said, 'to cover neo-Nazis, but one can get sidelined in the obvious places just as much as in the sticks. Somebody, I mean, can be filling the screen from Albania when the girl in Paris or Berlin is eating her heart out. What decided me to opt for Ruritania was the story about Rudolf Rassendyll being re-buried in the cathedral. I thought there must be more to come – I loved the books when I was a child. But I'm afraid I guessed wrong – there's only small-town politics.'

'You did well with the President,' I said, 'and you may turn up something better yet.'

'Can't be too soon for me. They've virtually forgotten my existence at White City.'

She went off below the road to pee and after she'd come back I did the same. As I was zipping up I heard them calling for me with a note of urgency and when I rejoined them on the road saw a lorry coming up the rise from the direction we were facing. It pulled up within a foot or two of our leading car and we were immediately surrounded by about fifteen soldiers with Kalashnikovs.

'Who are these?' said Clare nervously, flourishing her government permission without getting anybody to read it.

'Terrorists,' I said. 'You can tell by the scratch uniforms and informal headgear.'

They told us to lie face down on the ground.

'BBC,' said Clare desperately. 'From England.'

'Lie down!'

She did.

'We're making for Bilavice,' I said, 'to report on conditions there.'

'Lie down!'

'Are you from the Ruritanian Army of the True Faith?'

'Lie down!'

'Are you in touch with the Captain?'

I was the only member of our party still standing. One of the soldiers fired his gun, cutting up the ground near me. I didn't recognise any of them, but I thought some at least must have been present at Chostok or Previce at Christmas.

'Surely you know who I am?' I said in Ruritanian. 'And I've brought my friends from the BBC to tell the world about your struggle.'

They looked at one another uncertainly. They didn't seem to have any particular leader.

'Who are you?' said the one who'd fired the shots.

'I helped capture Bilavice,' I said, again in Ruritanian. 'I was a prisoner at Kapitsa. I was at Sebrikov, in Chostok on Christmas Day and later at Previce Castle. Did none of you see me in any of those places?'

They looked very confused now and more like the bunch of farm-boys they really were than the soldiers they were pretending to be.

'The Captain, Sergeant Vakisch, Corporal Radichev – any of them would know me immediately.'

A boy with a broad, fair-skinned face that seemed vaguely familiar came forward and looked at me more closely. He was growing a moustache and was probably about twenty. None of them was much older.

'Take off your hat!' he said.

I'd hoped to avoid that. I wanted Clare to file her Bilavice story before she got wind of my real identity. But the soldier's finger was flicking constantly at his trigger and his barrel was pointed straight at my chest from a few feet away. I lifted my hat, held it in the air for some moments and said:

'Karel Berg, you see.'

As I replaced the hat they were lowering their guns and staring at me with curiosity. The boy with the incipient moustache put out his hand.

'Venslar Yavelets,' he said. 'Tishkon was my brother.'

We embraced emotionally. He told me he had left his family farm to fill his younger brother's place and if possible avenge him.

I went round and shook hands with all the others in turn, while Clare and her crew, getting up off the ground and dusting themselves down, watched us with relief and amazement. The soldiers, it turned out, were a local patrol and got warning of us by phone from the

248

villagers. They had no radio, so couldn't make contact with their superiors, but their general instructions were to stop and arrest all strangers. Several of them had seen me from a distance outside the church on Christmas Day and everyone in Karapata, they said, knew of me by repute since my symbolic anointing by Yelena.

With the lorry leading the way, we drove on to the next village, where phone calls could be made and our way cleared to Bilavice. Tishkon's brother joined Clare and me in the front car and brought us up to date with events since the bombing of the dam. Conditions were rugged, but not impossible. Some of the villages and farms had their own generators and in any case they were used to working by daylight and keeping themselves warm with wood fires. There was more hardship, he thought, in Chostok and Bilavice, but emergency committees were making sure everyone survived and the net result of the bombing had been to bring over a lot of waverers to the nationalist cause. Everyone was nervous about what would happen in spring, but the main hope was that the government would be too weak by then to risk invading Karapata.

After stopping to make the phone calls in the next village, we said goodbye to Venslar and his comrades and left them standing behind us in the road, waving their guns enthusiastically in the air. Clare, sitting in the back seat next to him, had questioned Venslar carefully, but I had only intervened occasionally from my place in the front seat to help out Venslar's halting German with my own halting Ruritanian. Now she wanted to question me.

'What was so magical about taking off your hat?'

'They recognised me without it,' I said.

'It makes such a difference?'

'That's why I wear it.'

'Unfortunately I missed the revelation,' she said. 'I was lying face down in the mud.' She brushed irritably at a dried patch on her leather jacket. 'You gave your name as Karel Berg. Is that a pseudonym? Or is Ed Fenton a pseudonym?'

I have to admit this was a good moment. Like most people, I suppose, I have ambiguous feelings about television people. Is it a privilege to hobnob with them or is it a pain in the neck to have to put up with their self-esteem and general assumption of power and influence? It's a mixture, in fact, of envy and of enjoying being envied by people outside the charmed circle: humiliating either way. Clare Studebaker, being attractive as well as successful and highly conscious of both, touched this nerve in me from the moment I first saw her on Freddy's screen talking about Rudolf Rassendyll. We were

249

now climbing the escarpment below Bilavice and although the road itself was clear of snow, there was still plenty of it on the rocks and patches of forest that hemmed the road in.

'This story has an embargo on it,' I said.

'Yes? How long?'

'Until further notice. But if you give me your word to respect it, I'll give you mine that you can be the first to use it.'

'Is it such an important story?'

'Not in world terms, perhaps. It's royal, but not British royal. Still, for a journalist based in the back of beyond, it's probably as good as you'll get.'

'O.K.'

'You've heard of Rudolf Rassendyll. You've enjoyed the books. You may remember that when he was supposed to be dead of an assassin's bullet they buried a waxwork, while he went off to live in Cornwall as a bearded photographer called . . .'

'Edwin Fenton. And secretly married the Queen.'

'And they had a child, you see. Charles Gordon Rassendyll. And he had children. And one of those children had two sons, whom he named after his socialist heroes, Karl and Friedrich. Who are therefore the great-grandsons of Rudolf Rassendyll and Flavia Elphberg.'

She was leaning back in her corner of the back seat, watching me closely, one hand in her lap, the other holding the strap over the window as we took a steep bend. The sun shone directly on to her intent face and she half closed her eyes. I savoured my moment and, whle the driver was concentrating on sticking to the road, I lifted my hat and showed her my profile. She sat up, shading her eyes.

'Unbelievable!' she said.

'A good story?'

I put the hat on again. She moved to the middle of the back seat and leaned forward.

'And you think you can make it?'

'What do you think?'

'I'm glad I turned down Dresden.'

'You obviously have a nose for the right place,' I said. 'And incidentally you've still got mud on it.'

'Where?'

I touched the place and she immediately opened her handbag and, like a cat, began grooming herself.

Bilavice received us warmly and Clare was soon busy collecting interviews and shots of empty shops, though it must be said she didn't find anybody as emaciated or war-torn as her audience might have liked – even the hospital was doing business as usual with its emergency generator.

I saw Gerda again as soon as we arrived – she was running several of the emergency committees from the Town Hall – and we arranged to meet at a restaurant for supper, as soon as her committee-work was over for the day. She warned me to expect austerity rations, but in fact the meal was delicious: an excellent vegetable soup and chicken grilled on a wood fire, eaten by candle-light with an encouraging bottle of Hungarian red.

'Perhaps Karapata should go off electricity for good,' I said. ' "A way of life unchanged since the middle ages . . . the happy people of Karapata have turned their backs on the 20th century . . . yak rides to the tranquil waters of Lake Sebrikov . . ." Is the dam badly damaged?'

'Hardly at all,' said Gerda. 'But the machinery is. And they demolished the house.'

'The house?'

'The one you stayed in with Maria. Perhaps it was her they were aiming at or perhaps they mistook it for another part of the hydro-electric plant.'

'The house was empty?'

'No. It was very early in the morning. Maria's cook and her husband were sleeping there. They were both killed. But there was no damage to the barracks, where they might have killed and wounded a lot of soldiers.'

The news upset me.

'You look very sad,' Gerda said. 'Were you fond of her?'

'I hardly knew her. She was an excellent cook and . . .'

'And . . .?'

'She cheered me up a lot on one occasion.'

'I wonder what you mean by that?'

I didn't try to explain, though I could see that Gerda misunderstood me. I didn't want to talk about my relationship with Yelena and it involved going into that. I drank my wine in silence, thought about Anna – her noisy shoes and brief remarks – and then about Yelena. What results from her tests? Gerda left me to my thoughts for a while and then said:

'I have news of another lady who cheered you up on more than one occasion. Susha is expecting a baby. Everybody says it's a miracle: she and her husband without children for so long

251

and suddenly she has a vision of the Virgin Mary in church and conceives.'

'Is there a problem, then?' I said warily.

'On the contrary. She's very very happy. So is Mikos her husband. He's a changed man – not angry and mean any more, but optimistic, helpful. All this time, it seems, his only trouble was that he couldn't have children of his own.'

'Sounds very satisfactory.'

'One doubt remains, of course. What will this miracle child look like when it's born? Will it – perish the thought! – resemble the father?'

'Close resemblances,' I said, 'very often skip a generation or two. Look at my own red hair and long nose, for instance!'

'I should have thought your genes were more pushy than most,' Gerda said.

After the meal we went home to her place. Our relationship was almost entirely physical now. We didn't talk about Slav nationalism or my plans or hers. I didn't tell her I'd met the boss of *Corpus*, the people who'd tried to abduct her and eliminate me. She didn't ask me about Yelena – she probably wasn't even aware that Yelena was ill or that I was in touch with her. Gerda was making her life now in Bilavice and Bilavice was simply waiting for spring. The government would fall or it wouldn't, things would get marginally better or distinctly worse. Without the active presence of Yelena, Karapata's sense of a larger destiny had evidently faded. Gerda certainly had no suspicion that my prospects for the immediate future were any brighter than before.

Why should she, after all? People mostly see life as a slow natural shift of circumstances and I suppose I'd seen it like that myself until recently. The idea that circumstances can be completely altered by deliberate human interference is worrying, because humans have a low opinion of each other and don't trust others to interfere for the best, but assume purely selfish motives. That's probably broadly correct and accounts for the way any big interference is usually followed by a big reaction. If you start throwing stones in the pond and making rings, others just want to do the same from the opposite side. My task as I saw it now was to throw all my stones in the pond so neatly and rapidly that the rings would spread right across before anyone even had time to pick up a stone of their own.

252

26

Cavemen

Clare was very keen to interview Michael. He never came to Bilavice, which was a basically bourgeois place where he was not popular and regarded as little more than a bandit, even if he did make mayhem under the colour of Slav nationalism. I wasn't entirely happy about meeting him myself, in case he hadn't forgiven me for my disappearance with Yelena. On the other hand, he was one of the stones I needed to throw into the pond and I thought he might be manageable if I came in the company of Clare. So a meeting was set up. I didn't stipulate that Vakisch should be present – I thought that would only ensure Michael would leave him out – but I sincerely hoped he would be.

Michael chose the venue. It was to be neither Chostok nor Previce Castle, but Fisher John's place outside Chostok, where Yelena had gone into retreat. The roads from Bilavice up to Chostok were still partly snowbound and although we made an early start we arrived late for our appointment.

The house was large and modern, in Roman villa style. It was another communist big-wig's country mansion, set among beetling crags in a sheltered bowl open to the south, with a large central court-yard surrounded by a covered cloister. Perhaps it was that monastic touch which had appealed to Fisher and Yelena. There were a lot of soldiers about, including a few I recognised, and Fisher was there as well as Michael, but not Vakisch. Michael was very irritated by our lateness: he was worried about the light. He didn't want the interview filmed in the house, but about three quarters of an hour away by foot, in a mountain-cave which had been his original hideout and therefore the cradle of the Ruritanian Army of the True Faith. It looked as if Fisher had not only set up the religious side of the rebellion but at least connived in the early stages of the military side by occupying the house which acted as both supply-base and camouflage for the cave above it.

Michael's reception of me was cold and only just short of hostile. Fisher avoided me altogether, shaking hands with Clare when I introduced her at the front door, but immediately disappearing into the house as if he'd heard the telephone. We were given hurried refreshments and then set out in a long file – Michael, Clare, me, the cameraman and sound recordist and at least ten soldiers – up the steep path to the cave. Fisher stayed behind. I'd asked Michael, while we were snatching our meal, where Vakisch was and been told he was busy elsewhere. I'd given him news of Yelena – that she was still undergoing tests and was intermittently better – and received no reply beyond a grunt. On the way up to the cave he talked to Clare, walking just behind him.

When we reached the cave I asked him why he chose to publicise his hideout like this. Surely he might need it again?

'Do you think so? You have no faith.'

'But just in case.'

'As far as I'm concerned, it's win or lose now. This was not the best time of my life, living in this hole in the mountain for two winters. I'd rather be dead or leave the country than have to do it again.'

It struck me that the Count, by unwillingly putting the luxury of his castle and car at Michael's disposal, had sapped the rebellion at source more effectively than the army could have done with a frontal assault.

The cave was deep but not all that broad, its mouth concealed with boulders and stunted trees and facing a wall of rock, so that it must have been invisible from the air as well as from below. Inside, there were signs of its former use: empty ammunition boxes and kerosene cans, a makeshift fireplace near the entrance and a few bits of litter in corners. There was even an ancient telephone – it looked pre-war – connected to the house. The interview was done on the small flat area in front of the cave, where there was still a layer of snow and the light was good. The soldiers sat or stood around among the boulders and made a martial background, but I kept out of the picture by standing behind the cameraman.

Michael didn't give a good interview from the point of view of his own cause, though he was a natural from the viewer's angle. He looked nasty and he sounded vicious and intransigent. It was the sort of interview cameras usually get for only about ten seconds, before the corrupt official, gun-runner, crooked businessman or whoever has offended society's norms bangs the door or makes a snarling getaway in his car. But here the man revelled in making a bad

254

impression. Believing his opponents to be wholly and inexcusably evil, he considered that whatever means he used to destroy them could only be justifiable and admirable. When Clare asked him about the sufferings of civilians and people caught in the middle he showed no sympathy at all. The cause of Slav freedom from German oppression was so unarguable that nothing could sully it except failure. He was prepared, he said, to sacrifice his own life to it and he thought no life more valuable than his own. Clare, ruthless as she was herself in her own way, was quite unprepared for this sort of image-damaging honesty and kept trying to put a decent liberal gloss on his replies.

'You feel that no compromise is possible, that the German interests in Ruritania are not ready to sit down and discuss Slav grievances?'

'I'd never sit down with those people. It would be a betrayal.'

'But surely, when it comes down to it, you are all Ruritanians?'

'*We* are. They are interlopers.'

'Wasn't there always a partly German population in Ruritania?'

'I'm not interested in the past, only the future. The future I see is a Slav Ruritania.'

'Do you mean ethnic cleansing?'

'I don't use those dictionary words. We have to defeat the Germans and give Ruritania back to its Slav people.'

'But if you succeed, what happens to the German part of the population?'

'It will be a Slav country. Anyone who wants to be German can go and live in Germany.'

'But we're *speaking* German,' said Clare, genuinely puzzled.

'I wasn't aware you could speak Ruritanian, Mrs Studebaker.'

'No, I don't, of course. But do you, Captain?'

'Certainly I speak some Ruritanian. This is part of what we have to do. First we make a Slav nation and then we make a Slav language. But the nation must come first. I am not a language-teacher, but a soldier. I will do my part, then let the language-teachers do theirs.'

I began to understand why the military court in Kapitsa had taken such a dim view of my fighting for Michael. Certainly I never would have fought for him if I'd heard this interview first. It wasn't a cause anybody could identify with, it was just this man's way of putting himself on the map.

When the interview was over, I got a word with Michael myself.

'I have a message from Yelena. Can we speak privately?'

I drew him away into the cave.

'Why doesn't she tell me herself?'

255

'She's still in hospital. In Vlod. We arrived in Kapitsa just as the attack was starting.'

'You've brought a letter?'

'No letter. We thought – she thought a verbal message was safer.'

'How can I trust you? You always act for yourself alone. Why did you come here? Weren't you afraid? You cheated on me, you cheated on Fisher.'

'How did I cheat on you?'

'You took Yelena for yourself.'

'She was ill, very ill. You agreed she had to go into hospital.'

'Before that. You took her at Sebrikov.'

'I'd say it was the other way round. She got me out of Kapitsa and had them bring me to Sebrikov.'

'What difference does it make? She wanted you or you wanted her?'

I never think of myself as all that clever, just reasonably quick-witted, but now I felt really stupid. This was the first time I understood that we weren't talking politics but sex. The rivalry between him and me and perhaps also with Fisher took on a new dimension.

'Michael,' I said, 'you've got it wrong. I wanted her, of course, but she wouldn't have me. Not at all. She actually wrote me a letter to say so, to give me the brush-off. I wish I had it to show you. It ends up "never to be yours, Yelena", underlined.'

The man suddenly looked happy. His smile was still essentially a sneer, but a happy sneer.

'It's true?'

'Absolutely true. Anna could confirm it – she was there when I read the letter.'

I remembered then that Anna was dead and that reminded me that in my wallet I still carried the bunch of hair and the picture of the Virgin she'd restored to me. Perhaps she'd understood the situation a lot better than I had and her remark about 'amore' simple meant she thought I still had a better chance than either Fisher or Michael. We were standing well inside the cave, with the silhouettes of the soldiers and the TV team outlined against the light at the mouth. Clare came into view at this moment and called in English into the cave:

'Karl? Are you there?'

'Is this your woman?' said Michael.

'Not yet,' I said in a low, sly tone of the kind I thought he'd appreciate, 'but I have hopes.'

He actually patted me on the arm.

'Good!' he said. 'She is English. She's best for you.'

Clare should have recorded this – further damning evidence of his unabashed racism.

'Karl?'

'With you in a moment!' I called back.

'It's lucky we talked,' said Michael, holding my arm as we began to move towards the entrance.

'But that's why I came – because I wanted to talk to you.'

'You took a risk. You could easily have died.'

'I thought I could trust you.'

'I hadn't made up my mind. But Fisher thinks you're a mad dog.'

I told him then about my encounter with Fisher in the watch-tower and the whole history of Fisher and the statue. When he objected that Fisher didn't need money, I pointed out that his funds came from the members of his church and that he was obviously hoping to make a private profit from the statue. We were still talking in low voices just inside the cave, but had to break off when Clare joined us.

'Everyone's freezing,' she said. 'Can't we go down now?'

She looked from one to the other of us suspiciously, hating to be left out of the action.

Back at the house it was growing dark. While Clare and her team were warming up and getting something to eat, I went out with Michael into the cloister. It was cold but private and we could be sure of spotting anyone who tried to eavesdrop. At the centre of the courtyard there was a fish-pond with a thin layer of ice over its surface and a small fountain with naked cherubs playing under the frozen water-spout. I wondered if it had been put there by the communist big-wig or was another of Fisher's artistic acquisitions.

Michael by now had started to hate Fisher so much that, cheated of one assassination, he was seriously considering a substitute. The best thing you could say for Michael was that he wasn't devious; and deviousness in others was something he couldn't forgive. It was because he thought me treacherous that he'd seen me as rubbish and now he'd simply crossed Fisher off his list of human-beings. We left Fisher telling Clare about the True Faith and the Disciples of the First Instance and how their doctrines coincided or differed, but he too was obviously biding his time until he could get a private interview with Michael. The way he'd looked at me and then at Michael as we returned from the cave told me very clearly that he'd fully expected the party to be reduced by one on the way down. If he'd noticed us slip away into the cloister he probably assumed Michael was intending to dispose of the mad dog there.

I didn't feel as murderous towards Fisher as he did towards me. On the whole I thought it was better his relationship with Michael should remain undisturbed until the guerrillas had played their part in my plans. It was not easy to persuade Michael of this. He needed Fisher's funds, of course, but not right away; for the moment he had all the military supplies he needed or could cope with, given the rawness of his troops. More vehicles and some light artillery would have been useful, but they couldn't be brought in over the mountain border anyway. His view was that Fisher should be flown back to the folks in Tulsa, Oklahoma, in a wooden box, with a note explaining how he'd meant to betray, for private gain, the trust that both the Disciples and the True Faith had placed in him. I found myself defending the man, pointing out how much he must have done to make the rebellion viable in the first place, that he hadn't actually succeeded in removing the statue, that he probably regretted the whole episode now and that he'd done no harm to the cause except to sour relations between Michael and me. Greed, I pointed out sanctimoniously, was something that took hold of most people from time to time and distorted their outlook; Fisher was probably not rich himself and was worrying about his retirement. Michael's response was that, since he himself would be quite incapable of concealing what he felt about Fisher, even if Fisher was able to hide things from him, he didn't see any future for their relationship; but he said he'd give himself time to think about it.

It was almost dark now and I was afraid we'd be interrupted, so I plunged into the business I'd really come for. I'd been uncertain before whether I could risk telling Michael about the Cossacks, but there was no alternative if I wanted a co-ordinated plan. Now we were on such good terms I felt no hesitation. His reaction was mixed. He didn't like the idea of the Cossacks sharing the action and taking a greater part of the glory with their greater resources, but he did see that it would radically alter his own prospects for success. I didn't mention the 'circus' element, but left him to believe – what I hoped everyone would believe – that sixty fully operational tanks would leave the barracks in Plotla and move west; and I pressed him harder by presenting the plan as Yelena's, not mine. This, I said, was the message she'd sent with me and Michael's vanity glowed at the thought that Yelena and he were still the protagonists and I the mere go-between.

At this point I saw we were no longer alone. Somebody had

emerged into the cloister from the door on the far side. There was no time for further argument, but Michael still hadn't given me a definite answer. I peered across at the intruder, wondering how I could clinch Michael's agreement, thinking of Yelena perhaps pacing round the cloister while she prepared for Christmas and made herself ill in the process. It was an extremely cold place and would have been even colder then. Inspiration came. I turned my back on the shadowy person opposite, opened my wallet and removed the little bunch of Yelena's hair in its rubber-band.

'She sent you this, Michael,' I said, holding it out to him.
'What's that?'

Rather than hold it up to the light, I took his hand and put the hair in his palm, much as Anna had done for me.

'She knew you'd find it difficult to trust me,' I said, 'but she was sure you'd *never* fail her.'

He remained for several moments without moving, then his hand went to his heart. He was stowing the hair just where I'd kept it, in his shirt pocket. I hoped he wouldn't lose it in the wash as I so nearly had on at least two occasions.

'O.K.,' he said. 'Tell her I got the message and now I do trust you, Karl.'

'One more thing,' I said. 'Do you think that's Fisher across the way? He may be getting the impression we're too friendly. If you're friendly to me he'll hardly credit your friendship for him.'

'Who's that?' Michael called out. 'Is that you, Fisher?'

'It's me, Michael. The TV people are waiting to go. What's kept you?'

'Why not take a shot at me?' I suggested. 'It would make him feel happier. I'll break away and dodge round the cloister and trust you to miss. Otherwise – you're such an honest man – you'll never convince him we were *dis*agreeing.'

He laughed. It was almost the first time I'd heard him do it, but like his sneer-smile it was more sinister than cheerful.

'Run, then!' he whispered, 'and trust me!'

He took the revolver out of his holster and moved the safety-catch. I ran straight down the cloister as he fired. The noise was very loud. The bullet struck a pillar somewhere ahead of me. I turned the first corner.

'Save your shots, Michael!' said Fisher. 'He's got to make for this door. I'll head him off and you can corner him.'

As I reached the second corner, I saw Fisher coming towards me down the cloister and Michael running diagonally across the

259

courtyard. It looked as if I'd misjudged him – he was going to take Fisher's advice. I hesitated – whether to double back or fling myself straight at Fisher. As I decided on the second, Michael fired again and Fisher stumbled.

'I missed him,' Michael said, as Fisher collapsed slowly with some sort of pain-laden groan. 'But I didn't miss you, you greedy, treacherous bastard!'

He shot him again through the head and put his gun away in his holster. Soldiers were piling through the door now. Michael simply pointed to the body and led me back into the house.

Clare and her crew were waiting there aghast, looking even more so by the light of the oil-lamps. Michael ignored Clare's questions.

'Private business,' he said and hurried us all out to the cars. 'The only solution,' he said to me, gripping my hand as I got into the car.

'Shall I tell Yelena?' I asked.

He put his hand on his heart.

'Just thank her for this! And say, O.K.'

He shut the door on me, banged peremptorily on the car's roof and the driver pulled hastily away.

'My God!' said Clare, 'that man gives me the shivers.'

'I saw his better side,' I said. 'He shot the man that gave me the shivers.'

27

Manipulating the Media

Clare had booked us into a hotel in Chostok. Over dinner I gave her and the others an expurgated account of the death of Fisher John. The quarrel, I said, arose over a valuable work of art which Fisher was trying to export illegally. Michael, with his pathological hatred of any breach of trust, had killed Fisher in a moment of anger. On the face of it, it was a true account, but it left out Yelena altogether and I was fairly certain myself that the living virgin of Chostok had as much to do with Fisher's fate as the wooden one. Clare, of course, wanted the rest of the world to know the story right away and, since there was no communication with the outside world from Karapata, was anxious we should be on the road to Strelsau as soon as it was light.

'This is something, Karl. The Bilavice stuff and the interview with Michael may be dynamite for Ruritanians, but it's after all only what the West expects of a bleeding fragment of the former Soviet Empire. Whereas, when this same guerrilla chieftain goes straight home and puts a bullet into an American missionary, who has been trying to steal Ruritanian heritage – this begins to be world news. If I add that I'd been speaking to the victim myself minutes earlier and that the only witness to the shooting is an Englishman who just happens to be . . .'

'You don't add that,' I said in English, 'and you don't even mention it in front of our friends here.'

I realised now that Clare, who I'd intended to be an embarrassment to the government with her report on the hardships in Karapata, was likely to be a much more severe embarrassment to me. Even if she kept my identity secret – and I doubted if she considered any verbal promise sacrosanct when measured against the claims of Almighty News and her career – the last thing I wanted was to have the world's attention drawn to Ruritania at this delicate juncture. Fisher, at that rate, would reach out beyond the grave and have his revenge. I let the back of my mind tackle this problem while I asked Clare what Fisher had said about the True Faith.

'What he said was quite contradictory. He told me the Virgin Mary did appear in front of large numbers of people on several occasions. On the other hand, he didn't seem to think there was anything miraculous about that. The True Faith doesn't believe in miracles as such, though it also believes that from time to time these divine reincarnations occur. I suppose it just doesn't call them miracles.'

'Did he meet the lady himself?'

'Yes, he did.'

'And what was his own view?'

'He said she was very beautiful, very dedicated and very lovable.'

'Lovable?'

'That was his word. He said he would have done anything for her, as all her followers would, but this was human, not divine charisma. Physically she was completely human.'

'Where did he think she was now?'

'He thought she'd left the province immediately after Christmas. She tended to come and go, he said, but that didn't mean she was para-physical or extra-terrestrial. We were talking souls not bodies. All souls live in human bodies – the only question was whether this soul was special.'

It was strange to get Fisher's version of Yelena like this – doubly distorted. Evidently he'd kept very quiet about his part in making her soul special.

'Did he tell you anything about how he first became involved with the True Faith?' I asked.

'He was just bridge-building, he said, with his own people in the States.'

Since we were leaving so early, we broke up early. Clare sent the others off, but kept me behind at the table drinking Russian brandy. She wanted to find out what I planned to do: would I claim the throne, lobby for support, try to use the rebels for a *coup d'état*? I gave nothing away, just said lightly that I'd have to see how things turned out and whether I could be of any use to my country (public life breeds a hypocrite a minute). All the while I was thinking what to do about the Fisher/Michael story and it seemed to me there wasn't much to hang it on if we could lose the interview. I knew where that was, because the cameraman, before leaving the table, handed the video-tape and the audio-cassette to Clare for safe-keeping. She'd put them in her own shoulder-bag and it was under

262

her chair now, against her feet. As we got up to go, she picked it up and patted it.

'Valuable stuff!' she said.

I managed some sort of wincing smile and we went upstairs. In the corridor outside her door I offered to kiss her goodnight.

'If you like.'

It went on a bit longer than she liked.

'That's enough!' she said, withdrawing and pushing me firmly away.

'You'd better lock your door,' I said.

'I always do.'

'I only look like my great-grandfather,' I said. 'My character's completely different.'

'What does that mean?'

'He was a gentleman.'

'And you?'

'I hardly know the meaning of the word.'

'Goodnight, Karl!'

She did lock her door. Even if she hadn't and I'd got into her room by fair means or foul and stolen the interview – plan number one – I'd have been prime suspect. Plan number two was more trouble but safer. I went downstairs again and, after getting Michael's number from Vakisch at Previce, spoke to him personally. He needed a lot of convincing that his first major appearance on the world's screens should be postponed, but when I told him that it would be accompanied by the news of Fisher's death and that that might easily mean the Americans lending at least covert support to the Ruritanian government, if not pressing for Michael's own trial for war-crimes, he gave way.

Leaving Chostok at dawn on the road to Bilavice we were waylaid by a lorry-load of soldiers and escorted to the farm where I'd first been enrolled into the Ruritanian Army of the True Faith. There I paid my respects to the farmer and his wife while both cars and all our personal possessions were searched microscopically. Every video-tape or film, exposed or unexposed – including the footage of Bilavice and the private snapshots taken by one of the drivers – and every cassette was seized. Clare was devastated, of course, and demanded that I should exert my influence to stop it happening. I went back into the farm-house and pretended to phone Michael, returning to say that he was adamant and now thought he'd been a fool to give the interview; furthermore he was seriously worried about letting us leave Karapata at all and if we stayed to argue we'd probably be staying indefinitely. The only concession I'd obtained, I said, was that the material wouldn't be destroyed and might eventually be returned.

So we came back to Bilavice empty-handed. Clare would be able to tell the viewers about her experiences in front of some kind of still of mountain-scenery, but without any documentary material her story wouldn't rate high in competition with Bosnia, Afghanistan, South Africa, Kurdistan, Azerbaijan, Georgia, Colombia, Sudan, Algeria, Liberia, Rwanda, Guatemala, Angola, Somaliland or any of the other stew-pots of the world where warlords were terrorising civilians and eliminating rivals. I'd also lost my propaganda about the government's Sebrikov atrocity, but on the whole I'd thought it better to have everything seized and leave no room for error. I was sure TV people would stick at no deception in order to get their stuff safely out and, in fact, these ones had had a small extra camera called a Hi-8 attached to the main Beta camera, as well as an extra cassette recorder to back up the 'DAT'. Clare's distress at losing even this crafty stand-by material was sufficient to show they'd got away with nothing on this occasion. She was more or less hysterical when I came back with the bad news from my phoney phone-call and since Michael wasn't available, I took the brunt. I thought this fair enough: she'd got the right target even if she didn't know it.

By the time the search was over and Clare had finally accepted that her career was blighted, it was too late to do the long journey to Strelsau in daylight and less urgent anyway. There were no hotels on our devious route to avoid the army check-points, so we spent that night in Bilavice. I didn't look up Gerda but stayed in the same hotel as the others, an old German-style inn – with its own generator – called the 'Kakadu' (cockatoo). The name had the advantage for the owner of being exactly the same in Ruritanian. Clare's fury had burned down gradually to resentment and self-pity and she wanted me there to share it. It's extremely tiring pretending to be angry and upset when you're really relieved and cheerful and I also found her quite unattractive in this mood. So I had every incentive to give her other things to think about and took her out to the restaurant I'd been to with Gerda; we had the same menu too. Here at last, freed of her team's constant presence and in a town where I was already known, I could remove my hat in public.

Through all the millennia since they lost their fur, humans have not kept hair on their head for nothing. There's no doubt that, however basically handsome he is, a person who goes everywhere with a synthetic fur hat pulled down over his ears looks seedy and

264

unappetising. A candlelit meal with the reincarnation of Rudolf Rassendyll soon perked Clare up. I think I compared her before to a cat: now, having been badly excruciated with the equivalent of a bucket of cold water, she began to be sleek and proud again. I told her everything I knew about my family – it was all going to come out anyway and I owed her the first interview. But although she enjoyed being in my company and playing around with the possibility of my being king, she was also instinctively suspicious of such a reactionary idea.

'I suppose it might just work in a tinpot place like this,' she said, 'but it's bucking the trend.'

'Which trend?'

'Towards democracy. Nobody believes in kings any more.'

'If they can believe in the Virgin Mary, a king would be quite mundane.'

'Those are peasants.'

She'd have rapped me severely if I'd said anything so patronising myself.

'Democracy is a belief like any other,' I said, 'with periodic elections instead of holy communion. Where in the world have you ever seen a democratic election bring a real change of power or personnel? Whenever there's even a threat of it from outsiders to left or right, all the privileged people start to scream for the rules to be changed.'

'You're not a fascist, are you, Karl?'

'Just an ordinary egoist.'

'What would you hope to do for Ruritania if you did become king?'

'Constitutional monarchs don't usually have the power to do anything, do they?'

'Not directly, but they can make a significant difference to people's awareness of social problems, ecology, charities, etc.'

'You'd need to be trained for that,' I said. 'An ordinary egoist like me would just put his big feet all over other people's expertise.'

'We're talking PR, not expertise.'

It became a dispiriting conversation, because we were at cross purposes, talking about two different worlds: her highly-regulated western one, with sanitised 'agendas' and bus-lane 'correctness', and my still unformed, perhaps imaginary one, which was as much as anything, I suppose, a rejection of hers. Yelena was quite right. To become a king of the only sort Clare could envisage would be sheer misery. I began to wish it was Yelena sitting opposite me. But the odd thing was that the more Clare turned me off with her relentlessly prosaic version of my function, the more she turned herself on with my image, with *who* I was. She wanted to be able to control the reality and reduce it to some kind of wizened welfare dwarf, but she loved the glittering dream, the intimacy with the future King Karel. It was the same thing I'd noticed about her approach to the scenery: she couldn't see that paradise stopped being paradise with tourists in it or that a PR king wasn't worth having dinner with.

And so as the evening drew to a close we were at cross-purposes in another way. I'd fully intended not to be locked out of her room this time, whereas she'd made it clear when she accepted dinner *à deux* that no keys were on offer. Now as I looked into her blue eyes and screen-friendly face I had no desire to take her clothes off, but saw that she had that in mind. I put my hat on to go back to the hotel. The town was almost totally lightless and spring rain was falling. As we ambled side by side down the straight avenue from the bridge towards the church square, Clare took my arm.

'Thanks, Karl, I enjoyed that enormously. You cheered me up after that appalling start this morning.'

I murmured something deprecatory (*Nil Quae Feci*).

'Whatever you may say, I think you are quite like your great-grandfather.'

'In what sense?'

'You're more of a gentleman than you pretend.'

'Is that a compliment?'

'All I mean, I suppose, is that you're not a bloody-minded bastard like Michael.'

'Yes, he has behaved badly.'

'If I could cut off his head and kick it down this street, I would.'

Alcohol makes some people sleepy and others maudlin; it seemed to make her wrongs return to her mind with increased violence.

'I feel some sympathy for him,' I said.

She stopped, let go of my arm and virtually spat.

'Why?'

'He doesn't want to antagonise the Americans.'

'Well, he's antagonised me and not being a gentleman I shall never forgive or forget the way he's buggered me up.'

Not being a gentleman either, I hoped she'd never find out that he hadn't.

We arrived at the Hotel Kakadu arm-in-arm again, but with nothing fixed. Outside her door, in a very dim light, with the old boards, which must have been first nailed down at about the time of Rudolf V's coronation, creaking at every movement, I bent down to kiss her.

'Goodnight, Clare!'

She took off my hat, studied me with a serious expression and then allowed me to kiss her, which I did quite formally, on one cheek. She unlocked her door, opened it and stood in the doorway. Still unsmiling, she held out my hat, then suddenly put it on her own head.

'How do I look?'

'Fetching!'

She did, especially now she smiled. The hat – hiding her short, barbed, gingery hair – made her look, of course, Russian, but also frivolous, raffish, off-duty. We went inside together, locked the door and stripped completely in seconds, though I made her keep the hat on. The Count was right, it had magical powers. Visually her face was her strong point and her body rather square and homely, but the visual aspects never bother me at this stage of a relationship. Her breasts were larger than they looked when she wore clothes, she had broad hips, a flat stomach and shortish legs. She was a very ardent lover and we were busy much of the night, with intervals for rest. She bit and scratched quite a lot and by breakfast-time I was sore in several tender places and very reluctant to get up. She pulled me out of bed, picked up my clothes for me and when I'd got them on, transferred the hat from her head to mine.

'Ed Fenton,' she said, 'I *never* thought I'd sleep with you.'

We left Bilavice immediately after breakfast. It's a pleasant peaceful town, historically interesting, but for me will always be associated with war, death and very good sex.

28

The Elphbergs Come
to Town

I intended this account of my adventures to be as lean and mean as my great-grandfather's, but I've found myself including more detail than he did. That may be because people expect more detail these days or because ours is a more complicated world than his. However, it's time now to fast spool, especially since, with the arrival of spring, events began to move very quickly indeed.

But first things first. Soon after parting with Clare in Strelsau – she had a comfortable flat in one corner of a square in the gracious part of town – I went back to Vlod to check up on Yelena and the Cossacks. The Cossacks were doing fine, hammering in their workshops as busily as Wagner's Nibelungen and much more cheerfully, and I was able to settle a precise date for the circus with Colonel Stavrilev. Yelena was not fine at all. The hospital had diagnosed the disease her husband died of.

Among the recognised causes of leukaemia – which is basically white blood cells crowding out red ones, a sort of ethnic cleansing – are chemical pollution and radiation. Since she and her husband both came from near Kiev, the doctors thought they might be delayed victims of the Chernobyl disaster. But the cause hardly mattered, the question was whether the disease could be stopped and the doctors were practising their own form of ethnic cleansing with state-of-the-art drugs. At least, that was my understanding of the treatment: if we call the white cells Germans and the red cells Slavs and the problem is that the Germans are eliminating all the Slavs, then the straightforward remedy is for the Slavs to start eliminating Germans in sufficient numbers to restore the original balance.

I hardly recognised Yelena. Her face looked wasted – actually, she reminded me of the last photographs of Flavia – and she was nearly bald. I came bouncing into the hospital ready to juggle all my promising schemes in front of her like coloured balls, only to be diverted to an interview with a doctor which told me what I could hardly bear to hear. Now when I saw her I began to cry. Yelena wasn't upset or even surprised. Crying is no guarantee of feeling for others – one is usually crying for oneself – and she knew me well enough to guess this would be my reaction. She said nothing, but gently took my hands and stroked them until I stopped. After that we talked for a while, but not about anything I'd come to tell her – none of that mattered to me any more.

By the time I came to see her next day I'd decided to call a halt to all my arrangements and when she asked me what news I had, I told her my decision.

'Why?'

'Because I couldn't care less. I only care what happens to you.'

'You're very bitter because you think I'm spoiling your plans.'

'It's not that at all.'

'It's quite unnecessary. I shall not spoil your plans.'

'Do you mean you'll get better?'

'I'll be with the Cossacks – as promised.'

'How can you?'

'The doctor virtually guaranteed that if I underwent this treatment I would get better. Not necessarily for ever, but sufficiently. I didn't lose my hair and my looks, Karel, because I was afraid of dying, but because I was afraid of not being with the Cossacks at the crucial time.'

'I don't want you to do that,' I said. 'I don't want any of it.'

'If you'd mentioned that before, I would have refused the treatment.'

'But what is the point of it?'

It's very hard for sick people to become really angry. They lack the energy and usually they don't have sufficient interest in anything outside their own bodies to be made angry. But I never had a greater sense of Yelena's difference from other people than now. White, skull-like, hairless – only her head, shoulders and arms visible against the heaped-up pillows – she incandesced.

'*You* ask what is the point of *my* sacrifice? No, it's not for Slav nationalism, it's not for the True Faith, it's not even for myself. It's for *you*, Karel Rassendyll, and your bloody kingdom!'

The flame burnt out almost at once. Her energy was a very short match. I sat with her until she went to sleep and came back the next day to find her rested and ready to talk. I apologised for my first reaction to her illness, promised everything would go ahead as planned and gave her the date I'd fixed with Colonel Stavrilev. I also told her that Michael had agreed to co-operate and that Orlin and the corporal would drive into Karapata to give him the final details, including the date.

Then I told her about Michael killing Fisher. She took it calmly and said she'd begun to distrust Fisher well before the incident of the statue and his attempt to murder me.

'So why did you make me go through that hellish time with him at the chalet?'

'I didn't want him with me and I thought you deserved him. Even more, he deserved you.'

'But before that – were you lovers?'

For a moment I thought she was going to be furious again and no doubt she would have been if she'd been well. But obviously she didn't want to waste energy on something that no longer mattered, so she relaxed and spoke so quietly that I had to move nearer to catch what she was saying.

'I didn't find him physically attractive. He did a lot for me, though, he pulled me out of despair; and it took me a long time to lose my faith in him. He wasn't a bad man pretending to be good, he was a good man who thought he'd discovered a formula for being good. Of course there isn't one – formulas never fit properly – but having found one, as he thought, in the land of his ancestors . . .'

'He came from Ruritania?'

'His parents were refugees from the Nazis. They joined the Disciples of the First Instance in America because it shared some of the ideas of the True Faith, but Fisher wanted to get back to the real thing. And he really believed, when he and I met at the time my husband was dying and I joined the True Faith, that I might be the Virgin Mary returned to earth. But this was where his formula started to betray him. Instead of waiting to see if there was any truth in what he believed, he began to act as if the truth – the True Faith – was what he believed. Anything then could be done in its name – he didn't need to test it any further. If I was the Virgin Mary and he was my earthly sponsor, whatever we did must be good. Slav nationalism was good if we decided to support it, Michael and his guerrillas were good if we chose to enrol them under our banner. I suppose the business with the statue was only the squalid ending of an increasing addiction to his own certainty. I'm sure he didn't want to kill you so much because you threatened to expose him as because he'd begun to know that he'd lost his way. It was more like an attempt at suicide.'

I asked her about the relationship between Fisher and Michael.

'Michael never liked Fisher, but he was dependent on him.'

'For funds to buy weapons?'

'I don't know about that. I suppose you must be right.'

'For the use of his house as a cover and base for the cave.'

'Yes, but most of all for the alliance with the True Faith, which gave him his justification.'

'And with you, Our Lady of Chostok.'

'It sounds as if we were all cynical and conspiratorial, but I don't think any of us was. The True Faith *is* a true faith and comforts and supports many people, as I know myself. Fisher truly wanted to bring the true faith to others and he thought Providence had given me to help him. Michael thought the Slavs had to fight for their rights and territory and wanted to believe it was also God's will.'

'What about you?' I asked.

'I believed Fisher.'

She closed her eyes and seemed to go to sleep. I sat looking at her – it had taken me till now to be able to look at her without glancing away in embarrassment – and thought about the deceptiveness of appearances: Michael the ugly bandit hating treachery; Tishkon the shy nervous boy who could shoot better than anyone; Corporal Radichev who pretended to be a bully to conceal his soft heart; Clare who seemed so sophisticated and was so naive and even silly; Yelena. When Yelena was beautiful I'd been quite certain that, however inspiring she seemed, she was basically a power-woman, using the religious thing for quite obvious and not very attractive purposes of her own. Now she was ugly I could easily believe her body was really just an envelope for something more than herself. She opened her eyes, found me looking at her and stared back.

'What do you see?' she asked.

I opened my wallet and took out the creased, half-obliterated picture of the Virgin and gave it to her.

'The gaoler's wife sent that to me when I was waiting to be shot,' I said.

'Did it help?'

'Not in itself, but perhaps the thought counted. And it did seem significant that it came with the bunch of your hair which I'd stupidly sent to the wash in my shirt.'

'What bunch of my hair?'

'Don't you remember how I collected it in the train?' I said. 'After you'd thrown the rest out of the window. And I kept it in the rubber-band holding your message on to the stone that came through my window. Though, of course, I didn't know then it was a message from you.'

She thought about that and so did I.

'Have you still got my hair?' she asked, touching her bald head as if she hardly believed she'd ever had any.

I told her how I'd given it to Michael and how it had certainly made sure of his co-operation, though at a higher price than I'd realised at the time.

'I'd never have given it to him if I'd known it would be so difficult to replace,' I said.

'And if he'd known, he might not have wanted it,' said Yelena.

'Or all the more,' I said.

She shook her head. It was a painful subject and we were both glad to drop it. She gave me back the picture of the Virgin.

'When I went into retreat,' she said, 'and made Fisher move out to educate you, I was trying very hard to hold on to his idea of me. As some contemporary, living version of that vulgar image. But I didn't succeed.'

'Why not?'

'I saw how I'd taken myself in under his influence. The reason I could see that was that I was no longer under his influence. And the reason for that . . .'

'Yes?'

'I looked in the mirror.'

'So?'

'I saw a silly woman who had taken it into her head to make you King of Ruritania.'

I wasn't quite sure what she meant.

'Your letter?'

'And your letter, Karel. I took your letter to heart.'

'I certainly took yours to heart.'

'The last thing you would do now is tell me to look in a mirror.'

I still wasn't sure what she meant. I couldn't remember much about my own letter, though I knew hers, with the phrase about 'the silly woman', almost word for word.

She didn't want to talk any more that day and the next I had an urgent summons from the Count to go to Zenda. The body of Queen Flavia had been found in the grave of her first husband, King Rudolf V, buried under the stone marked 'Rudolf Rassendyll'. I called at the hospital, but Yelena was under treatment. I left a note for her:

Great Granny resurrected. Gone to Zenda. Love, K.R.

Then I took the train to Zenda.

My great-grandfather doesn't waste much space on descriptions in his book, but he does go into some detail about the Castle of Zenda, so I can leave that out, since it's hardly changed. The old fortress part, where King Rudolf V was kept prisoner, was used as a prison and torture-centre by the Nazis and then the communist secret police, but is now open to tourists. The 18th-century chateau facing it across the moat and drawbridge, however, still belongs to the security service, *Corpus*. It was here that, after taking a taxi from the station, I found the Count, Vladek and General Practsin.

Queen Flavia and Rudolf V were also on the premises, in the basement, but I saw no need to view the remains. As the Count said, it wasn't a sight for loved ones – even Rudolf Rassendyll would have had to rely on a dentist to identify them. But the Nazis, as I'd guessed, had been very punctilious: not only had they put Flavia in a decent coffin with a discreet brass label reading 'Flavia Elphberg', they had popped her crown in too. It wasn't, of course, the crown of state – she wouldn't have had that hanging on the hat-stand in the hall when the German tanks rolled into the square – but a simple, thin gold circlet. Vladek said it was very ancient, probably dating from the middle ages.

'When *my* ancestors were kings,' said the Count.

There it lay on the massive desk in front of General Practsin. It was badly kinked, but Vladek said he knew a goldsmith who could easily iron it out. He produced a tape-measure.

'Take your hat off, please, Karl!'

I looked at the Count, standing near the window, with a view of the old Castle behind him. We were on the first floor, in a spacious office which had once been the bedroom of the villainous Duke Michael. The Count smiled at General Practsin, standing behind the desk.

'You will not need a forensic scientist to identify this member of the family,' he said, then to me: 'General Practsin has a good eye and an excellent filing-system, but he confused himself after our meeting at the 'Royal Elphberg' by turning up the photograph of a wanted criminal in a proletarian cap: a mercenary known as Karl Berg or Edwin Fenton. You should give him a better idea now.'

I took off my fur hat and, when the General had walked all

round me and satisfied himself that I was real, Vladek measured the circumference of my head and wrote the figure on his wrist.

Then we sat down to work out a final timetable. Afterwards we walked across the drawbridge and had a private view of the Castle – it was after tourist hours – finishing, as all official tours did, with the dungeon at moat-level beside the main gate from which Rudolf V was rescued by Rudolf Rassendyll. Vladek took photos to be included in his exhibition. The Count soon became fidgety.

'I know what it's like to be a prisoner,' he said.

'Don't we all?' I said. 'But perhaps not you, General Practsin?'

'I was a prisoner here,' he said. 'In Zenda, though not in this particular room.'

'You must find it depressing to revisit – or even to look at from your office?'

'No, on the contrary,' he said, without any alteration in his permanently lugubrious expression, 'my spirits are always raised by being on the right side of the walls. Or, if I'm on the wrong side, by having the key in my hand.'

He swung the huge old key with which he had locked the inner door of the dungeon in case we should be disturbed. I was encouraged – he if anyone would surely know how best to stay on the right side and keep control of the key.

Vladek, the Count and I dined and spent the night at an expensive hotel on the far side of the small town of Zenda. 'The Tarlenheim' was a nineteenth-century French-style chateau perched on a hill with a view across to the Castle – my great-grandfather describes staying there when it was a private house belonging to Vladek's family. Now, like the 'Royal Elphberg', it belonged partly to the Count, but as he said to Vladek:

'You're happier without it, dear boy. The last thing artists need is a lot of property. Look at the way that promising young Spanish draughtsman ruined his art once he began to acquire real estate all over France!'

'Do you mean Picasso?' asked Vladek.

'Women and chateaux!' said the Count. 'What a wasted life!'

I learnt, incidentally, on this occasion, how Vladek made his living. It wasn't from selling his own pictures, but by brokering the sale abroad of old furniture, paintings and *objets d'art*. There was nothing crooked about this – Ruritanian museums were allowed to dispose of their unwanted possessions – but Vladek did nicely out

274

of selling in hard currency and paying the museums in Ruritanian krunas. It wasn't, obviously, a trade that could last indefinitely and he was pinning a lot of hopes on his exhibition in the Palace of Youth.

Two weeks before it was due to open the government fell, after losing a vote of no confidence. An election was scheduled for the early summer and meanwhile the President installed a caretaker government of moderates, led by the suave and popular foreign minister, Heinz Albert, who, although German, was sympathetic to Slavs and always at odds with the hard-liners in the government and the military. He was also a particular friend of both the President and the Count.

Albert and his moderate cabinet had only just moved into their new offices, when it was announced that the body of Queen Flavia had been discovered in the cemetery at Zenda and that she and her first husband would now join Rudolf Rassendyll in the royal vault in Strelsau Cathedral. Their grave at Zenda was to be left empty, with the stone reading 'Rudolf Rassendyll' still standing and the leader-writers of the Ruritanian press agreed this would be a fitting local monument to an elusive character and certainly not less of a draw for tourists.

At about the same time, but without publicity, *Corpus* began to investigate irregularities in the administration of the airforce. The main military airfield near Zenda was effectively occupied by units of the security force and the senior officers placed under house arrest.

The state funeral of the last king and queen of Ruritania received world-wide coverage, albeit as a curiosity item at the foot of front pages or the end of main news-bulletins on TV and radio. The train bringing the two coffins from Zenda was met at Strelsau station by the President with a ceremonial guard. Led by a military band and six mounted hussars, followed on foot by the President, members of the caretaker government and military chiefs – minus General Rischenheim of the airforce – the coffins were carried up the hill to the Cathedral on gun-carriages.

The Cathedral itself was packed with the Ruritanian great and good and foreign ambassadors and the cameras recording the ceremony were able to pan – as the coffins of Flavia and Rudolf V were laid side-by-side in front of the chancel steps – to the waxwork

275

of Rudolf Rassendyll, freshly installed in a glass case in the side aisle. The Archbishop of Strelsau – another good friend of the Count – described in his address the different kinds of heroism displayed by all three: the steady endurance of the royal prisoner; the flamboyant courage of his English cousin; the defiant patriotism of the queen, last of her line, in the face of Nazi aggression. Then he held up the very crown she had worn as she died, crushed by the tanks, but now restored to its original shape; and, as many patriots wept openly, he went down from his pulpit and placed the crown on the high altar.

But, as the service drew to an end, those watching it on BBC and Ruritanian Television were carried away from the Archbishop standing in front of the altar as he gave his blessing; briefly shown the two coffins with their ceremonial guards and the VIPs kneeling in the front row of the congregation – among them the President and his wife – and brought in close to the waxwork of Rudolf Rassendyll at the side. Then, rapidly passing over the main body of the congregation, these favoured viewers in Britain and Ruritania found themselves suddenly focussing on the outside end of the back row. Could this be true? It must be a trick of the camera. Rudolf Rassendyll – or it might be Rudolf V, come to that – appeared to be kneeling there in the flesh.

The congregation itself, of course, missed this *coup de théâtre* altogether and the two wayward cameras flicked almost immediately back to the main action, as the service ended and the VIPs, led by the President, began to leave their seats. The television viewers must have been still rubbing their eyes in disbelief as they were carried for a second time to the back of the Cathedral to catch another fleeting glimpse of the same red-headed, long-nosed figure as he hurried towards the door, pausing for a moment to stoop and kiss the toe of the famous statue of Our Lady of Wloczovar.

The mystery was cleared up next day by headlines in the Ruritanian papers and front-page news in the rest of the world's press. The heroic Queen Flavia was not the last of her line. The person who looked so like Rudolf Rassendyll was indeed his direct descendant by the secret marriage to Queen Flavia. What could be more natural or romantically appropriate than that Karl Rassendyll should attend his great-grandmother's belated funeral? In fact he had been in Ruritania for at least six months and had even found his way into the rebellious province of Karapata, where, according to the BBC's reporter, Clare Studebaker, who was to interview him that evening but had not known his identity at the time, he had behaved very much as his dashing great-grandfather might have done. Asked for his response to this astonishing news, the philosopher-president, Stepan Slobodjak, replied that he was delighted fate should have delivered this charming coda to a solemn and moving ceremony and hoped that Karl Rassendyll might pay him a call before he returned to London and feel free to visit Ruritania again at some time in the future.

My interview with Clare was rated a success. I turned off her questions about my activities in Karapata with careless replies about the kindness and hospitality of all Ruritanians and raved about the scenery. I realised, of course, I said, that there were political problems, but no one had expected me, as a visiting Englishman, to take sides and how could I?

'You had no difficulties making yourself understood?'

'None whatever. My mother was German, so it's, as you might say, my mother-tongue and as for Ruritanian I found it almost as easy to pick up as lying in bed.'

Karapata, of course, said Clare, was very beautiful and relatively unspoiled, but what of Plotla, which I had also visited? I replied that it saddened me to see the dire results of a command economy, but was sure the West, if properly approached, would be particularly sympathetic to Ruritania's needs.

'What makes you think that?'

'I'm recalling, I suppose, how they rallied round my great-grandmother, Queen Flavia, after the First War. And it wouldn't be hard to put a small, united country like this one back on its feet.'

'But Ruritania is sadly disunited at present.'

'It only needs a determined and fair-minded leader. I'm sure the election in the summer will produce the man for the hour.'

'Have you any thought of claiming your great-grandmother's throne?'

'Good Heavens, no! It's a lovely, romantic idea, of course, for Ruritania to become a kingdom again. Obviously it would do wonders for tourism. But a country isn't a piece of property. A country is its people and they must choose their own leader.'

'Suppose the Ruritanian people did want you as their king? Would you accept?'

'I wasn't brought up to be a king, you know, but just to make my way in the world like everybody else. I'd be deeply honoured, of course, and feel I owed it to my great-grandmother, who surely never wanted her crown buried with her, not to

277

refuse out of hand, but – Heavens! – I'm not sure I'd have the nerve.'

'Wouldn't you?'

'How can I tell?'

'I'm thinking of that occasion in Karapata recently when my team and I were stopped by a lorry-load of armed men and made to lie on the ground . . .'

'Yes, well, that's the sensible thing to do if people with guns are suggesting it . . .'

'But you were with us, Karl, and you didn't do the sensible thing – not even when one of the guerrillas fired at the ground just beside you – you kept on standing and talked us out of trouble. Wouldn't you call that nerve?'

'More like stupidity. I never believe anybody can really mean me harm. I always see people as basically friendly and reasonable. And, of course, it was useful to be able to speak a bit of Ruritanian.'

'You look remarkably like your great-grandfather – do you think you *are* like him?'

'I wish I was. But no – he was a real old-fashioned English gentleman and I'm just the son of a socialist schoolmaster.'

I genuinely hadn't known in advance that Clare would put in the heroic bit. She was, I suppose, genuinely impressed by it; but of course the explanation left out the fact that the guerrillas wouldn't have been so friendly if they hadn't known who I was and that depended on a lot of events in my Karapatan experience which were also being left out. So it was a disgracefully rigged interview, but what can anyone expect? People don't appear real under bright lights in front of cameras by *being* real. And who can blame Clare? She needed her own exclusive king to be real too, not a one-day wonder.

Vladek came in on the act next. He filled three rooms in the Palace of Youth with his accumulated paintings, but the last room was devoted to photographs, portraits and reconstructed scenes of 'Karl Rassendyll in Ruritania'. The photos from the dungeon in Zenda Castle were evocative, of course, but the portraits and reconstructed scenes looked as if they were drawn in barbed wire and blood and were quite dull in content, since the Count had censored any that suggested I'd fought with the guerrillas. The head-stand 'masterpiece' had also been left out in case it should seem too insulting to the President. The success of the show, to Vladek's chagrin, was his photo of me and Magda, posed in a window of Previce Castle and titled 'Karl and Karapatan Girl'. My red hair with the virulent green of her ethnic costume against the snow outside the window thrilled the public. Poster-size versions were sold by the hundred, postcards by the thousand.

A few days after the exhibition opened I took tea with the President, arriving by taxi in the palace square to find an enthusiastic crowd and a mob of press reporters and photographers. Vladek came with me, but I made a point of paying the taxi-driver myself, with a thick wodge of Ruritanian krunas (the Count had already paid in advance in dollars). As I reached the bottom step a little girl of about ten ran forward and held out a red rose. I took the rose and kissed her, then taking the rose in my teeth, lifted her off her feet and held her up for the cameras. As I put her carefully down again, reporters from the front of the crowd, which was being held back by police, shouted questions:

'What are your feelings, Karl?'

'It's a nice house.'

'Do you want to live in it?'

'Haven't seen the inside yet?'

'Do you think Ruritania needs a king?'

'It's already got a president.'

'What will you talk about?'

'Englishmen always talk about the weather.'

I ran up the steps two at a time, with Vladek close behind, and waved the rose nonchalantly from the top step before going in.

The drawing-room where the President and his wife received us was large and ornate, with chandeliers, mirrors, paintings, silk-covered chairs and big windows looking across the Volzer to the gracious part of the city. Vladek told me afterwards that most of the furniture and fittings were reproduction Second Empire, itself a mix-up of imitations of earlier styles.

The little President looked older than when I'd last seen him at the top of the steps. It might have been that he'd been improved by distance then or that he'd aged since with the anxiety of the Kapitsa Atrocity. His hair seemed whiter, his eye-sockets more cavernous and his flesh grey and flabby where before it had looked pink and chubby. He spoke hoarsely and he moved and sat stiffly, as if he had a perpetual pain in the lower back. His wife was taller than him – a thin, nervous, bird-like person with a high, fussy voice. They were more like a couple of retired schoolteachers than the head of state and first lady. The President, however, in spite of his used-up appearance, had the manner of somebody who liked being looked at, whereas she never quite caught my eye and I thought would have preferred not to be visible at all. A flunkey in a dark blue uniform with silver buttons served us from a side-board with porcelain cups of tea and German cakes. I asked if tea was a usual thing in the presidential palace.

'No, it's in your honour, Mr Rassendyll,' said Slobodjak, 'as an Englishman.'

I took the point. I was a visitor from a foreign country and had no business in his except as a tourist. Mrs Slobodjak rammed the point home by asking how long I was staying. I replied that I had no immediate plans to leave – I was enjoying myself too much. They both seemed edgy, probably because they'd witnessed my arrival and found it altogether too showy. The President asked me about my experiences in Karapata and when I replied that the people there seemed mostly friendly and peace-loving, said, with a touch of sarcasm:

'You never encountered any terrorists, then?'

'Probably,' I said, 'but what would they have against me?'

He left the subject abruptly and asked me what I did in England.

'Worked in the City,' I said, 'but latterly I was more of a philosopher.'

'Really?'

'Not professional, like yourself. But I thought about things.'

'What kind of things?'

'Life. Purpose – or lack of it. Forgive me, I haven't read your books. What's your own area?'

'Absurdity,' he said in his Louis Armstrong gravelly voice. 'The absurdity of all human endeavour in the light of history and our chance existence on a lump of matter in a mysterious universe.'

'It sounds very close to my own line of thought,' I said. 'Could I be a disciple of yours without knowing it?'

'The arguments are too bleak to live by,' he said, 'but philosophy is not a practical subject. Philosophers, you know, are often hedonists in ordinary life.'

He tucked into a piece of sticky chocolate cake.

'I know this is bad for me, but I like it. Mitzi tells me . . .' he glanced wearily at his wife, as if he knew she'd heard this one a thousand times before, but would have to hear it again and not for the last time either . . . 'that I deny the validity of cake but keep on eating it.'

280

'I also tell Stepi,' she said, her glance flitting about his head like a fly that couldn't settle, 'that if only he could prove its validity, perhaps he could give up eating it.'

My only real acquaintance with philosophy was my mother reading *Alice in Wonderland* to me as a child and we seemed to be quite close to that now. Vladek, however, began asking about the pictures and furniture and Mrs Slobodjak was a keen custodian of them. They moved about the room examining things.

'Come and see my library, Mr Rassendyll!' said Slobodjak.

It was more of a study than a library, quite small, with nothing much in it except the desk and chair and built-in shelves of books.

'Not so very many books, you see,' he said. 'A philosopher doesn't need to read all that much. You can never accuse a philosopher of ignorance, only of stupidity. I began to be a serious philosopher only in prison, in Previce Castle, as a matter of fact, when I had no books at all. I believe you have stayed there with Count von Wunklisch, our rich re-immigrant?'

I nodded, looking at the shelves to see if he kept Machiavelli handy. It seemed not: Mao, Marcus Aurelius, Marcuse, Marx . . .

'Your activities in Karapata are not unknown to me,' he said. 'My attention has been drawn to the photograph of a terrorist making an unequivocal sign of victory from the middle of a mountain stream. This terrorist, I understand, was an Englishman called Edwin Fenton who was later captured and condemned to death – a sentence never carried out because of a sudden mutiny in the barracks where he was being held. Naturally you did not refer to this episode in your TV interview. But I was surprised Ms Studebaker failed to. She can be a very sharp and even aggressive performer. If she had done any serious research, consulted the military authorities, for instance, she might have formed and imparted a very different view of you and given you a rougher ride, don't you think?'

'Not really,' I said. 'If I'd been making any political claims I'd have opened myself to tighter questioning, but I was only coming on as a kind of circus performer. You don't make the clown take off his flat cap and makeup and reveal himself as just ordinary Ed Fenton. That would spoil everyone's pleasure, wouldn't it?'

Slobodjak now lay down on a small *chaise longue* to ease his back and waved me to the only other seat – the chair at the desk.

'You said your father was a socialist. What sort of socialist?'

'A real one. A believer.'

'What did he think about his ancestry?'

'We never talked about it. I imagine he disapproved.'

'I should have liked to meet him. Well, if you're going home in a day or two, there's no need to spoil everybody's pleasure.'

'You really don't want me to stay around?'

'No, really not. We have enough troubles in the present without digging up the past.'

'Would a week be too long?'

'Say five days!'

'And you aren't as keen for me to come back some time as you said you were?'

'Some time in the future, Mr Rassendyll, I said. After about 2001.'

'Fair enough,' I said. 'I'll see you then.'

'No, I expect to be dead. No longer a fragment of the consciousness of absurdity.'

I got up from the chair – the very same chair I'm sitting in now to write this – and, running my finger along the books with authors beginning M, went to the door. Even a philosopher shouldn't be ignorant of Machiavelli if he takes a job as head of state.

29

The Key to the Kingdom

Five days was perfect. I'd suggested a week to be on the safe side, but fate – you can call it providence or the zodiac or God or the laws of chance if you prefer – made the philosopher of absurdity draw the line finer. At dawn on the day Vladek had tipped off his friends in the media that I was booked on the midday flight to London, the Cossacks enveloped Kapitsa and the Ruritanian Army of the True Faith erupted out of the province of Karapata and across the Volzer.

The Cossacks had sweated with such fervour in their workshops that nearly forty tanks actually rumbled into Kapitsa on their own tracks and seized the town and barracks. The Second Regiment immediately arrested their new senior officers and released their mutinous junior ones from custody, declaring themselves allies of their fellow Slavs from Ukraine. The units of the First Armoured Regiment which had remained in Kapitsa to police the Second Regiment lost two tanks and an armoured vehicle in a foolish attempt to defend the barracks against overwhelming odds, but their other three tanks – chocked up in the workshops for repair – were captured, as were a dozen or so lighter armoured vehicles.

Meanwhile – some measure of the invaders' confidence, as the newspapers put it next day – at least a third of their armament never even left its transporters, but was carried straight through the town and parked in a sinister convoy pointing along the main road to Zenda. The transporters drove so urgently through the streets that the people peering fearfully out of their windows as they were woken by the racket, had no time to observe – even if they'd been technically knowledgeable enough – that the tracks of the tanks they were carrying did not always even join up; and they had no way of telling that not one of them had a working engine, while many contained no engine at all.

At Kapitsa airfield the sudden arrival of three tanks at – and shortly afterwards through – the main gates convinced the sentries that resistance was useless, though they had time to ring the alarm. The tanks were followed by a yellow 4×4, which raced straight for the airfield's single helicopter and arrived beside it at the same moment as a green 4×4 carrying the airforce major in command of the airfield. This major was a large, clumsy man with a swinging beer-belly and flabby jowls either side of an untidy Zapata moustache. By the time he'd extricated himself from his seat, his driver and the helicopter pilot had their hands up and his bodyguard, who had immediately exchanged fire with two armed passengers from the yellow car, was lying wounded on the tarmac. The major's surrender was taken by a thin, white-faced officer, half his own size, whose recently-fired machine-gun trembled slightly, but whose hypnotic pale blue eyes never wavered from his face. The airfield was defended by only a small force of soldiers and the major had little choice but to give instructions over the radio in his car for all resistance to cease. Then he got into the yellow car with his diminutive captor, whose sidekick – a corporal in regular army uniform with the flashes of the Second Regiment – made the captured helicopter pilot and driver load the wounded man into the green car.

Shocked and dismayed as he was, however, the major still had hopes of saving the four aircraft in his care and he saw that three of them were already emerging from their hangars. The pilots scrambled as soon as they heard the alarm, but in their haste the ground staff reversed one of the tractors too abruptly and damaged both the coupling gear and the fourth aircraft. From the major's point of view, though, three out of four planes airborne would make good reading on the official report and, as the yellow car stopped in front of the main building and he lowered his legs to the ground and began to raise the great weight of his belly, he was overjoyed to see the three aircraft taxi forward. The nearest of the Russian tanks (was the Soviet Union reclaiming its empire already?) began to swivel its turret and depress its gun, but the major reckoned it would be too late to stop his pilots taking off. There was a light morning mist hanging over the airfield and the jets would be into it and invisible before the tank's gunner could get their range.

But as he stared gratefully at the mist he thought he'd begun to hallucinate. It was full of horsemen. From under the mist, like the foam under an incoming wave, came a long line of galloping Cossacks in traditional white astrakhan hats, tunics and breeches, some with drawn sabres, some with ordinary farm bill-hooks, and, stabbing and ripping as they broke like surf around the three aircraft, left them slewed and crippled before wheeling in a long arc and breaking round them a second time from behind. As the Cossacks re-formed and trotted demurely towards the main building, the traumatised pilots could be seen jumping out of their damaged machines and haring back to the safety of the hangars. The airforce major – whose description of the episode was published in the Ruritanian press some weeks afterwards – only fully believed what he'd seen when, half an hour later, the convoy of horseboxes which had deposited the Cossack chargers at the far end of the airfield drove in to collect them.

Kapitsa was seized almost without casualties, but the army checkpoints at the two main bridges over the River Volzer were each equipped with an armoured vehicle and put up serious resistance. However, when they called for air support from airforce headquarters at Zenda and were told that none was available, they gave up. Both sides had dead and wounded. Michael disarmed the surrendered troops and released those that were uninjured to walk the sixty miles or so to Strelsau, while he and his victorious guerrillas settled down with the captured armoured vehicles to hold the two bridges into Karapata and the main road linking Strelsau and Kapitsa.

By the time I reached Zenda Airport for my return flight to London, the news that Ruritania was in the grip of civil war had reached everybody. Disembarking from the Count's new crimson Mercedes at the airport entrance, I found only a small group of young reporters and photographers waiting for me. Their seniors were urgently filing what news they had or besieging the government, parliament and the presidential palace for more. Flanked by Vladek and the Count, with my rucksack slung over one shoulder, I gave a short statement:

'I'm not leaving Ruritania because I want to. Even less do I want to now that the country in which I've found so much happiness seems to be tearing itself apart. The President personally asked me to leave no later than today. He is a wise and fatherly man and I couldn't think of refusing such a request, even though it seemed a bit unreasonable, not to say authoritarian. I got used to that sort of treatment from my own father when I was a boy, but I thought now that I'm grown up . . . Well, even if I'd considered refusing, it wouldn't have made much difference, would it? Fatherly requests tend to turn into orders if they meet any opposition. So I'm going. But please make it clear that far from being a rat leaving a sinking ship I'm a cat being shoved out into the cold. And I'd swop this any day . . .' (holding up my EC passport) '. . . especially today, for one of yours.'

Then the three of us moved towards the departure desks in the concourse. Here there was a problem. We'd hoped that all scheduled flights would be cancelled because of the emergency, but the government had evidently been occupied with more important matters and whereas the various airlines had themselves cancelled incoming flights for fear of losing their aircraft, for the same reason they were only too eager to maintain their outgoing flights. All the desks had queues of anxious travellers and the departures board told us that the flight to London via Warsaw was still due to leave at midday. The Count thought we might have to invoke General Practsin to get it stopped on some specious excuse, but Vladek had a better idea. He pointed out that the desk issuing last-minute tickets was besieged with anxious foreigners and, while the Count and I joined the back of the queue to be checked in, Vladek made a quick survey across the way and found an elderly American woman standing to one side and clutching her heart with apprehension and despair as she watched the struggle to reach the ticket-desk.

'I have a ticket for tomorrow to Frankfurt,' she told Vladek, when he asked politely if he could help, 'but I know there will be no planes by tomorrow.'

'How would Warsaw or London do instead?' asked Vladek.

'London would be the greatest thing that ever happened to me – it's almost New York.'

So, followed by my two or three most persistent young press-hounds, I approached the woman and offered to exchange tickets. Seeing my entourage she became momentarily suspicious.

'Is this some kind of stunt?'

'The stunt that saved a kingdom,' murmured the Count, *sotto voce* in German.

That was an exaggeration, but the story and photo in the Strelsau *Abendstern* of Karl Rassendyll giving up his chance of safety and risking the wrath of the authoritarian president ('just like my father') for the sake of an unknown elderly woman ('perhaps she reminded him of his mother') was one more candle lit in front of my myth. Mrs Amstervan recognised her gallant saviour as soon as she heard his name and the exact spot where he kissed her cheek as he wished her a safe journey was still being shown to reporters when she reached New York the following day. What interested me most about the whole affair was Vladek's part in it. He, the idealist, not only had no scruples about such blatant media chicanery, he actually dreamed it up.

So we returned to Strelsau with a ticket to Frankfurt for the following day. I went to ground in the 'Royal Elphberg', while we waited to see what the President, the government and the military would do next. This was the most dangerous moment – the rocky narrows in our strategy. The military chiefs, who would surely have to resign and possibly face court martial if they sat on their hands, had nothing to lose by ordering what remained of the Ruritanian Army – based in Strelsau – to attack and if possible destroy Michael and his guerrillas. Even with its handful of tanks, armoured vehicles and artillery, the Army could probably win quite easily and if the airforce at Zenda became operational again, it would be a savage walkover. They couldn't, of course, take on the Cossacks in Kapitsa – especially believing as they did that the unused tanks were useable – but without air support it would be very risky for the Cossacks to advance further and impossible for them to hold Kapitsa indefinitely.

The President could only resign or side with the hard-liners. His equivocal part in the suppression of the Kapitsa mutiny had lost him the support of Slav nationalists and he'd never been liked by ex-communist Slavs because of his history of dissidence. With no chance of persuading the guerrillas to back off, he would either have to try clobbering them or give in to Michael's demands for semi-independence and lose the support of the German population. As for the Cossacks, they already held nearly a third of the country simply by sitting in Kapitsa with the whole unprotected province of Plotla behind them; and they seriously threatened both Zenda and Strelsau itself. The president's first move was to summon the Ukrainian ambassador and make a personal phone call to the President of Ukraine, but neither had any effect at all. The Ukrainians insisted they had no prior knowledge of the Cossacks' action, didn't condone it, were baffled by it and had no means whatever of rounding up a herd of elephants which had clearly gone rogue. They could only recommend that the President of Ruritania tell his government to be nicer in future to their Slav minority.

The caretaker government was also in difficulty. They couldn't ignore the President and negotiate with the rebel Slavs on their own account; nor did they want to use the army and were convinced that, if they did, they would lose the country to the Slavs. If they chose to fight they would certainly have to release General Rischenheim and his senior officers so that what remained of the airforce could take part. But if they ordered the release of General Rischenheim they would have to replace General Practsin as head of *Corpus* and if he refused to go and his security forces stood by him, then the

Army would have to deal with *Corpus* before going on to deal with the guerrillas, let alone the Cossacks. And although the personnel of *Corpus* – at least in Strelsau – were predominantly German, General Practsin kept a very tight grip of his organisation and would be difficult to oust or replace at short notice.

From the government side their position must have looked hopeless. The Count, who was in constant touch with them, told us that several ministers might have been glad to use my spare ticket to Frankfurt. But our position was also weak. I had never contemplated the military conquest of Ruritania, which was probably impossible anyway with the forces at my disposal and would certainly have started me off with the wrong image as king. Neither Michael nor the Cossacks had any plans to advance further or indeed any further plans period; and if the government havered long enough they might discover that the threat was less terrible than it appeared. In a way, it was all a much more fraught version of my head-stand in front of the President's palace: if the performance was taken seriously right away, well and good. But if not, I might just have to go right way up again and slink off. This time, though, I'd be leaving the guerrillas and the Cossacks still standing on their heads.

My room at the 'Royal Elphberg' looked down over the Volzer to the parliament building on the far bank. The Count, returning from his latest session with the prime minister, said that the cabinet had discussed whether they could ask me, as 'a new friend of Ruritanians on both sides of the ethnic divide', to negotiate with the guerrillas and their Cossack allies, but thought it impossible without the consent of the President. He was so angry about my antics at the airport, as already gleefully reported in the Strelsau *Abendstern*, that he'd ordered my arrest and forcible deportation if I was not in Mrs Amstervan's seat to Frankfurt without fail the next day. General Practsin joined us shortly afterwards and said he'd received the President's order and would either have to obey it or become an open rebel himself.

'Any chance of that?' I asked.

'You want me to seize the President and lock him up in the dungeon at Zenda?'

'Why not?'

'It would damage my reputation, Mr Rassendyll. Not to mention yours. In both cases fatally, I would think.'

'I wonder if the President would like Mrs Amstervan's ticket,' said Vladek.

It was a conundrum which, like a sudden stalemate in chess, I hadn't foreseen. Only the President could invite me to resolve the conflict between Slavs and Germans and so in effect hand me the key to my kingdom; but the President was the person who least wanted anybody to be king, let alone me. I asked the Count, if it would be possible to persuade the President to grant me a farewell interview.

'For what purpose, dear boy? Not to kick his teeth in, I hope? I have no particular affection for the man myself, but I think personal violence would be counter-productive from your point of view.'

'He's a philosopher,' I said. 'He ought to be willing to listen to an argument.'

'I doubt if you can assume that and I doubt if you are as good at arguing as you are at kicking teeth, but we can only try.'

The Count spoke to his friends the prime minister and the Archbishop of Strelsau and they spoke to their friend the President and I was given an appointment for half past nine that night, provided I came completely alone and without any press attention whatever.

Wearing my grey fur hat and a long coat, so that I looked and felt like a Russian assassin, I arrived at a side door of the palace, was admitted by a flunkey and taken straight to the President's library. He was seated at his desk, covered with papers; through an open door between the bookcases in one wall, I could see an office with a studious-looking girl in glasses busy at the phone. There was no sign of any security. However low Slobodjak's opinion of me, he obviously had no fear that I might do him an injury.

'Would you be so kind as to shut that door, Mr Rassendyll?'

I closed out the secretary and sat on the *chaise longue*. He laid his spectacles on the papers in front of him, put down his pen, rubbed his impressive brow and turned his chair round to face me. He looked another ten years older than when I'd last seen him less than a week ago and hardly had the energy to speak.

'What do you wish to say to me?'

'I believe I could help you avoid a civil war.'

'There already is one.'

'I could make peace between the Germans and the Slavs. With your help.'

'What makes you think that? I know you're good at imposing on the press, but this goes somewhat beyond publicity.'

'Everybody seems to see this conflict in crude material terms, as a struggle for political power or territory or even personal gain, but there are ideals at stake.'

He rubbed his back slowly with one hand but didn't interrupt and I went on to tell him about the True Faith and Yelena. I didn't reveal that I knew her well, but explained how powerfully she'd impressed me when I first saw her on the steps of the church in Chostok. It was listening to her, I said, that made me want to fight for the guerrillas (was that entirely a lie?). I described how I'd taken part in the capture of Bilavice and seen this extraordinary woman again, dressed as a soldier, just at the moment when Tishkon was dying. Then I told him about the train-journey to Kapitsa, the hair-cutting episode and my last-minute escape from the firing-squad in the turmoil of the mutiny. I didn't mention that the mutiny had been brought forward specially for me nor that I had gone to Sebrikov. After the escape, I said, I had lived quietly on a farm until Vladek and the Count were released and I could rejoin them in Strelsau. The President listened carefully and patiently, though we could hear the telephone constantly ringing next door and he must have expected to hear at any moment that the guerrillas or the Cossacks or both had begun to close in on the capital.

'So you see,' I said, 'that it's not this bandit chief of the guerrillas or even perhaps straight nationalism that you're dealing with, it's a belief. It's a crusade for the True Faith, led by this strange woman, a kind of Joan of Arc, who comes originally from Ukraine and must have inspired the Cossacks to follow her.'

He rose painfully from his chair, paced the length of the room and then came and sat beside me on the *chaise longue*. I made space for him so that he could put his back against the raised part.

'Thank you,' he said. 'I like your story and I like you better for telling it to me so simply and modestly. I'm sure it's an edited version and I'm sure your own part in these events was more important than you pretend. It's a story that makes me feel sad and old and out of touch. I see that I've been deceived about these guerrillas – or terrorists, as we usually call them in Strelsau. I haven't taken their aspirations seriously and although I'm mainly Slav myself, I've become a hostage to German interests. It is this, no doubt, which has exacerbated the divisions in our country and this which has brought us all – and myself in particular – to our present crisis. Greek Tragedy, you know, says it all: the truth will always emerge in the end, however you try to suppress it. I, who gave the best part of my life to proving that fact to communists, have now become an instrument for suppressing the truth. What is it you want to do, Mr Rassendyll?'

290

'If you and I were to ask to meet them . . .'

'Yes, by all means, arrange that if you can! But, for God's sake, without publicity!'

'I'm flying to Frankfurt tomorrow.'

He smiled faintly and wearily.

'I doubt it. All flights have been stopped. The airport is close to the military airfield. We couldn't risk a jet fighter colliding with an airliner, though I admit I had moments of wishing such an airliner might have contained you.'

'You were going to fight, then?'

'It was on the cards.'

'You didn't kick him in the teeth, then?' said the Count, when I got back to the hotel and told him of my success.

'It wasn't necessary. He saw that he'd been stupid. Also, oddly enough for a philosopher who pretends to believe in absurdity, he's really an idealist.'

I sat down and drank the whisky the Count had poured for me. As I did so, the sheath-knife pushed into my back pocket pressed uncomfortably against my buttock. I pulled it out and put it on the table next to the bottle of whisky. The Count looked at it and then at me.

'Did you have that with you, dear boy?'

'I borrowed it from Vladek. But it's not something to take to a peace conference.'

'What a risk if you'd been searched! How very rash and irresponsible you still are, dear boy! Did you imagine the old fellow would have a go at you, like that American missionary?'

'I didn't give it a lot of thought. I just felt that we haven't come so far to be stopped by one old man not being able to admit he was wrong.'

The Count picked up the knife, slid it out of its sheath and tested the point with his finger.

'I wonder how Ruritania will enjoy being a kingdom again when you wear the crown. But why are you showing me this?'

'Why not?'

'It would be inconvenient if I happened to mention it to anyone.'

'Why should you? We're on the same side.'

'But later? If we should fall out?'

'Perish the thought!' I said.

'You mean I should be an accessory after the fact?'

'You can put it like that. You can put it that Vladek is an accessory before. But among friends those terms sound a bit legalistic.'

He returned the knife to its sheath.

'You'd never have used it, Karl Marx. Not even to threaten him! I know you better.'

I shrugged. I didn't know the answer to that myself and was glad I hadn't needed to find out.

30

Never To Be Yours

It always rains on my birthday and my thirtieth was no exception. As the Count and I, in a hired car driven by his new Polish chauffeur, left the 'Royal Elphberg' for our rendezvous, it was raining so hard we could scarcely see the parliament building across the driver. The surface of the Volzer looked as if it was coming to the boil. We stayed close to the river most of the way; the rendezvous was an island near the small town of Dresch, about forty miles from Strelsau and twenty from the nearest bridge held by the guerrillas. On the island was a country-club (formerly Party membership only), with tennis-courts, facilities for boating and fishing (discontinued), a dance hall, casino, restaurant and self-contained chalets among birch trees. The place had evidently been created by some Russia-freak, perhaps in the early days after the communist takeover when Germans were still definitely bad and Russians thought to be good: the chalets were called 'dachas' and each was named after a Russian writer acceptable to the Party. The Count had rented 'Mayakovsky Dacha' and sent some trusted staff from the 'Royal Elphberg' ahead to stock it with refreshments and other temporary amenities, such as soap and towels, tissues and vases of flowers.

The owners of the country-club knew nothing of our meeting and, to maintain complete secrecy, there was no attempt to provide serious security. I was the guarantor to Michael and Yelena of their safe conduct and the Count and General Practsin guaranteed the President's and Prime Minister's. Yelena, driven by Orlin, came in a hired car from Kapitsa and collected Michael on the way; General Practsin brought the President with one bodyguard in a *Corpus* car; two more *Corpus* men brought the Prime Minister in another. By ten o'clock on the morning of my birthday, the morning after I should have flown to Frankfurt, the four cars had crossed the bridge from the main road to the island, circled the main country-club building without attracting any particular attention and parked beside 'Mayakovsky

Dacha'. The drivers and bodyguards took up posts round the house to keep out intruders and the rest of us assembled in the dacha's bare, wood-panelled living-room, while the rain continued to pour down outside.

Yelena and Michael were the last to arrive, she in a white round-necked shirt and light grey cotton jacket and skirt, he all in black imitation leather. He looked ill at ease and just what he was, a small-time bandit outside his natural habitat, a black beetle creeping out from under a stone. She was ethereally thin, her face, though, less cadaverous, her hair or lack of it concealed by a white woollen hat. As they entered the room, the others, drinking coffee and talking jovially, went silent. It was partly the sense that here at last was the enemy face to face, but still more, outright astonishment at the appearance and presence of Yelena. I saw at once that each one of these self-important people who thought they'd seen it all – the cynical, bantering von Wunklisch; the gloomy, watchful Practsin; the smooth, worldly Heinz Albert; and the old, disillusioned, exhausted President – was knocked sideways by her, just as I had been when I first saw her in Chostok – and was again now. I'd instructed her beforehand to treat me distantly, as if she barely knew me, but I hadn't imagined I'd need to instruct myself. It wasn't so much that I wanted to embrace her and kiss her restored face, though that would have been bliss, as to fall at her feet and kiss her toe. She gave nothing away herself, not a spark of special feeling for me in her face, but as I took her hand, she drew her little finger very lightly along mine and said in a strangled voice I hardly recognised as hers:

'Karel.'

I shook Michael's hand and introduced them both to the others, one by one, he just as Michael, she as Yelena Lopotska. He accepted coffee, she didn't; then we all sat down facing a wood-burning stove in the grate: an inner horseshoe of myself, in an upright chair with arms, flanked by the President and Prime Minister in armchairs to my right facing Yelena and Michael on a sofa to my left, with the Count and Practsin sitting a little apart near the window. There was no small-talk. The President, fascinated by Yelena, lost his look of exhaustion and began immediately to question her about the True Faith and her part in it. She replied simply that she'd been converted to it after the death of her husband, that she knew she had to lead the Ruritanian Slavs towards a better life, politically as well as spiritually; and that the Ruritanian Army of the True Faith was not a band of ruthless, professional terrorists but just what their name proclaimed them: ordinary people fighting for a belief which would otherwise be suppressed, as it always had been in the past, by Catholics and Orthodox alike. She never mentioned the Virgin Mary and regretted involving her countrymen and their tanks, but, after the atrocities and treacheries of the Ruritanian Army in Kapitsa and the ruthless efforts on the part of the authorities – especially the bombing of the Sebrikov dam, in which two innocent friends of hers had died – to bring the people of Karapata to their knees, she had seen it as a last resort.

'If I had not led out the Cossacks,' she finished, 'can you honestly say, Mr President, that the Ruritanian Army would not have crushed Karapata as soon as the snow melted and gone on to suppress the True Faith for another generation at least? One is only alive once and must do what one can in one's own time.'

The fact was, of course, that this peace conference was nothing of the sort. Everyone in the room, except the President, was already committed to a particular outcome. Even Heinz Albert, the caretaker prime minister, though he and I had never met before, had agreed with his friend the Count to edge the moderates towards a monarchy, if that could be achieved, as he put it, 'naturally, unemphatically, moderately'. He himself was a handsome, fit-looking 55-year-old, with curly white hair and a bronze complexion, who wore expensive Italian suits and hand-made shoes and loved the international circuit. The last thing he wanted was to continue as what he called 'Mayor of Ruritania' or 'second biggest frog in our local puddle'; he wanted to hop off again as Foreign Minister to the lily-pads of more stately ponds abroad. The Count, on the other hand, who had run powerful corporations and constantly increased his wealth and power by obscure board-room intrigues and manipulations, but never held any public office, longed to run a country, however poor and small. General Practsin's motives were less obvious – he was already one of the most powerful figures in Ruritania – but he thought as little of the other military chiefs as he did of Rischenheim and if they were toppled and he had a voice in their replacement, his own position would be virtually unassailable.

So what appeared to be a preponderance of Germans from the heart of the establishment negotiating with two Slav outsiders under a disinterested English referee was in fact a pressure group aimed at loosening the President's grasp on power in favour of the referee. Whether President Slovbodjak himself realised he was the victim of a velvet *coup* no one could be sure. Heinz Albert was too smooth an operator to suggest at any point that he wasn't, as he sat, confronting the two outsiders and shoulder-to-shoulder with his President. But the combination of undeclared interests all on one side with the military weakness of the Germans, plus Slobodjak's own sense of guilt at having betrayed the Slavs, would probably have been enough on its own to convince him he might as well let go. As it was, faced with Yelena, he became as soft and nearly as gooey as an overripe pear. Pity the philosopher who meets – or thinks he meets – an angel! He doesn't transform into a theologian, which is only another sort of arguer, but into a convert, a mindless worshipper of mystery and divine beneficence.

President Slobodjak fell in love with Yelena just as instantly as I had and Michael had and no doubt Fisher too (and Colonel Starvrilev and his Cossacks, for that matter, not to speak of half the population of Karapata) and was happy, like the rest of us, to think of it as something more spiritual than physical. Perhaps it was. Or perhaps it's simply physical abstinence that turns sex into love. I never succeeded in getting between Yelena's legs, but I 'loved' her far more intensely than I did Gerda or Clare or even darling Susha (to name only those sexual partners I've included in this story).

Anyway, by the time the Count's delectable cold lunch was served half way through the afternoon, the President would have ceded his palace there and then, if only Yelena had been the great-grandaughter of Queen Flavia. When the table of salads, with asparagus, caviare, smoked salmon, spiced chicken-legs, thin rolls of underdone beef, salami and cheeses was brought in by the 'Royal Elphberg' staff, Slobodjak himself filled Yelena's plate, carried it to her and sat beside her on the sofa. Had his eyes left hers for a moment he would surely have twigged the collusion of everyone else in the room, since we all – even Michael – exchanged little winks or smiles at this significant development.

During lunch the discussion turned from whether an agreement could be reached to how it could be implemented: what concessions could be offered by the Germans and accepted by the Slavs, how this might affect the constitution and the forthcoming election, how the True Faith could live at peace with the Catholic and Orthodox churches, and how security for the agreement could be guaranteed once the guerrillas dispersed to their farms and the Cossacks pulled back beyond Vlod. But would the Cossacks then pull back to Ukraine? Would Ukraine forgive them for causing trouble with a neighbouring country or would it punish them? I had to continue pretending that I had no knowledge of or contact with the Cossacks, so Yelena grasped this nettle immediately:

'The Cossacks must stay in Ruritania,' she said.

Consternation all round.

'For two reasons,' she said. 'First, because they've burnt their bridges with Ukraine. Secondly, because we Slavs of the True Faith owe our safety to them. We want them to stay and we make it an absolute condition of any agreement that they do. In any case, it would be useless to tell them to go. You might as well order them to go and shoot themselves as return to Kiev to be disciplined. They already have Kapitsa and they could seize Zenda tomorrow and maybe Strelsau the day after.'

So that potentially disastrous debt of mine was covered in advance and Yelena went on to propose that the Cossacks should be given land for their own semi-independent community in the foot-hills between Bilavice and Kapitsa, where they would remain as permanent guarantors of the good faith of Germans towards Slavs.

'Do you mean roughly the area where we dumped your hair from the train-window?' I asked, smiling at the President to remind him that he already knew this intimate secret.

'About there,' she said.

I could see that her latest devotee already liked the idea a lot.

'Goldenhair Valley!' I said, 'Land of the Ruritanian Cossacks!'

'This is how myths are made,' said Slobodjak, not disapprovingly.

'Are you suggesting they would be permanently armed?' asked Heinz Albert.

'All Cossack hosts are organised on military lines,' said Yelena. 'They will have to be attached to the State independently of the Ruritanian Army, directly answerable to the Head of State.'

There was a pause, while they all considered the implications both for the State and the Head of State, whoever that might be.

'Two separate armies?' said General Practsin.

'For two separate ethnic groups in one country,' said Yelena. 'Or you could say one body with two legs, two arms and one head.'

Outside it had stopped raining at last and through the windows a few visitors to the country club could be seen strolling through the trees. There were only a few because most were afraid of being caught between the guerrillas and the Army and broke off their spring holidays prematurely. Only the boldest and dumbest stayed and were able to boast afterwards of being present unawares at the historic Mayakovsky Dacha Treaty. There may be a moral in that.

Nibbling fastidiously at a slab of gruyère, Heinz Albert, with something of the creaky deftness of a famous but ageing matador,

297

now initiated the last phase of what had become a kind of bullfight.

'All these arrangements are very well so long as you remain President, Stepan. You can be trusted to stand up for the Slav minority and indeed our present constitution reserves more power to the Presidency than in many other republics for that very reason, as a counter-weight to the advantage held by the German majority in elections. But when – if – you should retire, we must remember that the next President will also be elected by a majority and that that person might not be so well trusted by the minority. Then all the arrangements we may make today, including this interesting proposal for a Cossack homeland, could unravel and bring about another civil war with less reasonable leaders on either side.'

The President misunderstood him – or perhaps, since politicians use a coded language of their own, understood him perfectly.

'You mean, Heinz, that the Slavs no longer trust me as they did and it will be hard to win their approval for these arrangements in the forthcoming election?'

The Prime Minister began to bite into a large red apple and put his head on one side as if he agreed but didn't commit himself to saying so.

'Should I perhaps step down and should Mrs Lopotska stand for the Presidency? Dare I say she might be equally attractive to both Slavs and Germans?'

He was joking, probably – at least everybody except Practsin smiled. Michael made his sneer and Yelena, who had risen from the sofa and was going out of the room to find the loo, bowed slightly in humorous acknowledgment.

'But I'm not a Ruritanian national,' she said. 'You should change your constitution more radically, Mr Slobodjak. You're lucky enough to have available a man everybody can love, a worthy descendant of your national heroine Queen Flavia. I think Ruritania should be a kingdom again.'

She went out, leaving us all embarrassed. This was exactly what we'd all, except the President, come here to bring about; but not so overtly. Our unspoken plan was that the ground would be opened and fertilised at this meeting and that its success through my agency would make the crop spring up more gradually in the minds of the press and public. Slobodjak was not a fool. He may never have realised that he was the victim of a preconceived plot, but as he looked round at us now he understood that Yelena had spoken for everybody. His eyes came back to his particular friend, Heinz Albert, and he spoke Latin:

'*Et tu, Brute?*'

'A wild idea,' said the Prime Minister, without dropping his eyes, continuing to munch delicately round the core of his apple, 'but if what we're really talking about is unifying the country, it's nearly as attractive as your own wild idea for Mrs Lopotska.'

Slobodjak went on looking at him as he thought about it.

'Could you get a majority in parliament on this platform?' he asked.

'Very likely. Especially if we achieve a good agreement at this meeting and make known who was its designer.'

That put the whole conspiracy in a nutshell, but if Slobodjak guessed he pretended not to.

'It bears thinking about,' he said.

Soon afterwards the Count's staff came in with a birthday cake and lit its thirty blue candles.

'A celebration?' said the President.

'A tribute to our young friend,' said the Count, waving at me, 'on reaching the age of discretion.'

The President examined the cake. It was iced all in white with a crimson script: 'Karl Marx Rassendyll'. Slobodjak turned to me incredulously:

'Is that really your name?'

'I said my father was a believer.'

'Just as well you're not,' he said.

I saw Yelena come into the room and stop in surprise at the cake.

'Not at least in *that* prophet,' I said.

I cut the first slice. Nobody mentioned a wish or sang 'Happy Birthday'. Everybody knew what the wish was and we none of us felt like pretending to be children. I put the slice on a plate and gave it to Yelena, who nibbled a crumb for form's sake.

'Red writing, white icing, blue candles,' she said. 'How tactful of the Count to remind us of your neutral nationality and how sly to put the Elphberg rose there too!'

She sounded and looked now like the victim of a vampire. She'd probably been doctoring herself in the loo. It struck me she must have put in her sudden sword-thrust about the kingdom because she was running out of puff and couldn't wait any longer for the others to bring the bull to his last stand. The bull himself, carrying his own slice of birthday cake, came and joined us.

'I can understand why you fought for those people,' he said, perhaps meaning both of us. 'You *are* very young and it's sometimes easier to be right when you're young than when you're old.'

The meeting broke up soon afterwards. The public would be told on the news that night that a truce had been arranged and they could sleep quietly. The details would be worked out in the next few days. Asked what exactly the public should be told, the President said:

'Where the meeting took place, those who took part in it and that the conclusion was peace and brotherhood.'

'I'd rather you didn't mention my name,' said Yelena. 'You can say a representative of the Cossacks.'

'And shouldn't we say to whom the credit for the truce is due?' asked the Count.

'The credit is due to all of us,' said the President, 'but principally to this lady and to the great-grandson of our last monarch. The lady cannot be mentioned, but perhaps the gentleman can. Not his middle name, however! That would confuse people.'

I was able to speak privately, though very briefly, to Yelena as I helped her out to her car.

'If it happens, will you come to Strelsau as soon as possible?'

'Perhaps.'

'And will you revoke your sentence of "never to be yours"?'

She stumbled – or perhaps deliberately pressed against me.

'I would, dear Karel, with all my heart, but one sometimes speaks the truth without meaning it.'

She kissed me on the mouth and got slowly into the car.

'Please thank Colonel Stavrilev and tell him what you've done for him,' I said.

'As he has done for us,' she said and lay back against the seat.

I couldn't disguise my red eyes and wet face from Michael as I shook his hand through the car window and Orlin drove away. Nor could I disguise them from the President who was waiting by his own car to shake my hand.

'She's very ill?' he asked.

'I'm afraid so.'

'I'm sorry,' he said. 'But she did the trick, didn't she? In my view, Karl – may I call you that? – she could very easily be the Virgin Mary. At any rate the Virgin Mary herself could have done no more than she did. And if gods come to earth at all, I'm sure they never do stay long.'

The President stayed in office until after the election, having promised he would readily step down and endorse a new constitution if the Royal Party of National Reconciliation (PRRN), led by Count von Wunklisch and Heinz Albert, gained a majority. My reputation rose like a gas balloon with the news of my role in averting civil war and postcards of the flat-capped guerrilla in the mountain-stream making his victory sign and of the Count and Rudolf Rassendyll's descendant smiling at one another in the grim dungeon of Zenda Castle began to sell even better than 'Karl and Karapatan Girl'. The PRRN swept to power and I became King of Ruritania.

I was crowned that autumn by the Archbishop of Strelsau with Flavia's own simple gold circlet, which was an excellent fit – thanks to Vladek's goldsmith – and generally thought to be a better symbol of modern monarchy than the sort of gem-encrusted wedding-cake normally used on these occasions. Since the Ruritanian crown jewels had long since disappeared, it was cheaper too. The ceremony was long and included rites performed by the Orthodox patriarch as well as rambling statements of good will from several members of the True Faith, during which a very new, still hairless sprog began squalling furiously and had to be taken out by its doting parents, Susha and Mikos.

There were many other old friends in the cathedral that day. From Bilavice came Gerda (now its mayor) and ex-sergeant Brobek with other ex-members of the Bilavice home guard; from Chostok or thereabouts came Corporal Radichev and Tishkon Yavelets' whole family, with other ex-guerrillas; from Previce Castle, Magda and her mother; from Kapitsa, the junior officers of the Second Regiment (many now promoted). Michael and Vakisch (both now generals in the Royal Ruritanian Army, from which most of the old high command had been purged) were there, as were Andrzej (now personal bodyguard and fitness adviser to His Majesty) and Anton Grabenau (one of the deputies elected for the PRRN). General Stavrilev and a mounted troop of the Royal Ruritanian Cossacks formed the guard of honour before and behind my open British-racing-green Bentley (not a charge to the State, it was acquired second-hand in Switzerland by the Count at his own expense), as we processed through the packed and cheering crowds, which flung innumerable British-labour-party-red roses, but fortunately no bombs or bad eggs (I was too much loved) on our way to and from the Cathedral.

Among the most important guests in the front rows of the congregation, with minor foreign royalties, ambassadors and third-rank international politicians, were, of course, my prime minister, Count von Wunklisch, my foreign minister, Heinz Albert, ex-President Slobodjak and his wife, and General Practsin, now in overall command of the airforce as well as the security services, since there could be little security for a ruler in such a small country as

Ruritania without tight control of the airforce. Also up front were Vladek Tarlenheim (newly appointed Director of Ruritanian Heritage, including all museums and historic buildings, which I hoped would leave him no time to paint); my distant (*le mot juste*) cousin, Lord Burlesdon, an elderly horsebreeding type who disapproved of my not wearing a robe and knee-breeches for the ceremony and flew home immediately afterwards; General Danzing (re-appointed Ruritanian Ambassador in London); an elderly couple no one knew from a barge on the River Volzer; and two British tourists from Hackney, delighted to find the exchange rate of the Ruritanian kruna still more advantageous than the year before, though it hardly mattered – except for buying souvenirs – since they were staying at the Palace and would accompany the King, all expenses paid, on his first ceremonial tour of the country. Freddy and Jennifer, I must say, took my new job extremely well. Freddy gave me invaluable advice on how to handle civil servants, while Jennifer immediately started to redesign the interior of the Palace for me and promised to order new furnishings and fittings from Heal's, unless, she said, I preferred cheaper things which would wear out sooner. I got the impression they were both quite confident that I wouldn't be in this position much longer than in previous ones, but as Jennifer said:

'The good thing about this job is that, even if *you* drop it, it doesn't go out of the family.'

Clare Studebaker was not, sadly, in the congregation. We quarrelled over the confiscated video-tapes and cassettes, which never were returned to her and which Michael – not, I think, meaning any harm – told her he only took on my instructions and had now destroyed, also on my instructions. She was posted elsewhere – some trouble-spot in Africa, I think – after General Danzing complained to the BBC about a hostile report she broadcast almost on the eve of my coronation.

Nor was Yelena there. She stayed in the hospital at Vlod until after the election and I visited her whenever I could spare the time, but she was dead before my coronation – at the end of which I kissed the toe of Our Lady of Wloczovar with such passion that one of the papers suggested I must be 'a truly religious man'. Yelena is buried with her husband the water-engineer at Chostok. In her honour the statue of Our Lady of Chostok was restored to the church (which remained otherwise bare and, regrettably to Dr Moritz, retained by the True Faith) and is becoming a shrine to her memory among all the people of Karapata of whatever denomination, as well as the third most popular tourist venue in the country, after Zenda and

Strelsau itself. Outside the church, in spite of the disapproval of the True Faith, there is always a lively trade in relics, especially small cellophane sachets of golden hair, said to have been picked up along the railway line to Kapitsa, but I'm sure most of that went to line birds' nests or fill some peasant's pillow and the only true hair is the bunch still possessed by Michael.

Tourism is what we are pinning our hopes to for the country's revival; plus, of course, foreign aid and the excellent opportunities for businessmen – briefly described in an article written by my trade minister over my royal signature in the latest number of *Open Sesame* – in a country now so united and, I must say, contented. And – to allay any superstition in financial circles about lending money to countries with green in their flag – there is now a measure before parliament to eliminate both green stripes from our national flag and substitute royal (or pollution) yellow, blue and white, with a gold circlet super-imposed. I should finish by inviting you warmly to book your next holiday – winter or summer – in laughing Ruritania and by urging other still woebegone nations with dismal pseudo-democracies to consider restoring their kings – they're a link with tradition, more glamorous than presidents and as long as you get the right bloke in charge and give him real power, they work. It is, after all, a much more tried and tested system than democracy. Anyway, as the old barge-woman said, Ruritania without a king is like a man without a bulge. I *should* finish there, but it would be pointless.

I'm writing this, as I said, in Slobodjak's library, which, although it is pitifully short of books since he moved his out, does at least contain a brand-new copy of *The Prince*. I sent Hackney Library's copy back with Freddy and Jennifer – she said it would save the postage, but made sure I gave her the outstanding fine in hard cur-rency. It was a translation dating from before *The Prisoner of Zenda* and, incidentally, not the same edition as the paperback bought by Danzing for our coded correspondence: he never understood a single message I sent him. My reason for writing this, while the facts are fresh in my mind, is that if I have any descendant in, say, 2094, he or she will be able to know as much about me as I do about Rudolf Rassendyll and Flavia and perhaps something too about Yelena – she might be back on earth about then – and learn from my mistakes as well as my positive qualities. Well, perhaps the real reason is that I'm a bit pleased with myself for not living up – or down – to the family motto. But for that same reason and although this narrative is mainly true and I'm happy with the style – especially considering my lousy education – it's not, obviously, brilliant PR for a new and much loved King. People still treat Machiavelli with suspicion five hundred years after his time. So I hope you're not reading this in my time and, if you are, it must be because someone has stolen the manuscript or I've lost my crown and am trying to scrape a living in retirement like other has-been personalities. Or it could be, of course, that I'm dead; unless I'm shamming dead, like my great-grandfather the waxwork.

KR
The Royal Palace, Strelsau

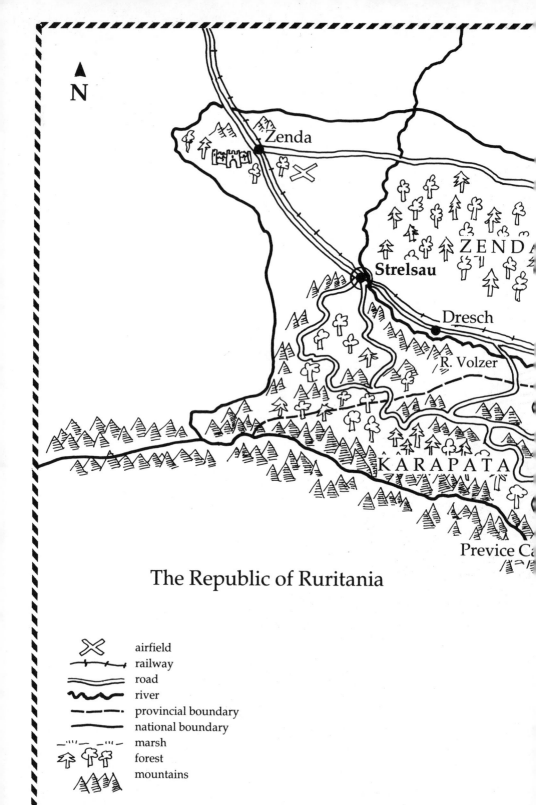

The Republic of Ruritania